# QUEEN OF LOVE

*Recent Titles by Alan Savage from Severn House*

ELEANOR OF AQUITAINE
QUEEN OF LOVE

*Recent Titles writing as Christopher Nicole from Severn House*

The Dawson Family Saga
BOOK ONE: DAYS OF WINE AND ROSES?
BOOK TWO: THE TITANS
BOOK THREE: RESUMPTION
BOOK FOUR: THE LAST BATTLE

BLOODY SUNRISE
BLOODY SUNSET

The Russian Quartet
BOOK ONE: THE SEEDS OF POWER
BOOK TWO: THE MASTERS
BOOK THREE: THE RED TIDE

*Recent Titles writing as Caroline Gray from Severn House*

The Devil Series
SPAWN OF THE DEVIL
SWORD OF THE DEVIL
DEATH OF THE DEVIL

WOMAN OF HER TIME
A CHILD OF FORTUNE

*Recent Titles writing as Max Marlow from Severn House*

GROWTH
SHADOW AT EVENING
THE BURNING ROCKS
WHERE THE RIVER RISES

# QUEEN OF LOVE

Alan Savage

This first world edition published in Great Britain 1995 by
SEVERN HOUSE PUBLISHERS LTD of
9–15 High Street, Sutton, Surrey SM1 1DF.
First published in the USA 1995 by
SEVERN HOUSE PUBLISHERS INC., of
595 Madison Avenue, New York, NY 10022.

Copyright © 1995 by Alan Savage

All rights reserved.
The moral rights of the author have been asserted.

British Library Cataloguing in Publication Data
Savage, Alan
  Queen of Love
  I. Title
  823.914 [F]

  ISBN 0-7278-4811-9

All situations in this publication are fictitious and
any resemblance to living persons is purely coincidental.

Typeset by Palimpsest Book Production Limited,
Polmont, Stirlingshire
Printed and bound in Great Britain by
Hartnolls Ltd, Bodmin, Cornwall.

# The Family of Eleanor of Aquitaine

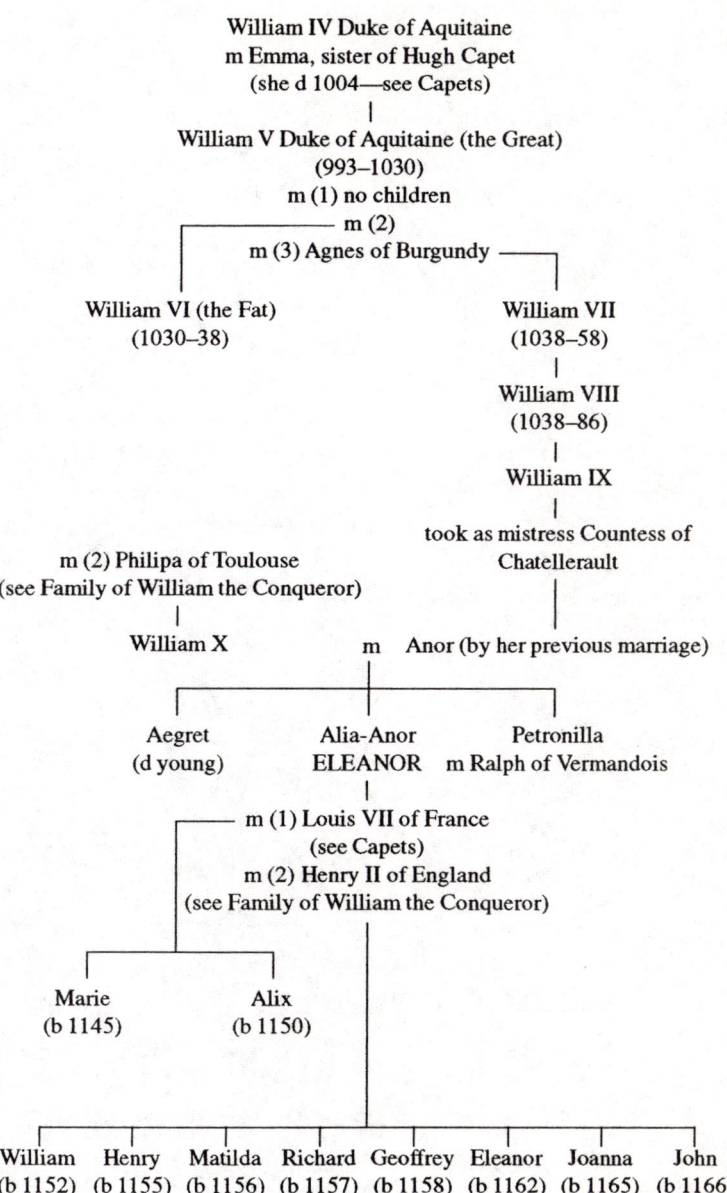

# THE CAPETS

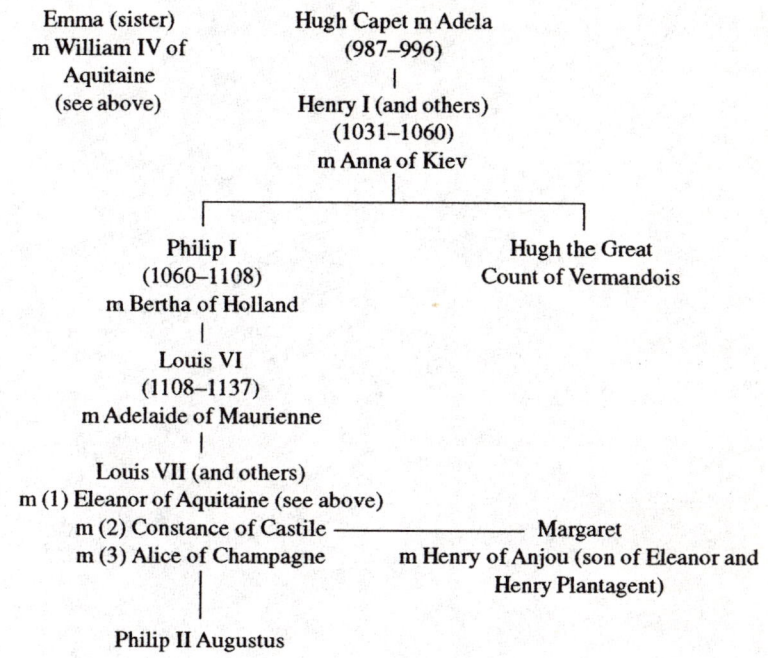

# Family of William the Conqueror

Robert I Duke of Normandy

William (the Conqueror)
(1066–87)
m Matilda of Flanders
|
Henry I Beauclerk (and others)
(1100–1135)
m Matilda of Scotland
|
Matilda (Empress) (and others)
m (2) Geoffrey of Anjou
|
Henry II (and others)
m Eleanor of Aquitaine

(by a separate mother)
Robert of Mortain
|
Granddaughter
Philippa of Toulouse
m William IX of Aquitaine
(see Family of Eleanor of Aquitaine)

# Chapter One

On 18 May 1152, I was married, for the second time. The wedding took place in the church of Notre Dame la Grande, in Poitiers, and my husband and I were surrounded by an eager and excited throng. Indeed, we had to be protected from the mob by a guard of nobles. There were shouts of "Vivat Eleanor!" and "Vivat Plantagenet!" all about us, and I fancy we made an imposing couple. My husband, who was introduced by his title, Henry, Duke of Normandy, was short and powerfully built, craggy-featured even at nineteen, a mop of unruly red hair flowing out from beneath his ducal coronet, his crimson robe worn beneath a cloak of ultramarine blue. Myself, tall and statuesque, at thirty still the most beautiful woman in Europe, with my long brown hair confined in two plaits falling from beneath my white headress and lying on the deep red of my own gown. My face was left exposed – showing it to be slightly aquiline but flawless in every feature, as my glass constantly reminds me. I could not of course claim to be a virgin. And, yes, I was eleven years older than my husband. Well, it may be said, queens, even ex-queens – or perhaps, ex-queens more than any others – need to marry where they may.

But there was a much more to this great event than expediency.

I suppose the most remarkable thing about my second

marriage, apart from the fact that it happened at all, was that it took place in the cathedral of Poitiers: I had had some doubts as to the wisdom of returning to my ancestral lands until I was more certain that I would be welcomed. This was because, when I went to the altar for the second time in my life, although I had been Duchess of Aquitaine for some fifteen years, very little of that time had actually been spent *in* Aquitaine, and apart from being an absentee duchess, the requirements of my first husband, who in addition to being King of France was, by right of his marriage to me, also Duke of Aquitaine, had meant that my people had been sorely taxed, time and again. This sort of thing does little to maintain one's popularity.

I had been popular once. When my father had died with such unseemly haste in 1137, the accession of his fifteen-year-old daughter Alia-Anor, corrupted by the unwashed into Eleanor, met with acclaim. Papa had had his faults, and here was a sweet-natured virgin of fifteen, already described as the most beautiful woman in Europe, to take his place.

Sadly, a sweet-natured virgin of fifteen, especially when she is heiress to vast wealth and power, and in addition is the most beautiful woman in Europe, seldom has control of her own destiny. Notwithstanding the well-known fact that I was already betrothed to Louis the Dauphin, every man with any nobility in his family tree, and who was either single, widowed, or possessed an eligible son, came thumping on my door. While I flatter myself that they undoubtedly wished to get their hands on my body, they were even more interested in getting their hands on my possessions.

From this disagreeable state of siege I was rescued by my betrothed and carried off to Paris in the most romantic fashion. I must be honest here and confess that

Louis was in every way a romantic, something which could hardly be said about Henry Plantagenet. Sadly, Louis was several other things as well. Principally, he had the mind, as he had had the upbringing, of a monk. He had been intended for the Church before the untimely death of his elder brother had made him the Dauphin. This combination of romantic flights of fancy, and an awareness that one's every action is sinful, would be dangerous in a cowherd; it is catastrophic in a king.

The story of my fifteen years as wife of Louis and Queen of France has been told in the first volume of these memoirs. Suffice to say that Louis possessed another outstanding male characteristic: when things go wrong, blame the wife. I would be the last to pretend I am white as the driven snow. Am I not widely regarded as the greatest lover in history? In my defence I will claim that when first I committed adultery I was driven to it by the maniacal changes of mood in my husband. And despite all that has been written in an endeavour to point the finger at me, his military and political disasters were his own doing. But I must plead guilty to the most cardinal of sins: I was Queen of France, and after fifteen years of marriage I had not given my husband a male heir! In this regard, bearing in mind that the French adhere to the Salic Law, which prohibits any woman from wearing the crown, my two daughters were as nothing. I was a failure.

Thus Louis, much as I know he still adored my body, came to the reluctant conclusion, or was driven to it by his advisers, that I had to be put aside and replaced by another younger, and hopefully more fecund, wife. But herein lay a problem. Unlike the Moslems, the Christian Church does not recognise divorce. A marriage can be terminated, but only by proving that it was illegal in the first place. This is usually achieved by discovering that the married couple are within the bounds of consanguinity, and discovering this as regards Louis and myself was not difficult. The problem arises because such an annulment necessarily means that the marriage never was. *This* meant that once the decree was passed my two daughters would become bastards, and far more important to Louis, his rights as Duke of Aquitaine, held, as I have said, as my husband, would immediately cease. And Aquitaine was more than half his kingdom!

I am fairly certain that Louis, with his high moral character, realised that he must accept this sacrifice. He no doubt still hoped to control events, as he remained my liege lord, and thus could forbid me to remarry without his consent, which of course would never be given. But I was very aware that there were others about his person who were considering a far more simple solution. If I were to *die* while still Queen of France, the duchy would pass to my eldest daughter, and Louis would retain practical possession of it as her father. Thus my precipitate flight from France to the protection of the greatest lady in Europe, at that time, Matilda FitzHenry, Empress Dowager of Germany, Countess Dowager of Anjou, and claimant to the throne of England.

It may be supposed that I was here jumping from the frying pan into the fire. Towards the end of my career as Queen of France I had had a brief but satisfying fling with this formidable lady's husband, Count Geoffrey of Anjou, and I had to suppose she knew of this. However, Geoffrey had died, recently and suddenly, and I knew Matilda to be a most logical person. Her attempts to oust the pretender Stephen from the throne of England had failed, through lack of men and money. I could promise her assistance in this direction, if she would give me shelter and support until I could re-establish myself as Duchess of Aquitaine.

I was proved correct in this judgement, and in fact Matilda and I so took to each other that we became the best of friends, notwithstanding a difference of some twenty years in our ages. But there remained the matter of my marriage. Knowing that whoever I married without permission, would not be recognised in some quarters as my legal husband, I might have been content to put off any consideration of this for some time, to let the dust settle, as it were. Others had different ideas. Including Matilda. She immediately had to rescue me from a variety of unwanted suitors, prominent amongst whom was Count Theobald of Blois, nephew of her hated rival Stephen. Obviously, until I was married, my life, and therefore hers, was likely to remain far too exciting for comfort.

But she was also working to a plan of her own. She had three sons. True, the eldest of these was eleven years younger than I. But he was Duke of Normandy, and he was her heir in her quest for the English crown. I might change my mind about supporting her: Henry Plantagenet, as Duke of Aquitaine by right of being my husband, would never do so. Thus before I really knew what was happening, and after a courtship which lasted hardly more than an hour and consisted mainly of rape, I found myself betrothed to this uncouth young man, not yet twenty years of age.

Marriage to Henry at least promised security, which was what I wanted a great deal of at that time. However, I envisaged a clandestine ceremony, which could then be revealed to the world (and my liege lord) as and when circumstances dictated.

Henry was not disposed to consider such trifles.

Having ascertained the position from me, he announced where we would be wed, and that was that. We accumulated his various retainers from all over Normandy, proceeded south, crossed the Orne and then the Loire, and made our presence felt.

Henry, of course, combined daring with commonsense and an appreciation of realities – quite unlike my first husband – and was not prepared to plunge too deeply into Aquitaine until we had tested the temperature of the water. He was well aware that to my Gascons, exchanging the rule of a simpleton for that of a descendant of the devil – as Henry was usually considered – might not universally be regarded as a step forward. We both knew that I was more highly regarded by my Poitevins than any other people. I will not say that they were not taken aback by our appearance as, like everyone else, they had no idea where I was or what had happened to me since my flight from Beaugency. Theobald of Blois had naturally not spread it about how he had been defeated in his attempt to gain possession of me. Nor, may I add, did he make the slightest attempt to interfere with our plans – he had a mortal fear of the new Duke of Normandy.

Bewildered as they were, however, my Poitevins were delighted to welcome me into their midst. Of course they had very little option, in view of Henry's army, but I flatter myself that much of their greeting was genuine. Besides, what people can resist a royal wedding? It was a great occasion. For us. As may be imagined, it caused a very great sensation elsewhere. In the first place, we were breaking every rule in the book. We had *not* applied for exemption from consanguinity. We had *not* applied to my legal liege lord, Louis, for permission. And I had personally broken his express command. These were serious matters, and I am sure provoked no end of discussion amongst the students of Paris.

Louis was the man we had to consider. It would simply have been too humiliating for him to have accepted such a slap in the face of his authority, not to mention the feelings of jealousy which must range through the heart and mind of any man whose still beautiful, and still young – I was only just coming up to thirty – wife takes off and gets into bed with someone eleven years her junior, with every indication of joy and happiness and without a by-your-leave. He had to take action. In this he was not short of allies: Theobald, naturally, and my new brother-in-law, Geoffrey of Anjou. He had also attempted to gain me for himself, only to see me rescued by his mother, and was now breathing fire and smoke at both his brother and me, and even Matilda herself, for the way he had been duped. Louis also, so we were informed, had hopes of Eustace of Boulogne, who was *his* brother-in-law, and who had every reason to bring down the son of his father's most bitter enemy (who, it had to be supposed, would now be dreaming, with the immense power at his disposal, of setting his mother on the throne of England). This was a position which, naturally enough, Eustace intended to occupy upon the death of *his* father, Stephen.

None of these idiotic men had any understanding of the man they were now intending to attack. But by this time I did, and I had not the slightest doubt about the outcome.

I suppose, looking back on those heady days when we rode from one triumph to the next, the aspect of Henry which most strikes one is his energy. It was such as almost to make one believe the tales of a devilish ancestor. From the moment my new husband rose in the morning until the moment he collapsed exhausted in bed at night, he never rested either his body or his brain for a moment.

He began the day by tumbling me. I may say that for me this was a continuing mixture of consternation and delight. The delight lay in his amatory prowess. It may have been gathered that I was not short of amatory experience myself. However, this had necessarily been limited to what may be called one-night stands. I may have tasted the cup of nectar on more than one occasion, but I had never been allowed to drain it to the dregs. This can be a most stimulating experience. The consternation lay in the realisation that this was to be my fate at least once in every day for the rest of my life, at least when my husband was about. I was of course being wildly optimistic in thus evaluating the constancy of man, but that is how it appeared to me in the first flush of love. At the same time I realised that such a prospect might possibly be *too* stimulating, and was not averse to taking advantage of my feminine infirmities.

This did not appear to disturb Henry. When I was not available he tumbled my maid Amaria, or anyone else who happened to be in the vicinity of our bedchamber. I did not object to this. I was still drifting along on a kind of cloud at having at last encountered a man who could surpass me – I knew I could never cope with his requirements all on my own.

When he left his bed Henry immediately called for his horse. While he was washed and dressed he dealt with various matters which had arisen overnight or on the previous day, issued orders, gave instructions, listened to petitions, while chewing a crust of bread and gulping a goblet of wine. His breakfast finished, he would hunt for some hours. He ate his dinner either in the saddle or standing up, talking all the while, and often playing a game of chess –

a pastime of which he was passionately fond – on the side.

When he returned from the hunt he would engage in passages of arms with his nobles – there were few who could stand against him – while again listening to petitions and judging criminal cases until darkness fell. Then at last he allowed himself to sit, to eat. Henry's supper table was always crowded, with food and wine and beautiful women as well as men and fools and hangers-on, and was always attended by at least a score of dogs, of whom he knew the name of each one. It was my pleasure to sit beside him while we indulged ourselves, following which it was his pleasure to listen to music. I know this art form is supposed to be able to soothe the savage breast, but the fact is that Henry, although he could be very savage when aroused, was, for all his uncouth exterior, a man of considerable learning and sensibility. He had been very carefully educated – his mother had attended to that – and not only in the trivium and quadrivium: Matilda had also seen to it that he understood statecraft and government, economics and the management of men. He was a very complete prince. In a word, for all his physical drawbacks, I found myself falling in love with my husband. Not every woman has been able to say this.

Following our marriage, Henry and I were separated for a few months. We both felt that I was absolutely safe in Poitiers, where the people vied with one another to show their loyalty to their returned Duchess, and thus he left me there while he went off to deal with his detractors. This he accomplished with masterly skill, utterly out-manoeuvering the allies as they advanced into Normandy, and forcing their withdrawal with hardly more than a skirmish. Louis had already seen one army swallowed up, in Palestine, and had little desire to have the same thing happen again. Besides, he had other things on his mind, although we were not at the time aware of this. Geoffrey, abandoned by his ally, very rapidly made peace with his brother on a promise of future favours. But Theobald merely fled.

Yet Henry was gone all summer, leaving me in a somewhat unsettled frame of mind. I would actually have preferred to join my mother-in-law in Rouen, conscious as I was that Matilda, although she had never shown me anything but affection and indeed love, was actually the guiding spirit behind much of what Henry did, or even thought. I did not really wish to encroach upon Matilda's prerogatives; I had seen enough of her to know that her temper – renowned throughout Europe – was extremely fierce when aroused. But I did feel that I should have some prerogatives of my own when it came to aiding and advising my husband. However, Henry deemed it best for me to be in Poitiers, and known to be there, as Duchess of Aquitaine.

At this juncture I feel bound to reveal that although Henry was the perfect example of knighthood – in the best possible sense, combining great physical strength and skill at arms with an interest in art, literature and music – he also possessed a temper which was even more terrifying than that of his mother. In these early days of our marriage I was immune from his rages, but others were not, and were subjected to fits of the most disturbing nature. The Duke would literally foam at the mouth, or hurl himself to the floor and eat the rushes, regardless of who might just have been standing there, or the condition of his boots. I had no desire to provoke such an eruption, and thus fell in with his wishes with apparent docility. But I was filled with a desire to do.

For the past two years and more I had been virtually a prisoner in the Capetian Tower in Paris, and for a year before that I had been a prisoner in Jerusalem. But before *that* I had adventured. And in between my two periods of incarceration I had again had some interesting experiences. Now here I was, trapped in what was admittedly a beautiful city, set in the midst of beautiful countryside, with nothing more to do than judge the odd civil or criminal case. Small wonder that I became increasingly restless.

As an added frustration, it rapidly became apparent that even Henry's furious assaults had failed to breach my citadel, and, more than anything, I was anxious to conceive and give birth for my new husband. This was not merely to please him, although I knew it would. I also needed to replace the two daughters I had to consider lost to me forever. My dream was to present Henry with a boy, which would be another slap in the face for Louis, for whom, at that time, I had conceived the most virulent dislike. It will therefore be seen that it was a most inopportune moment for Bernard of Ventadour to reappear.

Bernard had been my most constant male companion during my final years as Queen of France. As a troubadour, no one had been able to object to his entertaining me with the singing of songs. That when we were alone together (save for my most faithful lady Amaria) he entertained me with more than songs, was our secret. When I had fled, he and Amaria had been my only companions. But he had chosen to disappear after we had gained Rouen and discovered ourselves surrounded by Henry Plantagenet. Where he had gone no one seemed to know, not even Amaria. But of course his absence was a great relief to me. When one is in the midst of marrying and honeymooning nothing is more inconvenient than to have an erstwhile lover lying about the place. As it turned out, he had gone down into Gascony. The sad fact is that troubadours possess a freedom of movement far beyond that achieved by kings. As long as they are talented, and Bernard was perhaps the most talented in the land, they are welcomed in any knights' hall, being required only to sing for their suppers. His meal paid for, your songster is free to amuse himself and, if possible, find some attractive and willing female with whom to share the midnight hours. Obviously, it is a risky business to aspire to the bed of the lady of the house, even should her husband be absent, but every castle I have ever known is filled with females eager to accommodate passers-by.

This freedom of movement serves another very useful purpose, in that your observant troubadour can be of enormous value as a spy, or even a mere gleaner of scraps of knowledge. Bernard was very accomplished at this. From my point of view, however, his reappearance, although disturbing while I was in my fresh mood of accidia, was very welcome. Henry had left me a garrison to ensure my safety, but these Norman lords were a rough-and-ready lot, with scarce a word of conversation between them, and not one of them could read more than his name. Here was someone with whom I could converse, who could sing to me and tell me sweet tales, and even report on the feelings of my people farther to the south.

I therefore forgave him both his disappearance, without my leave, and his reappearance, without my leave, and bade him entertain me. This he did, by means of a kind of serial story, relating the adventures of Tristan and Isolde, with every conceivable detail conveyed with innumerable sighs and secret glances. I must assume that he made up a lot of it as he went along, certainly the erotic bits, but that made it even more interesting. It was not long before, as he sat on the floor at the foot of my couch, he had seized my ankle and was nibbling at my toes, which is something that Tristan never did to Isolde. Or either of my husbands to me.

I would like it to be understood that to this moment I had not considered being unfaithful to Henry for a moment. Quite apart from my understanding that Henry was not Louis and was therefore unlikely to dissolve into tears should he feel I had betrayed him, I was still very much in love with my husband. And besides, I was enjoying the rest. Equally, however, it is difficult to resist the temptation to be adored. At this early stage in my marriage I felt confident that Henry loved me. That is to say, he enjoyed my company, the use of my body and, even more, the prospect of the use of my lands. But the word adoration was not a part of his vocabulary. Equally, his love-making was of an intensely physical nature. I found this very pleasurable indeed after the rather short rations of the past couple of years, or indeed my unsatisfactory conjugal relations before then. But can there be a woman alive who does not, at least occasionally, sigh for the soft touch, the whispered word, the gentle caress and, above all, the acknowledgement on the part of her lover that what happens next is up to her, not him? Bernard possessed all of these characteristics to perfection.

Thus it was that I took to spending more and more time in his company, excluding all my ladies save for Amaria. It was necessary to have a lady present, to prevent gossip, but Amaria was almost an alter ego of mine, and her presence in no way inhibited me. Indeed we often shared the same embrace and moments of passion, courtesy of Bernard. And I did not commit adultery, certainly in the legal sense of the word. I often think that those precious few months in the summer at Poitiers were the genesis of the Courts of Love later made so famous by my daughter Marie and myself. All things begin in a primitive fashion, and there was nothing elaborate or ritualistic about my relations with Bernard. The three of us lounged in my bedchamber, usually in a state of extreme *deshabille*, more often than not naked, while Bernard told us stories and sang us songs, and we spoke of love and practiced the art, seeking sensuality in every part of the body as well as the mind, arousing ourselves over and over again until on occasion we were fit to burst, and on occasion, to be candid, we did.

As an exercise in the creation of intimacy, it was an unsurpassed experience, and the more so for me, as I was undisputed mistress of ceremonies; it was my whims they sought to please, my appetites they sought to sate, my body at which they worshipped. It was a happy time.

I would not have you suppose that I was entirely occupied with profane matters: I had learned from the misfortunes of my father that it pays to regard the sacred as well. It was during this comparatively restful period of my life that I first visited the Abbey of Fontevrault, not far from Poitiers, where the abbess was an aunt of Henry's. She bore the same name as his mother, Matilda, and gave me a hearty welcome.

I was able to assuage the pangs of my conscience by making her a considerable endowment.

All good things come to an end as, fortunately, do all bad things. In the autumn Henry returned, flushed with success, and filled with ambition. I was not aware of just what this ambition was. Neither was the Empress Matilda, who remained in Rouen, keeping Normandy in subjection. Henry's first consideration was to make sure of Aquitaine, and thus consolidate his enormous accretion of strength, for all the world to see. We thus set off on a vast *chevauchee*, to a large extent following the same path as Louis and myself took less than a twelvemonth before. I cannot claim that we were whole-heartedly acclaimed, but acclaimed we were by the people who mattered. My Poitevin and Gascon barons, eager to fight each other or rebel against authority on the slightest pretext, quickly understood that they had accumulated a master when Henry had hanged one or two of them and knocked down some of their castles. The realisation that their new duke was not yet twenty years old and would therefore be around for a very long time to come, God willing – or was it the Devil? – terrified them out of their wits.

We naturally also resumed our conjugal relations, and it was back to exhilaration and hard knocks; Bernard very sensibly again slipped into the background here, but Henry had heard of his reputation as a troubadour and would have him perform most nights after supper. The poor fellow was too afraid to even look at me too closely. However, Henry was too busy being his fulsome self to notice anything untoward. We returned to Poitiers in the autumn, when he informed me that he intended to go to England. I was entirely taken aback by this. "You mean to raise an army and invade?"

He sat on the side of our bed, his chin in his hands. As this was an unusually reflective pose for him to adopt, it was clear that he had a great deal on his mind. "I shall take an armed force with me," he said. "But not an army of invasion. You know that I was in England hardly more than a year ago?"

"I have heard this," I said, deciding not to add that I had also heard how that *chevauchee* had been a total failure.

"I actually went to Scotland, to be knighted by my great-uncle David, King of Scots," he explained. "But when that was done, I ventured into England, and indeed travelled the length of the country."

"But was overwhelmed by superiority of numbers," I suggested.

"Nothing of the sort. Stephen raised a vast army against me, but he could not defeat me. I decided to abandon the campaign only because Cousin Eustace, who actually commanded the army sent against me, began laying waste the countryside. My inheritance!"

"Or more correctly, your mother's inheritance," I suggested.

He had been half-turned away from me. Now he gave me a quick glance. "Why, yes," he agreed. "To be sure." I realised there were deep waters here. "The point is," he went on, "that I received promises of support everywhere. Under Stephen's mismanagement, the country has collapsed into utter anarchy, not to mention ruin. And the barons fear that if Eustace came to the throne, things would get a whole lot worse. Stephen may be an incompetent fool, but he is a very decent fellow and a gallant knight. Eustace is also an incompetent fool, but *he* is a vicious animal."

I could not help but wonder how my erstwhile sister-in-law Constance – Louis' younger sister – was getting on, if that was true. She had been married to this Eustace a few years before, as part of an alliance pact. But the business at hand was more important. "Yet these barons would not rise up and support you."

"Well, what would you? I was then a seventeen-year-old boy, with nothing save my name to offer them. But now, I go to them as Duke of Normandy, Count of Anjou, *and* Duke of Aquitaine."

"And as an emissary of your mother!"

Another quick glance. "Why, yes," he said. "I go as my mother's son, to be sure."

"I will come with you."

"No, no," he said. "That would be quite impossible. Think of the danger."

"Will I not be in more danger here, with you across the sea?"

"You will be safe here, my pet, because everyone will know that I am coming back. However, if you feel uneasy, you may go to Rouen and be with Mama."

Had it been Louis I might have argued. Indeed, had it been Louis, I might have insisted. But I had not yet reached the stage where I was prepared to challenge my second husband, and so I acquiesced. We had a merry Christmas in Poitiers, and then he hurried away, to visit with his mother in Rouen, before going on to Barfleur to take ship for England.

It may be imagined that I saw him go with a heavy heart, standing on the highest battlement of the Maubergeonne Tower in Poitiers to wave him out of sight. Supposing he never returned? What then? His brother Geoffrey would become Duke of Normandy and Count of Anjou, and I would revert to being Duchess of Aquitaine, with every man seeking my hand. But of course, the future is always unexpected. Henry sailed for England in January 1153, and only a month later I realised that I was pregnant.

# Chapter Two

I was delighted, and sent messengers chasing behind my husband, as well as up to Rouen to inform my mother-in-law. Matilda immediately returned her congratulations, but it was some time before I heard from Henry. He was, of course, very busy.

Matilda enjoined in me the greatest care, and this I practised for the whole of the winter and spring and early summer, despite the problems which cropped up all around me. For naturally the news of my pregnancy spread abroad, and reached Paris quickly enough. The result was that Louis, whether in a fit of pique or for general political reasons I could not at the time determine, proceeded to marry off both of my daughters: Alix went to the Count of Blois, and Marie to his brother, the Count of Champagne. Diplomacy or no, this was an intended slap in the face for Henry and me, as the Count of Blois, of course, was the same lout who had tried to marry *me*, while it may be recalled that Henry had originally had the idea of marrying Marie. As for the idea of marrying two sisters to two brothers, this could not possibly have been approved by any impartial church. But Louis was big with the Pope at this time. As Marie was but eight years old, and Alix was only three, any consummations were obviously some time in the future but, as was the custom, the two princesses were despatched to the courts of their chosen husbands for their education. My heart bled for them. I still conceived them lost to me forever.

On the good side of the coin, dare I say it, Bernard of Clairvaux died that summer. As I have mentioned earlier, a movement immediately began to have him canonised, and this was done only twenty years later, one of the quickest elevations to sainthood in memory, only to be compared with that of Becket. Undoubtedly Bernard was worth the honour: I doubt the Church has ever had a more staunch and determined champion. But I have still not entirely acquitted him of causing the death of dear Papa, even if only by the power of thought, while his consistent opposition to me in almost everything made my life a trial. On the other hand, if he had *not* opposed me in virtually everything, I might never have left Louis. For no sooner had Bernard departed, than I gave birth, on 17 August 1153 . . . and to a boy! The bells of Poitiers rang out that night, and thence northwards right across Maine and Anjou and Normandy. Their pealing might even have drifted across the Channel, because only a week later there was another most significant death: that of Eustace of Boulogne, Stephen's son and heir, and the principal stumbling block in the realisation of the ambitions of Henry and his mother.

Save that his mother, unbeknownst to her, was no longer in the running. Neither Matilda nor I had any idea of what was happening in England. Henry had departed, and only the wildest of rumours came back to us until he himself returned in the spring of the following year.

I was, of course, very sorry that he had not been present at the birth of his first child, as I then supposed, but I understood that he had his business to be about.

The child's name had long been agreed, if it was a boy. It was to be William, not only because most of my ducal ancestors had borne that name, including both Papa and Grandpapa, but because it was also the name of Henry's most famous Norman ancestor, the Conqueror. It will be understood that all our world was concentrated in this small body. I could have wished it was a slightly more robust body, but then history is littered with apparently weak babies who grow up to be strong and famous kings. I placed my faith in the future.

Thus I awaited my husband's return with equanimity, as I had at least received a letter from him informing me that he had survived the battle at Wallingford and had indeed triumphed over the usurper's army. Now this additional news of Eustace's death – from overeating, just like his Uncle Henry Beauclerk, it was said, although anger and frustration no doubt played their parts in his sudden demise – seemed even better. With this obstacle removed from Matilda's path we spent a very merry Christmas, the Empress having journeyed down from Rouen to celebrate the festival with me. She adored what she believed was her first grandson, and was the very picture of a drooling grandmama. She remained with me throughout the winter, and was thus with me when Henry arrived.

His first view of his heir was somewhat brusque, but he had a great deal on his mind. I was present, in a manner of speaking, when he had his first private interview with his mother since his return: I was listening from behind a convenient screen, unknown to either. "The news from England has been so varied," Matilda said. "I have not known what to believe. But now, your expression . . . you have lost a battle."

"On the contrary, dearest Mama, I have triumphed.

Without even having to fight another battle." A chair creaked as the Empress sat down. "You are unwell," Henry said.

I listened to Matilda sigh. "I am actually near to tears," she said. "And that has not happened for a very long time. To think, that after so many years . . . tell me what has been agreed."

Henry cleared his throat. "Following Wallingford, when it became clear to Stephen, and his adherents, that they could not beat me, we had a meeting. It was recalled what you and Stephen and Uncle Robert discussed during the truce of 1140. As you agreed then, we have decided that Stephen will retain the crown until his death, which I do assure you cannot now be far away. Never have I seen a man so decrepit and worn down. When he is dead, the crown of England will pass to the House of Anjou."

"And William has accepted this?" (This William being Stephen's younger son.)

"Well, no, he has not. He stormed out of London in a rage. But his father has agreed to it, and with his mother dead, and himself known to be a weakling, I do not think we need fear Cousin William."

"I entirely agree," Matilda said. "Oh, my dear boy, I do so admire you for your achievement. Do you know, there have been times that I doubted I would ever succeed? Well, if as you say, Stephen is on his last legs, I must prepare for my coronation. I will need new gowns, and jewellery. I must get back to Rouen with all haste."

"Ahem," Henry remarked. There was a brief silence, and I could imagine the pair of them staring at one another. "You will understand, dearest Mama," Henry said. "That this agreement is not merely between Stephen and myself. All the great lords and barons attended our conferences, eager to have peace restored to our fair land."

"Well, of course," Matilda acknowledged, her voice quiet. "Any agreement would hardly work without the whole-hearted support of the barons."

"I am glad you understand this, Mama," Henry said. "Thus I know that you will understand that I intend no disrespect when I inform you that the barons conveyed to Stephen and myself that they could never accept you as their queen."

"What did you say?" Matilda's voice rose an octave.

"I would suppose there are many factors involved," Henry went on. "But I think there are two of vital importance. One is the fact that you are a woman, and the other is that you are the Empress Matilda, a lady famed throughout Europe for her beauty and her courage, but also for her ruthless determination to have her way no matter who or what may seek to temper her decisions."

Of course this was mere masculine claptrap as, for instance, there could be no prince in Europe more determined to have his own way than Henry himself, but I was too busy trying to figure out just what it all meant for me. "Then what exactly is the intention of this agreement between Stephen and yourself?" the Empress inquired, her voice like a rumble of distant thunder.

I heard Henry inhale; if he feared any single living human being, it was his mother. "That upon his death, I should become King of England." There was another brief silence, and once again I could imagine the stares that were being exchanged. "It is my inheritance," he said as winningly as possible. I heard the sound of something smashing, and realised that the Empress was giving way to her anger, at the expense of some of my crockery. "You will always be at my right side," Henry protested. There was another resounding smash. "You will be queen in all but name, dearest Mama."

That gave me pause for thought, but before I could decide on an attitude I discerned from the sounds beyond the wall that he had evaded the next missile hurled at him, and reached her side, for his voice was lower and more dulcet. "Dearest Mama," he said. "I seek only your happiness. Will you not assist me in the great tasks that lie ahead?"

I was too excited to care about the exact relationship the three of us would enjoy. I had of course understood from the beginning that Henry aspired to the throne of England, but I had anticipated years of campaigning, and then possibly years of waiting in the wings while Matilda ruled. I had never doubted that Henry would succeed in his quest as he was not the sort of man who accepted failure. But to have the whole thing fall into our laps so suddenly and completely! What an empire we would rule! England, Normandy, Anjou, Maine, Poitou, Guienne, Gascony – and Toulouse – I could not see Henry failing to regain title to that long-lost province. The entire western seaboard of Europe from Flanders to Spain would be under the rule of one man, and that man would be the most powerful prince in Christendom, greater even than the Emperor.

And I would be his wife! Queen of England! I am sure I can be forgiven for indulging in a few caracoles, at least in the privacy of my own bedchamber. As for Matilda sitting at her son's right hand, it was my private determination that it should be at his *left* hand, but I had no objection to her giving him advice – she had been around a good deal longer than I: twenty years to be precise. And although it saddens me to have to admit such a fault of character, my principal thoughts were of how Louis was going to react to this startling news.

As a matter of fact, he reacted very well. I suppose that he too must have known that this would be Henry's eventual ambition, and if it had happened a good deal sooner than he might have hoped, there was nothing he could do but accept the situation. This he did to such an extent that during the early summer of 1154 he and Henry actually met, greeted each other cordially, and arranged the vexed matters of fiefs, with the result that Louis eventually retained only the homage of Toulouse, and this we had not actually regained as yet. These important matters resolved, my first husband took himself off to St James of Compostella on a pilgrimage, or so it was said. The truth of the matter is that he was looking for a hopefully more compliant replacement for me, and he duly returned with a Spanish princess named Constance.

I did not even allow this to upset me. Louis had put it about that the real reason our marriage had been annulled was because of my inability to bear France a male heir, and this scurrilous accusation had been widely accepted. Now it had been given the lie, and so Louis' claims that he was marrying the Princess Constance simply in search of such an heir sounded somewhat hollow. He seemed to be following in my footsteps at a very humble distance.

Our business now was simply to wait, but we used our time profitably. Henry had returned to France in April; by mid-summer I was again pregnant! From which it may be gathered that I continued to find my youthful husband's company a pleasure; so much so that I equally continued to overlook those faults of character – principally shortness of temper and a most roving eye

– which became more evident every day. Henry had never vented his anger upon *me*, and as for the other, I quite understood that when I was pregnant, or he was separated from me, he needed some comfort from time to time, or, in Henry's case, on a fairly regular basis. Well, was I not in the same case? My only reservation was that he should reserve his *love* for me, if not his body, and I saw nothing to disturb me in this direction. I actually conceived my fourth child in Rouen, whence Henry had removed Matilda and I soon after his return. He regarded Rouen as his natural capital, as it was the capital of Normandy. While I still dreamed of setting up a Constantinople-in-Western-Europe in Bordeaux, I had to acknowledge that Bordeaux was too far removed from where all the action was likely to be. Nor did I have any desire to be separated from my husband more than necessary.

As it happened, that autumn he was again required to take the field, for although he and Louis were ostensibly on the best of terms, my erstwhile husband was still intent on making trouble where he could, and the obvious place to do this was the Vexin, that parcel of land which lies between Normandy and France proper. The inhabitants had been required to swear allegiance, first to one side and then the other, for so many years that they were in a perpetual state of anarchy. Henry reckoned that it was necessary to settle this matter once and for all and with his customary energy he went bounding off.

By this time I was in the most debilitating period of child-bearing, puking all over the place and feeling thoroughly out of sorts. I was entirely content to sit back and let others do the running, Henry campaigning and Matilda ruling Normandy, while I spent my time with Baby William, who as yet was showing no signs of his dad's vigour and energy. From these maternal pursuits I was rudely awakened on 26 October by the arrival of a messenger from Archbishop Theobald of Canterbury, announcing Stephen's death. For the second time in my life I was a queen!

I remember the sense of exhilarated shock I experienced that week. Stephen was not yet sixty. He had, admittedly, suffered several personal misfortunes in the deaths of his wife and favourite son, but this is the lot of many men. One is more inclined to suppose that his spirit had been worn down by the realisation that the kingdom which he had grasped so vigorously and ambitiously nearly twenty years before had degenerated into a fought-over wasteland, and that his writ was entirely ignored by his barons. But no one had expected him to dwindle and die with such rapidity, of a chill, we were informed. Of the House of Anjou, only Matilda, myself, and my infant son were in residence at Rouen when the news arrived. Matilda was immediately aflame with energetic anxiety. She remembered too well the events of 1136. All the nobles of England and Normandy had sworn, on two occasions, to uphold her as Queen of England, and almost without exception they had reneged on their oaths in support of the first member of the royal family to reach England – Stephen of Blois. She was not going to let that happen again.

At the same time the thought of usurping her own son never crossed her mind. If Henry was afraid of his mother, she was equally afraid of him. Thus she sent messengers hurrying off to give him the news, enjoining them to have him abort the campaign in favour of this far greater enterprise. He was with us in a week. By then we had been joined by Geoffrey, who was also not prepared to risk usurping his brother, as Stephen had done to Theobald. Needless to say, he and I regarded each other somewhat coolly, this being the first time we had ever actually met, although he was by now aware that he had ridden in my company on that famous night two years before.

But all thoughts were upon the Enterprise.

It was decided that Matilda should remain in Rouen, and take care of Normandy while Henry seized the greater prize. There was some suggestion that William and I too should remain in Rouen, at least for the time being, but I was having none of that. I was not yet showing, I had got over my bout of morning sickness, and was as filled with energy as ever. Besides, this was my destiny as much as Henry's. As for William, it was even more his. Thus off we set for Barfleur which, despite its bad reputation in the House of Henry Beauclerk as having been the place from whence the ill-fated *White Ship* had sailed in November 1120 to drown Henry's heir, also named William – and cause all the chaos that had since followed – remained the principal port of embarkation for England. Here a small armada of ships was waiting for us, with England only a day's sail away. And here we spent a thoroughly miserable month.

I cannot claim ever to have been fortunate with ships or the sea. My first voyage of any consequence had involved that dreadful month I had spent getting from Satalia to Antioch. My second had been that equally unfortunate journey from Jaffa to Sicily, when I had counted myself utterly lost more than once. On this occasion we were not even able to put to sea, as the wind howled out of the north at gale force and above, causing huge seas to break on the rocks which shroud the port. Henry, naturally, put a good face on the situation. "Why," he proclaimed, "this inclement weather is the best of omens. Was not my mighty ancestor, William the Conqueror, beset for over a month in this very port by northerly winds? And did he not triumph in the end?"

This was perfectly true, but William had always known that he had only one head to cut off, as it were: Saxon England had been firmly in the grasp of Harold Godwinson, and possession of the island lay simply between the two men. In our circumstances, England wallowed rudderless, to be taken by the first man bold enough, and fortunate enough, to get there. No one possessed a claim equal to Henry's, but yet I could tell that he worried more than he allowed himself to reveal, even to me. My own frustration and anxiety was all but unbearable, for if I had not been showing when we arrived at Barfleur, I was certainly showing a month later, when we were still confined in the beastly place. Quite apart from feeling increasingly inhibited as to movement, of which I had to anticipate there would be a great deal once we actually got across the water, I was now effectively barred from Henry's bed and dependent upon the company of Amaria and my ladies, while I was in mortal fear that he would insist upon returning me to the care of his mother.

Actually, as he later told me, this course never crossed his mind. He was determined to be crowned, *en famille*, with his wife and son at his side. What is more, he was determined to be crowned, in London, before Christmas. So when December dawned and the wind showed so sign of abating, he grew more restless than usual. At last, on the morning of 7 December, he had the trumpets blown. His lords assembled. As the wind howled and the seas raged, I imagine they were under the impression that they were going to be dismissed to their homes until the spring. I had no idea what he was going to tell them, as he was not in the habit of confiding in me and was thus taken as much by surprise as everyone else when, without any preamble, he pointed out to sea and said, "My lords, across that narrow stretch of water lies my kingdom. I will wait no longer to claim it. I sail upon the noon tide. Let those who would ride to glory at my side accompany me. The faint-hearted may remain here in safety."

Those can only be called fighting words; what knight can remain a knight if he is accused of faint-heartedness? Suddenly the whole of Barfleur was a-bustle. Men shouted, women screamed, dogs barked and geese cackled. Cats prudently kept out of sight. Sails were bent on and rowlocks greased. Horses were manhandled on to the largest of the craft. And my ladies twittered. Amaria naturally came with me. We had adventured for too long together to be separated when it seemed certain we were bound for a watery grave. We, and William, embarked with Henry and his immediate bodyguard; our ship was nothing more than a smack, and with twelve passengers, sixteen crew and half a dozen horses, it was very crowded and soon became very noisome as well. However, the royal standard was set, the oars fell to, and we cast off.

The only time I had been at sea when it had *not* been blowing a storm I had been seized by pirates! But on all my earlier occasions I had been in a considerably more substantial boat than this one. And then, the Mediterranean, however often I may have criticised it, is a landlocked sea and the waves seldom get up to any very great height. The English Channel is exposed to the mighty Atlantic, that ocean which stretches clear to the edge of the earth and no doubt tumbles over that edge. Barfleur is actually situated in the Bay of the Seine, and thus, rough as it immediately seemed to us, we were initially slightly protected by the Cherbourg Peninsular. But that did not last long. Our sail was useless, as we were heading into the wind, but the oarsmen pulled lustily and we surged forward, while Amaria and I took heart from the immense fleet that was putting out behind us, rising and falling on the waves, sometimes half lost in the flurries of spray, but all following the leopards of Normandy.

When we left the shelter of the headland and were on the open sea, I had never seen anything like it. Great curling green monsters came rushing at us, blotting out the sky as they reared above us, their crests a mass of tumbling foam which hissed at us as if alive. Amazingly, very few of these great waves actually came on board, but as they broke against our sides or astern of us, or more often than not, on our bows, they sent showers of spray into our midst, soaking us to the skin, and filling the bilges. Thus could be seen the sight of the future King and Queen of England kneeling shoulder to shoulder in the bottom of this tub, together with their knights, baling with all our strength, while Amaria hugged Baby William and endeavoured to keep him as dry as possible. At least I was too busy to be seasick, although what effect the motion was having on the babe in my womb I did not care to think. He also must have become exceedingly hungry as the day wore on, for the only sustenance I had for close on twenty-four hours was some wine gulped from the neck of a flagon.

I think I can say without fear of contradiction that it was the longest day of our lives, and certainly it was an experience I never wished to repeat. Our only relief was at dusk, when our navigator pointed ahead and we made out high cliffs rising out of the foaming surf. "The island called Wight," he explained. "Once we are within her shelter, we are safe."

We had yet to gain that shelter, and although the navigator claimed to know the south coast of England well, he dared not approach the land too closely in the darkness. We spent a most uncomfortable night, tossing to and fro and having to continue baling, so that not one of us slept a wink, and sunrise found us in the midst of the same raging seas and flying spray as on the previous day, accompanied now by lowering clouds and flurries of sleet and rain. At least the land was now very close, and soon after dawn we were making our way up a narrow passage between some high white pillars of rock on our right hand, and a massive foam-ridden sandbank on our left. As the seas were even more tumultuous in this passage I apprehended that we were in greater danger now than at any time before.

What was equally disturbing was the total disappearance of our armada; there was now not a sail to be seen. Whether they had all sunk or had all put back was irrelevant; here were ten men, two women, and a babe – we could not count the sailors – seeking to seize a kingdom. Henry was not insensible to the situation, although his confidence remained unabated. His sole desire was to get ashore, and when we were actually through the passage and in that broad body of sheltered water known as the Solent, he wished to know how soon we would reach the port of Southampton.

"Well, your grace, Southampton is still some twenty miles away," the navigator explained. "And the tide is about to turn. It's running hard this time of the month. Aye, hard. I doubt we'll make the port afore tomorrow."

"Tomorrow?" the King shouted. "Have we been at

sea for twenty-four hours to have to spend another night at sea, when within hailing distance of the land?"

"Aye, well, your grace, 'tis the tides, see. They're strong in here. Aye, strong."

"Then put me ashore," the King commanded. "Somewhere. Anywhere. But put me ashore."

I entirely agreed with him. The thought of spending another night on this now virtually uninhabitable piece of wood was unbearable. Thus overwhelmed by our requirements, the navigator located a small creek meandering through the mudbanks which extended off the southern shore of my new kingdom. Into this we were landed, men, women and horses, a disagreeable business as we had to struggle through the mud, while the inhabitants of the hamlet situated a short distance inland, and called Lymington, stood around and gawped at us, quite unable to reconcile the royal standard with any one of the mud- and sea-stained knights before them. But we were ashore in England.

Happily, so were many others. Our lords may have been scattered by the storm, but not one of them intended to fail the King, save by actually drowning; Henry had that way with people. As we wended our way inland from Lymington and turned through the New Forest – it was now actually quite an old forest, having been created by William the Conqueror nearly a hundred years ago – for Southampton, people emerged from every direction to join us. Not all of these were our original force from Barfleur. All the local barons and their retainers turned out as well, anxious to make their mark with their new ruler. The most remarkable aspect of Henry's descent upon England was that no man's hand was raised against him, so weary were the people, knight and villein alike, from nearly twenty years of civil war and misgovernment. However, we could not be certain of this welcome, and there was some tension as we proceeded first to Southampton and thence to Winchester, where lay the royal treasury, and where, by tradition, any English reign began. By the time we reached Winchester, it had become apparent to us that we were going to be welcomed throughout the land.

My own reflections upon this new kingdom were necessarily coloured by my circumstances, for Henry decreed that I should not ride, but rather be carried in a litter, horseback riding being generally regarded as the most efficacious way of inducing a miscarriage, which neither of us wished; one son is a dream, but two are an insurance against the future! Thus I had more time to look around me, although the jolting I underwent in my moving bed was hardly less than I would have suffered on a horse.

I could by now claim to be a much-travelled woman. I had journeyed the length and breadth of France on more than one occasion, and been impressed by its size and the endless fields of vines, sunflowers or wheat. I had boated on the Danube, and been amazed at the fertility of the great plain traversed by the mighty river. I had penetrated the vastnesses of the Balkan Mountains, and been awed by their craggy peaks and sudden precipices. I had seen Constantinople and Antioch. I had made my way through the treacherous passes of Asia Minor, and I had crossed the desert to look upon Jerusalem. I had made my way the length of sunlit Italy, from Sicily to the Alps. And above all, my heart would ever lie in the many-faceted delights of my native Gascony. But this England over which I was now to be queen possessed a quality all of its own.

It had, it should be remembered, been fought over, especially here in the south, time and again for fifteen years. The evidence of this unending conflict was all around me, in burned and ruined villages, unharrowed and in some cases even unharvested fields. Only the many castles stood, grim and ghastly monuments to the vileness of man, dominating the landscape like creatures from another world. It was also approaching the dead of winter, and much of our time was spent travelling beneath leaden skies which often enough delivered themselves of rain, or sleet, or even snow.

Yet I had never beheld a land so patently bursting with the desire to deliver to man all that he required to live a goodly life. The woods were thicker, the grass was greener, the mud in the fields more clinging, than anywhere I had known. Neglected as they were, the fields yet retained the evidences of growth, and although it was late in the year the trees still drooped beneath the weight of fruit, mostly rotting on the limb. When to this indication of great wealth just waiting to be harvested one adds the obvious pleasure of the weary people who still turned out to greet us, it will be understood that both Henry and I had a great sense of achievement.

We were warmly welcomed in Winchester, but dallied there only a few days before pressing on to London, where we were even more well received. We approached the city with some apprehension, as we knew that of all England the Londoners had supported the usurper most faithfully. Indeed it had been the uprising of these people, following Matilda's great victory at Lincoln, when she had defeated and captured Stephen, which had caused the Empress to flee, and brought all her hopes tumbling to the ground. Now they were being approached by Matilda's son.

We need not have worried. Although they had suffered less, in terms of physical damage and despoilment, than the rest of the nation during the civil war, the Londoners yet conceived that they had suffered enough. They were a trading community. Their great wealth arose from their dealings with the continent, and especially Flanders. This had been greatly interfered with by the decrees of various barons, supporting first one side and then the other. They wanted peace, and a return to prosperity, and they conceived that Henry Plantagenet was the man to give them those things. Nor were they wrong. But that lay in the future. In the present, there was the question of where we were to set up home. We had naturally been taken, in the first instance, to the village of Westminster, which stood some little distance from the city, and where there was not only a splendid cathedral, built a hundred years previously by an earlier English king, so pious that he was known as Edward the Confessor, but also the royal palace. This too was a splendid edifice, on the outside. When we entered its broad portals, however, we were appalled. The place had clearly been looted and despoiled in every possible way. The drapes were torn, the rushes scattered, the furniture broken, and horses had been stabled on the lower floors.

Archbishop Theobald, an elderly fellow with a nervous tic, wrung his hands. "Times have been very hard," he remarked.

"They are scum," muttered Henry, Bishop of Winchester. This was actually the late king's brother, a very handsome fellow, but with a shifty reputation. From time to time during the war, he had supported Matilda against Stephen while seeking advancement; it was common knowledge that he had his eye on the pallium of Canterbury whenever Theobald decided to die (which, looking at the old fellow, did not appear to be a very distant prospect).

"If only we had known you were coming, your grace," Theobald explained. "We would have put the work in hand."

I found this specious. The Archbishop may not have known we were coming on this particular day, in view of the weather, but he had certainly known we *were* coming, in the not too distant future.

Henry, however, did not lose his temper. "That may be," he said. "But where are we to sleep?"

"I will put people to work immediately, your grace," the Archbishop promised.

"We are speaking of the here and now. I am not sleeping in this pigsty," I informed him.

Henry cleared his throat. Although he never prevented me from having my say, he disliked me to be too positive in public, at least in his company. "With respect, your grace," said a quiet voice.

We both turned, and saw an extraordinarily handsome man, about my own age, I estimated – he was actually four years the elder – dressed in clerical robes, to be sure, but very well set up, and standing almost arrogantly before the throng of priests and clerks and lords waiting behind the bishops.

"Who the devil are you?" Henry demanded.

"His name is Becket, your grace," Theobald said. "He is my Archdeacon at Canterbury. Thomas, this is a most unseemly interruption."

"I apologise, your grace," this Becket said, "but I wish to offer the King and Queen suitable accommodation, until this place can be refurbished."

"*You* have accommodation fit for a king?" Henry demanded.

Becket flushed; he did this rather readily. "Not I, your grace. But knowing of your coming, and of the condition of this palace of Westminster, I took the liberty of preparing a priory belonging to the Archbishop."

"Where is this house?" I inquired. I liked the look of this fellow.

He gave me a brief bow, while blushing all over again. "It is not far, your grace, a place called Bermondsey, just on the south side of the river, but in fact east of where we stand. It is hard by the Tower and the Bridge, and will offer every convenience. I have seen to this personally."

"Well, then, let us look at it," I decided, adding, "if you agree, my lord," to Henry. He did some more harrumphing, but as no one had any better suggestion, across the river we went. And I am bound to say that I was impressed. The house was by no means a palace, but it was a substantial place, and had been most thoroughly and tastefully decorated and furnished. "Why, Master Becket," I said, "you are to be congratulated, not only on your foresight and initiative, but on your understanding of what will please a woman."

He gave one of his bows, as well as one of his flushes. "I seek only to please my queen, your grace. May I say that you are more beautiful now than even when I first beheld you?"

"Of course you may. But . . . we have met?"

"No, no, your grace. How could that be? But I was in the throng on that unforgettable day when you entered Paris, nigh on seventeen years ago, a bride and a queen."

"Good heavens!" I commented, remembering the total disfavour with which I had looked upon that unruly mob of students. "Well then, I must also congratulate you upon your memory."

"That man," Henry commented when we were alone, "is going to end his days either as Archbishop of

Canterbury or on the gallows. He has an overweening ambition."

"Which he seeks only to place at our disposal, Henry," I pointed out. "He is clearly a man of ability. I think you should employ him." Thus do we gather sweet-talking vipers to our bosom, without considering that it is actually possible to end one's days both as Archbishop of Canterbury and on the gallows, in a manner of speaking.

As I had been so interested in the country I had travelled so far to rule, at least in a manner of speaking, I was even more interested in this city, which I had to suppose was going to be my home for the better part of the rest of my life. In this I was to be mistaken, but London nevertheless always held my interest, if only because it was unlike any other city I had ever beheld. All rivers are thoroughfares in some degree or other, as well as moats for the cities they guard. In Bordeaux, for example, as in Antioch, the river was situated on the northern side of the walls, as being the most likely to be assailed. In Paris, the river ran on both sides of the Isle de la Cité. But in London, the Thames ran right through the centre. Admittedly the old city walls, and those of the grim edifice of the Tower, and its sister castle, Barnard, rose on the north bank. The Tower, indeed, was almost exactly opposite our dwelling, but the houses and shops had overspilled the bridge onto the south bank, and around us there was a lively, bustling, generally good-humoured community. One of the first things that struck me about London, indeed, was the amount of trading that was carried on at every street-corner and in every shop. In place of masses of priests and students, here were masses of tradesmen, and tradeswomen as well. The bridge itself was an immense shopping arcade, so crowded with houses and people it was a miracle it stood.

Beneath its arches wherries darted to and fro, and downstream, massed along the banks with their sails furled and their oars shipped, were the trading vessels that linked London to Scandinavia and Flanders, Paris and Bordeaux, and even further south. For about the only good thing that had come out of the ill-fated Crusade of 1147 had been the diversion of a fleet of English knights to the assistance of the Prince of Portugal in his unending struggle with the Moors. The Englishmen had helped the Prince capture the Moorish stronghold of Lisbon, whereupon he had not only taken the title of King of Portugal, but had also bestowed great trading privileges upon his allies. Your true Englishman, it may be said, always campaigned with his sword in one hand and his account book in his other, but I suspect this was the Norman in his blood.

I have mentioned that there were far fewer priests to be seen in London than in Paris. This is because there were far fewer churches. These, in and around the city itself as distinct from Westminster, were universally of a small and insignificant sort, with hardly a stained glass window to be seen, much less a lofty spire. I'm sure, in view of my experiences – and those of my family – at the hands of the Church, that I cannot be criticised for feeling that this was no bad thing. Indeed it was a great relief to discover that English society was by no means as riddled with sanctity as was France. Quite the reverse, in fact. Bishop Henry of Winchester, although I knew him for a rogue, was both handsome and urbane. He was a man who enjoyed both wine and wenching, not to mention wealth, of which he had managed to accumulate a great deal. This was achieved principally by retaining hold of the diocese of

Glastonbury as well as that of Winchester, a procedure quite outside of Church Law, but that interested him not a whit.

Even Archbishop Theobald, aged and decrepit as he was, was not above a romp, while the lesser clergy were a very lively lot. And of them all, our new friend and servant, Thomas à Becket, was the liveliest. He had, in fact, just about every vice possible in a cleric, for quite apart from being as fond of the three w's as Bishop Henry, he also enjoyed ostentation, and was always dressed in the finest clothes. I could see that, despite his initial criticism, Henry was quite taken with the fellow, especially as Becket went out of his way to be helpful, and was always at the King's beck and call. Thus was our arrival at our new capital smoothed, as was every other arrangement, and on 19 December, the Sunday before Christmas, Henry and I were crowned, Prince William seated on my lap.

Being crowned is naturally an event of the utmost importance. It is of great significance for the hoi poloi, who cannot conceive of a man as their king until he has been properly annointed by God's representatives, and it is of even greater significance to the nobles, who are required to kneel before their new master and swear eternal allegiance. Believe it or not – and remembering the events of the civil war it is difficult *to* believe it – a large number of these people actually take their oaths very seriously, requiring considerable cause before they will break them. Being crowned is equally an experience of great importance for the principals, attended as the ceremony is by a great deal of mumbo jumbo and ritual. For a queen it is more disturbing than relieving, as it is hopefully the only occasion on which her assembled notables and their wives will ever see her in extreme *deshabille*. As a fifteen-year-old I had found this something of a challenge, in Bourges. But that had been somewhat farther south than Westminster, and not yet December. As a seven-months-pregnant thirty-two-year-old I found being publicly stripped to the waist and annointed with oil a distinct ordeal, and not only because of the chill. However, some unpleasant experiences are worth any ordeal. I was Queen of England!

The coronation ended my interest in political matters for a season, and early in February 1155 I gave birth to my fourth child, and my second son! I wondered what Louis would make of that! This child we named Henry, after his father and great-grandfather. And here was indeed a lusty babe. Henry I did not feed, as I was now prepared to take seriously any medical opinions about the risks to childbearing; I was married to about the most virile man in the world, in my experience, and I desired only to continue bearing him children for as long as he desired me to. As whenever he was about he was about *me* at least once a day, I could not see this happy state of affairs ever ending.

Meanwhile, I had a lot to do. Anyone who attempted to keep up with Henry always had a lot to do. He was first of all sorting out his kingdom. As this meant, in the first instance, sorting out his baronage, there was a considerable amount of travelling to be done. His invariable speed and his equally invariable secrecy meant that he was likely to appear out of the blue, quite literally, in front of some hapless castle, and before the lord could gather his wits he was commanded to pull his house down because he had built it without a licence. This was exciting, if occasionally alarming: Henry did not always have an adequate force at his back. Yet no one ever attempted to resist him or his command. It was as if the Devil were indeed abroad, but it was a devil intent on restoring England to that green and pleasant – and wealthy – land which had proved so attractive to William the Conqueror. Thus it was that William of Aumale surrendered his fortress of Scarborough; William Peverel fled Nottingham and took refuge in a monastery, where he remained for the rest of his life; and Roger of Hereford surrendered Hereford and Gloucester.

Henry could be magnanimous when he felt it politic. Thus William of Ypres, a bastard son of the Count of Flanders, who had been Stephen's chief general, was permitted to keep his castles for a period of three years; they were all in the south-east of the country and were Henry's whenever he chose to take them. But when Hugh Mortimer, the chief of the Marcher lords, controlling the border between England and Wales, attempted to resist, Henry systematically laid siege to and pulled down his castles, until he too was forced to surrender on bended knee. This event, at which I was not present, was very nearly fatal to all our ambitions, as an arrow fired from the battlements of Mortimer's castle was on the way to embed itself in Henry's breast, when a noble knight, Hubert de St Clair, stepped in front and sacrificed himself for the King.

Nor did Henry omit to put the Church to rights. He did not trouble Archbishop Theobald, who was certainly not going to trouble him, and he confirmed men such as Nigel, Bishop of Ely, always a faithful adherent of his mother's, as Treasurer, but it was intimated to Bishop Henry of Winchester that it might be for the good of all if he took an extended visit to the continent. As with most churchmen of that period who happened to have fallen out with their temporal lords, Bishop Henry retired to Cluny, while King Henry demolished every one of his castles, appropriating their wealth.

Certainly the commonalty saw him as their deliverer from oppression, especially when he accompanied his castle-destroying forays with the re-establishment of a proper legal system. This had actually been instigated by his grandfather, who had not been called Beauclerk for nothing, and was based upon a contingent of justices who travelled from county to county, holding assizes. People gathered in their thousands when they learned that the King's representatives were about, judging men according to their crimes rather than the whim of their liege lord. As such judges were accountable only to the King, it meant the power of the baron to tyrannize his people was severely limited – but it also meant that the system required a strong and ruthless king to make it a success. Thus it had fallen into disuse during Stephen's usurpation, and the villeins had again been left to the wrath and lusts of their local lords. Of course on these early *chevauchees* Henry had not yet had the time to reinstate justice, except in his immediate presence, but the people clearly could sense that they again had a *king*, and once it was known that he was in their neighbourhood, they gathered in their thousands to cheer him and even to kiss his feet, if he could be reached. Nor was I neglected in their approbation.

From which it will be gathered that I accompanied him whenever possible. But accompanying Henry was always an exhausting business. He would ride all morning, and then think nothing of summoning us to the hunt in the afternoon. I am as energetic as any woman I have ever known, and most men too, but Henry did have the advantage of eleven years. Besides, the business of kingship, whether it be in politics or sport, is less all-consuming to a woman than a man, especially when she is only a consort. There were other aspects to living which interested me equally. Principally this concerned my new home. The house in Bermondsey was comfortable enough, but by no stretch of the imagination could it be called a palace. However exciting I had initially found living in the very heart of such a vigorous community to be, the cries of the fishmongers – and indeed the smell of their fish – soon palled as an entertainment.

In these circumstances Becket was a boon. Henry had almost immediately made the young man Chancellor. I did not see that he could have made a better choice. Becket was the man that Henry himself would have been had he not been born a prince. They had almost everything in common, save perhaps for Becket's love of ostentation, but that was all to the good from my point of view, as I shall explain shortly. For the rest, here was perhaps the most intelligent and best educated king in Europe, possessing a Chancellor of equal intellect and learning. They would sit for hours, discussing things from the merest syllogism to affairs of state. I watched the immense friendship, the intimacy, springing up between them with a joyous heart. All kings need their male intimates, their great counsellors. Poor Louis had inherited Suger, and had never got around to replacing him, at least during my tenure of office as Queen of France, but what kind of relationship could they possibly have save that of monk and oblate? Neither man had ever had the slightest idea how to enjoy himself. From my point of view, Becket was even more of a boon companion. For, dare I say it, I was even better educated than my husband, and I doubt his intellect was any the superior. To converse with Becket was an unending pleasure. I had barely to mention a subject, be it my favourite romance, Tristan and Isolde, or my favourite city, Antioch, and he had something worthwhile to add to my reflections. He had, of course, never been to Antioch, but he had read of it, and his lively imagination could bring his learning to life. Equally his clerical life had limited his romantic interludes, but he knew the saga from beginning to end and, here again, he could imagine what was necessary.

I should make it clear at this point that there was never anything irregular between us, and this may appear odd in view of my previous confessions. Here were a beautiful woman and a handsome man often closeted alone together, and never a suggestion of physical intimacy? But the fact is that I never found him, however handsome and debonair and learned, the least sexually attractive. Nor did he give any indication of being sexually attracted to me. For me, he was too perfect, and besides, I quickly discerned his problem – indeed I had discerned it on the occasion of our first meeting: his dreams were filled with only one lure, that of advancement. But as he certainly appreciated that such advancement could only arise through the good offices of his king and queen, I did not see how this could be a bad thing. Certainly his desire to please accomplished miracles. When I returned from one of the King's parades early in July – Henry was about to go off and fight with Hugh Mortimer in Wales, and I had no desire to spend the summer campaigning in such a barbarous country – Becket was waiting for me with a most conspiratorial air. Before I knew what was happening he had me placed in a boat and taken downstream to Westminister, to show me the palace. Because it was now a palace. It had been completely refurbished, was clean and comfortable, and had the most exquisite apartments. I was delighted, and said so, and that pleased him. Even Henry, Mortimer conquered, was pleased to take up residence in this ancient home of the English monarchy and, by Christmas I was pregnant.

Was I then not the happiest woman in the world? Had I not triumphed over every possible adversity? Was I not married to the most powerful man in Europe, and also the most virile one? Did I not have all the intellectual company I could wish? Was I not the mother of two bouncing baby boys with another on the way? All of these things are entirely true. But happiness is a transient business, to be sure. In the new year, Prince William sickened and died. He contracted some kind of a cough, which he could not shake off, and despite all the surgeons could do he just dwindled away.

The death of a first-born is like the death of a part of oneself. I am speaking as a woman, of course. To observers, including my husband, these things are only important when they affect the course of history. Little William's death did not do that. He was not my *first*-born, although he was my first-born of Henry. He had been heir to the great possessions over which Henry ruled, but there was another heir and, hopefully, yet another waiting to take his place upon the stage. His death was a pity, but hardly a catastrophe.

Save for his mother. I wept for days after we had laid the poor little mite to rest.

# Chapter Three

Never have I felt so alone as at the death of William. I was in the worst possible situation for a mother, as I was several months pregnant – this was, in fact, some solace for my loss – and also husbandless, for the moment. Having satisfied himself that England was completely pacified in his favour, Henry's ambitions had begun to roam further afield, in the direction of Ireland, no less.

There was a great deal to be said for the idea of bringing Ireland within the Angevin fold. Quite apart from being the last known land on earth, it had been overrun by the Vikings some centuries before, and remained a nest of pirates indulging in continuous internicine wars with the native Irish – who were even more warlike – when they were not raiding the shipping off our west coasts. There was also the consideration that if we did not conquer Ireland, someone else might, which would be very inconvenient. However, it was a vast enterprise, and to me it made more sense to settle affairs closer to home. I was thinking of Toulouse, where the recalcitrant barons had had the temerity to set up their own count, some distant cousin of mine, apparently forgetting that I was their legal liege lady. Needless to say in taking this step they were encouraged and supported by my first husband, still out to prick me wherever he could.

Even if Toulouse might be considered too much on the fringes of our empire, and equally that an expedition against it might involve a full-scale war with France, for which Henry was not at that moment ready, there were countries far closer to home which also needed sorting out. I am speaking of Wales, which was filled with wild Welshmen, and Scotland, which was filled with even wilder Scotsmen. Now, both Wales and Scotland had supported the Empress against Stephen, but this was in the main because both Wales and Scotland delighted in nothing better than invading England, and supporting Matilda had actually provided them with a legal reason for doing so. Now that Stephen was gone, I had no doubt they would soon find a reason to fall out with Matilda's son, and indeed it may be recalled that the previous summer Henry had already clashed with the Welsh.

However, it was Ireland upon which he had set his sights, and realising that I was going to offer him no encouragement and, as I was no comfort to his bed in my condition, he had taken himself off, to discuss the matter with his mother. I am happy to say that Matilda was also against so rash an adventure, and indeed she put the lid on the whole idea, at least for the time being. But the fact is that Henry was in Rouen while I was stuck in London, grieving, and preparing to give birth. Here again Becket was a tower of strength. He entirely took over the management and education of Prince Henry. This may sound a bit far-fetched, as Henry was only a year old, but Becket began his education just as soon as the little boy could speak. It is never too young to learn.

I gave birth to my first daughter by Henry in the June of 1156. As we had agreed, she was named Matilda after her maternal grandmother. The very moment the babe and I were well enough to travel, we left England, accompanied by Prince Henry and Becket, to rejoin my husband as well as display the babe to her grandmother. We reached Rouen without mishap, where the Empress was delighted with her namesake. Henry was not there. He was in Anjou, dealing with brother Geoffrey who, although having supported us in our invasion of England, now claimed to have done so in the belief that once his brother was secure on the throne, he would be granted the counties of Anjou and Maine. These had, indeed, been willed to him by his father. But Henry had never had the least intention of giving up one yard of his possessions, and Geoffrey had taken umbrage. Thus Henry had marched south with an army.

"Brothers will fight," Matilda said equably. My mother-in-law was now in her mid-fifties, and was a most remarkably mellowed lady, at least by comparison with the tales I had heard of her temper in her youth. "But Henry will always have the better of Geoffrey."

I hoped she was right. "Do you not think I should go down there?" I asked.

"Of course you must not, until things are settled," she said. "Unless you intend to leave the babies here."

I did not want to do that, and so I sat patiently in Rouen for the next couple of months until, as Matilda had prophesied, Geoffrey surrendered, with the promise of Brittany. This he indeed secured, the reigning duke, Conan, having recently died. I can't say the Breton nobles were the least happy at receiving a Norman/Angevin ruler, but the people seemed content. Actually, Henry was as usual thrusting his fingers deep into the pond. He knew what I, for one, did not: that having spent a brief lifetime living way beyond his physical means, his brother was not long for the world. He also knew that Conan had left behind him a daughter – but once the good Bretons had become used to the rule of an Angevin duke, all things might be possible.

It was during this brief period of our separation that Bernard of Ventadour popped up again, having been put out to grass by my husband. Amaria was all of a twitter, as she appeared in my chamber and whispered to me that: "The minstrel is here."

I received him. He had done me some most important services in the past, and I was relieved to see him looking well and to discover that Henry had not in any way mistreated him. But our day was done. The wife of Henry Plantagenet had not the time for adultery, even when separated from her husband – quite apart from being unable to contemplate the consequences were she discovered *in flagrante delicto*. Besides, although I knew Bernard's touch was like velvet, I had become used to Henry's rough and ready methods, and was finding them quite to my liking. Thus we delude ourselves. The fact is that I was now deeply in love, and was foolish enough to suppose that my husband was also. At the end of the summer I was able to join my beloved, and we had a merry romp in which he succeeded finally in ending my grief over the death of William, following which, to my great pleasure, he determined on a *chevauchee* through Aquitaine.

This was more than merely a matter of showing the flag, as it were. It was necessary to remind my barons that they did have a duchess, and more, a duke. Several of them seemed to have entirely forgotten these important facts, and there were even some calls to arms. Henry quashed that idea by the simple expedient of arresting the most prominent of the would-be insurgents, and informing them that they were required to attend their master and mistress for the celebration of Christmas. Of course they understood that they were hostages for the good behaviour of their people, but they put a good face on it.

This was my first proper return to Bordeaux since I had left it, in the most murky circumstances, nearly twenty years before. In that time, I had revisited my ducal capital twice, but with Louis it had been a hurried, unsatisfactory affair, with the future looming too heavily in front of me, and when Henry and I had come this way in 1153 that too had been in a hurry, and again the future had been summoning us to be on our way. But now I was home for a season, together with my two babes, and a husband who had proved himself to be worthy of his great station. As far as I was concerned I was travelling with the present as well as the future. I had total confidence in this future. It was with the utmost pleasure that I showed Henry the delights of my city, boated with him on the fast-running Garonne, hunted with him in the woods south of the city, and sang songs to him in the high towers of the Ombriere. It was a happy time, the only sadness being the absence of Geoffrey de Rançon, called to his ancestors the previous year. But I conceived that I had obtained another Chancellor, even more talented and faithful, in Becket, who was holding the fort in England.

I was happy that Christmas in Bordeaux, perhaps more so than ever before in my life, and I believe that Henry was happy too. Certainly he spent every available moment in my company, and we slept every night in each other's arms. At thirty-four years old I considered myself at the height of my beauty, and at twenty-three Henry was at his most virile. The result was inevitable, and joyous. I suspect that while I would have loved my third son more than any of the others in any event, on account of his genius and his personality – and even his waywardness – I loved him before any of those characteristics were apparent, simply because he was conceived in the Ombriere, in Bordeaux, in sun-washed Aquitaine.

Naturally neither Henry nor I were aware that I was again pregnant when, with Christmas behind us and the New Year celebrated, it was necessary for us to resume the business of ruling. As, despite his hostage taking, Henry still felt he needed to knock a few heads together, it was decided that I would return to England, where he would join me in the spring. Thus, with Young Hal, Matilda and Amaria, together with a sizeable mesnie, I made my way north, visited Grandmama in Rouen, and in February crossed from Barfleur to Southampton. I may say that February is probably the least propitious of all months in which to cross the Channel, but on this occasion we made the voyage without the slightest mishap, there being no wind and the sea thus perfectly calm. I arrived in Westminster with my family at the beginning of March, to be greeted with the greatest pleasure by dear Thomas. I was filled with pleasure myself, for I by then knew that I was again well on the way to becoming a mother. My third son was born on 8 September, at the palace of Woodstock, outside Oxford, by which time Henry had rejoined me.

This was actually the first time Henry had been present at the birth of any of our children, and while in a sense I was very happy for him to be there, especially as this was by far the most difficult of my deliveries, he was something of an embarrassment. He stormed in and out of my lying-in chamber, shouting commands at the midwives, who knew very well what they were about, and at the same time carrying on state matters with various scribes who were waiting in the antechamber. Even Thomas was present, as well, of course, as the Archbishop. They all had a lengthy wait. My third son was far larger than any of my other babes, and took an unconscionable and painful time before gracing us with his presence. Indeed there were times when I did not think I would survive, but I did, and the witnesses gathered round to gaze at the lustily roaring babe. We named him Richard.

It was a few weeks following the birth of Richard that Henry came to sit with me, dismissing all of my attendants. This was a surprise. Richard was the first of Henry's children to whom I gave my breast on a regular basis, for while I saw no reason to doubt medical theory, I also felt that I had done my duty as a queen, and were I not again to become pregnant, I would have been perfectly content. Indeed, although I have loved all of my children in some degree, history may well have been better pleased had I lost my fecundity at that moment. This was not to be. But Henry, as always, was full of plans. "Young Hal," he said, "he must have a wife."

"Well," I said, "surely the matter can wait a year or two." Young Hal was only two years old.

"It cannot wait," Henry declared. "The time is ripe now. You are aware that the Queen of France has given birth to a daughter?"

"Poor Louis must be gnashing his teeth. He is capable of nothing more." I spoke with the utmost carelessness, not being able to conceive what my husband had in mind.

"Indeed. There is talk that he will put Constance away as he did you, and seek yet another wife."

"I beg your pardon," I said. "Louis did not put me away. I ended the marriage long before he got around to it."

"Yes, yes," Henry said impatiently. "The point is that a marriage between Young Hal and the Princess Margaret would hold out immense promise for the future."

I'm afraid I goggled at him. "You are proposing a marriage between my son and the daughter of my first husband?"

"There is no blood between them."

"There most certainly is. Have you forgotten that the Church refused you permission to wed my daughter?"

"Not the Church," he argued. "That old goat Bernard of Clairvaux. Well, thank the Lord, he is not going to interfere in this one."

"I am quite sure someone will be found to raise an objection," I pointed out. "What about Louis?"

"I think Louis will agree to it," Henry said. "Consider: he has no son. And he has virtually no prospect of ever having one, now. The French would never have a woman as their reigning queen. Well, as we saw with Mama, neither would the English, after having sworn to accept her. The French actually have a law against it. Thus Louis' only hope of avoiding the total break-up of his kingdom is to import a son, as it were."

"My son! Louis probably hates me more than any other person in the world."

"Louis has not got the personality to hate with any steadfastness. And he also will see immense gains to be made from such a marriage. Henry is my heir. Thus we would have the King of France who is also the King of England, the Duke of Normandy, the Count of Anjou, and the Duke of Aquitaine. Not to mention the Lord of Ireland," he added for good measure. "Could the Emperor of China claim to be as powerful?"

I knew absolutely nothing about the Emperor of China. But I did not much care for Henry's pecking order. Quite apart from putting Aquitaine at the bottom of the list . . . "And this superhuman emperor will firstly be King of France."

Henry tapped his nose. "That is a point of view. Why should he not firstly be King of England? I intend to have him crowned just as soon as he is old enough, so there can be no question of his inheritance. Think on this, my pet: I am a good dozen years younger than Louis, and in much better health. I am certain to outlive him. I will thus still be King of England when my son becomes King of France. Now is that not a pleasant prospect?" It certainly was a fascinating idea. But I remained sure that Louis, or his advisers would never agree. "We'll send Thomas," Henry declared. "That'll do the trick."

Becket was delighted to have been selected as ambassador for such a vast project. But as ever, his thoughts ranged far beyond the immediate. "I shall need a great mesnie," he said, when we discussed the project with him, at Christmas, which we celebrated at Lincoln, one of the premier towns in England, and where we again were ceremonially crowned to allow the people of the north to enjoy the spectacle. "The King of France must understand that he is dealing with a power far greater than his own."

I understood what the rogue was after immediately. He had been a penniless student in Paris some twenty years before. Therefore he undoubtedly had a great many memories of the place, and more important, the people. Some he would remember as having treated him well; others, many more others, one suspects, as having treated him ill. No doubt there were women involved as well; those who had spurned a pauper student, perhaps one or two who had granted him their favours out of pity. But all related to his then poverty. He intended to reveal to them how the wheel can turn.

"Take whatever you wish," Henry said carelessly, but even he was astonished at what Thomas did take. It was widely said that nothing like it had ever been seen in France before. The cavalcade commenced with eight wagons bearing the Chancellor's personal belongings, which included his travelling chapel with its great gilded cross, and his travelling bedchamber as well as his travelling kitchen, with all its innumerable appurtenances. Then came several carts laden with English beer, followed by barrel-topped wagons containing the Chancellor's vestments and carpets, not to mention his bedclothes. Behind these, twelve horses bore his table plate, his books and his rolls. Then there were grooms and hawkers, leading English hounds in pairs and bearing English falcons on their wrists. Then came two hundred and fifty English yeomen, who sang English songs whenever they passed through a village or town. They were followed by the knights with their squires, a perfect blaze of heraldry. And at the rear rode the Chancellor himself, accompanied by his clerics and dignitaries, all dressed in the finest clothes. The entire parade was guarded, left and right, by armed soldiers accompanied by fierce dogs, and on the back of each lead horse there was to be seen, seated with as much gravity as any bishop, a long-tailed ape.

Small wonder that it was reported to us they were saying in France, "If this is how the Chancellor of the King of England travels, how then does the King himself proceed?" Even Paris was found to be too small for such an army, and too poor for such wealth. Thomas was lodged in the Great Hall of the Knights Templar, and his largesse induced a galloping inflation into that tight little city. The most amazing thing about this totally vulgar display of ostentation – although I suppose we must give some credit to Thomas's diplomatic skills – is that Louis agreed to the proposed match. And the terms! For Henry wanted, as Princess Margaret's dowry, the Vexin.

I may have mentioned this parcel of land before. It is neither very large nor very rich, but sticks into the area where Normandy abuts Anjou like a dagger thrust, and commands communication between the two. This was bad enough when the Duke of Normandy and the Count of Anjou were different men. When they were one and the same, it was intolerable. My second husband has been recognised far and wide as a most formidable soldier, but he was a far more formidable diplomat. Now Louis, as I have said, agreed to the terms. Perhaps he considered himself safe, for the dowry was not to be conceded until the actual marriage, and Prince Henry was not yet three while the Princess Margaret was a babe in arms. But again, he did not seem to have taken the measure of King Henry. Nor did he, when the King, with far less pomp and ceremony than Becket, himself journeyed to Paris in the early summer to take possession of his son's bride.

I did not accompany him as, yet again, I was heavy with child. Before his departure, however, I had another serious chat with him about the future. "We are going to have no more disputed successions," he told me again. "As soon as he is old enough to know what he is about, Young Hal will be crowned King of England. Of course he will not in any way usurp my prerogatives, but everyone will know that he is there to step into my shoes the moment I die. Then I shall have Louis agree to the same procedure, so that the lad will step into *his* shoes the moment *he* dies."

It seemed to me that he was being very optimistic about all this, but I was not prepared to argue with him at that juncture. I had my own fish to fry. "And what of Richard?"

"Ah," he said. "I have been considering this." It was now that he told me he thought his brother Geoffrey did not have long to live. "He has quite debauched himself into premature senility," he said. "Thus all we need is to bide our time with patience, and in a year or two Brittany will lack a duke. But it will have a duchess: the baby Constance. We shall marry Richard to her, and he will become Duke of Brittany. As a fief of mine, of course."

"Oh, no," I said. "Oh, no, no, no."

He raised his shaggy red eyebrows. "You do not wish Richard to be Duke of Brittany?"

"That wild headland? That will not suffice for Richard. I wish him to be Duke of Aquitaine."

"Eh?"

"It is appropriate. He was conceived there."

"Hm."

"He would of course do you homage, and keep my lands as your seneschal," I pointed out. I can be quite winning myself when I choose. "And of course to Young Hal," I added. "In the course of time."

"Hm. But if he is to marry Constance of Brittany, he will have to be Duke of Brittany as well. That is too much."

"I have no wish for him to marry Constance of Brittany," I said. "I am sure we will find him a much more suitable bride. Richard should have a princess, not a duchess, as his wife."

"Then what of Brittany?"

"I am sure we will find something to do with it, in the course of time," I said. I already had ideas of my own.

In his haste to be away to Paris he agreed to all of this, leaving me to hold the fort in England. And in that summer, as I had hoped and anticipated, I gave birth to yet another son. This one I named Geoffrey, after Henry's father . . . not his brother. I was sure the King would be pleased.

It may thus be accepted that I was very content with my marriage. After my years of frustration and even humiliation as the unwanted Queen of France, I was now achieving greatness as the wife of the most formidable man in Europe, and was establishing a reputation for myself as the most formidable woman in Europe, saving perhaps my mother-in-law. I had also been most successful as a mother. Of course I still grieved for dear William. What mother would not forever grieve for her first-born, even if he had been my first-born second time around? But I now possessed a family of three boys and three girls, even if I continued to regard my two eldest girls as lost to me. I was thoroughly content. Thus in December I again crossed the Channel to join my husband at Cherbourg for Christmas, taking all my Plantagenet babies with me, and discovered that my family was even larger than I had supposed.

We arrived at Cherbourg only just in time to celebrate the festival, and I was disappointed to discover that the Princess Margaret was not there. "She is in Rouen, with Mama," Henry said. "We will go there in the New Year. Now let me see the babe." For of course he had not yet seen his latest child. I proudly took him into the nursery, where the royal nursemaids, commanded and marshalled by Amaria, waited. "A likely lad," Henry said. "What are we to call him?"

"Why, Henry," I protested, "we agreed on this. He is named after your papa."

"Ah," he said. "Yes. Did we agree to that? I do not remember. It will be confusing, to be sure."

"What will be confusing, sire?" I asked, feeling most peculiar.

"Well," he said. "Yes. Come here, boy." The King, as is the way with kings, was attended wherever he went by a horde of guards and priests and squires and lords and ladies and jesters . . . and various children. One got into the habit of hardly noticing these hangers-on; I certainly never did. But now I was required to look more closely as the little boy – he was hardly more than six years old – came forward. He was most certainly Henry's son, for he resembled his father more than any of my brood.

I felt quite hot and then cold in successive flushes. I have surely mentioned that I was aware my husband required comfort in his bed either when I was not present or in the throes of menstruation or pregnancy. This had never greatly concerned me, because these reliefs had always surely been incidental. That they might have an outcome – that indeed, by the law of averages, they *had* to have an outcome had equally never concerned me either. Such a child was the responsibility of his mother. Oh, no doubt the King would make some kind of settlement upon the woman, but there would be an end to it. I had certainly never expected to be brought face to face with such a love child. And to discover that his name was . . . "Geoffrey," Henry explained. "Well, he was born some time before *that* Geoffrey. He was my first child, you see, and so I named him after Papa." For only the second time in my life I was rendered utterly speechless. But Henry could see that I would soon recover my powers. "He is a charming child," he hurried on. "And intelligent with it. The fact is, my dearest Anor, his mother has recently died, and, well . . . he is a charming child. And my first-born."

I found this repetition of such a nauseating fact unwelcome. "And who was his mother, pray, sire?" I inquired.

"Her name was Ykenai."

I could scarce believe my ears. "Ykenai?"

"Well, yes, she had no pretensions to rank," he said. "Indeed, she had no pretensions."

"You mean she was a common whore!"

"Well, she lived by her body, yes. However, that is by the by. I would like to point out that when she and I conceived this lad, you were still married to Louis of France. I am no adulterer." Well, talk about stretching the bow. However, I still loved him dearly, and if he had produced this offspring before our marriage had even been contemplated . . . "You will like the boy," Henry said winningly. "He is just like me, in every way."

I could not be certain that was a recommendation. Henry was enormous fun as a husband, but had he not been my husband I doubted I could ever have been his friend. However, the boy was certainly attractive looking, and was giving me a bright, albeit anxious, smile. "He will go into the Church," I decided.

"Absolutely what I had in mind," Henry declared.

"Until then, why, he may join the family," I said. "He may serve the princes."

"Absolutely," Henry agreed again.

Thus was our first marital crisis surmounted, very successfully. I suppose it is a blessing that we mortals are not vouchsafed a glimpse of the future.

\* \* \*

In fact I found Geoffrey the Bastard (a necessary distinction from Geoffrey the Prince) a most pleasant companion. He was certainly as intelligent as Henry claimed, and he was entirely anxious to please me. And his mother was dead. There could be no obstacle in the way of our friendship. In the New Year I journeyed to Rouen in good heart. There I met Margaret of France for the first time, and was well pleased. It is not of course possible to form any judgement of character in a one-year-old child. One can only look for good health and some spirit, as well as, hopefully, some signs of intelligence. Margaret possessed all of these, and she and Young Hal appeared good friends from the moment of their first meeting.

It was also a great treat to be again with Matilda, a woman I grew more and more to like every time I saw her. She was, as always, delighted with her grandchildren, and even patted Geoffrey the Bastard on the head. But she reserved her special warmth for me. There was much we had to discuss, and it was now that she told me how she had put the idea of conquering Ireland out of Henry's mind, as she and I hoped, forever. "And I had a lot to contend with," she said. "Henry claims he has been given the place by Pope Adrian. Do you know anything of this?"

This was not altogether surprising. Pope Adrian was actually an Englishman named Nicholas Breakspear, and he was the first Englishman ever to achieve the giddy heights of pontiff. As he had needed Henry's fullest support to climb so high, it was natural that he should seek to reward his benefactor. But this seemed to be going over the top. "I have never heard of it," I confessed. "Can popes give away lands?"

"I really do not know the legality of it. But it would

set a very bad precedent for the future were an English pope to give the King of England an entire country. What happens when next there is a French pope? However, I have directed Henry's ambitions into a far more suitable direction: Toulouse."

I clapped my hands for joy. But it was here that Henry and I received the first check to our hitherto triumphant career.

The moment actually seemed entirely appropriate to regain my long lost territory. My usurping cousin, who was also named Raymond, although not a patch on the man who had been my uncle, had fallen out with the Duke of Barcelona, and there was a desultory war going on between the two territories, which abutted each other. Thus Henry contracted a treaty of alliance with Barcelona, and set out with all his panoply.

However, there were factors at work which were against us, in the main my beastly ex-sister-in-law, Constance. This young lady had been a nuisance ever since I could remember. It may be recalled that she had been betrothed to Eustace of Boulogne, over my objections, way back in 1140, and had thus, for the space of several years, found herself a pawn in the struggle between the Empress and the usurper Stephen. Again, as it may be recalled, the young princess – she had been under ten at the time – had been placed in the Tower of London, and had thus changed hands as often as London had changed hands. Whether, in all of this, she had actually lost her maidenhead has never been established, not even after she was officially married to her husband, as Eustace by then had been more interested in booze and battle, harlots and harrying, than anything as humdrum as a wife. Now Eustace had, like his uncle Henry Beauclerk, fallen foul of a plate of lampreys in 1153; why anyone ever touches this pernicious delicacy quite defeats me – I personally loathe them. This had left Constance a widow, and Stephen, then in his own last throes, saw no objection to her being returned to her brother. Thus Louis had had to find something to do with her, and he had determined to wed her to this Raymond of Toulouse. Some women, it seems, are just born to be wed to usurpers or would-be usurpers.

We did not assume that her presence in Toulouse would make much difference to either our plans or our prospects. Henry proceeded with his usual mixture of élan and caution, and with his Barcelonian allies encountered the Toulouse army north of the city, and defeated it, capturing the town of Cahors. He then moved towards the city itself, calling upon it to surrender and preparing to besiege it, when he received most unpleasant news: Louis had himself hurried south, on learning of his sister's danger, and thrown himself into the city. The force he had with him was small, and in a purely military sense his presence could make little difference to the situation . . . but he was the King of France, and he was, legally, Henry's liege lord.

Here was a syllogism, if you like. Henry decided that he did not wish to appear to the world as a rebel against his lord – especially while opinion remained divided on the ethics of his making off with his lord's wife – and returned to Normandy, leaving Becket to oversee proceedings in the south-west. But with orders not to attack the town, at least as long as Louis was inside it. This was, as I have said, the first setback we had ever received. But things now started happening in every direction.

While Henry had still been outside the walls of

Toulouse Pope Adrian had died. This was a potentially serious matter for us, Adrian having been such a loyal and indeed, as we have seen, over-enthusiastic supporter of our projects, but as it happened, his death had sparked the usual controversy, and as had occurred so often before, Christendom found itself with two popes. The cardinals in conclave chose the Papal Chancellor, Roland Bandinello, as their new head: he took the name of Alexander III. This did not please Emperor Frederic, however, and he insisted that the new pope should be Cardinal Octavian, who took the name Victor IV. Backed by the imperial power, Victor forced his way into Rome and Alexander had to flee, which he did in the best tradition, to France.

Thus he was now seeking support. He was sure of Louis, again traditionally, and equally because Louis and Frederic loathed each other. But the situation posed a problem for us, as while we had been loyal supporters of what might be called the orthodox Papacy as long as Adrian had lived, we were also traditionally allies of the Emperor, who I continued to remember most fondly. But Henry, as ever, was ready to take advantage of the situation. For yet another momentous event took place this autumn; Queen Constance of France died in childbirth. The babe was actually born, but it was another girl, who was named Alais. Louis just did not appear to have it in him to father a son. But he remained an optimist, even if it meant behaving with a sad lack of good taste. We were all sympathetic when he went hurrying back to Paris from Toulouse upon learning of his wife's demise, but equally we were all astounded when he had married again within a month. And not merely married: he had chosen as his third wife Adelaide of Champagne!

Now this really was playing fast and loose with moral

and political issues. Adelaide was the sister of the lout, Theodore of Blois, who had tried to get his hands on me. She was therefore the projected sister-in-law of my two daughters, who it may be recalled had been betrothed to Theobald and his brother. Now really, how may a man marry the sister-in-law of his own daughters? This was really throwing the concept of consanguinity right out of the window, and it was obvious to us that Louis had had a quick chat with Alexander, and informed him that if he wanted the continued support of the French Crown he had better humour its plan, which, it was now apparent, was to keep marrying again and again until someone – possibly *anyone* – produced a son. I was staggered. But Henry was always capable of outsmarting Louis. He also went along to have a chat with Alexander, and returned with an even greater prize. The business of betrothal until puberty was set aside before anyone had the time to object, Prince Henry and Princess Margaret, the one five and the other two, were solemnly married.

As mother of the groom, I naturally had to play a part in this business, and of course what mother can resist the marriage of her eldest son. Though it becomes a bit farcical when one has to lead him up the aisle by the hand, while his bride, somewhat overborne by her robes and her jewellery, has to be carried in the arms of her nurse. But married they were, although how legal the whole business was remained to be seen. "What do you intend to do about the consummation?" I asked Henry at the wedding feast; the bride had already fallen asleep. "Or do you propose to jam him into her? I may as well tell you, I will have no part in it. It is against law and nature, and common decency."

"They are married," he declared. "That is what matters. Who is to say when it will be consummated?

They are married. I have already given the command for the Vexin to be occupied."

As may be supposed, the Capetians were outraged, as was the House of Blois, now even more closely united to the French royal house. Indeed, the whole business began to take on a profoundly incestuous appearance. But Theobald's appearance was in keeping with his appearance in every other field. Henry merely took a couple of his castles and he retired again.

I am not going to pretend that I entirely approved of my husband's carryings-on, but this was in a purely moral and legal sense, and it may be said, as Henry did say, that I had no strong moral or legal grounds in my own past on which to base my objections. But I could not help but be wholly admiring of his ruthless determination to be the greatest man in Europe, notwithstanding the Emperor. We spent a very happy Christmas at Le Mans. By now it may have seemed apparent to some that our relations had cooled somewhat: it was two years since I had given birth to Geoffrey, this after a child a year almost since our first get-together. But this was simply because, owing to the siege of Toulouse and other campaigns, we had not been able to get together very often during the past couple of years. This was now put right, and by the spring of 1161 I was most certainly pregnant again.

This was most pleasing, and with Louis and Theobald discomfited, affairs going well in England, and our lands utterly under our control, we supposed there remained only the matter of Toulouse to be dealt with, at our leisure. And the slight aggravation with the Emperor over our support for Pope Alexander, to be sure. But these were scarce earth-shaking discordances. It seemed to me that we could look forward to a period of peace and prosperity. But it was never thus. At Easter, Archbishop Theobald died.

This was not unexpected. Theobald was very old, and had been Archbishop for more than a quarter of a century. He had in fact been bombarding both Henry and Thomas with letters for the past six months, begging them to come to his bedside before he passed on. Naturally, both King and Chancellor being very busy men – when they were not campaigning or arranging great diplomatic issues or hunting together they were fond of getting drunk together – these requests were ignored. And now it was too late. Yet at the very least the Archbishop's departure was most inconvenient. In a constantly changing world Theobald had been like a rock. His endeavours had never been for either of the Houses in the dispute over the succession, but for the peace and stability of the realm. He had thus failed to support the Empress as he might have done during the Civil War, convinced as he had been that she was a disruptive element, and would remain so, even were she triumphant. This had not endeared him to the House of Plantagenet. But he had whole-heartedly embraced the succession of Henry, even before Eustace had died, because in my husband he had seen the elements he wanted in a King of England. And since our succession, he had been our strong right arm. The question was, with whom was he to be replaced?

The news was brought to us in Rouen by Bishop Henry of Winchester, the late King Stephen's youngest brother. It may be recalled that when King Henry had taken the throne he had suggested to Bishop Henry that he take a prolonged holiday, and this the Bishop had done. But that was in the past, and in recent years he had returned to his see of Winchester, not to mention his other see of Glastonbury. It so happened that the

Empress was with us when the Bishop was announced, and I observed with interest the expression on her face as he entered, because I was aware of the rumour that he and she had been lovers during the early stages of her campaign – against his brother! He had certainly supported her with all his power. So it had been a case of mutual ambition. The fact was that they were both very handsome people; twenty years before they must have made a splendid couple.

But there was no warmth in her expression as Bishop Henry kissed her hand. "Your Grace." And then to the King. "Your Grace." And then to me. "Your Grace." Well, clearly he was after something, and one did not have to be a genius to know what it was. "This is sad news," Bishop Henry said. "Sad news indeed. He was a great man."

Matilda gave what can best be described as a snort, as she more than anyone could recall how Bishop Henry had done his best to denigrate the Archbishop during the war. And how, indeed, he had challenged Theobald for the pallium. In fact, it had been his brother's refusal to support his ambition that had caused him to go over to the Empress in the first place. "But now," Bishop Henry went on, "we must face the business of replacing him with someone no less worthy."

"We?" King Henry inquired.

"It is a matter for the Church as well as the State, your Grace," Bishop Henry said severely.

"And you would put yourself forward," I suggested.

He spared me a glance, although clearly he counted me of little importance in this matter. "I am the most senior prelate in the land," he declared, importantly. "I am also of royal blood, and a most faithful adherent of the House of Anjou."

"Ha!" commented Matilda.

Bishop Henry addressed her. "Your Grace may recall that you promised me the pallium whenever it became available."

"Ha!" Matilda commented again. "You demanded the pallium, cousin, in payment for delivering to me the entire support of the Church. Well, you reneged on that. You are a rogue."

"I am the most suitable person to be the new Archbishop," he argued, amazingly neither taking offence at the Queen Mother's stricture nor appearing to realise that if he accepted it and still claimed the pallium it did not speak well for the Church in England. But his skin was as thick as a suit of armour.

"It is a matter to be considered," King Henry said. "Thank you, my lord Bishop, for putting yourself forward for such an arduous position. I will let you know what I decide."

Bishop Henry looked decidedly taken aback at this. "The decision needs to be taken very soon, your grace."

"I am aware of that. Thank you, my lord Bishop."

Bishop Henry looked as if he would have argued further, but then thought better of it, and withdrew. "That man will only be archbishop over my dead body," Matilda declared.

"And you are not yet ready to die, dearest Mama," Henry said jovially. But his smile was short-lived. He clearly had deep considerations on his mind and that night he came to my bedchamber. This was unexpected, as I was now four months pregnant, and neither Henry nor I believed in conjugal relations in these circumstances. "I would have an opinion," Henry said.

I was flattered. "You shall."

"An archbishop," he mused, sitting on my bed. "*The* most important man in the land, after myself."

"And the princes," I protested.

"After myself," he insisted. "The princes will take their order of precedence after us. But we must have an archbishop who is entirely subservient to me, who sees life from my point of view, whose loyalty will be to the King rather than the Church."

"As the archbishop has to come out of the Church, that man will be hard to find," I commented.

He glanced at me. "That man is in this very building." I frowned, for the moment unable to imagine who he had in mind. "Thomas," he said.

"Becket?" I was incredulous.

"The very man."

"That is quite impossible."

"Pray tell me why?" The fact that he was not losing his temper when opposed should have warned me that he was very serious, but the idea was indeed impossible.

"The reasons are legion, Henry," I said. "His age! He is not yet forty."

"Does one have to be in one's dotage to be an archbishop?"

"His habits. He drinks and fornicates like any king."

Henry grinned. "Like this king. He is my friend."

"He is ambitious."

"And I am offering him the highest post in the land, second to my own. Where can his ambition go after that, save to serve me ever more faithfully?"

"But he is not even an ordained priest!"

"That can easily be put right."

I played what I considered my trump card. "The Pope will never agree."

"Alexander will agree, because he dare not disagree."

"Henry . . . have you discussed this with your mother?"

"My mother does not like Thomas," he growled. "This is well known. Now you tell me why you are so opposed to my suggestion. I had supposed you and Thomas were the best of friends."

"We are," I acknowledged. "And I wish us to remain so."

"How can his becoming Archbishop change that? I would have supposed it would make you even closer friends."

There was nothing more I could say. Because I was acting on a woman's instinct. Thomas was four years older than I. That is, he was fifteen years older than the King, and although he was still in the prime of life he was inclined to be bossy. Well, so was the King. But all too often he agreed with what Thomas projected. It is the business of a chancellor to advise and recommend, and it is the business of a king to decide whether to take the advice or not. An archbishop is an entirely different kettle of fish. He is the head of the Church in England, virtually a state within a state. When he advises or recommends there are already a horde of priests and monks eagerly waiting to do his bidding. Theobald had never interfered in affairs of state. Thomas was already virtually running the state. I was profoundly uneasy about this. As it turned out, my fears were entirely unfounded, but the end result was even more disastrous than I had apprehended.

I was present when Henry informed Thomas that he had determined on his elevation. Having heard my objections, he hurried through them before Becket could even draw breath. "I know you are somewhat young, Thomas," he said. "That but means you will serve me longer. As for not being ordained, I have already written to England to have that arranged."

"You have thought of everything, sire," Thomas muttered.

"Well, then, let us prepare, eh? I will have a word with the Pope."

Thomas stroked his chin; he was, as always, clean-shaven. "You do me great honour, sire."

"I honour my best friend and greatest ally. Is that not fitting?" Not for the first time I found his choice of words disappointing, but I reminded myself that he was trying to achieve a goal.

Thomas was not looking convinced. "I doubt I am worthy of it, sire."

"Stuff and nonsense. You are the most worthy man in my kingdom."

"I was thinking of my capabilities, sire."

"Your capabilities? They are the equal of my own!"

"Ah, but sire, you serve but a single master: yourself. Had you to serve two . . ."

"There is only one master in my empire, Thomas, as you rightly say."

"Do you not concede that the Pope is your master, your Grace?"

"Not within my domains," Henry asserted.

"As Archbishop of Canterbury, I would have to serve the Pope, your Grace."

"After me," Henry said. "There is no conflict. I assure you that Alexander understands my point of view."

Thomas bowed, and withdrew. "He is distressed," I observed.

"You mean he is overwhelmed. A merchant's son can hardly have dreamed of rising so high. He will get used to the idea."

Matilda was less sanguine. "This will turn out badly," she told me, when we were alone together.

\* \* \*

There was no immediate indication of this, and in any event I had more pressing matters on my mind, and on my stomach. My fourth daughter was born at Domfret in September. After some consideration we named her Eleanor. We spent Christmas at Bayeux with our now numerous family, and had a very pleasant time of it. Thomas was with us, as we were still awaiting confirmation of his appointment from Alexander. He was as merry as always in the past, and seemed entirely reconciled to his coming elevation; but when he supposed he could not be seen I noticed his face settling into a contemplative expression, and he certainly drank less than usual. But I could find nothing to criticise in this. Becoming Archbishop of Canterbury was an immense responsibility, quite apart from being, as Henry had pointed out, the summit of any man's ambition where he could not be king.

In any event, he departed in the spring, as soon as the weather was good enough. We sent Prince Hal with him. The boy had grown very attached to his mentor, for Thomas had certainly become that, and both Henry and I thought he could not be in better hands. We kept Margaret with us, for the time being; she was the ideal playmate for her sisters-in-law in the nursery. We ourselves remained on the Continent throughout the year; Henry did not wish it to appear that he was interfering in Church matters by being on the scene when the new Archbishop was consecrated, which took place on 3 June 1162, almost immediately after he had been ordained. We had intended to join him for Christmas, but the weather that year was extremely bad and we were kept in Cherbourg.

So again it was the dead of winter when we returned

to England. Henry, I may say, was in a towering bad temper. It was more than four years since he had last been in England, and he knew there was going to be a lot needed doing; this was evident from every report which came across the Channel. Thus he was going to need all the assistance he could obtain, from those in his confidence and familiar with his methods of government. At the top of the list of these men was obviously his Chancellor and boon companion. But while we were still celebrating, if that is the appropriate word in the circumstances, Christmas, there arrived a missive from Thomas to the effect that he could not combine the duties of Archbishop *and* Chancellor, and that, as the one was irrevocable, he must resign the other.

Henry had not recently indulged in any of his more spectacular outbursts of rage, but perhaps he had just been saving them up. Now he flew into nothing short of a frenzy. We were at table when the offending letter arrived, and the first thing he did was hurl his goblet at the unfortunate priest who had read the words. This missed, fortunately, for the cup was made of heavy gilt, but it was followed by a shower of knives and joints of beef which belaboured the poor cleric and left him senseless upon the floor. There he was immediately joined by his king, for Henry vaulted over the table, paused only to sweep various utensils to the floor, and then hurled himself behind them. My first impression was that he intended a physical assault upon the prostrate man, but actually he was merely reverting to his old rush-chewing antics, while working his features in a horribly distorted mask and kicking his feet to and fro.

Our attendants would have gone to him, but I waved them back, as I also indicated to Amaria to take the children from the dining hall. Poor little mites, they were aghast, this being the first time they had seen their father entirely lose his temper, and as Prince Hal was in England with Becket, the eldest of our children with us, Matilda, was only seven years old. She was quite hysterical. Henry of course got over his maniacal outburst, as I knew he would. But he immediately conceived a violent dislike for his erstwhile friend, who he decided had let him down. While I hoped he would get over this also, his mood deepened as news arrived from England, of how the new Archbishop was acting in a most high-handed manner, principally in reclaiming for the Church all the lands alienated, for whatever reason, during the reign of Stephen. Not even Henry had sought to do this, for the Crown, in the interests of the peace of the realm; now he was besieged by angry barons who claimed they were being ruined.

Law was of course on Thomas's side, but this did not in any way alleviate Henry's temper, as he revealed in a somewhat spiteful fashion when, on our finally gaining England, he commanded Thomas to give up the Manor of Berkhamstead, which had been a gift from Henry some years before. He was quite entitled to do this, of course, but it was mean of him to rub salt in Thomas's wounds by electing to celebrate Christmas there. The quarrel thus commenced dragged on for some time. It is fairly well known, and I do not propose to go into details about it – during this period I had a fair number of problems of my own, and while I felt sorry for Thomas, placed in such a dilemma as having to choose between King and Church, I am bound to admit that he made life unnecessarily difficult for himself.

The point at issue was far more complicated than a mere matter of ultimate allegiance. It was the Church's concept that its minions were above civil law, and if guilty of a civil crime could only be judged by the Church itself. This was a very good idea, where it was properly carried out. But where the churchman in charge, be he bishop or archbishop, was concerned more with the prerogatives of his office than with justice, it could assume sinister aspects. Sadly, most of the English clergy had had to survive the anarchy of Stephen's reign – if they had not done so they would have been no trouble. To survive, they had had to adopt the habits and behaviour of those who sought to loot their lands, and such habits die hard. Thus we had a regular succession of clerics being accused of rape and robbery and even murder. Despite the gravity of these crimes, all hanging offences, the Church insisted upon the miscreants being handed over to its own jurisdiction. No doubt the villains were punished, by an extra Hail Mary or hour working in the garden, even, perhaps, by chastisement, but never were they handed back to the civil authorities to suffer a just fate. This caused great resentment amongst the common people. There was also the matter of whether or not the Church should pay adequate taxes, and who had the appointment of the various livings as they fell vacant, and even more, the various dioceses.

It was a sad business, which quite embittered the court, and indeed, distracted all Europe, as both sides appealed to the Pope, thus placing Alexander in a most invidious position. For while his instincts, and indeed the requirements of his position, were all in favour of Becket, the necessities of maintaining his papacy against the unremitting hostility of the Emperor meant that he needed the friendship of Henry, and thus his judgements were apt to change from day to day as he perceived his own fortunes rise and fall. For myself, as I have said, I was sorry that Thomas should find himself in such a pickle, and that we no longer could indulge in our lengthy but good-humoured disputations about every subject under the sun, but also as I have mentioned, there were other matters which, to a wife and mother, were of considerable more importance than Church politics.

Although one of my main problems was connected with the quarrel. Henry naturally brought Prince Hal back into the family fold. He regarded it as a form of rescue. Young Hal took an opposite point of view. He was now eight years old, and as bright and intelligent as we had all hoped he would be. But he was also the son of both Henry and myself, and the grandson of the Empress, and the great-grandson of Beauclerk, and the great-great-grandson of the Conqueror. Blood will out, and if I may mention that he was also the great-grandson of the First of the Troubadours, and enjoyed art and learning and poetry and gallantry, he also had inherited a most determined disposition which would brook little opposition. He conceived that he had been wrenched away from where he had been happiest, Becket's house, and as a result developed a dislike for his father almost as strong as that his father had developed for Becket. I naturally did my best to smooth things over, but it was difficult, especially as when, the following year, Henry virtually brought Becket to trial at Clarendon, with the upshot that the Archbishop had to flee the country and the see of Canterbury was actually confiscated to the Crown, Prince Henry was required to sit beside his father in passing judgement upon his old friend and tutor. This was clearly trying for the lad.

Then there was the disgusting business of the marriages of my two eldest daughters. Marie was actually well past the age when she should have been married: she was nineteen. Alix was only fourteen, but that is not too young to be bedded as by all accounts she was fully nubile – I of course had not seen either of them since 1152. But it was the idea that they should be marrying their father's brothers-in-law that was obscene, and in fact that the marriages had been delayed for so long revealed that even Louis must have had some reflections. No doubt pressure was eventually brought to bear on him by his new young wife, as early in the new year we received the information that the Queen of France was definitely pregnant.

Henry of course regarded this as a joke. "Another little princess to be found a home," he chortled. I was profoundly depressed by the whole thing, as I was even more certain that I would never see my darlings again, while the idea that their new half-sister, whenever she was born, would also be their niece-in-law and God knows what else was simply appalling.

I should point out that in the summer of 1162 I reached my fortieth birthday. This is a most depressing milestone, for anyone, but more I think for a woman than a man, and most of all for a woman once accounted the most beautiful of her time. At forty there could be no disguising the fact that I was growing old, and that even my beauty was fading. In addition, forty brings with it the approach of the dreaded end of fertility, and what has a woman got left? I may say that these were the opinions of my ladies, at which I snorted my derision. But that was a façade. Within myself I was disturbed, and took refuge in recalling all the adventures I had experienced since the age of fifteen. But one cannot live upon memories. Had anyone then told me that I had not yet reached the halfway stage of my life, or that the future held even more adventures than those I had already enjoyed, I would have spat in his face. But there it is. One should never despair, because none of us knows what is around the corner.

However, not every surprise can be a pleasant one, by the nature of things. My feelings at reaching forty were about to be compounded in a most severe manner. Consider me, then, marshalling my household, taking the greatest delight in Richard, who was growing into a most commanding young fellow, even at seven years old, able to swing his little sword with great endeavour, while I regarded my other children with maternal affection, concluding that they were all the hopes of my future, when two things happened in rapid succession.

Henry was now busily pursuing his plan to have Prince Hal accepted by Louis as the Heir of France, and Louis was as busily putting him off until the birth of Adelaide's child, just in case a miracle happened. Henry thus decided to press the matter more closely, and at Lent departed for the Continent, to meet Louis beneath the great oak at Gisors, where traditionally differences between the Duke of Normandy and the King of France had been settled, and twist his arm, at least mentally. I remained behind, for I had just discovered that I was again pregnant. This was an enormous delight in my circumstances, and it was arranged that I would follow my husband as soon as the babe was well established. It was while I was alone in London, figuratively speaking, that I first heard the name of Rosamund Clifford.

## Chapter Four

We were, in fact, in the throes of packing up for my departure to France, as I wished to cross the moment my baby was secure, but before I had begun to swell. It was a Sunday, and I had attended mass and was leaving the Abbey, surrounded as usual by my ladies, and watched by a motley crowd of spectators, always anxious for a glimpse of royalty. They were of both sexes, but I was suddenly taken by a young woman of quite exquisite beauty, standing with a group of friends, all women, and none much over twenty. This girl was as different to myself as it was possible to be. She was perhaps below medium height, whereas I am well above it. She was inordinately slender, although her breasts were full enough, whereas I can best be described as voluptuous. But it was in her colouring that the contrast was most marked: I am green-eyed and dark-haired, and perhaps a little swarthy of skin, but this girl was blue-eyed and flaxen-haired – indeed her hair was almost white – and her skin was so pale as to be virtually transparent.

I was taken by her. "Whoever can that be?" I asked Amaria.

Who to my surprise seemed extremely embarrassed by the question. "She is the daughter of Sir Walter de Clifford, your Grace."

I knew the name; Henry counted this Clifford one of his most faithful supporters, as he had always been loyal to the Empress and was indeed one of the knights who had escaped with her from Oxford across the frozen Thames. "I did not know he had a daughter, much less one who is such a beauty," I remarked. "Do you not suppose we could find a place for her amongst my ladies?"

Amaria looked positively terrified. "I doubt that would be wise, your Grace," she stammered.

I frowned at her. Amaria was no longer a girl. She was in fact in her mid-thirties, and having shared all of my adventures for the past eighteen years was a woman of some experience. For this reason she remained my most utter intimate, and surely could not suppose she could ever be replaced. "You are not jealous, I hope?" I asked.

"Jealous, your Grace? Good heavens, no. But I would beg of you, do not bring that girl into your home."

Obviously she had either said too little, or too much. I considered it the former. But I held my tongue until we were alone in my bedroom. Then I commanded her, "Now, out with it. What is the matter with this girl? What is her name, by the way?"

"Rosamund, your Grace."

"Rose of the World," I mused. "She is certainly fair."

"That is how she is known, your Grace: the Fair Rosamund."

"How quaint," I remarked. "Now tell me what is the matter with her?"

Amaria sighed. "She is known to the King."

I raised my eyebrows. "You mean she has been known to the King." Henry never maintained any mistress for very long.

"Lady Clifford has been known to the King for a very long time. It is said that he played in her nursery when he was a boy." Which was certainly not yesterday.

"I understand," I said. "As you suggest, Amaria, I will not invite her to join my household."

I may say that I consider I took the whole thing very calmly. I may even be accused of not taking it seriously enough, at the time. It is of course very disconcerting for a woman of forty to discover that her husband is liaising with a girl half her age, and who could only be called an outstanding beauty. But I reflected that at least Rosamund Clifford was better born than someone like Ykenai, and I was prepared to field any child that might appear and pitch him also into the Church, where he could only help my own sons. While, if she were to produce nothing but daughters, these, even if illegitimate, were always useful for marrying off to various members of the nobility one sought to bind more closely to the Crown.

Besides, this young woman, if undoubtedly most attractive, could not possibly be my equal in either intellect or sexual experience. It will be noted that even at forty I suffered from the dangerous weakness of over-confidence.

Thus I sailed for France in perfect equanimity, and found Henry the most loving of husbands. But as I have mentioned, this was to be one of those troublesome years: in fact, we were about to enter a distinctly troublesome period. Henry was in any event preoccupied with the machinations of the foul Becket, who was rushing about hither and thither – principally between the courts of Louis and Alexander – drumming up support. Henry did not then regard this as very dangerous, as he still reckoned that Alexander had more need of him than of Becket, but there was another problem which *did* threaten to become a nuisance: the projected coronation of Young Hal. This was still dear to both our hearts, but it had come to be accepted that a king in England could only be crowned and consecrated by the Archbishop of Canterbury.

This situation clearly needed thinking about but we had barely got together when there was an uprising in North Wales, and Henry determined to deal with it personally. He assured me he would be back in a few months, and I believed him. In my delicate condition I could not accompany him. In the normal course of events I would have remained in Rouen until my delivery, but there were two factors militating against this. One was the extreme age and ill-humour of the Empress. My mother-in-law was only sixty-three years old – I use the word "only" as I sailed past that age without a moment's hesitation – but it is a great age to many people. Matilda had lived life to the very fullest, not always of her own accord, and she was beginning to feel the strain. This was making her very querulous and difficult. In any event she was devoting most of her time to the Church – no doubt in anticipation of having to enter its bosom in a most literal manner before very long – which meant that she was not a wholehearted supporter of our quarrel with the Archbishop: she had, it will be recalled, advised against the appointment in the first place.

The other was that there had also been some trouble in Anjou, and Henry wanted a representative on the spot. As Prince Hal was accompanying his father, and none of the others were old enough, I was the obvious choice. Thus, one might say, factor one made me more amenable to accepting factor two.

In fact I looked forward to a congenial summer in

Anjou, where the sun shone more often than in England, and where the ancestral castle of the Plantagenets had been made into a most comfortable home by Matilda when she had gone there as the young bride of Geoffrey the Fair. Equally did I look forward to being able to exercise some executive authority after having been for so long merely a wife and mother. I also had a most pleasant surprise, soon after arriving in Angers: I was visited by Raoul de Faye. Raoul was by way of being an uncle of mine by marriage, and had always been one of my favourites; he was a most delightful fellow, and a bit of a troubadour himself. When he came to me at Angers he was somewhat saddened, as his wife had recently died, and he was, shall we say, at a loose end. But I soon cheered him up. Indeed, after several years spent mostly in the company of Henry, Raoul cheered me up as well.

I wish no one to suppose that I had as yet fallen out of love with my husband, but I am sure I have related enough of our life together to illustrate that being Henry's wife was not an easy business. I am not speaking of his infidelities, or his terrible rages. It was simply a matter of his excessive energy. Even when we were locked naked in each other's arms I was never sure he would not raise his head and bellow for some cleric to come bursting in and take an order of which he had just thought, to be delivered immediately, while this business of eating half of our meals standing up or in the saddle was most enervating. I thoroughly enjoyed masculine company. Indeed, I preferred it to the endless gossip and mindless chatter of my ladies, but when one is married to a king one needs to be careful about spending too much time conversing with other men. I had been allowed to do so with Becket, and had always found his intellect most stimulating. But now he was gone. Thus Uncle Raoul was like a breath of fresh, but cool, gentle air, not a rushing tempest.

I welcomed him with open arms, quite literally. And for the next couple of months we were inseperable. In this I was undoubtedly thoughtless. But of course there was no possibility of impropriety between us: I was seven months pregnant. Yet people do choose to see evil in everything they can. I was Eleanor of Aquitaine, and the most ripe source of gossip in Europe – and even possibly Asia. I had been very close – too close in the opinion of many – to an uncle in the past. Now here was another uncle almost sharing my every waking moment, as often as not with no one else present. And there *are* women who permit the sexual habit down almost to the moment of delivery, however uncomfortable, and perhaps even unnatural, this may be for both partners. As I was reputed to have permitted just about everything else in my time, why not this? Needless to say I remained in total ignorance of the rumours that were rushing about my head. I was even ignorant that the Bishop of Poitiers had seen fit to write a letter to my husband, in which he indicated in guarded terms that it might be wise for the King and Queen of England to be united rather than apart.

There was not any immediate response to this disgusting missive, at least as far as I was concerned. But this may well have been because that summer brought about the second event to disturb my tranquillity, and was something that none of us, myself least of all, had ever supposed possible: Adelaide of Champagne gave birth . . . to a son. It may well be imagined that the ringing of bells in Paris all but disturbed our slumbers in Angers. Certainly the news reached us rapidly enough. Louis called the babe Philip, and both to indicate his hopes and to make sure there was no confusion with any earlier Philip, added the title Augustus.

This event threw all of Henry's plans into disarray. There was now an heir to the throne of France, and the marriage of *our* heir to the daughter of France was meaningless. I could imagine him hurling himself to the floor and eating a whole parcel of rushes in his anger: I was quite pleased that he was still occupied with the Welsh. I personally was less regretful. I had always felt that his concept of a union between England and France in the person of a single prince, and for no other reason, was really storing up a great deal of trouble for the future. Now I felt that we could get on with our own business, like reclaiming Toulouse, and even, perhaps, conquering Ireland. Not being prescient, I did not suffer any apprehensions that this highly named babe in arms, being the son of such parents, could ever possibly be a nuisance to either my husband, myself, or *my* sons. Thus, business as usual, and shortly after Louis' triumph I gave birth to my fifth daughter, who I named Joanna. But my pleasure about this was very rapidly dissipated when I received a letter from Henry informing me that owing to various problems in England, he would be unable to join me for Christmas. This was a jolt. We had never been parted for Christmas, no matter what emergencies might have pressed upon us. "And where, pray, will his Grace spend the festive season?" I inquired of the messenger.

"I understand it is to be at his house at Woodstock, your Grace," the worthy answered.

Amaria gave a little gulp at this, and I hastily dismissed both the messenger and my other ladies. "Out with it," I commanded.

"It is rumoured that Mistress Clifford has been given apartments at the Palace of Woodstock, your Grace."

I glared at her, and briefly considered throwing a raging tantrum myself. But again my innate confidence restrained me. If it was true, and I had no cause to doubt it, that Henry *was* delayed by affairs of state, then obviously he could not come to me. And if he could not come to me, then obviously he had to spend Christmas somewhere. And if he had to spend Christmas somewhere, then obviously he would, lacking me, prefer to spend it in the proximity and thus the arms of his current favourite woman. I should hate to be mistaken for a fool. I know there are many women who absolutely refuse to contemplate infidelity in their husbands, sometimes even when the proof is displayed to them; this is of course foolish, because there is no such thing, in my experience, as an utterly faithful man when it comes to sex, and kings are by their very nature promiscuous, because there are so many opportunities placed in their way – what woman, in her right mind, is going to refuse an invitation to a king's bed? I am of course, speaking of *men*, and not half-monks like my first husband. A sensible woman, understanding that her husband will stray, accepts the situation, and endeavours to learn the identity of the current mistress – sometimes even to choose her – so that as far as possible she remains in control of events. This is what I was now endeavouring to do.

But I cannot pretend I spent a very happy Christmas myself.

Henry returned to me in the spring. Indeed, he had to because I sent for him, most urgently. This had nothing to do with our conjugal relations, or lack of them. His barons in the County of Maine, which was part of the patrimony of Anjou and not Aquitaine, decided that it was against the laws of nature that they should be ruled by a woman, and rose in revolt. I still had Joanna at my breast when this occurred, just after Christmas, and there was little I could do about it, so I shut myself up in Angers and sent an urgent message to my husband. He crossed the Channel in the middle of March, and dealt with the recalcitrant lords in his usual brusque and irresistible fashion – he was a great believer in knocking people on the head when they offended him – before coming on to spend Easter with me.

I was somewhat uncertain how to receive him, and how to approach the matter which was by now becoming uppermost in my mind, despite my attempts at calm reason. It was in fact difficult to get at the matter at all because Henry, however he had been spending his nights over the winter, seemed overjoyed to see me, in every possible way, and life became one long tumble. Then there was Baby Joanna to be presented and played with – he had not previously seen the child.

Henry was as ever full of plans. Brother Geoffrey had by now, as prognosticated, died, sadly unlamented. "Now those beastly Bretons seem to feel that their child-Duchess Constance is to rule them, while they seek out a marriage that will enable them to maintain their independence," he grumbled. "Do they really suppose I am going to permit an independent duchy in the heart of my empire?"

I entirely agreed with him, although I would have preferred him to refer to *our* empire, as my lands were at least half of it. But I did not feel he was in the mood to indulge in an argument, nor did I wish to upset him, in view of the subject I wished to praise as soon as possible. "What do you plan?" I asked.

"Why, simply to continue with our original idea: we shall marry Constance to young Geoffrey."

"I had gained the impression that the Bretons were not very keen on that," I remarked.

"Ha, ha," my husband grinned. "Then we shall knock enough heads together to make them agree, shall we not?"

"I see. When will this romance commence?"

"The negotiations for the marriage will commence immediately. If the Bretons are not amenable, then the campaign will commence in the summer. But we have other matters to attend to, and consider before then. Husbands for Matilda and Eleanor."

"Already?"

"Already?" he bellowed. "You mean it is late, already, since that scoundrel of an ex-husband of yours has managed to infiltrate a son into his wife's bed."

I frowned. "Are you suggesting that Philip Augustus is not Louis's son?"

"Well . . ." he had the grace to blush. "It took a long time, did it not? But that is by the by. The situation has now changed, dramatically. In every way. Did you know that Alexander has managed to get himself back into Rome? And do you know who is there with him? That villain Becket. They are all plotting against me."

"Oh, come now," I protested. "What possible harm can Alexander or Becket do you? In any event, does not Alexander rely on your support to maintain himself?"

"He conceives that he no longer needs my support," Henry growled. "Not while Louis is flexing his muscles. No, no, we must look to the future, and return to our old pursuits. Germany! The Empire! They are our traditional allies. I did not tell you of this before, but last year Barbarossa sent an envoy to Rouen, to discuss some marriages. He had in mind linking Matilda to

Henry of Saxony, and Eleanor to some other of his dukes."

"Did you not suppose I might be interested in such matters?" I inquired, keeping my temper with some difficulty. "We are speaking of my daughters."

"Well, you were busy at the time." Pesumably he meant being pregnant. "In any event," he went on, "I put him off. Henry of Saxony is a powerful magnate, but I didn't much like the idea of Eleanor being stuck with some petty duke. Besides, at that time, I still had the French throne in my sights. Now all has changed. Did you know that the Empress has given birth to another son?"

The Empress being Beatrice of Burgundy, whom Barbarossa had married, when, with just a little patience, he could have had me! "I did hear of it," I conceded.

"He has been named Frederick, after his father, and he will be Duke of Swabia. I have sent an envoy to Barbarossa suggesting that I will permit the marriage of Matilda to Henry of Saxony, if at the same time I can marry Eleanor to young Frederick."

I was beginning to be rather irritated by this constant "I will do this, and I will do that", when we were discussing my children. However, I could not help but be intrigued at the idea of Barbarossa and myself being linked through the bodies of our offspring. On the other hand . . . "Why cannot Eleanor marry his first-born, Henry?"

"Because," my Henry said, with a good deal of patience, "Prince Henry is already betrothed, to Constance of Sicily. It will all turn out very well, you'll see."

Actually, I was inclined to agree with him, if only because I conceived that it might be considered necessary for us, or me at least, to accompany Eleanor to her marriage to a possible emperor, should Prince Henry die before his Sicilian wife had given him an heir. I dearly wished to meet Barbarossa again. However . . . "There is one small matter you have overlooked," I said. "You will then have married off all of our children, with the exception of Baby Joanna . . . and Richard. He must be found a suitable bride, immediately."

"It is never advisable to have favourites amongst one's children," Henry pointed out. "However, I have already given the matter some thought. Why not Alais."

"You mean the other daughter of Louis and Constance?" I was amazed.

"Why not? So he and Hal will be married to sisters. That might turn out very well. And after all, Louis set an example by marrying your first two brats to those Blois brothers."

I realised that he had not yet abandoned his idea of dabbling in French politics when Louis died. But I could not really object to the idea of marrying Richard to a French princess: we were not going to do better than that and as no one had raised the subject of consanguinity between Hal and Margaret, I could not see anyone doing so between Richard and Alais. In fact, I became quite excited about the idea, and shelved the matter of Fair Rosamund until I had broken the good news to my favourite son. Imagine me, therefore, tripping along the garden path to where I knew Richard was to be found, quite literally full of the joys of spring. Actually I was even fuller than that, thanks to Henry's pleasure at being reunited with me, but none of us knew this as yet.

Richard was now nine years old, and even had he not been my favourite from birth, he would have become so, because, having just attained puberty, he was as tall, strong and vigorous as most boys three and four years older; he towered above his brother Hal. I saw in him the reincarnation of myself, had I been born a man. His only interests were martial, and as I approached I could hear the cries and the sounds of wooden swords clashing as he and his whipping boy, a youth named Giles who was two years older than his princely playmate but no bigger, faced off against each other. They did not hear my approach, and I paused behind the last of the hedge to watch them, filled with motherly pride.

They were both stripped to the waist, early in the year as it still was, and their youthful muscles gleamed with sweat, while their handsome faces also glowed. They seemed to tire of their game at the same time, and threw down their swords, still quite unaware of my presence. I watched them each extend both arms, to hold each other, and then to embrace each other. This is truly how warriors should end even a mock combat, in mutual admiration, but I was a little taken aback when their heads, pressed together ear to ear for several seconds, moved back together, so that they could look into each other's eyes, and then moved forward again, so that they could kiss each other on the lips. Well, men do kiss each other on the lips, although this was the deepest and longest kiss I had ever seen exchanged between people of the same sex. But then I saw Giles' hands slip down to close on my son's buttocks, while Richard's hands slid down Giles' sides to find his breeches, and unfasten them.

I realised then that this was not the moment to discuss his future marriage with my son, and fled.

Perhaps, not for the first time in my life, I acted hastily. But I felt I needed to think. Homosexuality in a prince, or a princess – recalling my own games in the baths at Constantinople – is a forgiveable vice, certainly when compared with so many others available to those with all but omnipotent powers. The important point is that it remain a game. Once it assumes the proportions of a desire, or worse yet, a way of life, it can be calamitous. My own immediate family had had none of it, but as I was now married into the house of the Conqueror, I could not help but be aware of the catastrophe that had been the reign of my husband's great-uncle, William II, known as Rufus, who had allowed his undoubted qualities as a soldier and perhaps even a king, to sink into a sea of vice and the indolence it induces. Partly this was because of the condemnation of the Church, and its unrelenting opposition to his desires. But then, the Church had not changed in the least during the past fifty years – possibly because it too was riddled with this peculiarity . . . as men are all made the same, and those in the Church are specifically forbidden the use of women, it would be amazing were it to be otherwise.

But morality aside, the consequences of total homosexuality – that is, a determination to have nothing *whatever* to do with the opposite sex, even in the line of duty – can be disastrous in a king. To this day no one knows whether or not Rufus was murdered. The man who fired the fatal bolt, Walter Tyrell, fled England the same day. For all of his life he protested that it had been an accident, but not too many people seem to have believed him. There are quite a few, indeed, who suppose that it was my grandfather-in-law, Henry Beauclerk, Matilda's father, who inspired the assassination of his brother in order to obtain the throne for himself. But had Rufus had a son waiting to step into his shoes, such a consideration could never have entered Beauclerk's mind.

Now, obviously it appeared unlikely that Richard would ever be a king. Young Hal was fit, strong and married, even if the event had not yet been consummated. But I still looked to a clutch of grandsons, young and strong and vigorous, to protect my old age. In this, as it turned out, I was to be sadly disappointed: I have had to protect my old age by myself, and flatter myself that I have not done too badly. But at forty I was not that prescient. I took refuge in the fact that Richard was still a small boy, while resolving to see to it that his companions from now on included a goodly number of pretty little girls. In my defence, I can only say that it was difficult to imagine a son of Henry Plantagenet, who from all I had heard had begun his career of sexual debauchery long before the age of nine, being anything less than a menace to anyone wearing a skirt.

Nonetheless, I would dearly have liked to discuss the situation with my husband, but even in my short absence, things had taken a decided turn for the worse: papal commissioners had arrived from Rome. Henry was closeted with them when I returned to our apartments, and he did not join me for some time. When he did, I could see he was extremely angry. "They threaten me with interdict and excommunication if I do not take Becket back," he shouted.

Now I am sure I have made it plain that I of all people was not afraid of either interdict or excommunication: I had seen too much of it already to take it as more than rhetoric. However, there were these other several matters on my mind. Regarding Becket, it was chiefly the coronation of Young Hal. "Might it not be in everyone's interests to end this quarrel?" I suggested.

"What?" he bellowed. "What?" And he pointed at me. "You're on that scoundrel's side. Admit it."

"Of course I am not on his side," I said. "I merely

seek the furtherance of our mutual plans, and it appears to me that this quarrel is sadly interfering with them. We wish Hal to be crowned. How do you propose to accomplish that without an archbishop?"

He glared at me. Now, obviously, I was not so stupid as even to consider bringing up the subject of Rosamund Clifford or Richard's deviance while he was in such a mood. But at the same time I remained Eleanor of Aquitaine, and I was not in the habit of being browbeaten by anyone, while my temper, dare I say it, was quite as sharp as Henry's even if I kept it under more control. I mention this because of what now happened. I had apparently angered him more than ever by my suggestion that it might be more comfortable for everyone if he patched up his differences with Becket. He now decided to cross the bounds of personal criticism.

"I am surrounded by plots," he declared. "So, pray tell me, what was hatched between Raoul de Faye and yourself last summer?" I was taken by surprise, being, as I have indicated, unaware that there had been any gossip about my relations with my uncle, much less any reportage to my husband. "Aha!" Henry cried. "You are struck dumb."

"Raoul is my uncle," I said. "He came to see me, and kept me company for awhile."

"Kept you company," he sneered. "Well, that is not how it was related to me. By the Bishop, no less."

"Indeed?" I asked, as coldly as I might. "Then he is a lying scoundrel."

"A bishop?"

"Bishops can lie, as you well know. It even applies to archbishops. Whatever he told you was a lie."

"Because Raoul is your uncle? And what of that rascal in Antioch, eh? He was your uncle."

"Whatever the Bishop told you was a lie," I repeated evenly, "for the simple reason that I was seven months pregnant during Uncle Raoul's visit."

"And that is supposed to reassure me?" he demanded. "You, with your oriental habits?"

At that, I lost my temper. "And what of you, with your blue-eyed child whore?" I demanded.

I at least had the satisfaction of rendering him speechless in turn, for a few moments. Then he uttered a roar and leapt at me. I evaded his initial rush and retired behind the bed. "She is as pure as you are foul," he shouted.

"I see," I said, restraining the temptation to throw something at him. "You mean that associating with someone as foul as yourself is not contagious."

He gave another roar, and threw a chair at me. This too I evaded easily enough, and by now the racket had aroused the castle, and there was a crowd at the door, Amaria well to the fore. "Get out," Henry bellowed. "Away with you."

But by this time he had chased me round the bed to the side nearest the door. "Wait just a moment," I told them. "I will accompany you."

I half expected him to come behind me, but he did not. To say truth, I was unsure whether or not I actually wanted this to happen. One serious quarrel – this was our first – does not end a marriage, of course. But the *cause* was serious, and it was the first stone to be removed from our mutually impregnable edifice. I did not see it so at the time, although I was very angry. So, it appeared, was Henry. We had not been reconciled by the time that the Pope's chivvying in respect of Becket became quite serious. Thus he came to see me. "Are you for me, or against me?" he demanded.

"My dear Henry," I said, "I am always for you. Provided you are always for me."

"We are a team, you and I," he said.

"Of course."

"Well then, I can tell you that this matter is becoming critical. I am informed that if I do not take Becket back immediately, I shall be excommunicated. And so will you. And the kingdom placed under an interdict."

"Rhetoric," I said scornfully.

"That may be so. But you know as well as I that we have a score of other problems that need attending to, and which will but be encouraged by an open break with the Pope. I have been neglectful of that angle. Now I must correct it."

"You mean you will accept the Pope's demands?" I was astonished.

"Never," he declared. "I know this Pope. He is the same as all other popes. A few threats, and a liberal donation to his coffers, will bring him back to our side. But to accomplish that, before we are excommunicated, I need time. Now tell me this, is there not a Church law which says that a king may not be placed under the interdict when he is ill?"

"Why, I believe there is. But you are not ill."

"You think so? As of this moment I am desperately ill. We will go to Chinon. No one will be able to get at us there."

Henry's ability to cope with every situation that was thrown at him very nearly amounted to genius. He left Angers in a litter with the curtains drawn, and only Amaria and myself were ever allowed behind them; he gave some convincing groans whenever anyone else approached too closely. While, as he had said, once safely behind the walls of the castle of Chinon, perched high above the Loire, he could keep himself in the severest purdah. The papal legate who arrived in Angers to deliver the fatal interdict found himself with no one to excommunicate. He duly came along to Chinon, but was refused entry on the grounds of the king's illness, and was forced to retrace his steps to Rome, utterly confounded. By the time he got there, Henry's envoys were also there, armed with their bags of silver. As we later learned, it was never even certain that this donation was necessary, for things had turned out badly for Alexander: a quarrel with Barbarossa had brought Imperial troops south of the Alps, together with a potential anti-Pope, the citizens of Rome were as revolting as ever, and all-in-all Alexander needed all the help he could get. Thus it was that he advised Becket to submit to the King, at least for the time being. Thomas, needless to say, refused. This was undoubtedly very honourable of him, but there are times when practicalities are of greater value. The upshot of this affair, at least in the short term, was that all talk of excommunication was dropped, and Alexander even went so far as to suggest that in cases where the Archbishop of Canterbury was not available, the Archbishop of York might do just as well!

Henry recovered his health with a rapidity which was the marvel of the medical profession. He was encouraged even more by the discovery that I was again pregnant. But by then, it was the beginning of summer. It was also apparent that the Bretons were going to be recalcitrant: he called in his troops for a campaign which would, hopefully, convince the wild inhabitants of that peninsular – they do not claim a relationship with the Welsh for nothing – that their future lay within the Angevin Empire, and that they could hope for no future outside it.

This left me, quite literally, at a loose end. Being again pregnant I could not accompany my lord and master on a campaign, and besides, I had some very personal matters to consider. For all our apparent reconciliation I understood that Henry and I had now entered a phase of mutual interest rather than mutual admiration, or indeed love. As I have mentioned earlier, I do not believe that I had as yet fallen out of love with my husband, by which I mean that I had not yet even considered replacing his image as that of the finest man of my acquaintance. Obviously, after a dozen years of mutual tumbling there was no longer any great inspiration in his embrace, even if he had been the most inspiring man I *had* ever embraced. But yet that essential intimacy of the mind which can be shared by two people, and which *needs* to be shared by husband and wife if their relationship is to endure, had suddenly gone astray. Yet I swear I hoped it could be regained – and it seemed to me that it was I who was going to have to attend to the matter.

I was, of course, still naive enough to suppose that Henry remained in love with me. But the fact was that, while I do not consider that I had lost any of my looks, my energy, or my charm, I was now forty-four, which many men consider old in a woman. While Henry was thirty-three, which most men consider to be the prime of life. My hope of conjugal bliss was thus perhaps already lost. But I was never a woman who admitted defeat. I determined to return to England.

There were several factors influencing me here. One was to discover an entirely suitable place for the birth of my child. Angers had lost its charms for me since it had been made plain that I was not wanted as its ruler. This indeed went for all of Anjou, and Maine. Poitiers or Bordeaux beckoned me strongly emotionally, but these ancient centres of my family's greatness were also simmering with the embers of rebellion, inspired by Henry's harsh rule, and stoked by yet another uncle of mine, William Taillefer. Uncle William was a completely different sort of man from either Raoul de Faye or Raymond of Antioch: he lacked the gentleness of the one and the chivalry of the other. I had no wish to find myself seized and held as a hostage for the restoration of ancient rights. Perhaps I feared that Henry would merely say, "Do your worst." Then there was Richard. Weaning him from his relationship with Giles was proving to be difficult. I determined to solve the problem by the simplest possible method: that of separating them, and thus left Giles behind. Some might say there was an even simpler and more permanent method of ending their relationship, but I had not yet had the necessity to turn to murder. Besides, dare I admit that I was already a little afraid of the reactions of my nine-year-old son?

On our voyage across the Channel, however, I took the opportunity to speak seriously to Richard. "Yours is a future lined with greatness," I told him.

"As a younger son, Mama?" This from a boy of nine.

"Now, who has been filling your head with such absurd notions?" I inquired, and then held up my hand. "No, it would be better that I should not know, else I would be forever angry with him. Or her," I hastened to add for good measure, although I had no doubt at all it had been Giles who was responsible. "As soon as you reach manhood, you will be made Duke of Aquitaine. You will be ruler of the greatest contiguous realm in Europe."

"Held in fief of my brother."

"As your brother will hold Normandy in fief of the King of France, who holds France in fief of the Pope, who holds Christendom in fief of God, if you wish to be entirely legal about it," I pointed out. "It is the ruler who matters, not the legality of it. Your father has pledged fealty to Louis for Normandy, but does that prevent him doing as he chooses?" Richard considered this, his eyes gleaming, and I realised that perhaps I had said too much; it was certainly not my intention to cause a rift between my sons. "In any event," I went on, "are not you and Young Hal the best of friends?"

"I hardly ever see him," Richard grumbled. "He accompanies Papa everywhere, and I accompany you."

"Do you then find my company distasteful?"

"Of course I do not, Mama. It is merely that Hal and I hardly know each other."

"You shall know each other better when you are older," I promised him. "Now, let us talk about your marriage."

"My marriage?" He was dismayed.

"Is Richard going to get married?" Matilda asked. "Why can't I get married?"

"You are going to get married, my poppet," I assured her. "Just as soon as the negotiations have been completed. You are going to marry a German duke!"

"Oooh!" she screamed, and I swear that had we not been at sea she would have jumped up and down. "Will he have a beard?"

"All German dukes have beards," I promised.

"I want to get married too," Eleanor complained.

"Of course you do, my darling. And you are. You are going to marry a German prince!"

Eleanor's eyes were as big as saucers. Matilda pouted. "How is it that she is going to marry a prince, and I have to make do with a duke?" she complained.

"He is a very great duke," I said. But I was more interested in Richard's reaction to all this.

"Who am I going to have to marry?" he now asked.

"Your wife will be the Princess Alais of France."

"Oh. Will I have to bed her?"

"Well, of course you will have to bed her," I snapped. "She is very pretty." I had actually never seen the girl, and was acting upon report. "She will give you many strong sons. Plantagenets!" He did not look very happy about the prospect.

We landed safely and, as I had sent ahead, were met by the usual crowd of lords and prelates, showering me with adulation. But they were less happy when I announced my intention of proceeding immediately to the Palace of Woodstock. "Apartments are all ready for you at Westminster, your Grace," they protested.

"I wish my babe to be born in the country," I told them. "Somewhere peaceful and beautiful. I have chosen Woodstock."

"But will you not at least visit London first, your Grace?" they begged.

"I will not. The less travelling I do the better, in my condition. I will proceed immediately to Woodstock." Not one of them dared raise the question of why. If I wished to keep my travelling to a minimum, would I have not merely gone to Rouen for my lying-in, or indeed, not left Angers at all? So off we set.

I swear I undertook this journey with no clear idea of my intentions. As with, I fancy, a good many women in my position, my thoughts were confused with a variety of issues, and possible denouments. I do know that I wanted to find out more about this young beauty who had so turned the head of my husband. But I imagined that I would do so by viewing her surroundings, rather than the woman herself: I had no doubt that messengers were already galloping north, ahead of me, to warn Lady Clifford to be away as rapidly as possible. And no doubt this was another idea at the back of my mind: that I should display to her the difference between us. She might be the plaything of a king, but I was the Queen, and every palace in the kingdom belonged to me, not her. Thus I could eject her as I chose. This is not very complimentary to me, but an injured wife does not take kindly to sleeping tenants, so to speak. What never crossed my mind was that this young woman might seek to defy me. In my entire life no woman had ever done that. Thus I arrived at Woodstock, three days after leaving Southampton

We had had a pleasant journey. In early summer, when it is not raining, England can be a most delightful place. The fields were green and filled either with barley or cattle or sheep, the people seemed contented, and both Richard and Matilda were old enough to appreciate and enjoy their surroundings. Richard now had his own falcons, and he hunted as we rode along, encouraged by the members of my mesnie, who kept telling me what a strong young man my son was. We arrived at Woodstock just on dusk, and I was assisted from my saddle. I smiled at the waiting crowd of domestics, and turned towards the steps leading upto the knight's hall, and gazed at the woman standing there.

"Welcome to Woodstock, your Grace," she said.

I think I was the most calm of my entire party, except of course for the children, who had no idea there was anything to be agitated about. Amaria nearly swooned, and some of my male attendants looked equally close to collapse. I went forward and up the steps, and Rosamund Clifford dropped into a deep curtsey. "Are you then my housekeeper?" I inquired.

She flushed as she rose. "If it pleases your Grace."

"Well then," I said. "Let us see what sort of house you keep, Mistress Clifford." I stepped past her into the hall, and regarded the row of bowing menials. As I have said, it was all but dusk outside, but in here torches flared in their sconces, and it was bright. I thus turned to the girl, and inspected her most closely. Of her beauty it would be impossible to speak too highly. It lay less in her features, although these were good, than in her complexion, which was quite flawless, and rendered the more attractive when, as now, there were pink roses in her cheeks. Her hair, as I had noted on the occasion of our first meeting, was quite startling. This did not mean I felt any the less vicious towards her. "Were you expecting me?" I asked.

"I was informed of your coming, your Grace."

And chose to sit it out, I thought. Well, you will have to pay me rent, my pretty maid. "Children," I said. "Come here and meet Mistress Clifford. She has been looking after the palace for us."

The three came forward, while Joanna was brought by her nurse. "You're lovely," Matilda remarked.

"Thank you, my lady," Rosamund Clifford said, but she was looking at Richard for approbation. And was disappointed. He merely glanced at her, then looked around him at his surroundings. "There is no defence for this castle," he said. "I noticed this outside."

"It does not need defending, my lord," Rosamund said. "Your father has no enemies, in England."

"It is very late," I said. "We will have supper, and then bed. But I would like a bath. See to it, mistress." Rosamund curtseyed again, and gave the necessary instructions. People scurried in every direction, while

Rosamund herself escorted me up the stairs to my apartment. Amaria came with me, of course, while the children were also shown to their rooms. The bedchamber in which I found myself was in every way fit for a queen, but I was now in a fine fury. "And where do you sleep, Mistress Clifford?" I inquired.

"On the floor above, your Grace."

"Show me." There was only the slightest hesitation, then she led me up the next flight of stairs, to a room much smaller than mine, and less luxuriously furnished. "I do not think you sleep here every night," I remarked.

"I sleep here, your Grace, unless I am commanded to sleep elsewhere."

A reply which but made me the more angry. "Well then," I said, "I command you to sleep elsewhere, tonight."

"As you wish, your Grace."

"But first, you will attend me."

"As you wish, your Grace."

I stamped back down the stairs, where Amaria waited, looking distinctly frightened. Maidservants were scurrying to and fro with buckets of hot water as my bath was prepared. It was all but ready. I entered the room, and they hurried out. Amaria and Rosamund waited in the doorway. "Leave us," I told Amaria.

"Your Grace . . ." her voice trembled, but whether she was more afraid for me or for the girl it was difficult to say.

"I wish to speak to this lady alone," I said. Amaria glanced at Rosamund, who stood quite still, features composed. Then she curtseyed and left the room. "Close the door," I told Rosamund. She obeyed. "Now come here and undress me."

What did I intend? Do you know, I have no idea even now? At that moment my personality seemed to be divided into several different aspects. Certainly there was a part of me which wished to seize her and drag her round the room by the hair, kicking her all the while. It was not merely the fact that she was the first of Henry's mistresses I had ever met face to face, at least knowingly. It was not even entirely the fact that she had had the effrontery to ignore the warning messages she must have received, and in preference to fleeing had chosen to remain and welcome me as if this were indeed her castle, and I merely a visitor, of superior rank to be sure, but nonetheless a visitor. It was her calm arrogance, her certainty that I would never dare harm her, because she possessed Henry's love, that was eating into my mind. I might not be able to harm her, but I certainly intended to humiliate her, and not merely by having her act the maid, either.

But another part of me was curious. Just how much courage *did* she have? How much resilience, how much ability to withstand insult and injury, as I had had to do so often in my life? And yet a third part of me was reaching into the recesses of my mind, remembering, and imagining. She was a truly beautiful woman. And she had shared a bed with my husband. As had I. Here was curiosity with a vengeance. It was a matter of which of my feelings towards her gained the ascendancy.

She showed not the least resentment at being forced to play the lady's maid, and it occurred to me that she was as curious, and perhaps as confused, as I. She must know that she was in my power, were I to become overwhelmed with jealousy. But her fingers were quick and accurate, as well as soft, and within a few seconds I was naked. My pregnancy, at four and a half months, was not immediately obvious. "Shall I test the water for you, your Grace?" she asked.

"Yes," I said, and as she moved towards the steaming tub, pushing up her sleeve, added, "Not with your hand, girl. With your ass." She checked. Her back was turned to me, yet I could see her cheeks beginning to glow. I had at least obtained a reaction. "Quickly," I said. She bit her lip as she untied her girdle, and then let it and her gown slip to the floor. Her figure was slender perfection, caught in that glowing translucent skin. "Now get in," I said.

She hesitated again, then stepped into the tub. Immediately a great red heat spread up her legs, but I knew that the water, if certainly very hot, was far from boiling or even hot enough to scald. Daintily she lowered her body, holding onto the sides of the tub which, being made of iron, would also be fairly hot by now, and dipped her buttocks into the water, then straightened again, her whole body glowing. "It is ready, if you like the water hot, your Grace," she said, stepping out.

"I did not give you permission to get out," I told her. She drew a deep breath, and stepped into the water again. "I cannot have it too hot," I explained. "As I am pregnant." She shot me a quick glance, while standing quite still in the water. "Four and a half months," I said. "I will not show for a few weeks yet. This will be my tenth child."

"Your Grace is blest," she acknowledged.

"Is the water cooler now?"

"It is difficult for me to say," Rosamund said. "I have become used to the heat."

I stopped beside her and put my hand in the water. It was quite acceptable. Leaving my hand under the water I placed it on her ankle, and then slid it up the back of her leg, slowly straightening as I did so. My hand coursed up her thigh and over her left buttock, then moved up to her shoulder. All this time she remained absolutely still, but despite the heat she was shivering; her hair, lying in a damp cloud down her back, trembled. "How many children have you had?" I asked.

"I have had no children, your Grace, as . . ." she bit her lip.

"As yet?" I let my hand continue on its way upwards, driving my fingers into the thick hair at the base of her skull. Her trembling increased. "Then no doubt you are betrothed," I suggested.

"I am not betrothed, your Grace."

"A girl of your age, with some pretensions to beauty, and not betrothed? That is unbelieveable. Have you then, some blemish? It is not readily apparent." I brought my hand out of her hair and back to her shoulder, then slid it in front, down to her breast, to cup it and hold it, and gently pinch the nipple. Would you believe I had never done that to a woman before, at least in such circumstances.

"I know of no blemish, your Grace." Her voice was hardly louder than a whisper.

"Then I must find you a husband, lest your desire to be a mother lead you into lewdness." My hand moved over her stomach, sliding down to the pale silk at her groin.

"I . . ." she turned towards me, violently, scattering water, her nerves at last giving way. "You are playing a game with me, your Grace."

"A game of your choosing, miss. Or you would not be here with me."

We gazed at each other, then I smiled. "I think the water is the right temperature now. I will sit in it, and you will bathe me, Mistress Clifford. And we will talk."

# Chapter Five

Rosamund Clifford was an enchanting child. I took her to my bosom, in every possible sense, and conceived that I had won a great triumph. Henry's favourite mistress was in my pocket, again in every possible sense, and therefore I supposed that I was entirely in control of all our lives. My ladies, not to mention my gentlemen, not to mention most of all Amaria, were in a complete tizzy by the manner in which I had handled the affair. There were undoubtedly the usual number of secret spy-holes in the various drapes surrounding the royal bedchamber, and I have no doubt that we were constantly overlooked. Certainly the fact that we had shared a bath, because after she had soaped me I had her in the tub on top of me, and as the water had flowed out our mutual desires had flowed in, was very rapidly known and disseminated. From this, again I have no doubt, arose many of the later legends, which were to grow to such proportions as to become almost absurd.

No one seems to have any doubt that I eventually murdered the girl, by a variety of methods, each one more horrible than the last. The most popular theory, however, is that I made her sit in a hot bath, opened her veins with a knife, and jeered at her while she bled to death. This story had to arise from somewhere. It is at least no less fanciful than the one of how I only discovered who Rosamund was, and where she was, by following an unrolling ball of thread which had somehow become attached to Henry's spurs as he left his lady-love's arbour. As if Henry ever sought any lady-love when I was in close proximity or, indeed, that we were ever all at Woodstock together. The most important point is that in 1166 Rosamund still had ten years to live, and I can certainly, and indeed sadly, prove that it was quite impossible for me to have any hand in her death.

For the moment, I was well pleased with my handling of the affair. If I could not doubt that the next time he was in England Henry would seek her out, or that she would melt into his arms as willingly as she had melted into mine, I was equally sure that at least I would know what he was about . . . and I doubted that he would achieve any greater triumph than had I.

Meanwhile, he campaigned against the Bretons, Richard hunted, Matilda dreamed of her forthcoming marriage – which Richard was obviously not doing – and I grew larger by the day. Finally, on Christmas Eve, 1166, I gave birth to my tenth child and fifth son: I obviously have an orderly disposition.

He was also my last child. But this was as much in the nature of things as my growing estrangement from Henry. Perhaps for this reason, combined with this birth date, he was my second favourite. He could never replace Richard, who had a special place in my heart whatever his vices, but he developed a good many of Richard's virtues: military skill and a shrewd brain amongst them. And who was to say that he would not gain even greater triumphs than his brother? I named him John.

This was the second consecutive Christmas that Henry

and I had spent separately. At least I had the satisfaction of knowing that he would not be lying in the arms of Rosamund Clifford, although I could not doubt that he would be lying in *somebody*'s arms. Just how seriously he might be doing this I did not consider. In fact I had very little desire to lie in Henry's arms myself again for awhile, and was entirely content with my surroundings and my company. I thus elected to remain in England throughout 1167. This was in part dictated by events on the Continent, where Henry seemed to be fighting people in every direction. Apart from the Bretons he managed to have a clash with the French this year and, worst of all, Uncle William Taillefer, proving to be a skilful general. My husband was carrying fire and sword – a pastime at which he was expert – the length and breadth of Aquitaine. I had no desire to be at his side when he was destroying my own subjects and their homes and livelihoods.

I was also preparing Matilda and Eleanor for their departure for Germany. It was a busy time, but a rewarding one. Matilda was now eleven, and a very grown-up young lady. Eleanor was six, and remained very much of a child, but she was going to a much greater household than that of the Duke of Saxony. Or so I supposed. One may imagine then my astonishment and chagrin when a letter arrived from Barbarossa to the effect that the marriage between his second son and my second daughter could not take place, for reasons of state. Astonishment and chagrin were very rapidly replaced by fury, and I sent letters in every direction, with very little result: my old "friend" Barbarossa's thoughts were apparently moving in other directions. I fear therefore that when the envoys of the Duke of Saxony arrived to collect Matilda I did not give them the welcome they had anticipated. Not that I stinted upon my eldest daughter's trousseau or appointments. I spent lavishly, and even accompanied her across the Channel to see her on her way.

"Will we meet again, Mama?" the dear girl asked, as we embraced for a last time.

"All things are possible," I told her.

To say truth, I had another reason for returning to France: news had reached me that the Empress was dying. She and I may not have had a great deal in common in recent years, but we had experienced much together, and I could never forget that she had come to my aid at the most perilous moment of my life. Besides, she had never seen either of her two youngest grandchildren. So with all my remaining children I hurried to Rouen. Henry and Hal arrived shortly after us, and all of us knelt around Matilda's bedside. Margaret, now grown into a pretty little girl, was already there; I was only sorry that Matilda's namesake could not be there too. The Empress did not appear to be in any great pain. But equally, unlike her, she was not very talkative, and she slipped from this world a good deal more quietly than she had lived. We buried her, as she had designated, in the Abbey of Fontevrault.

Although it hurts me to confess it, looking back I am more and more convinced that Matilda's death was the most important event of Henry's reign. Although it was not always apparent to the uninformed eye, she had dominated his life. Whatever he had done, or not done, had always been governed by the same principle: will the Empress approve? Even when he had agreed to usurp her right to the English throne, he had been able to convince himself, and eventually her, that this was the best course for both of them. Now he was rudderless. There had been two other people in his life who might, and should, have now been able to help him in his ambitions, and his plans: Becket and myself. But he was estranged from the one, and in the course of becoming estranged from the other. I would not have had it so. But sadly, I had never established a sufficient mastery over my husband. This was in part the result of the circumstances surrounding our getting together, when I was a fugitive and he had the world at his feet; in part because of his sheer physical dominance; and in part because for our entire married life to this moment I had either been pregnant or nursing, and thus content to leave affairs of state, and even domestic decisions, in the hands of so masterful a man, happy that he should be governed by so masterful a woman. Now, just as I had completed my term as a mother, Henry began to look at me with hostility.

Here again, Matilda's influence had governed him all of his life, with respect to both the Archbishop and myself. Matilda had never truly liked Becket, and it may be recalled that she had advised most strongly against giving him the pallium. When Henry had gone his own way, she had spent the rest of her life trying to mediate between King and Archbishop. She had not been successful, but it is impossible not to feel that as long as she lived neither man could consider going to extremes. Similarly as regards myself. Henry certainly felt, much as I did, that his mother had most skilfully engineered our marriage while appearing almost to oppose it. Equally he knew that she and I had been very close in our initial relationship. Thus again whatever his growing number of differences with me, he had always felt that I was his mother's friend and protegee, and required to be treated as such. Now that too no longer pertained.

All the above is written with the advantage of hindsight. We are seldom aware of the vast changes in our circumstances while these are in motion. Certainly Henry and I spent some tender moments as we mutually mourned his mother. I do not know if he was aware of my meeting with Rosamund, but if he was he gave no sign of it. He was delighted with his youngest son who, in fact, gave every indication of being the nearest of our children to his father, in looks.

We spent Christmas together at Argentan, where I discovered that our circle had been joined by a young girl named Lampagie de Porhoet. Her father was the Viscount Eudo de Porhoet, a prominent Breton noble, and I gathered that Lampagie was one of several hostages being held by Henry to ensure her daddy's continuing support and good behaviour. This was a common enough practice, and I could find nothing unusual or sinister in it. I did discern that Lampagie was a most attractive child, possessing a wild beauty shrouded in a mass of curling tawny hair, and equally did I discern that Henry found her quite as attractive as I did. However, as she was only twelve years old, I regarded her as a possible problem of the future, but hardly of the present. My present was filled with good cheer, and although this was the first time we had enjoyed the festive season together without there being very shortly an enlargement to my circle, as it were, neither of us – I certainly – took this omission very seriously. Indeed I felt glad of the rest, especially as Henry was full of ideas, as usual.

In fact he made a very strange announcement, for

Henry. "I am done with warring," he said. This was of course said in the privacy of our bedchamber, so there was only myself to be amazed. Well, I was, and could think of nothing to say in reply. "Louis is equally anxious to arrive at a peaceful settlement of our difficulties," he went on. "So we have arranged a meeting, at Pacy. I will take Young Hal and Geoffrey and Richard, and we shall do homage for our lands in France; that is, Young Hal for Normandy, Geoffrey for Brittany, and Richard for Aquitaine."

I scratched my head. "None of them have been granted those lands, as yet."

"But as we are agreed it will happen, my poppet, it is best to get these formalities out of the way now."

"You have said nothing of Baby John."

"Well, there is nothing to say about Baby John, is there? He has no lands to do homage for."

"That is exactly it. Some provision must be made for him. He cannot go through life as Prince Lackland."

"I shall have to consider the matter." He grinned at me. "What of Ireland?"

"Henry, Ireland does not belong to you. So how can you give it to John?"

"But it will belong to me," Henry declared. "I am resolved on it. And I still have the Papal Bull promulgated by Adrian, granting me the right of conquest. Oh, yes, Ireland. John can be Duke of Ireland. When he is a little older."

I scratched my head some more, but it sounded very grand, and I had known my husband long enough to know that he usually made his plans materialise. "What of Eleanor?"

"Yes. That Barbarossa is a scoundrel. I am working on it. How does Castile take you?" He had not lost his gift of surprising me. As he knew. "Castile," he repeated, warming to his task. "It is on its way to becoming a great nation."

I considered this rather speculative. Castile was doing very well, but the fact was it was still a small country, had recently lost Portugal, thanks to our English Crusaders, and half of the Iberian Peninsular remained in Moorish hands. All it required was the emergence of another Abd-er-Rahman to unite and lead the Moslems, and Castile could find itself wiped from the map. On the other hand, my forefathers had always maintained close relations with the Spanish kingdom, as they shared a great deal in common. I was at least assured that my little girl would be going to a broad-minded court . . . and she would, after all, be a queen. It would also serve to show Barbarossa that he and his sons were not the only fish in the sea. Henry, as usual, took my silent consideration of his proposal as an acceptance. "I will open negotiations right away," he said.

"But are you sure it is safe?" I asked.

Castile was in the throes of a regency, and regencies are always uneasy states of affair. Alfonso VIII was only nine years old. He had actually succeeded his father, Alfonso VII (who was known as the Emperor because he had achieved so much) at the age of one. Since then there had been considerable ups and downs for the Spanish monarchy. "As Alfonso and his advisers have survived eight years, it must be getting safer every day," Henry said. "And a marriage alliance with the House of Anjou will strengthen his hand."

Not for the first time I was resentful of his way of putting things, but I had no desire to quarrel over Eleanor's future, which now again looked quite bright. Even the Moors did not actually make war upon queens, and I reflected that if Alfonso fell, Eleanor would be returned to me. So I merely said, "And in the meantime, do you wish me to take the little ones back to England?"

"Ah . . . no." This was the first indication I had had that he might not want me to spend too much time in England – certainly at Woodstock. "I think," he went on, "that it would be best for you to spend a season in Poitiers, or Bordeaux, if you prefer. The duchy is completely pacified since your Uncle William surrendered, and you should have no trouble at all. However, just to be sure of this, I will send Patrick, Earl of Salisbury, with you to act as your seneschal. I shall of course join you, with the boys, as soon as I have concluded my business with Louis. I trust that is satisfactory?"

I would have preferred to return to England. However, the prospect of being able to spend the summer in sunny Poitiers was most attractive, especially as Henry had promised to come to me himself, as soon as he could. "I find that very satisfactory, sire," I told him.

I set off to return to my ancestral lands just after Easter. My party was not large – there was a considerable garrison awaiting us in Poitiers – but perhaps for that reason was a merry one. Patrick of Salisbury was a genial fellow, but I was even more attracted to his nephew, a young lad named William Marshal, who was at once handsome and outgoing, and clearly a great admirer of his queen. Now it may have escaped anyone who reads these words, but to this moment I had never, over a period of thirty years of married ups and downs, committed adultery, at least from my point of view. When I had played with Uncle Raymond and surrendered to Saladin, my marriage to Louis had already been over, as far as I was concerned. Bernard of Ventadour had attempted to re-enter my life after my marriage to Henry, and I had thoroughly enjoyed his company, but however much we had fondled had not permitted him the ultimate. For the rest, one might say that enjoying – if that is the right word – such a period of fecundity, I had had no time to think of dalliance. But actually, as I have endeavoured to establish, I had never felt the need. Henry was a most consuming husband.

Now I found my attitudes changing. I suppose that meeting Rosamund, and being aware that she was Henry's bedmate whenever possible, was having its effect. I could see little point in becoming jealous. But I was beginning to feel that what is sauce for the gander should also be sauce for the goose. It was not so much that I any longer aspired to great feats of sexual endeavour, but that I dreamed of the chase, the excitement of a new personality bubbling into my life. It followed that such a personality needed to be young, and manly, and handsome, and intelligent, and well-educated. William Marshal was all of these things. Of course I did not realise this upon the occasion of our first meeting, although he was certainly handsome enough. I simply found that I enjoyed his company.

Now, Henry had assured me, as he had assured Salisbury, that Aquitaine was entirely quiescent since the surrender of Uncle William. Thus, as I have mentioned, we had neither a large body of men riding with us, nor were we taking any serious precautions, such as putting out either an advance guard or a rearguard. This was my country, recently pacified by my husband, who was about the most feared warrior in Christendom, and I was proceeding to my favourite city. Our surprise was thus the greater when, as we traversed a bridle path through a wood, and not all that far from Poitiers itself, the air suddenly became filled with humming arrows, screaming women, and falling men. Amaria and I, riding together as was our wont, drew rein and looked left and right, while Salisbury and his nephew drew their swords and called their men to action. But we were both outnumbered, had lost several men already, and were too surprised by the ambush to take effective measures. The arrow hail ceased, and large numbers of armed men issued from the trees to either side. To my amazement there was no concealment about their heraldry: they all wore the crest of Lusignan, as did their banners.

  A word about this family may not be amiss. They were, and had been for several generations, amongst the most prominent and warlike of my Poitevin nobles, owners of vast lands and thus some considerable power. But they had always been staunch supporters of my family, and it may be recalled that the present head of the House, Hugues de Lusignan, had accompanied me upon the Crusade. But that had been a long time ago. Hugues was now an elderly man, and I realised at once that my assailant was his son Guy. Sadly, Guy, and his father, had been amongst those who had condemned my behaviour in Palestine, and our relations had become somewhat strained. Not that I had seen a lot of them over the intervening years. But here was Guy making a serious attempt to lay hands upon my person, and if in a sense this was flattering, I had to be realistic about it and admit that few men kidnap a forty-five-year-old woman simply to take her to bed. Nor, as I was married, could Guy hope to use my hand to gain control of Aquitaine. I did not believe that he meant my death, as that would have involved him in a lifelong contest of revenge with my husband. So, supposing that he had not entirely lost his senses – which was always possible with Guy of Lusignan – his project had only to be to gain control of my person, and use me as some kind of bargaining counter in dealing with Henry.

This was of course outrageous, as well as being a little frightening as, not for the first time in my life, I had a lurking fear that my current husband might merely say, "Do your worst." It will therefore be understood that when gallant Salisbury slapped my horse on the rump and cried, "Ride, your Grace, ride! We will cover you," I did just that without a moment's hesitation. While Patrick, his nephew and my guards swung their swords most lustily, Amaria and I spurred our horses out of the melée and up a nearby hill.

There I drew rein to look back, and was horrified to see Salisbury tumbling from his horse, blood pouring from his head. I was even more concerned about William Marshal, but he was laying about himself like a lion, although dismounted and surrounded by enemies. My heart went out to the gallant young man, but now our would-be kidnappers were beginning to be interested in what might have become of me, and were looking up my hill. It was necessary again to spur our horses and gallop away. By nightfall we gained Poitiers, where the commander of the garrison, Rohan de Rais, was aghast at the sight of his queen arriving with only one attendant, and in a state of some agitation. He immediately sent messengers to summon the King, and to do him justice, Henry forthwith abandoned his get-together with Louis at Pacy and hurried to my rescue. Or at least, to my vengeance.

This was carried out in Henry's usual, and in this case entirely suitable fashion. The Lusignan lands were devastated, their castles burned, their captains hanged, their women violated, until they bowed their heads in total surrender. But Henry was still not satisfied, and demanded that Guy take the Cross, and himself, to

Palestine, and not return. This actually set in motion a rather curious and ultimately catastrophic course of events, as the wretched man found the Palestinian sun much to his liking, so much so that he eventually wound up King of Jerusalem! But of this, I will speak in its proper place.

My immediate concern was the well-being of the gallant young William Marshal. He had been captured, finally overborne by sheer weight of numbers, and been held for ransom. This I insisted upon paying myself, regardless of what anyone might make of it. Thus I could demand that the youth be brought before me, that I might thank him for his gallantry, and he thank me for my rescue of him. I was, I swear, considering nothing more than this, certainly as I expected Henry to be at my side when I received my champion. But Henry was not at my side. He had no sooner dealt with the Lusignans when there was more trouble in Brittany. "His Grace sends his deepest regards, your Grace," explained the messenger. "But Viscount Eudo of Porhoet is in arms, and must be dealt with."

I frowned. "Eudo of Porhoet? There is something familiar about that name." At this, the messenger went very red in the face. "Out with it," I commanded.

"I know naught of such things, your Grace," he protested. "I only know that Viscount Eudo's daughter Lampagie was sent as a hostage to the King, and, well . . ."

"The Viscount claims the King has debauched the girl."

"Well, your Grace . . . violated is the word being used."

"He does bring his troubles on himself," I said. "Very well. I will do the best I can here, until my husband is free to join me." I was fit to spit. A twenty-year-old Rosamund Clifford I could just put up with. A twelve-year-old Lampagie de Porhoet was really quite unacceptable – and virtually under my very eyes! I could now envisage Henry prowling the corridors of a lying-in house, seeking babes in arms! I almost took horse and rode up to Rouen. But I had not yet made up my mind to do this before I had a distraction of my own: William Marshal arrived at Poitiers.

I know it will be said that as William was just twenty-one and I was forty-five, while if Lampagie was twelve, Henry was thirty-four, the gap in ages between each of us and our respective partners was greater in my case. On the other hand, there could be no doubt that William was a grown man, not a recent arrival at puberty. Not that considerations of this nature crossed my mind for a moment as he came into my presence. I was appalled. The tall, strong youth who had fought so gallantly to allow me to escape had dwindled to an emaciated wreck. Even his height seemed diminished by reason of his bowed shoulders. "My God!" I cried, myself taking his hands to raise him from his knees.

"The Lord of Lusignan is a harsh and cruel man, your Grace," he said.

"We shall see about that," I declared, examining his wrists, chafed with the irons which had been attached there.

"I shall be forever grateful to your Grace," he assured me.

I smiled at him. "You will be more grateful yet, my dear William. It will be my business to nurse you back to health."

To say truth, this was not a difficult business. William had a strong constitution, and although he had been kept chained in a dungeon existing on a diet of bread and water for long enough to destroy a weaker character, he recovered his strength rapidly when fed good meat and better wine, and even better company. It was now that I discovered his true worth, the extent of his education, the brilliance of his mind. Did I set off with the intention of seducing him? I do not think so. But the idea was undoubtedly there. It had been planted by Henry's rape of Lampagie, for it can have been nothing less than rape. Thus it grew as we spent long hours together, and I watched the strength flowing back into his muscles. It was not long before he wished to indulge in passages of arms, to regain his skill as well as his power. But this inadvertently took us another step down the slippery slope which led to an affair. For Henry, before bustling off to Brittany, had sent Richard to join me; he had taken Geoffrey with him, as it was Geoffrey's future he was about.

Richard was now ten, and taller and stronger than ever. He had been delighted with the proceedings at Pacy, and only irritated that they had been interrupted. But the entire agreement between Henry and Louis was due to be signed and sealed as soon as possible. Sadly, he revealed no interest whatsoever in the Princess Alais, who was also due to be handed over at the formal treaty-signing. I asked him about her, and he merely shrugged, and said, "She is as other women, Mama."

Now it seemed obvious to me that Richard should be taught some more of the use of weapons by William. I will confess that I seized every opportunity to oversee them surreptitiously, and with some concern. But there was never anything the least suspicious in their actions together. Yet it was magnificent to watch them; the boy, only recently arrived at puberty, but already almost as tall and as strong as the young man, who now that he had recovered most of his health was a splendid sight, all rippling muscles. I should say that, as they jousted in the privacy of the innermost gardens of the Maubergeonne, they wore nothing but their hose, without even the inconvenience of a codpiece for modesty. Thus they might as well have been naked, and perhaps were even more attractive than if they *had* been naked, those most exciting portions of a man's anatomy being, as it were, at once constrained and yet delineated.

Thus there came a morning when I could control my natural impulses no longer, and so stepped from my protecting arbour on an occasion when they had lowered their swords for a moment. Richard was surprised at my appearance, William embarrassed. Both bowed deeply, sword points resting on the ground. "The pair of you dazzle me with your brilliance," I remarked. "Run along and dry your sweat, Richard. I would speak with Master William."

Richard bowed again, cast William a curious glance, and then hurried off. I watched him disappear before again turning to William, who was holding his sword in front of himself somewhat protectively. "Come now, William," I said. "I have had two husbands and five sons." I considered it best not to bring up the subject of past lovers. "Do you suppose I am unused to the sight of naked men?"

The poor lad blushed. "Forgive me, your Grace. I have had little to do with women. And you . . ." he bit his lip.

"Go on," I invited. "What transpires is between you and me, William. No one shall ever hear of it."

"You are so great. So beautiful," he added, which was what I wished to hear. "So . . ." again he bit his lip.

I entered the arbour, and sat down. "Go on," I again invited.

"So . . . I do not know the word, your Grace."

"Then use the first one that comes into your head."

"So . . . so majestic."

"Why, that is charming. Come here." He advanced towards me, slowly, apprehensively, certainly, but not reluctantly. "Would you possess such majesty?" I asked.

"Your Grace!" Now his face was the colour of beetroot.

He was standing immediately in front of me. "Let me find out for myself," I suggested, and released the cord holding his hose. This promptly slipped about his ankles. Or certainly tried to do this. But it was impeded, and so, with dainty fingers, I helped it on its way. In truth, I had already discerned the answer I sought, as a gentleman's hose is not as a rule made of the thickest of material, but it was far more impressive when revealed in its natural state.

"Your Grace," he muttered. I gained the impression that he was begging, but for what, there was the question.

However, I had some desires of my own, and proceeded to indulge them, being careful not to stimulate him to the ultimate.

"Now," I told him, when my lips were free, "you have the power to make me the happiest woman in the world."

"Your Grace?" He was anxious.

And I realised that the entire business would have to be in my hands. Well, it was, most literally. "You may commence by helping me out of my clothes," I suggested.

\* \* \*

In cold terms, of course, my seduction of dear William was entirely reprehensible. But one needs to consider the situation. I was distinctly put out with my husband because of the Lampagie de Porhoet affair, and sought a tit for tat – although it would probably be more accurate to say I was offering a tit for tat to dear William. Then I was, I think without properly realising it, coming to realise that my marriage was ending; this being the case, I had no intention of again finding myself in the position I had been in when I had fled Louis in 1152. To begin with, there was no Matilda left to welcome me with open arms. I would have to provide my own salvation. I had great faith in my sons, but these were yet boys. I needed strong, and utterly faithful young men about me, to see to my safety. These are both eminently sensible reasons for my behaviour. But I would be untrue to myself did I not admit there was a third, and far more compelling, attraction for me in the young man. This had less to do with his masculinity than with my own, insidious but nonetheless demanding, awareness of omnipotence – in certain directions. If I was going to be forced, by circumstances beyond my control, to set up a court of my own, while I had no desire, at that moment, to attempt to wrest my dominions from Henry's grasp – it would have been an immense undertaking, as I was soon to discover – I had every intention that it should be a court of my own design, and my own control. I had, heaven knows, a great deal of experience on which to draw, and if I entirely discarded almost everything to be found at the courts of my two husbands, well, surely the fault was theirs rather than mine.

What I did draw upon were my observations of Constantinople and Antioch, added to my memories of Bordeaux when Papa had ruled and I was a small girl. These became to me the epitome of grace and beauty, of knightly behaviour, of love. Of course, one feels one's way towards perfection. There are very few of us – and none in my acquaintance – who, like Athena, are enabled to spring from their father's forehead, fully fledged, armed and armoured for the battle of life. My concern was, in the first place, beauty in every aspect. This is to be found *in* every aspect of life, if one knows where and how to look.

As a woman, I looked first in a mirror, and then into the various aspects of my ladies. Nor did I seek only the deeply curved breast or buttock, the sheen of leg or arm, the wealth of hair. Beauty can equally be found in a smile or a laugh, or better yet in a voice. Obviously this applies equally to men. But beauty can most of all be found in the mind, in quickness of wit and intelligence, in learning, to be sure, but learning can always be acquired whereas the others are innate. Knowing that I would probably never have the opportunity of ruling, I set myself to create a court of beauty. From that there was but a short step to the court of love. The credit for this has been given to my daughter Marie. But she learned from her mother.

Into these preoccupations I sank all my time, while I possessed it. Let Henry pursue his scarcely nubile Rosamunds and Lampagies: I was seeking the true substance. Henry was pursuing more than young women. He scarce seemed to notice my absence as he went about his affairs, which, in many directions, were my affairs as well. He did not come to me for Christmas – I did not miss him – and in January he resumed his negotiations with Louis, at Montmirail, on the Sarthe. To this meeting I was required to send Richard. I toyed with the idea of accompanying him, but since I had found an interest of my own I really had no desire to be closeted with Henry and have to accept his violent approach to life. So Richard went by himself, with a suitable escort, and returned a few months later, having done homage for Aquitaine, as Young Hal had done homage for Normandy, and Geoffrey had done homage for Brittany. Richard indeed returned in fine fettle, for in addition to Aquitaine he had also done homage for Toulouse, thus gaining acceptance from both his father and his stepfather that all my ancestral lands were his – whenever he could lay hands upon them. This was a brilliant accomplishment for a boy of twelve.

He also returned with the Princess Alais, his fiancée. She was a pretty little thing, although it was easy to tell that her head had been filled with the most dreadful notions regarding the ogre that would be her mother-in-law; she regarded me with abject terror, and trembled whenever I spoke to her. This of course could be overcome by kindness. Far more serious was the obvious fact that to Richard she remained a thing.

Richard also had news regarding Becket. For Henry had in his pocket that Papal Bull permitting the coronation of Young Hal to be performed by the Archbishop of York. Were that to happen, all of Becket's credit and standing would fly away like dust in the wind. Thus Thomas had also appeared at Montmirail, suggesting that he was ready for a reconciliation. I do not know what Henry's true feelings were regarding this, but of course Thomas found a ready supporter in Louis. My first husband was not entirely two-faced. Indeed, there will be many who will insist that he was not two-faced at all, but merely always found the business of being a monk at heart and a king in fact impossible to reconcile. Thus he always inclined towards the Church in any quarrel between

Church and State, especially when it did not happen in his own dominions, and thus it was obvious that he would side with Becket in a quarrel with the English crown. At the same time, however, as he was not a complete fool, he must have known that the return of Becket, if accepted, would be a considerable thorn in Henry's side. He also had to be aware of something else, which Richard put into words in his own succinct fashion. "My brother is very fond of the Archbishop," he remarked.

It would have been odd if Young Hal had not been fond of the Archbishop, as for several years before the rupture Becket had had the upbringing of the future King of England. It is my opinion that in this relationship lay all the tragedy that was to come. For the time being, however, it seemed that very little had changed. Pressure being brought to bear upon him, Henry had been prepared to accept the Archbishop's return, but Becket had immediately ended any prospect of a reconciliation by excommunicating two of Henry's churchmen of whom he disapproved, and there had been yet another quarrel.

I was determined to take no part in this ongoing controversy, unless invited to do so. I was not so invited. What is more, Henry did not come near me for the entire year, and preferred to spend that Christmas with Geoffrey and his bride Constance in Rennes, Brittany, and even the Viscount of Porhoet, having finally accepted the inevitable. For all I knew, Henry had Lampagie with him as a bedwarmer. I was not even informed of the impending coronation of my eldest son, and had to learn of it from other sources, as Henry intended that it should take place in the spring of 1170. "Is he to be crowned by the Archbishop?" I asked the messenger.

"Of York, I understand, your Grace." the fellow replied.

I again had half a mind to re-enter Henry's world. It was, in any event, a great insult for my eldest son to be crowned without my even being invited to be present. But apart from that, it promised to be a most interesting occasion, supposing Becket happened to be in England at the time. However, I again resisted the temptation. For one thing, I was busy preparing Eleanor's trousseau, and the girl herself for marriage and Spanish custom. She departed for her new life before Easter, while I reflected that I was now down to a single daughter, five-year-old Joanna, and for her too Henry had marriage plans, to William II of Sicily, grandson of King Roger who I had met in Italy twenty years previously. This lad was aged seventeen, having like Alfonso of Spain, succeeded his father while still a boy. His mother, also a Spaniard, Margaret of Navarre, had conducted affairs very well, and his kingdom was actually in much better order than Castile, but it was a little disturbing that he was succeeding a father known as William the Bad. On the other hand, Henry wrote jovially, William the Bad had been so very bad that his son could only ever be known as William the Good! What was most interesting was Henry's shift entirely away from northern Europe to the Mediterranean when seeking marriage alliances. Indeed, how much his ideas were turning in this direction only became apparent later on. For my part, I was determined, again, to carry out my own plans. Thus I wrote letters to all the interested parties, and that spring Richard and I set out on a *chevauchee* through Aquitaine. Alais naturally accompanied us, but as yet she had no great part to play, nor, I feared, would she ever have.

But that was for the future. In which I was now

dealing. On 31 May 1170 Richard was enthroned in the church of St Hilaire in Poitiers, receiving the lance and banner that were the insignia of the Counts of Poitou. From there we travelled down to Limoges, where Richard was invested with the ring of the virgin martyr Saint Valerie, and solemnly pronounced Duke of Aquitaine. With me on these auspicious occasions I had Joanna and John, while Uncle Raoul performed the duties of Master of Ceremonies, and generally conducted the whole proceedings. I may say, and I can add, needless to say, the Bishop of Poitiers disapproved of this taking matters into my own hands. He had remained implacably opposed to Uncle Raoul and I, not only because of the scandal we had created a few years previously but because he was a supporter of Becket and conceived that we were necessarily in the other camp. Well, he was by no means wrong there.

Meanwhile, Henry was also pressing ahead with his plans. Learning that Becket had regained the ear of the Pope, and that the Bishop of Worcester was on his way from Rome with a Bull revoking the earlier permission for the coronation, Henry acted with his usual speed and resolution. He took the Prince and crossed to England, leaving even the Queen-elect, Margaret, behind, in the care of the Constable of Normandy, Richard du Hommet. Hommet was also commanded to seize the Bishop, whenever he appeared, and prevent him from crossing to England himself. This the Constable did, with great aplomb, and on 14 June, safe from any interference from papal bulls, Young Hal was crowned King of England. There now followed the final act of what can only be called a tragedy. Faced with a *fait accompli*, it appeared as if Becket had surrendered. The coronation completed, Henry returned to France, and met with both Louis and Becket. The Archbishop and the King were officially reconciled, Becket was allowed to return to England, and it was arranged that Young Hal would be crowned again, this time with his wife – Louis was rather miffed that she had been omitted from the earlier ceremony – by Becket. What could be more civilised than that?

I may say that I was not informed about all of this. I gathered from various messengers that Henry was not pleased at the manner in which I had forwarded my own plans, but as he had agreed to it, and as Richard had already done homage to Louis for Aquitaine, there was nothing he could do about it. However, I was not invited to join him at the castle near Bayeux where he intended to spend Christmas – no doubt he was still finding Lampagie de Porhoet a bundle of joy. So I celebrated Christmas with Richard and Alais and my two babies in Poitiers: I had William Marshal to enjoy. Looking back on what was about to happen, I sometimes think that I was well out of it. On the other hand, I equally sometimes think that had I been present at the King's festivities, a great deal of unpleasantness might have been avoided.

For Becket had by now returned to England, eager to resume his duties and more important, his prerogatives. It is impossible to say whether or not he genuinely intended to make a go of it this time, but whatever his intentions they soon became soured when he realised that Henry had little intention of restoring to him any of the manors that had been confiscated when he had been expelled. Thus any milk of human kindness that might have been roaming through his system also became soured as well, and within a few weeks he was back at his old tricks, protecting the most criminal monks from the long arm of the law, and holding forth against the King whenever he found himself in a pulpit. This naturally jaundiced Henry in turn, and I gather that he was the more angry because he had honestly thought the matter resolved, and the Archbishop committed to toeing the line – the King's line. Thus he reckoned that he had been stabbed in the back, for a second time, by his old friend and confidant.

As I have said, I was not present to discern his mood and perhaps control it. The first I knew of what had happened was a white-faced messenger bursting into the Maubergeonne to stammer out, "Your Grace, your Grace, the Archbishop is dead."

I did not, initially, regard this as remarkable. Becket was a choleric fellow, he was nearly fifty years old, and a seizure was entirely possible. So I merely remarked, "How sad. I shall say a prayer for him," while reflecting that this was excellent news for Henry, who would hopefully come up with a more suitable replacement.

"You do not understand, your Grace," the fellow gabbled. "He has been done to death."

"Becket? Murdered?"

"Struck down before the altar at Canterbury, your Grace."

"Good heavens! Who did this?"

"There were four knights, your Grace."

"Four knights have murdered the Archbishop? Does the King know of this?"

"They are saying the King commanded it, your Grace."

I could not believe my ears. Archbishops had of course been murdered before – by the Vikings. It simply was not done by Christians, at least, out in the open, so to speak. Popes had certainly been done away with in the past, but by means of a poison introduced into their posset. One had actually recently died as a result of a street brawl, as I have recounted. But to cut a prelate of such distinction down before his own altar ... I was aghast.

I later learned that Henry had not commanded the murder to be done in so many words, but at the dinner table, when steeped in wine and having recently received news of some more of Becket's insolence and intransigence, had suddenly shouted, "Will no one rid me of this turbulent priest?" At which four of his most faithful knights – their names are Richard Brito, Hugh de Morville, William Tracy and Reginald Fitzurse, all most staunch and loyal supporters of the King – sprang up and left the hall. They took ship to England, reached Canterbury, and did indeed cut down the Archbishop before his altar.

No such event had taken place in Christendom within the reach of history, and the entire continent was staggered. Henry, by his rough and ready methods, had a whole host of enemies just waiting to drag him down. Now he had put himself beyond the pale, as it were. There had been a large number of people in the hall when he had made his outburst, and there were few who would argue that the four knights had been but obeying their master's command, however much he may have regretted giving it. In fact, Henry had sent messengers to recall Fitzurse and the others the moment he had realised their probable purpose, but they had not been reached in time.

However, as I am sure I have managed to convey in these pages, Henry was above all else a realist and a pragmatist. He had never had the weakness of stubborn assumptions of position which afflicts so many rulers. Now he had, unintentionally caused a catastrophe. Excommunication was inevitable, with all the evils that follow. I personally may always have scoffed at this ultimate of the weapon Church, but I had never misunderstood the powerful incentive it gives to the dissatisfied. A king needs above all else to be obeyed, and a king depends above all else on the homage and loyal service of his feudal tenants. Take away the necessity to obey, the requirement of service, for an excommunicated king can command no one, and rebellion is immediately in the air. Henry may have felt that he was powerful enough and ruthless enough to put down any revolt in England or even in Normandy, but he dreaded a return to the anarchy of Stephen's reign, and England and Normandy were only parts of his empire. In both Brittany and Aquitaine he had only just finished putting down revolts. He might feel he had triumphed there, but he could not be certain of the loyalty of the barons if he was under an interdict. He therefore acted with all of his customary energy. Almost before the news of Becket's death reached Rome Henry's messengers were there too, not only bearing large donations to the papal coffers, but assuring Alexander that Henry had not intended the crime, and indeed was overborne with remorse. The story was quickly spread about how he walked the corridors of his palaces in the midnight hours, crying out for Becket to be returned to him, and if there may have been many – I was one of them – who took the genuineness of this display of guilty grief with a pinch of salt, there could be no gainsaying the startling picture presented to Christendom of the most powerful king in Europe being scourged on his bare shoulders before the shrine of the martyred Archbishop.

Equally did Henry swear everlasting fealty to the Church, and promise to obey the Pope in all things. This whole charade was entirely specious, of course. Henry knew his man. Alexander was above everything else an empty showcase; the spectacle of a King of England, who was also Duke of Normandy and Aquitaine and Count of Anjou, abasing himself before the Church was too attractive to be rejected. He also must have had in mind, unless he was a complete fool, that a Henry rejected and perhaps rendered desperate, might become a very dangerous man indeed, and Alexander was still deep in the midst of his quarrel with Barbarossa, with the threat of an anti-pope being put forward continually hanging over him. Henry, if a dangerous enemy, could also be a most useful friend and ally. The result was absolution. Thomas was sanctified, within two years of his death, about the quickest canonisation in modern times; he was even so elevated before Bernard, as I have mentioned.

Henry was forgiven, and was soon back to his old ways. But of course he had to hurry slowly, especially as he needed papal support for his latest brainchild: Ireland. Thus it seemed that nothing had changed, save that the Emperor was now definitely our enemy, as he would have preferred Henry to defy pope and clergy. But this was less important to Henry than it may once have been for, quite apart from Barbarossa's reneging in the matter of Eleanor's marriage to his son, his thoughts were already roaming in other directions; Ireland was only one of the great things that he had afoot. And, of course, that Becket was dead. Henry was not about to make the same mistake twice. He actually kept the archbishopric vacant for more than two years, and then had the post filled by one Richard, Prior of Dover, a most humble fellow, who was entirely Henry's own nominee.

I think it is fair to say that in this dismal affair, as in so many others, my husband's triumph was absolute.

# Chapter Six

As I have said, I remained aloof from these matters. This was simply because, although one might have said that this was his hour of need, Henry did not turn to me. The decision was his. But it would be idle to pretend that I was not put out. Our estrangement seemed complete. And why? This was the dismal question. We had not quarrelled over any great matter. I had accepted his peccadilloes without protest, as he appeared to have accepted mine. Between us we had achieved everything we had set out to do. And yet my husband had turned his back on me. It could only be that he no longer found me desirable. I assume this is a state of affairs that is liable to overtake any woman unfortunate enough to marry a man eleven years her junior. It is not the more acceptable for that. And it is even less acceptable when I was clearly still very desirable to a large number of men. Or was I? Were they only fawning at my feet because I was the Queen? This too was a disturbing thought. I began the year 1171 in a most depressed frame of mind.

From which I was very quickly aroused by the arrival of my eldest daughter in Poitiers. I was taken entirely by surprise when Amaria scuttled into my boudoir and said, breathlessly, "Your Grace, the Countess of Champagne is here."

For a moment I had no idea of whom she was

speaking. Then I bounced to my feet. "Marie? Here?" I ran from the room, my skirts held high so that I should not trip, and almost fell down the stairs.

"Mama?" asked the woman standing in the centre of the knights' hall.

I gazed at her almost in awe. Marie was now twenty-four years old. I had not seen her for all but eighteen years. I remembered a child of six. And I was looking at an utterly beautiful woman, tall and slender, but voluptuous enough to earn a second glance from any man; light-brown-haired – a mixture of Louis and myself – and blue-eyed; those she got from her father. But her face was mine, and she stood like me. It only slowly dawned on me that she was wearing black. "Oh, Marie!" I said.

She came forward, and was in my arms. We hugged each other so tightly I ran out of breath, but so did she. When she released me I could at last look around me. There were a good many people in the hall, but they were all mine. Only two strange women stood just inside the doorway. With them was a priest, a young fellow, and quite handsome. "Tell me," I said.

"Henry of Champagne is dead."

"And you?"

"Am in mourning, Mama, as custom requires."

"Nothing more than that?"

"He was a brute."

"I believe you," I agreed, remembering his brother. "But why are you fleeing?"

"To prevent Papa getting his hands on me, and marrying me off to some other brute."

"I see. He will be very angry."

"He cannot touch me, if you will give me shelter, Mama."

"My dear girl," I said. "My dear, dear girl. I will give you shelter."

I did not tell her that she might just have jumped from the frying pan into the fire, as Henry was quite as capable of marrying her off as Louis. But I was resolved that he would only do that over my dead body.

Having Marie to live with me gave my life an entirely new dimension. It was far more than the reunion of a mother with her long-lost eldest daughter and first child, for whom I naturally had always had a special affection. It was a coming together of two grown women who had the same background and aspirations, as well as the same blood. I had sadly not had the upbringing and education of the girl, and I doubt that Henry of Champagne had paid too much attention to the intellectual side of her personality, but she was my daughter, and she had steeped herself in learning, history and legend, in philosophy and syllogism. Equally, as my daughter, she had never allowed her desires, in any direction, to be limited by religious points of view.

She had had what, to many women, would have been an almost unbearable life. It was distressing to consider that such a life could have been mine, had the Empress not protected me when Theobald came knocking on our door. But again, as my daughter, she had taken the importunities of her husband in her stride, while being resolved that she would never submit to another. Henry of Champagne's love-making had apparently been in the true Norman style, containing a great deal of rough masculine self-satisfaction which had left his wife and victim quite cold.

Not that Marie was frigid. Again, she was my daughter. But she had a different approach to life, and had not the opportunity of my experiences. Thus, where I had fled Louis accompanied only by Amaria and Bernard of Ventadour, Marie had fled Champagne accompanied only by two maids . . . and a chaplain. I was not inclined to delve too deeply into her relationship with her two ladies, but I was somewhat taken aback by the obvious intimacy she shared with this priest. Of which she was not the least bashful. "His name is Andrew," she explained. "He is a dear fellow. And also learned. He is writing a book."

"On your adventures together, no doubt," I remarked, with a touch of sarcasm.

"On love," the dear girl said seriously. "Is that not a universal subject?"

Who was I to argue with that? And even less when she allowed me to listen to Andrew reading aloud his latest chapter. He was certainly bashful, when he realised he was required to bare his all, metaphorically speaking – at least on this occasion – to the Queen of England who was also the Duchess of Aquitaine. And with good reason. This chapter dealt with what a man should seek to admire in his lady, and I am bound to say that he called a spade a spade. Alarmingly so, but also most stimulatingly. As he warmed to his task, and described the exact length it is desirable that a woman's pubic hair should be, and how – and by whom – it should be clipped, I could not forbear to glance at Marie and observe her reaction. But this was all excitement, slightly parted lips and heaving bosom, as she gazed at her lover: I could no longer doubt this. Well, he was a handsome fellow. I could not entirely suppress a spark of jealousy – for all my adventures I had never been bedded by a priest!

Andrew was also equipped with a new story for my titillation. It told of the marriage of the fabled King Arthur with Queen Guinevere, and of Guinevere's adultery with the great knight Sir Lancelot of the Lake. Well! It could have been a recounting of my marriage to Henry – although he had never thought of anything as romantic as a Round Table – and my affair with William Marshal. Perhaps it was intended to be. I enjoyed it thoroughly, while reflecting that I was certainly not going to retire to a convent on being found guilty!

It was natural that two such fertile minds as Marie's and mine, thrown together, should have acted as an inspiration, one upon the other. Marie, with her vivacity and effervescent humour, as well as her overwhelming interest in the flesh, was a tremendous hit with her young half-siblings. John and Joanna adored her, and even Richard sought her company whenever he could. Indeed, I had a flashing thought that had she not been his sister she would have made the ideal wife for him – she was, after all, not much older than him than I had been his father. But she was equally kind to Alais, who was really a rather miserable little girl. She as much as anyone was aware that she aroused not a spark of affection or even interest in her future husband's breast. But it was I who was Marie's principal attraction. Not merely because I was her mother. She regarded me as the ultimate woman. Well, in many ways I suppose I was. Marie had been prevented from *living*, thus far, by the dull boor to whom she had been tied at so early an age – it was no wonder that she was resolved never to marry again. Now she sought to live, at least vicariously, through the exploits of her mother.

It was a great experience for me to recount those exploits, and not only to Marie; Andrew was always present and, with my permission, making notes. Much of what I told him he added to his manuscript. I found this exciting, as I had already made him read to me his earlier chapters, and found these of equal interest, as he disserted on such things as the correct length of a man's penis and what relation it bore to the length of his nose! How much of what he has written down will ever be made public is impossible to say, or indeed, if *any* of it. But if it is, I suspect there will have to be some considerable editing to avoid a charge of obscenity. I should mention that I was at this time totally bereft of what might be called positive masculine company, William Marshal having found it necessary to return to Normandy and England to see to his affairs. I anticipated his return to me, but for the time being I certainly had to exist on memories.

Andrew was interested only in recounting history, of various aspects. Marie sought life, and would sigh most heavily as she realised that she was unlikely ever to have any experiences that would match mine. "Do you not still dream of Constantinople and Antioch, Mama? Of dark-visaged men, and burning sands? Of moon-filled nights and balmy breezes?"

"Well, of course I do," I said. "Although I have to say that it was not all milk and honey."

"Because of your circumstances. But now you are mistress of your circumstances. Would it not be grand to recreate Antioch here in Poitiers?"

I hugged her, because that had always been my dream.

"Would that it could be possible, my dearest child," I said.

She accepted defeat in this direction, but her brain continued to seek an outlet for her tumultuous thoughts. This came in a most unexpected fashion a week or so later, when Amaria brought a young woman to see me.

I was, as usual, closeted with Marie and Andrew but was not put out by the interruption, for the woman, she was hardly more than a girl, was most attractive. "Her name is Isabeau Doucette, your Grace," Amaria explained. "And she seeks the favour of your advice."

Marie clapped her hands. "Let her explain her situation, and she shall have it."

It turned out that Isabeau was the wife of a prosperous merchant in Poitiers, and in that role was content enough. But her husband was more than twice her age, and not very interested in matters of the flesh. She had accepted this as her portion, and had not sought to alleviate her desires, until very recently she had been approached by a member of my court, a young rascal named Flaubert de Rais – he was in fact the son of my garrison commander. Flaubert wished her to grant him her favour, but she was a well-brought up young woman, and shrank from adultery. Yet was the temptation, and Flaubert's importunities, increasing with every day. So she had hit upon the idea of seeking advice from the most famous lover of the day. Marie was delighted. "This must be debated," she declared. Isabeau was made to sit between us, and required to answer every question my daughter could think of, ranging over both her relations with her husband – whenever these took place – and what she hoped for from Flaubert. The girl was quite embarrassed, especially when we were joined by three other of my ladies, who also wished to know everything. "Well then," Marie said. "We have all heard all the evidence. Let us now vote."

Poor Isabeau was clearly wishing she had stayed at home, but there was nothing for it: she had to sit and hear each of our judgements. As it happened the verdict of the court was unanimous; all seven of us –

as Andrew had remained – voted that she should refuse Flaubert her bed. She didn't look the least pleased. "But what am I to do?" she wailed, "when next he comes to me?"

"Send him away," Marie told her. "And tell him that he must be worthy of you."

"But how may we know that?" the poor girl asked.

"It is up to him to prove it," Marie said sternly. "Let him, hm . . ." she appeared to consider, but by now I knew my daughter well enough to be sure she had long decided on her recommendation. "Let him cut off his little finger to prove his love for you."

"Do *what*?" Isabeau screamed.

"It doesn't have to be his sword hand," Marie explained.

"I couldn't possibly ask a man to cut off his finger for me, your Grace."

"Then you do not love him," Marie said severely.

"But I do!"

"Then the finger it must be."

Isabeau twisted *her* fingers together, and looked at me. But I was bound to support Marie, and kept my face stiff. Isabeau stood up. "If . . . if he cuts off his finger, may I allow him into my bed?"

"Of course," Marie said. "If he still wishes to have you. But there is one essential you must observe."

"Yes?" the girl asked eagerly.

"The amputation must take place before you."

"Oh, your Grace, I should faint."

"I would not recommend it," Marie said. "Now, off you go. And be sure to report to us on the outcome of your trial."

Isabeau stumbled off, shaking her head. "Marie," I said, "that was heartless of you."

Marie laughed. "Do you really suppose so, Mama?

Consider this: Isabeau will ask Flaubert to cut off his little finger, before her. If he is a man of courage, and if he is truly in love with her, he will immediately draw his knife to fulfil her requirement. But if she is a true woman, and truly in love with *him*, will she not then say, at least to herself, those noble ladies must have been mad, prevent him from mutilating himself, and take him to bed anyway?"

Sadly, this is not what happened. Flaubert refused to contemplate cutting off his finger! Isabeau was quite upset.

Naturally Isabeau's experience soon became widely known, at least amongst the younger set of my courtiers, and before long we were approached, this time by a young man, who sought our advice and judgement on how he should deal with a young lady of whom he was enamoured, and who, he was certain, reciprocated his love, but who was afraid to allow him the ultimate, principally because her father had forced her to take a vow of chastity until he could find a husband for her — apparently his short list of possible suitors did not include our young supplicant.

This was clearly a matter requiring considerable thought, involving as it did not a mere getting together, but the questions of oaths, when forced, of virginity before wedlock, and a whole host of subsidiary problems. Marie therefore determined to require the judgement of the entire court, or at least, those who were, as she considered, of the right age and mentality. Here again the young man found himself in an embarrassing position, as he stood in the midst of a semi-circle of my ladies, amongst whom were several other gentlemen, while Marie and I, Amaria and Andrew, sat on a specially-constructed dais above the throng. In these enervating circumstances he was required to tell us everything we thought pertinent to his case, whereupon we passed our verdict, which was that he should collect everything that fell from his lady's window, including the contents of her chamber-pot, for a period of a month, at the end of which time he should present his collection to her, as a token of his love.

The occasion was a great success, and set a precedent. From then on scarce a week went by than we sat in judgement on some affair of the heart, while Andrew copied it all down. When there was no case to be heard, we composed songs and stories, vying with each other to be the most risque. It was enormous fun.

It may well be said that I really had more important matters to consider than other people's love affairs, and this is probably true. I was enjoying myself, ruling my own inheritance for the first time, without any interference – Henry was far too busy, as I saw it, coping with the repercussions of Becket's murder to worry about me. In fact, he *was* very busy, but being Henry, he had already settled the matter of his guilt, at least to his own satisfaction, and was fully engaged in other directions. In the spring of this year I knew he was again campaigning in Brittany to ensure Geoffrey's portion would be safe. I half anticipated a visit from him, but he never appeared. I was therefore the more taken aback when a messenger arrived to inform me that my youngest son, John, was to marry the Countess Alice, daughter of Count Humbert of Maurienne, upon whose death John was to inherit the entire province of Maurienne, which occupied the south-east corner of the quadrangle formed by the Alps, the Rhine, the English Channel, the Atlantic and the Pyrenees, or what is generally regarded as France, even if the French King only rules a third of it! This Humbert was of course a nephew of my ex-mother-in-law and of that idiot with whom I had been involved during the Crusade.

Here was a complete surprise, and one which both explained a lot of things and created a lot of problems. It first of all explained several of Henry's recent actions. In marrying Eleanor to Alfonso of Castile he had formed close relations with the main Christian Spanish power. He already possessed, or at least was suzerain, of all south-west France, that is, Aquitaine and Provence. Now he clearly sought to establish his power in south-east France as well. He would become arbiter of the western Mediterranean, and as such an even greater influence upon the conclaves of Rome than was the Emperor, sulking north of the Alps. These were heady dreams, but they did not take into account the aspirations of his sons. John of course was only six, and not yet old enough to *have* aspirations, but his three older brothers most certainly did. Of them all, Richard was the most offended.

Richard was going through a difficult period at this time. He was now fourteen years old, and was already a full-grown man, with all of a man's instincts. But he was in the first place bedevilled by the perversities of his flesh, which was accentuated by the presence of Alais of France in our midst. Many a man, certainly many a prince, has been forced to wed, for reasons of state, where his heart is elsewhere. Most accept the situation, bed their wife, get her pregnant as rapidly as possible, and seek the solace of their mistress's arms. For someone to whom a woman's arms, *any* woman's arms, were positively repulsive, this duty called for a considerable amount of will, especially as he was aware that the arms he would have preferred were frowned upon by Church and society, and more important than either of these, his mother.

I suppose I can be accused of softness here, and I would admit the charge, freely. It was difficult to behold such a tall, strong, manly figure, so accomplished at arms, so intelligent, so much the product of my own womb, and find fault, however much I knew that his sexual instincts were pregnant with disaster. I had thus far managed to keep them from the knowledge of his father. Indeed, they were known only to Amaria and myself, although Marie, with her keen intellect, quickly discerned the truth of the matter, and, I have no doubt, confided them to her Capellanus – she confided everything else. My own instincts remained optimistic. It was obvious that Richard would never bed Alais, whom he regarded entirely as a sister. Thus my thoughts were already ranging to getting rid of the girl, and replacing her with someone more attractive to him. This course was filled with danger, as Louis might well be sufficiently offended at the repudiation of his daughter to take up arms. Even more important, the negation of one of the cornerstones of his policy might anger Henry! So it will be seen that I did have more on my mind at this time than Courts of Love. While I cogitated, I surrounded my son with all the most beautiful girls in Poitiers, and prayed that one of them would come to my door to complain about a distended girdle. But this did not happen.

A boy growing up in this uncertain mental dilemma is clearly not going to be entirely happy, and Richard's personality problem was accentuated by his overweening ambition. I do not think he ever considered rivalling Young Hal. He was too much the believer in primogeniture as the proper way to conduct a monarchy. But by the same token he was not about to allow any of his younger brothers to usurp *his* position, either as second heir to the crown or as second in line when it came to wealth and power. Well, it may be said that in possessing Aquitaine he was indeed second only to his elder brother in the power at his command. But was it at his command? I certainly endeavoured to let him rule in every possible way, but his father left no one in any doubt that the Duke of Aquitaine was but his agent, as were the Duke of Brittany and the Duke of Normandy. All taxes belonged to the King; it was his pleasure to disburse them, or part of them, back to his sons as he conceived it necessary. Richard constantly grumbled that he never had sufficient funds. Well, I agreed with him. But Henry would have it so. It was the same with the army. We disposed of a sizeable force in Aquitaine, but the commanders of the various garrisons were equally left in no doubt that it was their business to await the King's commands, and not engage in any flights of fancy that might enter the head of their Duke. In fact this was probably no bad thing, for Richard was so ambitious of military glory that, given his head, he might well have gone charging off to fight the Moors beside his brother-in-law Alfonso. But the restriction rankled.

And now came this John business. Soon after we received the news I found Richard stretched on the floor with some of his playmates, half across a map of Europe. "If this map is accurate, my baby brother will be the most powerful of us all, Mama," Richard said.

It became apparent to me that, much as I disliked the idea, it was absolutely necessary for Henry and me to have a get-together and a most serious chat about the future. But this proved difficult to arrange. It was difficult even to discover where I should address my letters. For Henry was not allowing the prospect of getting his hands on Nice and Savoy – as the Maurienne lands were known – to distract him from his other ambitions. Having settled Brittany, he immediately took himself off to Ireland.

These unhappy people had already been invaded and conquered by Richard of Clare, known as Strongbow, who had acted in Henry's name. Strongbow had allied himself with Dermot MacMurrugh, King of Leinster, in a war upon the High King, Rory O'Connor, the terms of the alliance stipulating that Strongbow should marry Dermot's daughter Eva, and succeed him as King of Leinster. After defeating Rory outside Dublin, Strongbow had married Eva on the field, and thus established English sovereignty. Actually, this sovereignty hardly extended beyond the limits of Dublin Castle, but it sounded very fine, and Henry, having carried his usual tactics of fire and sword some distance inland, apparently liked the place so much – or was it the red-haired Irish women? – he spent Christmas there. My messengers finally caught up with him in Dublin, but it was well into the new year before they returned and then the replies they brought with them were most unsatisfactory.

Henry agreed that we needed to confer – almost as if we had been rival potentates – but indicated that this would have to be at his leisure rather than mine. His calendar, needless to say, was already a full one, his principal objective for this year being to receive absolution for Becket's death and to have Young Hal crowned again, this time with his wife. It may be recalled that the crowning of Hal without Margaret at his side had annoyed Louis, and the matter had been going to be set right by a second crowning, by Becket. Well, that had gone by the board, but Louis still wanted it done, and it was finally accomplished on 27 August. Naturally, I was not invited. It seemed to be Henry's determination to keep me out of England. Presumably Rosamund had been tattling. As ever, I was tempted to gatecrash the party, but decided against it. I conceived, with good reason, that it was necessary to work with Henry rather than against him, to avoid any clashes with our sons, and was prepared to wait. And at last an invitation did arrive, for Richard and Joanna, John and Alais and myself to join Henry at Chinon for Christmas.

Marie was not included in this invitation, but I told her she could come if she wished. She decided against it, having no desire to get too close to her step-father, who had once been a suitor for her hand, and who was well-known to demand sexual satisfaction from any woman pretty enough to attract him, whatever her rank or affinity. No doubt she was wise. And in fact she did not miss much, except the final disolution of my marriage! We set off in high spirits, and found those at Chinon quite the reverse. Christmas necessarily involved the second anniversary of Becket's death, but as Henry had by now received full absolution for that crime, this should not have borne so heavily. In fact, he had far more serious problems on his mind, as I recognised at once.

We embraced, with as much warmth as could be expected. Truth to say, I was a little taken aback at his appearance, and recalled his father. Geoffrey the Fair had been some years short of forty when I had met him, and had looked far older – it may be recalled that he had, in fact, only a few months to live, and if his death might be considered an accident, it surely would not have overtaken a thirty-seven-year-old man had he been in good health. Henry was now actually forty, and he too looked at least twenty years older. His red hair was flecked with gray, and his movements, though still clearly governed by his enormous energy, too often suggested a certain hesitation, as if the relationship between brain and muscle, for so long the terror of all Europe, was beginning to weaken. I should say at this point that although I was fifty-one, there was not a gray hair in my head.

Henry's exhaustion, hardly to be surprised at in view of the life he had led for the past twenty years, was one very good reason for his not being in the best of spirits. The other reason was far more obvious . . . and disturbing. "When are Young Hal and Margaret arriving?" I inquired, when we were alone together in my bedchamber. That he had signified his intention of calling upon me in private had both Amaria and myself in something of a twitter, and she had left me reluctantly to cope with whatever might be coming my way. But for the moment it appeared that he sought only to unburden himself of his various problems.

"They are not arriving," Henry growled.

I raised my eyebrows. "I understood this was to be an assembly of all the family?"

"So it was. But that young scoundrel has gone scuttling off to Paris to spend Christmas with his father-in-law. Now, what do you think of that?" Well, of course, there were several ways to take this. If I was entitled to feel put out in that I had seen neither Hal nor Margaret since their coronation, and indeed, it was several years since we had spent Christmas together, it would have been even longer since Louis had seen his daughter. Thus the incident could be put down to mere thoughtlessness on the part of the young couple, as regards myself. Henry did not see it this way. "The fact is that Hal has turned against me," he grumbled. "Perhaps he was turned against me, years ago, by Becket. Now he blames me for Becket's death." He glanced at me, daring me to say the obvious. But I was here to make peace within the family, not provoke trouble. "And of course," Henry went on, "that little bitch of a wife of his is constantly whispering in his ear."

"That is not unnatural, for wives," I ventured.

"You do not know what she says."

"And you do?"

"Of course. Several of her ladies are in my pay. Her theme is that I do not give Hal sufficient authority, and that he should no longer lurk in the wings, as it were, merely a sub-king awaiting my death. I can tell you that she has turned him against you, as well."

I could believe that, even if it was disagreeable to hear it. However, I determined to pursue my strategy of peace at any price. "I will not accept that a son of mine could possibly plan a revolt against his father," I protested. "But this is the very question I wish to discuss with you. These sons you have, these splendid young eagles, they are your flesh, Henry. And mine. Hal is seventeen. He is only two years younger than you when you became Count of Anjou and Duke of Normandy. That was fortuitous, but surely you can appreciate how he feels. The same goes for Richard, and Geoffrey, I have no doubt. And so will John, in the course of time."

"Are you suggesting that I should abdicate?"

"I am not in the mood for jokes, Henry. I am suggesting that you could delegate some authority to the various dukes, allow them to manage their own dukedoms without interference. If they prove failures, well then, at least you will know to replace them in time."

"Indeed, madame? And do you not suppose that if I sought to replace them, I would be faced with armed opposition?"

"Henry," I said urgently. "My fear is that if you do not grant them something more than empty titles, you will most certainly be faced with armed opposition, and sooner than you think."

He glared at me. "You are telling me there is a conspiracy?"

"Of course there is not a conspiracy, Henry," I protested. "But we are speaking of young men of spirit."

"A conspiracy!" he bawled. "And you . . ." he pointed, "are at the heart of it."

"Me?"

"Do not trouble to deny it! You have been conspiring against me from the day we met. Nay, before we even met. When I remember how you inveigled me into your bed . . ."

Well, really! When he had virtually raped me! "You are talking nonsense," I pointed out, coldly.

"Nonsense, is it? By God . . ." I braced myself for an assault, but instead he turned away from me and stalked to the door. There he turned again, to point again. "I know of your schemes, madame. Be sure of that. And be sure that I shall deal with them." With which he left the room. So much for my determination to keep the peace!

I cannot say that this was the end of conjugal relations with my husband: these had ended some time ago. But it was certainly the end of any prospects for a merry Christmas. Geoffrey and Constance of Brittany duly arrived a few days later, and were greeted by Henry with glowering looks. This was the first time I had met Constance, who was a dour child, and a little uncouth in her personal habits – she was clearly terrified of her father-in-law. I did my best to be kind to the girl, as I was to Alais, but I could not help but feel that they were helpless pawns in a den of lions, the more so as I observed Geoffrey and Richard in constant conclave, while John trailed around behind them, saying little but obviously listening to everything that was said.

My own feelings were ambivalent. To me Henry was invariably cold. Yet I could not help but reflect that the Henry of my youth would have vented his anger with more than angry looks or sudden departures. Perhaps for the first time I realised that my husband might not be any longer capable of dealing with large crises. Because he had some small ones of his own, but they were of the nature to appear large to a man, especially a man such as Henry. This was confirmed to me one night only a week after I had arrived in Chinon, and that was a week after Henry and I had had our abortive conversation. I was indeed still studying the matter, and wondering what was best to be done as it was clear that anything to be done would have to be done by me to prevent the clash between father and sons I could see coming and of which I was mortally afraid. It must be remembered that although history in general is littered with events of this nature, there had never been a case in the history of any of the families with which I had been connected. Papa would no more ever have thought of rebelling against Grandpapa than Grandpapa against Great-Grandpapa. I had never met my first brother-in-law Philip, but I could not imagine either him or my first husband daring to raise a hand against Louis the Fat. Eustace of Boulogne might have been a despicable lout, but he had always fought faithfully for his father Stephen. And none of William the Conqueror's sons, fearsome warriors though they were, would have even considered rebelling against their far more fearsome father. True, the Empress Matilda had more than once attempted revolt against *her* father, Henry Beauclerk, but she had never been successful.

Now there was almost something ironic in the possibility that there could be a revolt against a man who could be quite as fearsome as the Conqueror. In a sense it was something to be proud of, because these young eagles, as I called them, had my blood in their veins. But it was nonetheless a frightening prospect. Or was it? As I have said above, I had scarce been in Chinon a week, brooding on the situation, and had retired for the night with, as usual, only Amaria for company — we were now no more than two very old and loving friends; gone was the ardour of our youth together — when there came a gentle tap on my door. Amaria sprang up in an instant, arming herself with a dagger. I sat up also, but I could not imagine that Henry would send me an assassin. Amaria stood against the door. "Who is there?"

"I must speak with the Queen," a voice said.

Amaria looked at me. But the voice had definitely been that of a woman. "Let her in," I commanded. Somewhat reluctantly Amaria pulled the bolt, and the door swung inwards. Standing in the gloom was a slight figure, wrapped in a cloak. "You may enter," I told her. She stepped inside, and Amaria closed and bolted the door again. "Reveal yourself," I commanded.

The woman hesitated, then threw the cowl from her head. I was taken aback. It was five years since I had last seen Lampagie de Porhoet. Then she had been a pretty child of twelve. Now she was a very beautiful woman of seventeen, neither tall nor particularly voluptuous, as I have indicated, but with the most perfect features, shrouded in that curling tawny hair which reached her waist. "You," I said, "dare come to me?"

"I have things that must be said, your Grace."

"Is that so." I swung my legs out of bed and stood up. Even at fifty-one and ten times a mother I feared comparison with no woman. Yet did I wish to know what Henry found so much more attractive. "Take off your robe," I said. She hesitated, then obeyed, while staring at me. I stared back at her, while I slowly put on *my* robe. Beneath she wore a single garment, a kind of Spartan chinon. "And that."

"Your Grace?"

"We must be sure you are not armed," I told her.

She heard Amaria behind her, and half turned her head; she knew Amaria was equipped with the dagger. Thus she released the tie at her shoulder and the garment slipped to the floor. "Bring the candle, Amaria," I said. She obeyed, and held it above the girl, while I looked at her. Now she was flushing, but she kept still, and silent, proving that she had courage. Now, as the fire had burned low, the chill was beginning to reach her, and she started to shiver. I returned to the bed and got beneath the covers. "Join me," I invited.

Again she hesitated, and again cast Amaria an anxious look. Then she licked her lips, and came to bed with me. Amaria got in on her other side. "Tell me why you are here?" I asked, stroking her hair. As I had conquered Rosamund, so would I conquer this one, I was determined. "Do you grow tired of my husband?"

"Your Grace, oh, your Grace." Without warning she burst into tears.

I took her in my arms, while Amaria, sensible child, got out of bed to pour a goblet of wine from the decanter on the table. "My dear girl," I said. "What can the matter be?"

I made her sit up, still in my arms, to sip the wine, and that seemed to give her some courage. But she said, "Oh, your Grace, I am so afraid."

"Of what, Lampagie?"

She licked her lips again. "Of the King, your Grace."

"Does he ill-treat you?" I could not believe that the violence of his love-making would frighten her now, when she had been his mistress for five years.

Her head moved against my shoulder as she shook it. "No, no, your Grace. Well, not intentionally. But . . . there are times when he is desperate, and they grow with every day."

"Desperate? You mean he cannot complete?"

"Sometimes he cannot even enter, your Grace."

"Then what does he do?"

"He . . . he squeezes me and throws me about. Sometimes he whips me."

"And you do not call that ill-treatment?"

"It is not intended to hurt me, your Grace. Only to bring about an erection." It occurred to me that perhaps this girl loved Henry far more than I had ever done, simply because she was prepared to serve him without question or ambition of her own. "But it is the other which is the worst," she said.

"Why? Does he hurt you then too?"

"Sometimes. Afterwards. But it is when he is trying, your Grace. He heaves and humps and pours sweat and pants most heavily . . . I can hear his heart beating, your Grace. It is like the beating of a drum."

I gave her some more wine and then gently eased her back on to the pillow, assisted by Amaria. "Why are you telling me this, Lampagie?" I asked. "Do you suppose I can help you?"

"I wished you to know, your Grace. If his Grace should die while . . ."

She fell silent, and I kissed her mouth. "You would not like to be executed for having caused his death. I entirely understand. Well, perhaps I would protect you." I watched her changing expressions; she had sought more than a perhaps. "If in turn you will obey me," I went on.

"Anything, your Grace, anything." She gave a most attractive little wriggle, sliding her legs against mine to indicate that when she meant anything, she meant anything. Well, she was a most earthy little thing. But there were more important matters on my mind.

"Does the King ever confide in you?" I asked. Suddenly her face was watchful. "Of course he does," she said. "And no doubt speaks to his confidantes in your presence. I wish you to remember everything he says, either to you, or to anyone else, that you may overhear, and come to me, and tell me of it."

"But your Grace, if his Grace should find out . . ."

"He would probably have you impaled. But then, he would have you impaled now, if he knew you were here. So, you see, you have very little choice but to obey me."

What would you? I have often been accused of ruthlessness, but this was not only the future of my boys at stake, but that of myself as well. And in fact Lampagie, in addition to being a bundle of joy, was also a mine of information. Henry, it appeared, had received information from Cousin Raymond of Toulouse – wretched man! – that his sons were plotting against him, encouraged by Louis. I am bound to say that this was news to me, at least as regards Richard. What Young Hal and Geoffrey might have been doing in Winchester and Rennes was another matter entirely. But Henry, while again apparently resolved to quash any incipient revolt in the bud, was also most anxious that nothing should happen to interfere with his plans for the Maurienne marriage contract. The child-bride Alice was due to arrive in Aquitaine in the spring, and so we seemed to have that much breathing space before any open break was likely to take place.

This placed me in yet another quandary. If, as now seemed obvious, my marriage was over, then I needed to look out for myself. As long as Henry lived and we were married – and there was no hope of another annulment, even if I was closer in blood to Henry than I had ever been to Louis – then he would remain Lord of Aquitaine. It was my business to be patient until he was no longer about – even then I never had the slightest doubt that I would outlive him. The point I had to consider was what happened when he did die. Young Hal would succeed as King of England, Duke of Normandy and Count of Anjou. There could be no argument about this: he had already been crowned. As King of England and head of the House of Anjou he would also claim suzerainty over Brittany, Ireland, whatever lands John might inherit . . . and Aquitaine. And I could hardly consider Young Hal as a friend, much less a dutiful son, in view of his recent ignoring of me, while I could not doubt that Margaret had indeed been filling his mind with absurdities about me.

It was obvious, therefore, that on Henry's death it would be necessary for me to resist Young Hal's claim, and declare Aquitaine an independent entity – ruled by Richard. Towards this I had been working, perhaps without even being fully aware of it, ever since Richard's birth. For this I had been prepared to overlook any minor vices that might have appeared in his character. And for this I was prepared to risk everything. I am sure I will be criticised for devoting so much of my love and ambitions to but a single one of my sons. But I have just explained that circumstances, or rather, Margaret of France, had conspired to drive a wedge between Young Hal and myself – as had been confirmed by Henry himself – and equally I had seen very little of Geoffrey virtually since he had left my breast. Richard and John were the two who had been with me constantly, and I knew that John worshipped his elder brother – could I be blamed for imagining a new empire arising in southern France, with Richard ruling from the Bay of Biscay to the Rhone, and John from the Rhone to the Alps, in mutual strength and harmony? It will thus be understood that the safety of my two youngest boys was of paramount importance to me. But that safety, I recognised, would have to be the subject of much caution. Therefore, firstly, I could not just gather them up and flee to Poitiers. That, to Henry, would be proof of a conspiracy, and I had no guarantee that the garrison in Poitiers would follow their youthful duke against his fearsome father.

Secondly, I dared not even warn Richard of his danger. Because I knew that he would react violently, and possibly even challenge his father there and then. Thus I had no choice but to sit it out until we were able to return home, and Henry had departed upon yet another adventure. Then I would have to set about making plans and reminding my people that I was their lawful duchess, and my son their lawful duke. Thus do we make plans. But Henry was making plans too. And so were others.

Christmas over, I made preparations to return to Poitiers, but to my consternation Henry refused to allow the family to divide. "We are all going to Limoges," he informed me. "To receive Alice de Maurienne. Hal is joining us there."

He had apparently written to our eldest son in the most peremptory terms, demanding his presence. Hal obeyed, and was already in Limoges when we arrived. It had been a difficult journey, for Richard was in a mood of the deepest resentment against his father. "He hates us all, Mama," he confided, riding beside me in the long cavalcade.

"He is undergoing a difficult time," I suggested, mildly.

"That does not mean he will not suddenly turn on us," Richard said. "Mama, we are deep in my duchy . . ." we had left Poitiers some distance behind us, "and these are my people. Is that not true?"

I would have preferred to refer to them as *my* people, but there was no way I was going to quarrel with Richard. "I am sure of it," I agreed.

"Then should we not settle the matter now?"

"You cannot be contemplating killing your father?"

"I said nothing of killing, But he could be seized, and imprisoned . . ."

"Richard," I said. "I do not wish to hear you speak like that again." My uneasiness grew.

As I have said, Hal was waiting for us in Limoges . . . but not Margaret. "She is unwell," he explained, embracing both Henry and myself. "I thought it best to leave her with her father for the time being."

I could see that Henry did not believe him, and the tension in our circle grew. I was very pleased to see Hal again, if only to reassure myself that he was fit and well. He was indeed the very epitome of a prince, taking after me much more than his father, and thus at eighteen was tall and strong and handsome. And soon enough he came to visit me, in private. He was not a man to mince words. "How do you stand in this business, Mother?" he asked.

"What business?" I countered.

"This quarrel between my father and myself."

"I did not know there was a quarrel between you," I said. "But whether there is or not, I would beg you to be patient."

He glared at me. "Then you are on his side."

"I am on no side. I only know that this family will destroy itself if it wars upon itself."

"You are on his side," Hal said again and left the room.

Alice de Maurienne arrived a week later. She was only two years old, and had nothing striking about her. John seemed delighted, but Richard, Geoffrey and Hal stalked about the place looking more angry than ever. "Now," Henry told us. "It is time for us to be about our duties. Anor, you may return to Poitiers, with Richard and John, and the princesses. I wish you to remain there until further notice." I opened my mouth to protest about being treated like a servant, but Henry was hurrying on. "Geoffrey, you and Constance will return to Rennes. Again, you will remain in Brittany until further instructions from me."

Geoffrey looked at Richard, then nodded. "And are you returning to England, Father?" Richard asked, innocently.

"I am returning to Chinon," Henry said. I presumed this was because he had left Lampagie there.

"Then I am to go to England," Hal said. "To remain there until further instructions, as well, eh, Father?"

"No," Henry said. "You will come with me, to Chinon."

Hal's head came up. "What am I to do at Chinon?"

"You will remain there, for the time being. You will write to your wife and tell her to join you there."

Hal's face was stiff. "You mean I am to be a prisoner."

"I mean you are to stay at Chinon until I say you may leave," Henry said.

It will be understood that the atmosphere at Limoges was not a merry one. Henry and Young Hal left the following day, for Chinon. I followed more slowly, with the rest of the family, for Poitiers. The boys were now very upset, and I found it difficult to contemplate the future. In all the circumstances, I refused to let Geoffrey continue to Rennes, but bade him accompany Richard and John, the girls and myself to Poitiers. There I was delighted and relieved to find Uncle Raoul waiting for us. "I have been hearing strange rumours," he told me.

"They may be strange but I doubt they are rumours," I said.

"Then what is to be done?"

"We must wait on events."

"Well," he said. "I am going to do some recruiting."

"Be careful, I beg of you," I told him.

But we had not been in Poitiers more than a few days when a messenger came galloping towards the Maubergeonne. I received him with my boys around me, as well as the princesses. "Your Grace," he panted, having been given a hasty glass of wine to revive him from his exhaustion. "I bear a message from the King."

"Indeed? Tell me."

"His Grace commands that the three princes be sent immediately to Chinon."

There was a moment's silence. "I'll not go," Richard declared. "I am not to be a prisoner."

I laid my hand on his arm to restrain him. "Does his Grace offer a reason?"

"The reason . . ." the messenger licked his lips.

I frowned. "Has something happened to Prince Hal?"

"Prince Hal . . . the Prince has left Chinon, your Grace."

My frown deepened. I was bewildered. "Left Chinon? Where has the King sent him?"

"His Grace has not sent the Prince anywhere, your Grace. The Prince escaped the guards the King had placed over him, and rode into the night. It is believed that he has gone to Paris."

"Hoorah for Hal!" Geoffrey shouted.

I was inclined to agree, in the short term. But it placed me in a serious position: there could be no doubt that Hal intended to start a rebellion against his father, and that Henry knew this, and thus that *he* intended to have his other sons under his hand, as prisoners, to prevent them from joining their brother. I could not contemplate that, with all the possible consequences that might flow from it. But if I refused to send them . . . Richard might have been able to read my thoughts. "He will march on Poitou next," he said.

I looked around their faces. Richard was aglow: it was his nature. Geoffrey was less positive. John was jumping up and down: he would follow Richard's lead, in whatever direction. Constance and Alais looked terrified. Joanna was bewildered. And little Alice was of course too small to understand what was going on. "Let him come," Richard said.

I looked at Uncle Raoul. "I can raise ten thousand men," he declared.

"And who will lead them?"

"I will lead them!" Richard cried.

How splendid he looked. But . . . "No," I said.

He frowned. "I am not afraid of Papa."

"I am sure you are not. But you would surely regret it the rest of your life were you to kill him."

"You cannot ask me to surrender."

"No, I will not do that, Richard." My brain was racing. Could I, or rather, Uncle Raoul, defeat Henry in battle? Raoul was a capable soldier, but Henry was . . . Henry. Were we to lose a battle, he would march on Poitiers, and probably demand the surrender of his sons on pain of devastating the countryside. That would put me in an intolerable situation. Thus the boys would have to flee, to safety, and leave me to cope with Henry, hopefully by reasoning, but if not, by force of arms. I was not afraid of this; but I had no desire to undertake a campaign while looking over my shoulder in fear for my children. But where was safety, from Henry? Anywhere in Aquitaine was dangerous. Cousin Raymond in Toulouse had already proved himself a black-hearted rogue. England was firmly under the thumb of Henry, as were Normandy, Anjou and Ireland. Humbert of Maurienne was his ally. That left . . . Louis!

Louis was obviously actively encouraging Hal to rebel against his father. He would most certainly give shelter to Hal's brothers. The point I had to consider was that, as Hal's brothers were, like Hal, *my* sons, if I sent them to him, would I ever get them back? Has ever a woman been faced with a more tricky decision?

I opted for Louis. Our differences were twenty years

in the past. Odo and Galeran were both dead, as were all those others who had tried to bring me down. I felt sure Louis would deal honourably with my children. When I told them my decision Richard was furious. "Do you suppose I am some girl, to be sent away so I shall not be hurt?" he demanded.

"I suppose that you are the Duke of Aquitaine," I told him.

"And does that not mean I should remain and fight for my duchy?"

"It is not a case of fighting for your duchy, Richard," I said. "This is a personal matter between your father and the rest of the family. I will represent the rest of the family, and see what arrangement I can come to. Once I have achieved that, I will send for you."

He hesitated, glancing at his brothers. But Geoffrey and John both clearly wished to go. His shoulders sagged. "And the girls?"

"The girls will be safe here in Poitou." Henry had never waged war upon women. Perhaps on this I was relying too heavily.

The boys departed, and I sent a message to Chinon that they could not attend the King as he wished, but that if he wished, *he* could come to Poitiers to discuss the situation. I understood this was tantamount to a declaration of war, and had scouts posted along the banks of the Loire. Meanwhile, Uncle Raoul and myself prepared ourselves for the coming struggle. In more ways than one. As I have recounted earlier, Raoul had long been one of my favourite uncles; indeed, he ranked second only to Uncle Raymond of Antioch in my esteem. It may also be recalled that it had been our intimacy – an entirely innocent intimacy at that time – that could be said to have driven the first nail into the relationship between Henry and myself. Now that my marriage was at an end, it was Raoul who was prepared to remain at my side and fight for me. Nothing could have been more natural than that we should find it both necessary, and desirable, to spend much time conferring together, often deep into the night, or indeed, throughout it.

I am well aware that there are those youthful innocents who assume that once a woman has passed the age of child-bearing she at the same time loses all interest in matters of the flesh. Nothing could be further from the truth. Indeed, in most cases, exactly the opposite obtains. In my fifties, and long after, I found sexual matters filled a good part of every day. And what matters! I had experienced almost everything that two people can do to each other. Thus I knew exactly what I liked and what I did not like, what filled me with joy and what left me totally disinterested. Equally had I been around long enough to understand that the mere fact of a man getting inside one is not the crowning achievement of a relationship, nor is his inability to do so, for whatever reason, necessarily a catastrophe while he still has fingers and lips; this can be a very important consideration when dealing with men who may be as old, or even older, than oneself. Uncle Raoul and I had a happy few weeks together, and this is important, because it was the last happy few weeks I was to know for some time. Early in June our scouts came galloping back to inform us that the King was crossing the Loire, with his army.

It may be supposed that we should have taken our position on the banks of the river. But that would have been pointless: there were several fords available. We reckoned our best prospect lay in giving battle closer to home, and on a ground of our own choosing. This we did. Raoul of course commanded, but I refused to skulk inside the Maubergeonne. If we won, there was no need; if we lost, my tower would not resist Henry's siege machines for very long, and I wished to put neither that beautiful old pile nor the girls at risk. So we chose our ground, and gave battle. I remained with our baggage train, but I dressed myself in full armour, well, as full armour as a woman may bear. I was thus on the ground to see the speedy and total disintegration of my forces. Sadly I must confess that Uncle Raoul, for all his charm, was not in the same class as Henry as a soldier. He fought gallantly, but was overborne by both strategy and tactics, not to say numbers. "We must flee, your Grace," said Flaubert de Rais, commanding my bodyguard. He might not have been willing to cut off his fingers to oblige his lady love, but he was certainly anxious to look after me.

"Flee where?" I demanded, watching the chaos in front of me with a sinking heart.

"Back to Poitiers," he suggested.

"And stand a siege?" I shook my head. "We must make our escape and hope to raise another army."

"Whither, your Grace?"

I squared my shoulders. This was not something I had ever been able to contemplate, before. But now I only wished to be with my sons, and above all, Richard. "We will ride for Paris," I said.

So off we set. I had made Amaria remain in Poitiers with Marie to look after the girls, and so, apart from myself, we were a totally masculine party. Although I was dressed as a man, this was not obvious to any passers-by. Not that it mattered. Fast as we rode, Henry's people rode faster. I can only assume some rascal had told him I had been on the field. We had not travelled twenty miles when we found ourselves surrounded, and forced to surrender. "Not a word," I told Flaubert, and he nodded.

But that too was unavailing. The commander of our captors rode straight up to me, and himself raised my visor to look at my face. "His Grace awaits you, your Grace," he said. "And may God have mercy on your soul."

# Chapter Seven

My captors treated me most courteously, but yet left me in no doubt that I was a prisoner. I felt less sanguine about my escort, from whom I was separated. But then, I had a great deal to think about myself, as I realised I was being taken to my lord and master, against whom I had raised my hand in anger. The royal army had already begun its march on Poitiers, but Henry was in camp and at his dinner when I arrived. He was, naturally, surrounded by his lords and his fools and his dogs, but to my relief there were no women present. Had Lampagie been there I have no doubt I would have had a seizure. As it was, I composed myself to look my usual imperturbable self. To my enormous relief, Henry also looked imperturbable. "You must be hungry, madame," he said. "Sit, and eat."

What I really wanted to do was drink, and this I did, gulping an entire goblet of wine, following which I felt more able to face the day. And the King. Henry gnawed at a bone, and then threw it to the waiting dogs. "Male attire suits you, Anor," he remarked. "However, you do realise, I am sure, that for a woman to dress herself as a man exposes her to a charge of witchcraft?" About to swallow my first mouthful, I all but choked. "It is the law," Henry pointed out. "I do not make the law. I am only responsible for carrying it out."

"I am really not in the mood for jokes, Henry," I remarked.

"You should be, madame. You are in so serious a situation that only laughter is left to you. Now, we have just established that you are guilty of witchcraft. I would say that it is also fairly well established that you have recently been in arms against your king."

"I acted as Duchess of Aquitaine," I pointed out. "As we are now in Aquitaine, you are an invader, and I am a prisoner-of-war."

"I am the ruler of Aquitaine," he argued.

"In my name," I riposted. "I have now withdrawn that privilege from you."

"Madame, your effrontery is startling."

"I am Eleanor of Aquitaine." At moments like this it is always best to stick to the essential facts.

He considered this for some seconds, and I hastily drank some more wine and ate some more food, as I had no idea what was going to happen next. "If you imagine," Henry said at last, "that I am going to place you on trial, where you can use your oratorical skills and your beauty to turn things upside down and hope to enlist the sympathy of the world against me, you are gravely mistaken. You may be Eleanor of Aquitaine, but before that you are my wife. I shall treat you as a wife, who has erred against her husband, most seriously. You will spend the rest of your life in total confinement, madame. And do not dream of escape and revenge. You shall have no sons to plot with. You shall have no one at all, to plot with."

I could not believe my ears. "You mean to place me in solitary confinement?"

"You may have that creature of yours to keep you company," he said.

"Be sure I will be avenged," I told him. It was all I could think of to say.

I naturally felt at a very low ebb. My first husband had contemplated locking me up, and I had been able to face him down. Henry was a very different kettle of fish. My imprisonment commenced that very day, as although I was returned to Poitiers, it was under guard. My people gathered on the streets to stare at me, but even more at the sombre figure of the King, who rode before me. Once inside the Maubergeonne, I again found myself under guard. I was not even allowed to see my daughters and prospective daughters-in-law. But Henry kept his word and sent Amaria to me. "Oh, your Grace," the dear girl said, hugging me to her breast. "What are we to do?"

"Wait," I told her.

This may be considered an outrageous flight of fancy, as I was eleven years older than the King, and indeed, when I was confined I was past fifty, which is an age when too many of us begin to consider turning our backs on an active life rather than making plans for what I had to assume might yet be a distant future. But wait is what I was determined to do. To be sure, it was difficult exactly to determine what I was waiting for. Henry's death? As I have said, he was considerably younger than I. Richard to avenge me? This certainly, in the first instance. But I was to be sorely disappointed.

As I have related, my imprisonment commenced immediately. I remained in my apartment in the Maubergeonne for some weeks, while Henry investigated the exact situation regarding the anticipated revolt of his sons. When he realised that they meant business, I was transported to England, together with

Joanna, Queen Margaret and the Princess Alais, as well as the Countess Constance and Alice de Maurienne. Henry intended to keep his hands on all of us. Marie he entirely ignored, much to my relief.

In England, I was separated from my family, even Joanna being taken from my side. Henry certainly intended to punish me. But his behaviour only hardened my resolve to regain the upper hand. Amaria and I were sent to Salisbury Castle.

At that time I had every reason to regard the future with some optimism. It seemed that all the world was in arms against my husband. There were several uprisings in England; the Scots, under their redoubtable new king, William, called the Lion, invaded from the north; and Young King Hal was rousing all Normandy and Anjou, aided by his brothers. The only disappointment was that there was not much doing in Aquitaine. But perhaps they were the wise ones. For with total and consummate skill Henry dealt with all of his foes, and within a year the rebellion was history. The English rebels faded away when confronted by the King; the Scots were defeated in battle and the famous Lion taken prisoner; and my sons were simply bought off. I do not wish to be hard on them: even Hal was hardly a full-grown man, and they were utterly dependent upon the support of Louis. This, as we have seen often enough, was akin to riding after a fox with a pack of kittens rather than dogs. Louis' character had not stiffened in the least in the years since the Crusade. He was as fond of making bellicose statements one day and being overcome with remorse the next as ever in the past. Besides, he had a mortal fear of having to confront Henry in battle. And Henry remained a master politician. He now suborned Louis by offering him peace, and suborned my sons by the simple procedure of offering them what I had requested he offer them at Chinon. Hal was confirmed as Duke of Normandy, with additional rights and privileges, and a guaranteed income of fifteen thousand Angevin pounds a year, and Margaret was restored to him; Geoffrey was confirmed as Duke of Brittany, with additional rights and privileges, half the revenues of his dukedom, and Constance was restored to *him*; and Richard was confirmed as Duke of Aquitaine, with additional rights and privileges, and half the revenues of Poitou. However, Alais was not restored to *him*, as he made it a condition of his surrender that she should not be. Henry did not quibble with this, for a reason which I only discovered later, and retained possession of the girl, announcing that she was still betrothed to his son. Louis was so relieved to have got out of his scrape without having to fight a battle that he raised no objection. What Henry did not know, and what saddened me greatly, was that Richard would now be left to his own devices – and we all know what they were.

To be sure, there were hiccups. Poor Alice of Maurienne very rapidly sickened and died, and thus that whole project fell to the ground. This seems to have been more of a disappointment to John than his father, less on account of the death of his future wife than because of the ending of his dreams of being the next Count of Maurienne. Of course there remained Ireland, but the Irish were in their usual state of revolt, and ruling them was going to be no sinecure, even had it been at all practical for a lad of eight. Henry thus felt constrained to give his youngest son some castles in Normandy. To be sure, this was a cause of complaint on the part of Young Hal, but by the end of 1174 the King was once again in complete and dominant control of his empire.

\* \* \*

I remained in my prison. For Henry had absolved my sons of any guilt for their rebellion against him by another very simple procedure: he announced that I was the instigator of the revolt, and was thus the sole guilty party. It was obviously a great disappointment to me than none of my sons endeavoured to stand up for me. But I determined to suppress any resentment and attempted to understand their points of view.

Hal and I had never been close. For this it was possible to blame Becket, and my support of Henry against the Archbishop, not to mention Margaret's dislike of me. But there it was. The same thing could be said for Geoffrey, while John was too young to have any influence upon his father. But what of Richard, my favourite, and who knew he was my favourite, too? Richard later told me that he had begged for my release, without avail. I am sure he did, but I am equally sure he did not press too hard at that time, for the very good reason that had I been released, I would undoubtedly have found my way back to Poitiers, and he would have had to put up with me. He was well aware that I disapproved of his peccadilloes, and no doubt wished to flap his wings – and presumably other parts of his body – for a while.

So there I was, and there I stayed. My confinement was not rigorous, except that merely being confined is rigorous. I had books to read, and I could write songs. I could walk the battlements and look out over the tumbling countryside – but I could not venture into it. I could walk the castle gardens and enjoy the flowers. I had Amaria for company, but we could do little more than reminisce. I received letters of support, from Richard, to be sure, from Walter Marshal, who even dreamed of rescuing me, but I put him off the idea as I feared it might involve his execution, from John, as he grew older, from Eleanor down in Toledo, from Matilda in Dresden, and from Joanna in Messina. And best of all from Marie, who had returned to Champagne and was again conducting her courts of love. All of these eagles of mine loved me and wished to help me, and all were constrained by their fear of Henry: I did not know if I would ever see any of them again. Thus my misery grew, as day followed day, week followed week, month followed month, and then year began to follow year. I have always been a woman who was up and doing. Now there was nothing to do.

Then I received a quite unexpected but greatly appreciated boost. The castle was under the command of Sir William de Wykham, and the distaff side of arrangements were controlled by his wife Marian. They caused me no hardship, partly I suspect because they had been so commanded by Henry, and partly because they were afraid of me. But in truth, they were both pleasant people, who I entertained often enough in my apartments. They never failed to let me be aware that in keeping me confined they were carrying out the instructions of the King rather than acting of their own volition. Now one day early in 1175 Marion de Wykham called on me, and with some embarrassment said, "There is someone to see you, your Grace."

I had not received a visitor in all the nearly two years of my imprisonment, thus far, and indeed Henry had told me that I never should. "Is he from the King?" I asked.

"In a manner of speaking, your Grace. That is to say, he has the King's permission to speak with you."

My imagination flew immediately to William Marshal, although why Henry should relent to the extent of allowing a man who was fairly well known to be my lover to visit me was a mystery. "Then show him in," I said.

Marion hesitated. "This gentleman . . . he is a monk."

"A monk?" I could think of no monk who would wish to visit me.

"A monk, your Grace. And . . ." she flushed.

"Tell me."

"Well, your Grace, I would say that he is not wholly a man."

I stood up. The only eunuch with whom I had ever come into close contact was Galeran, and as far as I was aware he was dead. My curiosity was fully aroused. "Bring this person to me," I commanded.

She bowed, withdrew, and returned a few minutes later with a black-robed figure, who walked with his head bowed. But when he found himself in my presence, he immediately ran forward. For a moment both Amaria and myself assumed I was the victim of an assassin, and Amaria boldly threw herself in front of me. But the monk only wished to kneel at my feet. "Your Grace," he said. "Oh, your Grace! How I have dreamed of this moment."

Now he raised his head, and I stared at him in consternation. His voice, high-pitched and slightly harsh, had certainly suggested the eunuch, now his beardless face confirmed that impression. But the face itself was familiar. "Do I know you?" I asked.

His animation faded. "There is no reason for so great a lady to remember one such as I," he said. "But once we sat side by side to discuss a poem."

"Albert!" I cried. "Albert! My dear, dear, boy." This was stretching a point, as he was a year older than myself. But how the memory of the carefree days of my girlhood came flooding back. I embraced him. "But

". . . what do you here? And what happened to you, all those years ago?"

"Your present husband gave me permission to be your chaplain, your Grace. He seemed rather amused when I related how we had known each other as children, and how I had suffered a most unfortunate fate."

"Who commanded it?" I demanded.

"Sadly, your father, your Grace. But I have no doubt that he was influenced by the Archbishop Geoffrey."

It is of course a waste of time feeling anger against the dead. So I said, "I am so terribly sorry, Albert."

"Your Grace, it was a long time ago. And besides . . ." he cast a glance at Marion, who had remained standing by the door. "If I may speak with you alone . . ."

"Thank you, Marion," I said. "That will be all." She hesitated, then curtseyed and withdrew. Amaria hastily closed and bolted the door. Albert looked at her in turn. "I have no secrets from Amaria," I said. "Nor should you. Now tell me, you bring a message from Duke Richard?"

"Sadly, no, your Grace. The message is from myself."

"But you are here?" I was bewildered.

"About myself, your Grace."

"Tell me."

"Your father commanded that I be seized and cropped, your Grace, and at the same time banished from Bordeaux. I was taken out of the city, clandestinely, and south to the town of Dax, where I was handed over to the monks in an abbey there. These men knew of a suitable surgeon to carry out my sentence. And this was done, but at the request of the good fathers the deed was done in a special manner."

I was intrigued. "Go on."

"Well, your Grace, I was cropped as regards reproduction and, indeed, manhood. But . . ."

"Good heavens!" I said. "You have retained your shaft!"

I had heard of this practice while in the East, for it is apparently a popular one amongst the ladies of the harem, as while the eunuch is definitely a eunuch, he is perfectly capable of erection and indeed, as he can never spend himself, can maintain himself for hours on end, so it is said. This is clearly of inestimable value where a hundred or more women are officially only allowed the satisfaction of knowing a single man.

As for two women – for I shared everything with Amaria – confined entirely without male company, such a fellow is a boon. Thus my imprisonment was not quite so arduous as Henry had intended. And Albert was a great asset in more than just sexual companionship. Throughout my life I had never maintained a truly personal chaplain. I had never found any compelling reason to trust any churchman absolutely, and once a confessor becomes a permanency, he is likely to take over one's life, rather as Andrew had taken over Marie's. Thus I had insisted upon confessing to, and taking the eucharist from, different priests on a regularly rotating basis. I now abandoned that system, and surrendered my every thought to dear Albert.

But being imprisoned remained nonetheless arduous, for while I was confined a great deal was going on.

I have related how Henry appeared to have achieved the most complete triumph by the end of 1174. But he remained perplexed by the problem that had always confronted Louis. He felt, no doubt sincerely, that I was his enemy, and certainly, that I could no longer be considered his wife. Thus he would like to take another. In Henry's case, this was not in search of an heir; he already had far too many of those. It was sheer libidinity. In the event, Albert, Amaria and myself were confounded when only a few weeks after Albert's reappearance in my life, Marion de Wykham informed me, all of a twitter, that there was a Papal Legate, no less, waiting to see me. I could understand the good beldam's excitement, for a Papal Legate, it should be remembered, carries with him the full authority of the Holy Father himself, and as such ranks above even an archbishop. But what, I asked myself, could such an eminent churchman have to do with me?

This man's name was Cardinal Huguezon. I had never met him before, and he put my back up immediately by offering me his finger to kiss. When I declined to do so, he looked quite put out, and he was a shifty-looking fellow in any event. "I trust your Grace is comfortable?" he inquired.

"I am sitting quite comfortably at this moment," I acknowledged.

He cleared his throat, glanced at Amaria and Albert, who stood one to each side of my chair, and decided that I was not in the mood for small talk. "I have just left the King," he announced. I raised my eyebrows. I had no idea the King was in England. "He is in Southampton," the Cardinal explained. I waited. "It is he bade me inquire after your comfort."

"Then you may tell him what you see."

"His Grace has in mind that you might wish a change, of scenery and situation." I regarded him for several seconds, but did not speak. I saw no reason why I should make his task easy for him. Huguezon cleared his throat again. "His Grace is of the opinion that your marriage is at an end. He is sure that you also are of this opinion." Still I would not speak. "It is therefore against all the laws of nature that the King should continue to be constrained by a wife who is not a wife," the Cardinal said. "I may say that this is also the point of view of the papacy." I continued to gaze at him. "His Grace knows your Grace's abiding interest in matters religious . . ." he paused here, as if aware that he had just uttered an absurdity, "as he knows how generously you have endowed the Abbey of Fontevrault, where his own mother lies buried. The Abbess of Fontevrault has recently died. His Grace would make you a gift of the Abbey, and the role of Abbess, so that you may end your days in peace and comfort, and some happiness."

"How can I be an abbess when I am not a nun?" I asked, gently.

"Well, of course, it would be necessary for you to renounce this world and take the veil," the simpleton agreed.

Shades of Guinevere, but I was not Guinevere. "And my lands?"

"Well, you would renounce them as well, your Grace."

"I see. And is Henry also going to renounce the world, and take the tonsure?"

"Well, no, your Grace. He is the King of England."

"And I am the Queen of England and Duchess of Aquitaine. It is not my intention to exchange my crown or my lands for a veil."

He opened and closed his mouth several times, like a fish gasping for water. "Do you mean that you refuse his Grace's offer?" he managed at last.

"That is what I mean, yes."

"You are aware that your marriage was never approved by His Holiness?"

"We never asked for his approval."

"But your union with the King is illegal, as being within the bounds of consanguinity."

"Is that so," I remarked. "Well, you may tell King Henry, and the Pope, that if they try to pull that one again I will turn both kingdom and papacy upside down. I will make such a fuss that no one will have any doubt that all Henry's children will be declared illegitimate. He will have no heirs, only rebels. I will retain Aquitaine. And I will publish my account of the Pope's double-dealing in the business of the annulment of my first marriage."

The Cardinal did some more gasping, and then took his leave.

It may be supposed, and indeed, Amaria and Albert feared, that I was again inviting assassination. But Henry was a "knife in the back" man even less than Louis. I have no doubt that when he heard of my refusal he chewed up a few rushes and broke some furniture, but he knew he was challenging a will as strong as his own, and besides, he had a personal problem of his own, of which I only learned later, but which would have made any public wrangling dangerous.

The remarkable aftermath of my conversation with the Legate was a considerable relaxation in the rigour of my confinement. A year later I was allowed to travel to Winchester to assist Joanna – she was now eleven and Henry was as usual hunting for alliances – in being outfitted for her marriage to William, King of Sicily. I was pleased about this, having such fond memories of William's grandfather Roger, and of course it was a great treat to be given as much money as I wished to spend on the girl . . . and on myself for a change, for my wardrobe had become sadly diminished. An even greater treat was that Matilda of Saxony paid a visit to England at this time, together with her children, and we were able to get together and I to meet my grandchildren for the first time. These were my only grandchildren, and I was not too sanguine about ever obtaining any more, as John and Richard were unmarried, Hal and Margaret had been married now for several years without producing, as could be said of Geoffrey and Constance. Still, there was always Eleanor, enjoying the heat of Spain, and in fact around this time she began sprogging with a fecundity which almost equalled mine.

Matilda was clearly distressed that I should be under restraint, which was fairly obvious even when I was not inside a castle, but she had too severe problems of her own to involve herself in what was really an affair of state, and we contented ourselves with personal matters. Her situation was indeed sad, for her husband, Henry of Saxony, like William of Scotland known as the Lion, had quarrelled with Barbarossa and been banished from the Empire for seven years. This was an unheard of punishment for perhaps the leading noble of Frederick's realm, and worse, it had carried with it the confiscation of all Henry's estates and wealth. Thus, virtually penniless, Matilda was entirely dependent upon the goodwill and support of her father, and could offer me nothing more than sympathy.

Joanna's marriage meant that all of my girl children were now away, but yet I did not lose touch with them, for we corresponded regularly.

It was on this visit to Winchester, that I became aware of the latest scandal on Henry's domestic front. I had been told, almost immediately following my incarceration, that when Henry was in England he was living openly with Rosamund Clifford as man and wife. This did not surprise me. It had surprised me, however, to be told that the King had entertained the Papal Legate at Southampton rather than at Woodstock. Now I discovered the reason why: Henry had a new mistress – Princess Alais of France! In fact, it was rumoured that Alais had given her prospective father-in-law a son.

Now I am sure everyone will agree with me that this was going over the top, or perhaps under the bottom, even allowing for Henry's rampant libidinity. I refuse to blame the girl. Alais, as I have recorded often enough, was a lovely child who, through no fault of her own, had been left as about the longest-waiting fiancée in history. Under my care she had been carefully educated, and I had never ceased to hold out the carrot of expectation that Richard would eventually marry her. But she had, it seemed, been absolutely rejected in the settlement of 1174, while still belonging to the Angevin household. And I had suddenly been removed from my role as guardian. Alais had neither the means, and in her circumstances I doubt she had the will, to resist the king she had come to regard as a father when he came knocking on her door. But however one looked at the matter, it was at least moral incest.

At that time I had no idea what Richard thought of it, although I could guess; he would use it as a reason never to marry the girl. What would happen then I did not care to imagine, but as it was Henry's pot of boiling oil he would have to get out of it as best he could. I was prepared to be interested, and await events. However, someone who took the news very much to heart was Fair Rosamund, and that summer she sickened and died. She was well short of forty, and naturally there were not lacking those who suggested that she had been encouraged on her way. But by whom? As I have mentioned earlier, the finger has swung round to point at me, but as I was securely walled up in Salisbury Castle that summer I have the best of all alibis. Nor, again as I have suggested, do I suppose for a moment that Henry would ever stoop to murder, even to get rid of an unwanted mistress. No, I suspect Rosamund just could not face the fact that she had been utterly replaced, and forever. She had sacrificed her life to Henry, in that she had never married, or had children. She had had only the King. When he repudiated her, she had nothing at all, save the reflection that those who give their all to kings are invariably treated thus. And presumably, she has secured herself a place in history – if only as my victim!

What Lampagie de Porhoet felt about it, I have no idea. I never saw or heard of the woman again.

Thus the years dragged by. Not without incident, but they were incidents I had to witness from the wings, as it were. Not all of it was edifying, at least to me, such as the spectacle of Henry and my favorite son, Richard, campaigning together. I seemed to have been entirely forgotten. I could not help but wonder what Louis thought of it all. No doubt he was rubbing his hands with delight at the thought that the proud beauty who had so humiliated him had been brought down at last. But I was to have the last laugh on both of my husbands.

In 1179, young Philip Augustus was fourteen years old, and Louis determined to follow Henry's example and have the boy crowned King of France during his own lifetime. I believe my first husband may even have had some idea of abdicating in the not too distant future – he was now appoaching sixty. The event was set for mid-August and was to take place at Rheims. As may be imagined, Louis was determined to make this the greatest happening of his reign; as unlike Henry he had no quarrels with any of his clergy or the Pope there was no necessity for clandestine comings and goings as had bedevilled Henry's crowning of Young Hal. All the crowned heads of Europe were invited to attend. Henry did not go, but he sent Young Hal to the investiture of his brother-in-law. I have no idea whether I was invited or not, as I certainly never received an invitation. But it is more likely that Louis never sent one than that Henry troubled to suppress it; it was the custom in Europe at that time to pretend I did not exist.

In the event, like almost every spectacular organised by my first husband, it was a disaster which turned out to be a catastrophe. The French royal party duly arrived in Rheims, and King-elect Philip duly went hunting with some friends. He got separated from them, and discovered himself to be lost. All alone in a forest, poor lad. It was some hours before he was found, and was then also discovered to be virtually a gibbering wreck from fright! Well, he was Louis' son: shades of Pamphylia!

Philip in fact soon recovered from his ordeal, although his behaviour had scarcely been that of a king; the real sufferer was his father. I am sure that I have amply illustrated that Louis' world was one overcast by considerations of sin and divine punishment. His principal dream had always been to have a son to carry on the monarchy. His inability to procure one from my womb he had related to our consanguinity, as well as punishment for his various sins, Vitry, etc, etc. That Constance of Spain had similarly failed to deliver he had put down to a continuation of that divine displeasure. The triumph of Adelaide of Champagne meant that he had at last been forgiven. Rejoice! Rejoice!

However, she had given him no more sons, and now

he was at an age where he could hardly expect more. Unlike Henry, who from time to time raged that he had too many sons, every hope of Louis' future rested in this frightened boy. When he was told that his heir was lost in the forest, and could be dead, the King of France swooned in despair. Like his son, he recovered from this attack. But unlike Philip, the recovery was far from complete – he had in fact suffered a stroke – and the following year he died.

I am sure Henry put on a good display of grief for a brother monarch. I did not trouble to, as there was no one to admire any display of mine in any event. Perchance I allowed myself to recall some of the glorious adventures I had had as Louis's wife . . . but apart from our first night together he had shared in none of them. And the truth of the matter was, that however publicly Henry mourned, Louis' death was an enormous relief to him. Not only did it mean that France was now ruled by a fifteen-year-old boy who seemed entirely lacking in any martial backbone, but this boy was also brother-in-law to the next King of England, and looked upon his sister's father-in-law with all the respect and fear that Henry managed to inspire in everyone who came into contact with him.

What is more, Philip immediately became encumbered with domestic affairs, as he got married, to a Dutch lady named Elizabeth of Hainault. In view of what we all now know of Philip's proclivities, which were in fact far more pronounced than Richard's, this was a supreme act of duty, and what is more, he managed to get his wife pregnant, although to be sure not for several years yet. I never had the opportunity of meeting Elizabeth, and therefore am unable to pass an opinion on who did what and to whom and at which end. But I have certainly met their son, as I shall explain in due course.

Marriages, or at least betrothals, were in the air around now, as I was informed, not by Henry I may say, that my little John was to be betrothed to Isabella of Gloucester. This was a considerable catch, as Isabella was heiress to all the vast west country lands of the earldom of Gloucester, and John would therefore immediately become a wealthy man. The drawback was that as she was the Empress Matilda's niece, and therefore Henry's first cousin, she was John's second cousin. That was really getting too close for comfort, but no one seemed to object to the idea, and I was not allowed to.

With France totally preoccupied, the Angevin Empire thereupon entered upon a period of great stability and indeed, prosperity.

It was now that Henry was able to carry out those legal reforms which have made his name great, and entirely to remake the face of Britain and Normandy, not to mention the other parts of his far-flung empire. I hope it will be noted that I desire to detract not one iota of credit from his immense achievements. The stability that he created was to stand us in good stead after his death. Because this was not to be long delayed.

Louis had died on 18 September 1180, and as I have indicated, for the next three years Henry was supreme. It was, in these circumstances, not unnatural for an over-active mind like his to seek fresh fields to conquer. Ever a realist, Henry understood that the death of Alice of Maurienne had ended forever his dream of extending the Angevin Empire to the domains of the Pope. He may even have felt that this was not necessarily a bad thing: almost everyone who became involved, politically, with the Papacy, came to a bad end. But there remained the ultimate dream of every king who was also a knight and a man of ambition: Palestine!

The cause of the trouble was the rise of Saladin to power. My old friend had, as I had supposed might be the case, replaced his uncle as commander of the caliph's armies, and was now well on the way to becoming ruler of the entire Saracen nation. If he accomplished this, then the Christian states in Palestine would be in great peril: their survival so far had been largely because of Arab rivalries. In these circumstances, what better finale could there be for a career of unbroken triumph than for King Henry of England to lead his army to Palestine and do what Louis of France and Conrad of Germany had so signally failed to do?

Henry was, I believe, attracted by this idea as far back as 1177, and had actually discussed it at a meeting with Louis that year. Needless to say, Louis was all for it. The idea of Henry being removed from the affairs of Western Europe for a few years would have been a most attractive one to my first husband; the possibility that Henry might come an equal cropper must have been even more attractive. From my point of view, I cannot help but wonder what would have happened *had* the most successful man of his time – and Henry was most certainly that, at least in Christendom – led his army against the most successful man in the Moslem world. It truly would have been a clash of giants, and one suspects the entire course of history might have been changed. However, it was not to be. Various other projects had got in Henry's way. With the death of Louis however, once he had put his empire into order, he began to take the concept seriously, as I was informed from various sources. Naturally the Pope was also in favour of the idea, and men actually began to be assembled, when Henry was again distracted, by a violent quarrel between Young Hal and Richard.

This had always been likely to happen, and my policy, as may have been noticed, was to keep my various sons widely separated, with the exception perhaps of Richard and John, for John worshipped his elder brother and would never do anything to harm him. Henry, however, in his usual fulsome manner, had always refused to accept that his sons could no more be together for any length of time without either plotting together or quarrelling together than a dog and a bear be locked up together without fighting, and so for the Christmas of 1182 he had the whole lot of them at Chinon. This included their various wives or prospective wives as the case may be, which could not have helped the atmosphere, presuming that Alais was also present. Also present was William Marshal, and, just to get the festive season off to an enjoyable start, Young Hal immediately accused William of having had an affair with Queen Margaret.

Naturally I was not very pleased when I heard this rumour, and it appears to have been founded in fact – although William offered to defend his honour, and that of the young queen, against his accuser. Henry of course could not let this happen – there was no way Young Hal could face such a warrior as William in the lists. So William took himself off. This did not leave Young Hal in any better humour, and the new year had hardly begun when he and Richard were at each other's throats. Or rather, Hal was at Richard's throat, invading Aquitaine. The fact is that Richard, like myself and like my father and grandfather, had found the Gascons difficult to deal with. However, Richard had very little in common with either Papa or

Grandpapa, save that, like them, he enjoyed composing songs. For the rest he had a streak of martial ardour which they had quite lacked, and which was clearly inherited from his father's side of the family. Thus when his barons became unruly he dealt with them as Henry would have done, and as, dare I say it, he was actually a superior soldier to his father, they found that they had caught hold of a tartar. Richard even managed what no one else had ever done before, and stormed that "impregnable" fortress of Taillebourg where Louis and I had spent our first night together as man and wife.

Now, as I have said, this was the sort of treatment the Gascons had received from Henry, and been forced to accept. The difference between Henry and Richard, however, was that in Henry's case there had been no one to whom the Gascons could turn for assistance. In Richard's case there were his brothers. Both Geoffrey and Young Hal were jealous of Richard's military prowess, and if Geoffrey was of little account, Young Hal was the next King of England. Now he undertook an invasion of Aquitaine upon some flimsy pretext or another. This upset Henry greatly – he seems to have had the idea that Hal would accompany him upon the crusade he was planning – and he sent messengers posthaste to command an end to the fighting. Young Hal appears to have accepted his father's diktat. But in the meanwhile he had been ravaging Richard's, and my, domains with a totally careless abandon, actually looting the sanctuary of Rocamador and in the process stealing the sword of his great ancestor Roland, for more than three hundred years regarded as sacrosanct by all the many berserkers who had wandered across Aquitaine. There are those who claim this was responsible for what then happened. I prefer not to pass judgement. Certainly it is, however, that just as he was preparing to pass to the north Young Hal was stricken with a fever of the stomach, and died. The date was 11 June 1183, ten years to the day since I had been captured by Henry and locked up.

I am no believer in dreams and omens, as I am sure I have indicated. But the fact is that I dreamed of Hal's death before I ever received the report of it. And did I mourn as deeply as I should? Sadly, no. I have said enough to establish that Hal and I had never been close. Circumstances had prevented this when he had been a boy, and then his wife had seen to it when she and her husband were approaching maturity. I had, in fact, been faced with the doleful prospect of becoming a prisoner of my eldest surviving son, on Henry's death. But my eldest surviving son was now Richard. It was he who was heir to the throne. This was an entirely different situation.

Evidence of this was immediate. Within a month of Hal's death heralds arrived to summon me from my prison, to journey to France, no less. It may be imagined with what delight Amaria and myself packed up and went.

The reason Henry required my presence was that following Young Hal's death, Philip Augustus had laid claim to some territory which he said had been Hal's only in right of his wife, the now widowed Margaret. Henry contended, correctly, that the lands had gone to Hal through me. I was thus required to swear to this, as I did. Neither Henry nor any of my sons were present; I had not laid eyes upon any of them for ten years. I did not know about the boys, who I had to assume were busy doing this and that, but that Henry should be avoiding me I regarded as at least a minor victory: he was afraid to face me after having treated me so unjustly for all of those years.

And that he now had to consider Richard's point of view became increasingly apparent. Although, having sworn, I was required to return to England, it was to find myself in an entirely different situation. Far from being sent back to Salisbury, I was placed in the care of Richard Fitz-Stephen, who was given a most liberal allowance for my needs. When I indicated that it would suit me greatly were my mesnie to be increased, he willingly agreed, and Amaria at last found herself in charge of an array of servants after having to do so much herself during the preceding decade. Best of all, there were no more prisons. I could travel wherever I wished, providing I made no effort to leave England, and made no effort to escape Fitz-Stephen. Thus I spent the Easter of 1184 in the house at Berkhamsted, which Henry had seized from Becket following their quarrel, and from there went on to Woodstock, of such compelling memories.

While there I was apprised that Henry of Saxony and his family were coming to England, and to my delight, when I intimated to Fitz-Stephen that I would like to see them, he raised no objection. I thus hurried down to Winchester to meet them. This was the first time I had met Henry of Saxony. He was an attractive man who was bearing up very well under his troubles, and, having completed his pilgrimage, was quite optimistic of making his peace with the Emperor and regaining his lands. While wishing him well, I was more interested, naturally enough, in my daughter, who had greeted her husband so enthusiastically upon his return – this being some months in the past – that she was heavily pregnant. I took them back to Woodstock with me for the birth; it was the first time I had been present at the birth of one of my own grandchildren, and I was delighted.

Pleasurable as this was, it was succeeded by an even more enjoyable occasion. It may be recalled that after leaving the see of Canterbury vacant for more than two years, Henry had finally appointed a new Archbishop, a man called Richard of Dover. This fellow had not been at all popular with the clergy because, although he had been a close associate and supporter of Becket, he now turned his coat so thoroughly that Henry had but to lift his little finger in the direction of the Church and his wishes were immediately carried out. Richard had obviously been chosen with great care. But in this summer of 1184 the fellow was so careless as to suffer a colic and die. It has often occurred to me that the deaths of archbishops, at least in England, have caused more upheaval than the deaths of popes in Rome. Certainly it is that as Richard's death was unexpected, Henry had no one in mind as a successor. Now it so happened that that summer he was in England, carefully avoiding me, as usual. He was in fact in Worcester – which is actually not all that far from Woodstock – when the news of Richard's death was brought to him. I assume he ate a few rushes and broke a few tables. But while he was thus cogitating, Worcester was itself disturbed by a tumult.

The story goes that a citizen of the town, one Ralph of Plumpton, had been arrested and convicted of the crime of abducting an heiress with a view to marrying her and obtaining her estates. It will be noted that Ralph was not charged with rape, which in this context was far the lesser crime. Now he was sentenced to be hanged. The Bishop of Worcester, however, one Baldwin, felt that he was innocent of any crime, that the lady had been quite amenable, and that what had been an elopement

– which was no crime – had been turned into an abduction – which was a capital offence – by jealous relatives who did not care to see their family's holdings thus dissipated. As these relatives had the ears of the town magistrates, Bishop Baldwin's attempts to save the young man had thus far proved unavailing. But learning that the King was arriving in Worcester on the very day of the execution, he hit upon a stratagem which was as simple as it was effective. The noose was already around poor Ralph's neck and the horse about to be driven off when Baldwin leapt into the cart, and himself seized the offending rope, declaring to the astounded spectators, and the even more astounded executioner, that they were breaking the law by hanging a man on a Sunday.

Well, it was certainly a Sunday. However, as Sunday is the most popular day for executions, as being the day upon which most people can get out to see the sport, if the legality of the Bishop's argument were to be admitted it would clearly mean a considerable change in the social habits of the people of England. There was, as may be imagined, a considerable to-do, and Baldwin was required to appear before the King. This he did, to plead his case so eloquently that not only was Ralph acquitted and returned to the arms of his ladylove, but Henry there and then appointed Baldwin to succeed Richard as Archbishop of Canterbury. This caused an even greater to-do, Baldwin being quite unknown outside of Church circles, but at this stage of his life no one was prepared to argue with Henry about anything.

It may well be asked what has all this to do with my situation, except in so far that we are all affected, in some degree or another, by the appointment of an

Archbishop of Canterbury. The point is that Henry wished the consecration to take place immediately, and in the presence of his three sons. I was not invited to this ceremony: I had not expected to be. However, to my consternation as well as to my delight, I now received a letter, from the King, inviting Matilda and Henry of Saxony and their children, and myself, to join him for Christmas at Windsor. It also stated that if I wished to come on ahead, I could meet with my sons at Westminster.

For the first time in many a long year, I broke down and wept.

# Chapter Eight

I find it very difficult to put into words my emotions as I came face to face with the male members of my family for the first time in ten years. This is partly because I had great difficulty in determining my attitude to this reunion. I consider I was entirely justified in continuing to feel some resentment, against Henry principally, but I also remembered that none of my surviving sons had been obviously forward in endeavouring to obtain my release. Although I also bore in mind that my new comparative freedom had only come about after the death of Hal, and therefore the loss of any influence on the part of Margaret, and the rise of Richard to be heir to the throne. But all feelings of resentment were lost when I actually found myself in the same room with them. Most of them, at any rate.

I was naturally surprised. Ten years is a considerable time, and although I flatter myself that I had not changed all that much, my children had become grown men, while as for their father . . . it had occurred to me back in 1173, just before the rebellion, that Henry was going the way of *his* father. Now I beheld an entirely old man, with scarce a wisp of red amidst the gray of his hair, while his beard was entirely white. Gone too was the unfettered energy that I remembered from his youth. He was, quite literally, burned out. I could only reflect, how are the mighty fallen? Yet this aged man was still master of the largest empire in Europe. We greeted each other formally. "Madame," Henry said, and kissed my hand. "You are looking well."

"But you, your Grace, are looking tired," I riposted. We might never have shared a bed.

With him was the Princess Alais, Richard's betrothed – and Henry's rumoured mistress. I could not help but be resentful of *her* presence, which I had to consider a studied insult to myself, as Henry had to know the rumour had reached me. But the girl was clearly terrified, while Richard seemed not the least concerned by her company, and indeed from time to time laughed and joked with her, as if they were still soon to marry. Alais was in fact now a handsome young woman of twenty-four, not very large as regards either height or figure, but then, when one considers Rosamund Clifford or Lampagie de Porhoet, this was apparently how Henry liked them as he grew older, no doubt as a contrast to me.

In any event, any lurking anger I may have felt at her presence was immediately dissipated when I beheld my eldest surviving son. Richard was now twenty-six years old. I remembered a strapping teenager. I now beheld quite the most splendid-looking man I had ever seen. Several inches over six feet in height, he was built to match. I had supposed he was like Uncle Raymond a man of immense strength, but Richard would clearly have broken him in two. His features were no less striking than his build. He wore his beard short, and thus the thrust of his chin was hardly concealed. His eyes were a brilliant, piercing blue, his lips sensual, his nose prominent, his forehead high. Every aspect denoted as much strength of mind as there was of body. I felt them both as he embraced me. "Mother," he said. "Dearest Mother! We must never be separated again."

I took that as a promise, and hugged him tightly in return.

From the sublime, as they say, to the ridiculous. Geoffrey was only a year younger than Richard, but it was really almost impossible to suppose them brothers. Geoffrey took after his father, and was short. Unlike his father, however – certainly at twenty-five – he was gross, his face half lost behind his jowls, his belly thrusting out of his breeches. His eyes were dull and his hair was thinning. He was just about repulsive. I found Constance had grown into a quite attractive little thing, the more so as she was pregnant. Was I at last to have a male grandchild? However, her humour was a dour as ever.

And then, John. He was eighteen, and as my baby had an enduring right to my continued love. Nor was he the least disappointing, physically. He was, in fact, a scaled-down version of Richard, slightly shorter, clearly less powerful, but only marginally less handsome. He obviously modelled himself on his hero, and even wore his beard in exactly the same fashion, although where Richard's was dark his was fair. But he clearly lacked the tremendous confidence of the one brother, or the careless arrogance of the other. This is often the lot of the youngest child in a family, but I could not help but wonder if John was still affected by his failure to obtain Nice and Savoy. I was equally concerned to observe that like Richard, John had no wife in tow. But at least he also was betrothed! He seemed delighted to see me, and embraced me every bit as warmly as had his brother.

There was naturally a great deal of wassailing to be done at such a family reunion, which we continued over Christmas, at Windsor, where we were joined by

Matilda and her brood as well as her husband. Geoffrey and Constance had by now left us to return to Rennes, as she wished her first child to be born in her ancestral home, but they were not greatly missed. The rest of us had a thoroughly good time.

But of course it was not all fun and games. The future was looming, and Henry had at last been forced to accept that I had to have a part in it. He therefore required me to remain in his company when Richard returned to Normandy in the early spring, and I was thus able to attend the knighting of John at Winchester, following which he departed for Ireland to take possession of his principality, at least formally. Nothing much had changed across the Irish Sea, however, and although John's princedom looked imposing on the map, the territory he actually controlled consisted of nothing more than a few square miles around Dublin Castle. John's problems were only a part of those that Henry now wished me to help him solve. "He is jealous of his brothers, of course," he told me, when we were alone together.

I should make it plain at this point that there had been not the slightest suggestion of any resumption of conjugal relations between us, and when I say that we were alone, I mean that we were seated at one end of a long chamber, with his lords and my ladies gathered at the other end, out of earshot but able to see us. "But if he is to be Prince of Ireland . . . and what of the Gloucester lands?"

"Ireland is a meaningless title, as you well know. And this girl Isabella is proving recalcitrant. It seems she has got wind of John's reputation as a roué. Well, what did she expect? He is a Plantagenet. Anyway, Gloucester! That is an earl's portion, not a prince's. Now, it seems to me that it would be entirely proper that Richard, as the future King of England, and Duke of Normandy and Count of Anjou, should not also be Duke of Aquitaine."

"You wish John to be Duke of Aquitaine?"

"As I say, that seems proper."

"And what of Geoffrey? Will he be satisfied with just Brittany?"

"Geoffrey is incapable of ruling Brittany, much less anything larger." Harsh words from a father, but I could not argue with them. "So, madame, will you assist me?"

"No," I said. His eyebrows, as shaggy as ever if no longer red, arched angrily. "Aquitaine is Richard's, and must always be Richard's," I said. "We will have to find something for John elsewhere."

He glared at me for several seconds, but I would not lower my gaze. "Well, madame," he said at last. "Then let us discuss a more domestic matter." He cleared his throat. "I have had a communication from Philip of France, wishing to be informed when his half-sister's marriage to Richard is to take place."

We gazed at each other. "Have you lost your senses?" I demanded.

He cleared his throat again. "It might cause a considerable problem were the marriage *not* to take place," he remarked.

"You *have* lost your senses."

"Royal marriages, madame, are undertaken for reasons of state, not of love, or even affection."

"I see. You are saying that you never felt the slightest love for me, or even affection. You wished only to get your hands on Aquitaine. Do not be afraid to tell me the truth."

He had the grace to blush. "Perhaps I was one of the fortunate ones, madame. When you and I became ... partners, I found much to admire in you."

"Well, thank you for those kind words."

"However, there is a case in point. You were another man's wife. I did not know, I did not wish to know, how many men's mistress you had been. And I was a good deal younger than Richard now is, and thus, shall we say, less mature and therefore more inclined to weigh matters like virginity in the balance. In addition, madame, I was aware that one of the men to whom you had granted your favour was my father."

"Henry," I said, as earnestly as I could. "The circumstances were a trifle different. I was not living in your father's household as your affianced bride. Nor, then, did I ever conceive that it could be possible for you and me to get together."

"These are matters of degree," he argued.

"Nor did the whole world know of it," I added.

"The marriage must take place," he said stubbornly.

"What you mean is, you are now tired of the girl."

"My personal feelings have nothing to do with it. There are great things afoot. I am to take the Cross."

Well, it was seven years since first I had heard that rumour. "You?" I asked. "With respect, Henry, but you are far too old to face the Palestinian sun."

"What?" he bellowed. "Me? Old? Shall I tell you who is coming with me? Frederick Barbarossa. Now, talk to me about being old." I could not credit my ears. Barbarossa, returning to Palestine? To the scene of so many dashed hopes and broken men. And now forty years older? Had he too lost his senses? "In any event, it is my duty," Henry went on. "Have you ever heard of a Saracen scoundrel named Salah-ud-Din?"

"Saladin," I breathed, aware that there was heat gathering in my cheeks. I gazed at my husband. Was he teasing, or did he really not know? "I have heard the name."

"Well, this loathsome infidel has succeeded in uniting Syria and Egypt. There is now a great Saracen power arisen about Palestine."

I had never doubted he was destined for greatness.

"And so Baldwin of Jerusalem is calling for help. He is dying, you know, of leprosy."

"Poor fellow," I muttered. Saladin, riding to glory at the head of his paladins. I wondered if he still remembered me? But how could he possibly forget me?

"I suppose you are aware that Baldwin and I share the same grandfather?" Henry went on. "How can I refuse his call for assistance? He has even sent his Patriarch of Jerusalem, a fellow called Heraclius, to beg for my help. Do you know that, as he has only a sister, he has offered me the Kingdom of Jerusalem, as his successor? That is exactly what his grandfather did to my grandfather. Grandpapa Fulk accepted. I have refused it of course, as I have more here than he did. Well?" he demanded. "What do you say to that, madame?"

"That you were very wise to do so." My brain was doing handsprings. "But if you are determined upon succouring your cousin . . . I will accompany you."

"*You*, madame?"

"I have been there before. I know the country and the problems. I will be able to assist you." And I may even see Saladin again, I thought.

"The idea is quite out of the question. I intend this crusade to be a triumph, not a disaster." Well! I could have slapped his face, but decided against it. "In any event, the whole point is, I must leave tranquillity behind me. I cannot afford to give this boy Philip the slightest excuse for causing trouble in my absence. And he would have a considerable reason were he able to claim that his half-sister had been dishonoured."

"You can say that with a straight face?"

"Listen, woman, you can moralise until the cows come home. I have already reminded you that you do not have a leg to stand on in that department. And even if you did, this is a state affair, not a domestic one. Will you help me or no?"

Quite apart from the fact that I understood a second point blank refusal might cause my re-incarceration, this was actually a matter in which I was as interested as he – if not for reasons of state. And besides, I was not without hope that I might still be able to persuade him to take me back to Palestine. "What would you have me do?"

"I wish you to persuade Richard to marry the girl. For God's sake, that is all he is required to do. Let him marry her, ram her sufficiently to get her pregnant – he won't find that a hardship, I can tell you; she is a most accomodating little thing, and pretty with it – then he can forget her and live his own life. Providing the babe is a boy, of course. We must have an heir."

I realised that Henry still did not have the slightest idea that Richard would indeed find ramming – to use his own vulgar choice of word – Alais a hardship. But I also realised that it was Richard's duty, as Henry had said, to produce an heir to the throne; the thought of his dying without doing so, and leaving all this empire to Geoffrey, was quite frightening. Well, the thought of his dying was terrifying enough. "Of course I will help you in this matter, Henry," I said. "But . . ." I glanced at him. "It will be necessary for me to go to him. To summon him here would not only put him on his guard, it would also put his back up."

He tugged at his lip. "You wish to go to Poitiers?"

"I consider it necessary that I go to Poitiers."

"To plot against me all over again, with that young cub."

"Do not be foolish," I said. "I am too old for plots."

"If you will swear an oath of fealty to me, I will restore you as Duchess of Aquitaine."

I am afraid I goggled at him. I had never actually supposed I could cease being Duchess of Aquitaine just because he had chosen to lock me up. But . . . "What of Richard?"

"He is Duke of Normandy and Count of Anjou. That is enough for any man to be going on with."

Well, well, *well*. That Henry might fear to leave Richard in total control of all his empire save for Ireland and Brittany, while he went on his Crusade, I could understand. But that he should turn to *me* to hold half of his empire . . . how the wheel does turn, I thought again. And then also felt sorry for the poor old fellow. He was turning to me because he had nowhere else *to* turn. Geoffrey was an impossibility, and John . . . I realised that my husband was perhaps being more devious than I supposed. What he really wanted was to have John Duke of Aquitaine. But he knew that Richard would never agree. Yet Richard would never oppose his mother and from my point of view, I was sixty-two years old, and an entire new life was opening in front of me. Or perhaps I should say, my old life was being offered back to me, with knobs on. "Oh, very well," I agreed. "If you insist."

And so I returned to Poitiers. In absolute triumph. Ten years before, when I had been threatened with lifelong imprisonment, I had never supposed I would ever see the Maubergeonne again. And here it was, opening its gates to me. What is more, as I had sent ahead, Richard had the entire city waiting for me, *en fête*. The tower itself had been refurbished and was as lovely as ever my grandfather had intended it to be as a home for his Dangerosa. And I was home, and re-united with my favourite child. Two of my favourite children, indeed, for Matilda accompanied me, as well, of course, as Amaria. And with us, naturally, were Matilda's children. Matilda was going through a trying time as her husband attempted to reach some kind of an agreement with Barbarossa, and I was disturbed about her health, which was visibly failing. My heart went out to the poor girl, but at the same time it was a great treat to be able to give her a home for as long as she needed it, and besides I was hoping that the presence of his nieces and nephew might stir something in Richard's breast.

I may say that around now Constance of Brittany gave birth, to a girl, whom they named Eleanor, no doubt in the hopes of winning me to their side in whatever trials lay ahead. However, as the line of succession now read Richard-Geoffrey-Eleanor, and I recalled the chaos of Grandmama Matilda's efforts to get hold of her inheritance, I could see nothing but trouble looming unless Richard did his duty. But here was a possible weapon, and I used it to the best of my ability, explaining to Richard the catastrophe it would be if he were to die without an heir. To my amazement he listened most carefully, and said, "I have been giving the matter much thought."

"My dear boy," I said. "Oh, I am so relieved."

"I thought you would be. I have been studying the lives of the Roman Emperors. Did you know that, whenever the male line seemed likely to fail, the reigning emperor simply adopted a son, Or more than one, as the case might be."

My jaw sagged. Of course I knew all about Ancient Rome, probably more than he did. But as far as I was concerned, Ancient Rome was a different planet. No English king or Norman duke had ever attempted to circumvent the laws of primogeniture by foisting an adopted child on their turbulent baronage. That was the quickest possible way to civil war. I could see that I had my work cut out, especially as it was now my unpleasant task to inform him that he was no longer Duke of Aquitaine. It was the turn of his jaw to drop. "Does my father suppose I will give up what is mine at his whim?" he demanded.

"Richard," I said gently, "you are not giving up what is yours. You are giving up what is *mine*, that I gave to you, back to me. This is because your father fears you. I have accepted the situation because I wish to keep the peace between you. But do you not suppose that when you are King of England, I will restore to you every right and privilege that you have ever held?"

He glared at me. "On the condition that I marry some puling girl. Well, I will tell you this: I will not marry my father's leavings, if I must die in a monastery."

My task grew more difficult by the moment.

In all the circumstances, I considered my only course was to report to Henry, and to this end I returned to England, where Henry was, in the spring of 1186. He was not amused. "You may regard him as the finest male specimen in the world, madame," he grumbled. "I, being a male myself, may think otherwise. I know you are entirely innocent about masculine matters, Anor, but I must tell you now that there have been disquieting rumours about this Richard of yours."

My heart sank, even as I reflected that Richard now appeared to be entirely mine. "I find that impossible to believe," I protested.

"You would. Was ever a man so cursed? An heir who dies in infancy. Well, then, another heir who did nothing but plague me and is now gone. Well then, another heir, who turns out to be a pervert. Well then, have I not yet another heir? Who is a gross, senseless pig. So, madame . . ." he stared at me. "I have at least one other. One other, whose vices would appear to be all Plantagenet. Now there is a man. There is a Plantagenet. There is the true future ruler of England."

I was aghast. I loved John dearly, as my baby. But . . . "You cannot mean to set John up against Richard and Geoffrey."

"Ha! Suppose I commanded you to make over Aquitaine to John, as its duke?"

"I should refuse."

"Madame, you try me too far."

"I would refuse," I said quietly, "because it would mean war between Richard and John. Do you really wish that? What price your crusade then?"

Henry let the matter drop for the time being, but needless to say, word of our conversation leaked out. I assume that he discussed his ideas with members of his court, because certainly I never mentioned them to a soul save Amaria and Albert. However, there can be no doubt that Geoffrey soon enough learned that his father was considering making John his heir should anything happen to Richard, and took himself off to Paris in high dudgeon. Although, as we later discovered, he may have had a politically-innocent reason for this action. But as we did not know this at the time, it merely seemed to us that Geoffrey was out to make trouble wherever he could find support. Henry was livid.

I do not know if it is necessary to restate this fact, but although Henry and I were now invariably to be found beneath the same roof, there had been no restoration of conjugal rights between us. Henry belonged to that masculine school of thought which assumes that a woman does not have sexual desires after the age of sixty – or fifty for that matter. I was content that it should be so. For although he was entirely wrong in his supposition, it is true to say that I became somewhat less libidinous as I grew older. I also I sought a quieter existence in my bed, and that entirely ruled out any consideration of my husband. Now, indeed, would have been the time for Bernard of Ventadour to reappear. However, he did not, and I believe he was dead. But I was not bereft of stimulating company. For conversation I had Amaria and Albert, and I could call upon a variety of troubadours to amuse me in one way or another. One of my favourites was a lad named Blondel de Nesle, not much over twenty, but oh, so ardent, in every direction. Of course I was not so stupid as to suppose that Blondel, or any of the others, would have so readily answered my every summons and gratified my every whim had I not been Queen of England, but what is the point in being a queen if one cannot call upon the support of one's subjects?

I may say that even William Marshal paid me a visit. But although it was a delight to see his face – he remained as handsome as ever – and listen to his voice, I had not yet forgiven him for the affair with Margaret. Besides, perhaps out of a guilty conscience, or perhaps merely because he was a penniless knight who must always seek the main chance, he had now become a loyal servant of Henry's, and that made him half an enemy. Thus I was contented enough until the autumn, when the most dreadful news arrived from Paris: taking part in a tourney, Geoffrey had fallen from his horse, and been so badly injured that he was dead.

I say the news was dreadful, because the news of the death of one's child must always be dreadful. On the other hand, both Henry and I had already seen the death of two of our sons, and I must be honest and confess that if we had had to make a choice of which of the remaining members of our family should be the next to go, son or daughter, we would have chosen the Duke of Brittany. But needless to say, his death caused another crisis. It was now that we learned of his relationship with Philip Augustus. Philip, indeed, had been so besotted with our son that he had to be forcibly restrained from throwing himself into the grave beside his lover's body. Henry was appalled, and in the circumstances I take off my hat to Marie, who was in Paris at the time – Philip was of course her half-brother as well as Margaret's and Alais' – and who funded a perpetual mass to be said for her dead half-brother's soul.

However, to return to politics, the tragedy obviously left Brittany without a duke. Henry, not unnaturally, regarded this as entirely his business. But now Philip, having apparently recovered from his grief, stuck his oar in. Brittany was, technically, a fief of France. So, of course, were Normandy, Anjou, Maine and all of Aquitaine, and Henry, and his sons, had all done homage for their continental lands to the youthful French King following his coronation. Philip was therefore technically within his rights to claim the disposal of the duchy, which meant the wardship of the

Duchess. But it was a bold liege lord who would dare so challenge a liege man such as Henry Plantagenet. Philip was no doubt just stirring the pot. What was disturbing was that we could not doubt that he had been encouraged to this step by Geoffrey, pre-posthumously, as it were, and that the two men had been laying a plot together. But now Philip's claim to the wardship of the widowed Duchess took on a new twist: Constance announced that Geoffrey had left her pregnant. This left both Philip and Henry somewhat agitated. In the first place, Philip could not possibly contemplate marrying off a pregnant widow to the man of his choice. In the second, were Constance to give birth to a boy, he would be Duke of Brittany, and all pot-stirrings would come to a dead end.

I may say that, in view of what we had learned of Geoffrey's carrying-on with Philip in Paris, it was a mystery to me just how Constance had accumulated this bun in her oven. Or, indeed, who had really been the father of Eleanor!

From our point of view, if the babe *were* Geoffrey's – and there was no way we could prove anything different if Constance insisted upon it, as she was bound to do – and if it turned out to be a boy, it would also mess up Henry's plans for the succession. The infant Duke would of course take precedence over his sister and be next in line for the throne of England, after Richard. It may be imagined that an anxious winter was spent by all, not least Constance, who with a degree of spirit no one had suspected her to possess, locked herself up in her castle in Rennes and defied anyone to attempt to lay hands on her, whether to marry her, pregnant or no, or to induce a miscarriage, or merely to solve the entire conundrum by murdering her before she could give birth. When the stakes are as high as a kingdom, all things are possible.

Henry even suggested, as Constance seemed so determined to withstand any male invasion, that I should go to her myself. "After all," he pointed out, "you are the nearest thing to a mother the poor girl has. You should be at her side when she is delivered."

"You are not, I hope, contemplating what I suspect you are contemplating," I remarked.

"Heaven forbid, Anor. I am ashamed that you should think such a thing of me. But . . . if we are to have a grandson, don't you think it would be a good thing if, how shall I put it, we got our hands on him first?"

I could follow his line of reasoning; it would certainly be a disaster if our grandson, and, the way things were turning out, the future King of England, should be removed to the court of Philip Augustus to receive his education and his opinions, either political or personal. But, while I would quite happily have gone to Rennes, I did not intend to make that journey only to find the gates of the castle slammed in my face: Constance had never liked me, nor I her, when you come down to it, and I knew she had been miffed because I had not gone into raptures over the baby Eleanor, who was apparently a pretty child, and was being touted as the Pearl of Brittany!

I thus wrote to her, asking if she would not like the comfort of me at her side. It was just as well I did this, for the answer returned was a most emphatic no. I decided to leave it at that. And everything we had all anticipated and feared came to pass. In March 1187 Constance did give birth to a son. She called him Arthur. Now there was a challenge. Not only was she deliberately casting aside all our usual family names, even those of her own family, but by resurrecting the name of the national hero of Roman Britain she was throwing down her gauntlet for the future.

John had been with Henry and me for Christmas, which we spent at Winchester, while Henry made plans for dealing with Philip. The French King was becoming obstreperous in his demands for the wardship of the Duchess of Brittany, and had resurrected an earlier claim, for the return of the Vexin, since Young Hal's death. In this last he was again legally correct. The Vexin had been Margaret's dowry, and when a wife went home a widow, it was usual for her dowry to go home with her. But Henry had never the least intention of giving up any of his territory, whether he was entitled to it or not; he had offered a cash settlement, which the French had refused, and now he was determined to teach Philip a lesson. Thus, in February, he and John crossed to the Continent, Richard having been sent for to join them with his forces, and it looked as if we were going to have a full-scale war on our hands, especially as we were informed that Philip was also calling out his vassals. But in March the boy Arthur appeared, and as I have said, the main reasons for going to war came to an abrupt end. Our people all went home, as did the French . . . and Richard went to Paris!

This news reached me somewhat belatedly, as I had prudently decided to remain in England until the men had sorted themselves out. It came in the form of a letter from Richard himself: *'This is such a splendid city,'* he wrote. *'I can well understand how happy you must have been here, dearest Mama, during the early days of your first marriage.'* I wondered where he'd got *that* piece of information from? *'I would willingly spend the rest of my days here.'* I began to frown. *'Philip is such a splendid fellow. He and I go everywhere together, do everything together, share our every moment. We are never apart.'*

I put down the letter. Oh, my God, I thought. Did this lout intend to seduce all the male members of my family? I had never laid eyes on Philip Augustus of France – but I had heard reports that he was a comely lad. I wondered how he would get on with John! What was to be done? Here I must confess that, for the first time in my life, I simply could not think of anything I *could* do. I had never had any doubt that I could keep Richard's desires in check, even when he became King, by reminding him of his duty, by encouraging his greatness, even if this meant also encouraging his desire for military glory at the expense of all else. But this was only possible in so far as he sought his lovers amongst his own servants or liege men. If he had fallen in love with the King of France, I did not see how I could cope.

I therefore took refuge in that ultimate arbiter, time. Those who fall violently in love are apt to fall out of love again with equal violence. In this, my judgement was absolutely correct. What I did not take into account was that there is no accurate timescale for these events, and some take longer than others. For the time being I sought what crumbs of comfort I could with the reflection that the two princes were at least no longer likely to go to war over Richard's rejection of poor Alais! From these domestic matters we were all recalled to reality by the news of Hattin!

I do not suppose any event in recent history has had such a momentous effect upon all of our lives, one way or another. The fall of Edessa had descended upon us like a thunderbolt, but that had been a single city, and had been caused by the total neglect of his duty by the

Count of Edessa, Jocelyn. Yet the results, as I have recounted them, were catastrophic enough, with the loss of innumerable fine men and a few fine reputations as well. Hattin was not a city. It was an obscure place in the Palestinian desert. But it had entailed the entire destruction of all the Christian forces in Palestine.

Briefly, what had happened was this. As I have mentioned, in the forty years since he had held me in his arms, Saladin had grown in strength and power and genius, as I had never doubted he would. Yet that genius had always forced him to understand that to embark upon a military action to drive the Christians out of the Holy Land might be a task even he could not undertake with equanimity. The Crusader states, if short of manpower, were long in defence. Their castles were at once the wonder and the fear of the Arabs. There has never been a castle as strong as the Templar stronghold of Krak des Chevaliers, and there were several others hardly inferior. The Saracens had no knowledge of siegecraft. Thus from their mighty towers the Crusaders could issue forth whenever the moment was propitious, raid or defeat an infidel caravan or force, and then rush back to the impregnable safety of their curtain walls, their towers, their glacis, and above all, their bottomless wells, for the sites of their castles were always most carefully chosen. I have no doubt that Saladin was pondering this situation with a view to finding a solution, but pending that solution, he found it most useful to remain on as good terms as possible with the Christians, and this was done by a series of truces, much as Uncle Raymond had maintained with Saladin's uncle Nur-ud-Din. Thus an uneasy peace had been maintained during the lifetime of the leper-king, my cousin-in-law, Baldwin V. But Baldwin, as Henry had prognosticated, died, in the spring of 1185 and almost immediately after his appeal for help. This left Jerusalem without a king, and the Crusader states without an acknowledged leader, for Baldwin left behind him only a sister, Sybille. She was already a widow. Now the whole future of Christendom in Palestine rested upon the man Sybille should choose to marry.

Sadly, this girl does not appear to have been very bright, although, like all queens, she has been described as very beautiful. But her choice as her second husband fell upon none other than that itinerant scoundrel Guy of Lusignan, who had once tried to get his hands on *me*, as a result of which, it may be recalled, my irate husband had sent him packing off to Palestine, where he had remained. No doubt, by marrying Sybille, he felt he was getting very much the better of the bargain than if he had succeeded outside Poitiers. He was soon to find out that he had thrown himself upon a bed of nails. The Frankish baronage, and I am here using the word in its generic sense, to cover not only the French, but the Germans, the Normans, the English, the Angevins and the Poitevins and Gascons, had always been, and remained, a turbulent lot. The slightest weakness on the part of the ruling king, and as we have seen in England during Stephen's reign, the country lapses into anarchy.

This is what now happened in Palestine. Guy had not the strength of will to command his barons. He had the sense to realise that the only hope of preserving his kingdom was to maintain peace with Saladin, but there was nothing he could do to enforce that peace on his people, and one scoundrel in particular, named Reynald of Chatillon, kept raiding Saracen caravans, despite the truce. Saladin appears to have been prepared to take no notice of these pin-pricks, but then Reynald went right over the top and attacked and plundered a caravan which not only belonged to Saladin's sister, but included the lady! Saladin immediately declared all truces at an end and mobilised an army of twenty thousand men. Guy called in his vassals. Amongst these was one of the few sensible Frankish leaders, Count Raymond of Tripoli. He obeyed the summons of his king, even though it meant leaving his fortress of Tiberias dangerously exposed. In the fortress, as *chatelaine*, was his wife the Princess Eschiva. Now, to the consternation of the Crusaders, Saladin's host moved on Tiberias, on the shores of the Sea of Gallilee.

From my memory of Saladin, I find it difficult to believe that he actually meant to wage war upon a woman, and prefer to suppose that he was hoping his manoeuvre would bring the Christians after him. Although men do change as they grow older – I have had sufficient evidence of *that* – and it may well be that even Saladin felt that as Reynald had warred upon his sister he was entitled to war upon any Christian princess he could get his hands on. In any event, his strategy worked liked a charm. Informed that the Saracen host was marching upon her castle, Eschiva promptly sent to her husband for help. I do not think the good lady can be blamed for this. Women are not expected to be grand strategists, and all she could see was the reports that a huge infidel force was about to descend upon her and the few score men-at-arms Raymond had left for her defence, no doubt with rape and pillage in mind. It is on record that when the messenger reached Jerusalem, Raymond, although his wife was the one in danger, strongly advised against going to her rescue. The month was July, the hottest of the year, and the march lay across country which was not only open, but mostly desert. He knew that the only hope of defeating Saladin was to let him dash his men to pieces against the Christian walls.

King Guy and his advisers, prominent amongst whom was this lunatic Reynald, would have none of that. They still fondly remembered the First Crusade, when a few hundred charging Christian knights had defeated several thousand Saracens, not once, but often. They forgot that times had changed, and so had men, and in Saladin they were confronted by a military genius. So off they set, with all their power. Saladin was as aware as anyone of the damage armoured knights could do to his lightly-clad warriors, and Guy had more than a thousand men-at-arms. But Saladin also knew that the past victories of the knights had always been gained when the horsemen had had the support of a body of disciplined infantry, who served them as a base from which they could regroup to launch their charges. Thus, as the Christians toiled across the desert beneath the burning sun, boiling inside their armour and very rapidly running entirely out of water, Saladin cunningly separated the cavalry from the infantry, and proceeded to massacre them. And it was, a massacre. Of the great lords, a large number were killed, together with nearly all their people, making a last stand on the hillock known as the Horns of Hattin. Raymond cut his way out at the head of some sixty knights, but was so badly wounded he died shortly afterwards. Guy was taken prisoner, together with Reynald. Guy, Saladin set free, on parole; Reynald, he slew with his own hand.

The news of this catastrophe struck Europe like an earthquake. But worse was to follow. Despite the disasters of the Second Crusade, in the ninety years since the First it had seemed that a Christian presence in Palestine, and especially a Christian-held Jerusalem, were permanencies, which would last until the end of time. Now in a matter of a few months all this was swept away. We had not recovered from the news of Hattin when we learned of the fall of Tiberias, and Acre, and Ascalon. And then came the crowning blow: after a siege of less than a fortnight, Saladin took Jerusalem. The Moslem world had triumphed over the Christian! Not so, shouted Richard. Not so, shouted Philip Augustus, not quite so loudly. Not so, bellowed Frederic Barbarossa, even if his beard was now white. Not so muttered my husband. John said nothing at all; he had no intention of disappearing into the sands of Palestine, when he and little Arthur were the last remaining Angevin princes.

Richard immediately took the Cross, and suggested his father do this also, as he had been threatening to do for some ten years now. Henry pleaded age and infirmity. Well, he was not altogether lying. Thus Richard was forced to have second thoughts. I played my part in instigating these. I owed Henry nothing, and all my hopes for the future were based on Richard. At my suggestion, therefore, Richard demanded of his father an absolute guarantee, sworn before representatives of the Church, that nothing belonging to him would be given to any other person while he was in Palestine; he was specifically referring to his right to the Crown of England, to the Dukedom of Normandy, to the Counties of Anjou and Maine, and above all to the Duchy of Aquitaine. Henry prevaricated, and by doing this made it plain that he would do Richard down the moment he left. Thus the idea of a Crusade was left hanging in the balance while father and son differed. I recognised that this was the crux of the entire reign, and wished to leave England myself, with the intention of joining Richard in Poitiers. To my consternation, and my anger, I was prevented from doing so by order of the King, and was indeed once again placed under strict confinement. I did not know whether I was a hostage, or whether Henry was afraid that I would encourage Richard to arms against him, as he presumed I had done once before. Well, had I been able to escape, I might well have done so, I was so furious. It was a tense period, a sort of cat-and-mouse game being played between the three parties, or were there really four parties, or even five?

Richard dreamed only of the military glory to be gained by going to Palestine and defeating Saladin, following which he would retake Jerusalem and earn himself immortality. This could be described as the Gascon in him. But the Norman in him wished to be quite sure that all his inheritance would be waiting for him once he returned. Thus he would not leave until this matter had been resolved. Philip wished to prove to the world that he was as great a Christian hero as his lover aspired to be, and he was also motivated by an urgent desire to avenge the humiliation suffered by his father forty years before, but he was statesman enough to know that he dared not abandon France for perhaps a year while all the Angevin might remained behind him. Thus he would not leave until at least Richard did.

My point of view was entirely that of Richard's. I still dreamed of going on the Crusade with him! As for if he and Saladin were ever to meet in battle . . . perhaps I could throw myself between them and bring peace to that troubled region. No doubt I shall die as I have lived, the granddaughter of the First of the Troubadours. Constance no doubt rubbed her hands together in the security of Rennes, and considered that the babe in her arms was the hope of England.

Henry encouraged Richard to leave by all the means in his power. I do not believe he ever intended to disinherit him. But he certainly wished to have John take over Aquitaine, and he now realised that I was never going to permit that, so I would have to be overborne, and that could never be done while I had Richard at my shoulder. And John . . . John was pursuing a game entirely his own. I am sure I have said enough to leave no doubt that as my very last child John has always had a very special place in my heart, but I am bound to confess that as he has grown to manhood and beyond he has revealed a quality of secret intention which at times is hard to fathom. As he has now realised all of his ambitions, I believe, and hope and trust, that he will prove the great king that his father was, and that Richard, I am sure, would have been had he been spared. But at the same time I must confess that some of his actions in recent years have been confounding, to say the least. At this time, however, the prospect of his ever being King of England seemed intensely remote. What did seem likely was that his doting father would engineer matters so that he became Duke of Aquitaine. Thus all he seemed to require was patience. And yet . . . I must let events speak for themselves.

As I have said, being again under restraint was an intensely annoying business. But as before, I was also prepared to practice patience. Henry meanwhile returned to Normandy to deal with his foes, amongst whom he naturally counted Philip. Here things did not go entirely to plan. For the first time in his life Henry was defeated in the field, for ranged against him were not only Philip but also Richard. Perhaps my favourite son was taking up arms in my defence. More likely he considered that he would never have a better opportunity to bring to a successful end the feud between his father and himself which had really lasted since 1173.

As it turned out, this campaign might have been Richard's last, for in a skirmish outside Le Mans he was unhorsed by none other than William Marshal, fighting as valiantly as ever but now in Henry's cause. I may say at this point that William was the only man I ever heard of who could unhorse Richard the Lion Heart, as my son was now being known. So there was Richard facing death, at the hands of his boyhood friend. Indeed, it was to that friendship that he appealed, as I heard the story. Marshal spared his life. He may have done this because of that friendship, or because he knew that Richard was my favourite son. He may even have done so because he understood that of all my surviving children, only Richard was capable of grasping, and keeping, the crown when Henry died. Or he may have meant what he said, in reply to Richard's appeal: "Let the devil kill you, for I will not."

Either way, Richard survived. Defeated, Henry could do nothing better than call a conference, which, as always in the past when the kings of England and France had met in solemn conclave, was held in Gisors, beneath the great oak. Here England and France solemnly signed a peace treaty, in which Henry gave away far more than he got. What Philip really thought about it all was revealed when, Henry having departed, he had the great oak hewn down! Henry was now at a low ebb of health, both mental and physical. He spent Christmas 1188 in Saumur, and in the spring retired to his favourite fortress of Chinon, to contemplate the situation. It was there that the fatal blow was struck, and not by a dagger either. Henry was undoubtedly in a depressed state of mind, and he did not help matters by daily having to contemplate a painting he had commissioned some years before, of a huge eagle whose vitals were being torn out by four eaglets. When one is young, and strong, paintings of this nature are perfectly acceptable, and perhaps Henry bore it in mind as a warning of the future. Now that future had arrived. Hal, Richard, Geoffrey, three of my eaglets, had all twisted their claws in his vitals. Only John, always his favourite, was left.

But one of the clauses of the treaty with Philip was that each side should exchange a list of their adherents, that they might know who to trust in the future. It was at Chinon that Henry opened Philip's list, and found at the head of those who had been in arms against him, John. There is actually not a great deal of evidence of his actually having taken part in the war against his father, and indeed John has always strongly denied it. It is therefore possible that Philip placed the name there out of spite, although given John's reputation for deviousness, who can say? In any event, the stratagem worked beyond their wildest dreams, or was it really their worst nightmares? Henry read the name of the son he had grown to love more than any of the others, turned his face to the wall, and died.

Henry died 6 July 1189, and the news reached me, or at least Fitz-Stephen, four days later; someone must have ridden like the wind. The first I knew of it was when Fitz-Stephen presented himself at my apartment, looking distinctly uneasy. "Your Grace," he said, "I have the most terrible news."

As he spoke, he regarded me somewhat quizzically. Of course I had been in his care, on and off, for sufficient time for him to know there was little love left between Henry and myself, and thus he could not be at all sure that I *would* consider his news so terrible, while with Henry dead . . .!

"Tell me," I said. I am sure I had a presentiment.

He knelt at my feet. "The King is dead, your Grace. Long live King Richard."

He raised his head, and we gazed at each other. I had never truly doubted that I would outlive Henry, especially when I had seen him for the first time in ten years, back in 1183. And as I have just intimated, there was no love or even affection left between us. Yet even so, the certain knowledge that he was dead left me with a feeling of breathlessness. It was as if, one day, the sun had failed to rise. It left me wondering what would happen now. Richard was King, certainly, but a Richard whose personal problems had not yet been sorted out, who remained, so far as I was aware, the lover of his greatest rival, whose efforts at ruling seemed to have been one long conflict with his Poitevin and Gascon subjects. And a Richard who was not yet married. But still, a Richard who was King. "Then you may unlock the doors, Fitz-Stephen," I commanded. He hesitated. "You cannot suppose that King Richard will wish me kept in confinement," I pointed out.

He needed only the briefest reflection to determine that I was probably right. "I will unlock the doors, your Grace."

"And have horses placed at my disposal," I told him.

He hurried off. "Where will we go, your Grace?" Amaria asked.

I looked at her, and then at Albert. "Why," I said. "For a gallop, without guards at our shoulders."

This we did. I needed to think. Because the truth of the matter was, I had nowhere to go, simply because I had no knowledge of my standing. I loved Richard dearly – but did he love me as well? Even if he did, he could have no doubt that we differed on several fundamental issues, in every possible sense of that word. It was inconceivable that he would wish to keep me locked up, as I had said to Fitz-Stephen. But on the other hand, would he wish me around? That raised another point. I did not know where he was. Filial duty would demand that he would go to his father's deathbed. But he was unlikely to stay there very long. And then, the duty of being a monarch would require him to hasten to England, and indeed to Winchester, where, as I have indicated, all English reigns began. Thus *he* would know where to find *me*. We returned to the castle, and waited.

And it was only two days later when from the battlements we saw a body of horsemen approaching us at the gallop. I peered at them, seeking Richard's bulk, and not finding it, and then frowning as I recognised the banners. As did Amaria at the same time. "Are those not the colours of William Marshal?" she asked.

"Yes," I agreed, biting my lip. There could not possibly be any reason for William to be hastening towards me save an attempt to have me oppose my son. But that I was not going to do – even if it meant sacrificing William.

I decided to wait for him in one of the small reception chambers, and soon enough I heard the clanking of metal and the jangle of spurs. He entered, and fell to his knees before me. "Your Grace. I bring tidings of the utmost importance."

"My husband is dead. I am aware of this. Are you in search of sanctuary?"

He raised his head. "Your Grace?"

"I am aware that you and King Richard are enemies," I pointed out.

"I fought for the King, your Grace. While he lived, his enemies were my enemies. Now he is dead, I still fight for the King."

I frowned. "You are reconciled with Richard."

"The King has honoured me, your Grace, as I buried his father."

"You buried Henry? Where?"

"Alongside his mother, in the Abbey at Fontevrault."

"Then I honour you also, William. And I am pleased that you and the King are reconciled. Now tell me, he wishes me to go to him?"

"No, your Grace. He wishes you to remain here. Or at least in England."

"Oh!"

"King Richard is determined to leave immediately on the Crusade, your Grace. To this end he has signed a treaty with King Philip, who is also about to leave. As is the Emperor. This will be the greatest Crusade the world has ever seen. It will mean the end of the Saracens."

I would have liked to argue that point, but I had more pressing matters on my mind. "How can King Richard consider going on a Crusade, absenting himself from the kingdom for perhaps a year and more, when he has not even taken possession of it? He has not even been crowned. That is madness."

"The King will be crowned, your Grace, as soon as he can get to England, which will be within a few weeks. In the meanwhile, he considers that the kingdom will be well held for him, your Grace. He has appointed a regent."

I stared at him. "He has not given John the kingdom?"

"No, no, your Grace. The King has appointed one to rule in his stead of whom he has the highest regard, the utmost trust, the total confidence that his crown will be well preserved in his absence."

"And whom may this paragon be?" I inquired.

"Why, yourself, your Grace."

# Chapter Nine

"William," I said. "Oh, William!" I took him in my arms, and then into my bedchamber. All was forgiven between us. As all was forgiven between him and Richard. Richard, indeed, honoured him above all other men save for his brothers, and gave him the hand of Isabel, the daughter and heiress of Strongbow and Eva. Thus at one bound my old hero leapt from being an impecunious knight to heir to one of the great fortunes in Britain. I was so happy for him.

It was a busy time, for I knew that Richard was in a hurry. The entire ordering of the coronation was left to me, and I undertook it with great gusto. This involved travelling all over the country, with Marshal at my side; he was a great assistance, as were Amaria and Albert, all filled with the energy of realised dreams. In the middle of this news arrived that Matilda was dead. Even if I had known it was likely to happen, it was still a most severe shock. I sat down and wept for some time; I might have lost three of my sons, but never a daughter.

But with so much to do there was no time for mourning. On 13 August Richard landed in England.

I received him in Winchester. We hugged each other for several minutes, before sitting down together.

"Everything is arranged," I told him. "But afterwards

". . . will you really go on the Crusade immediately? There is so much to be done here."

"I have taken the oath. Do not fear, Mother. Philip is coming with me. Barbarossa has already left. It will be the greatest Crusade in history." He squeezed my hand. "And you will rule here until I return. Thus, you see, I have total confidence in the future. Under you, and to assist you, I have appointed Hugh de Puiset and Walter de Mandeville as your justiciars. Do not fret; there will be no clash of authority. As Bishop of Durham, Puiset will be in charge north of the Humber. As Earl of Essex, Mandeville will be in charge south of that river. But both will be subject to your authority."

"You dear boy." I kissed him. But there was so much still on my mind. "Crusades can be dangerous things," I told him. "I do not fear for your life in battle; there is none can bring you down." Not even Saladin, I felt. "But in that heat, there are fevers, and poisons . . ."

"Would you have me stay at home like a girl?"

"I would have you consider the succession."

"I have done this, Mother."

"Can you really see Arthur of Brittany as King of England? Constance as Queen Mother, telling him what to do?"

Richard grinned. "It makes a pretty picture, does it not? Do not fear. I am to wed."

"Richard!" I clutched his hands. "I am so pleased! But you mean that Philip will accept Alais back?"

"No, no, Mother. All the world knows how she was dishonoured by Father. There is only one way to put that right. I am to wed Alais." I stared at him in consternation. "Well," he said, flushing. "It is what Philip wants."

"You will bed the girl?"

"Well . . ." his flush deepened. "I will do my best."

"But you cannot find it in your heart to love her?"
"Love her? She is utterly loathsome to me."
"Then how can you possibly marry her?"
"I am King. I must do my duty."
"If you knew how much that relieves me. When is this wedding to take place?"
"The very moment I return from Palestine."
"But . . . we have been discussing what the situation will be if you do not return, Richard."
"I will return, Mother."

I cannot pretend that I was happy with the arrangement, but I dared not press too hard: the mere fact that Richard was going to take a wife was an enormous step in the right direction. I could only pray that he came back safe and sound. Well, I would have done that anyway, but now it became doubly important – the entire life of the kingdom was at stake, or so it seemed to me. I was also unhappy at the tales I was hearing about the King's urgent search for money to finance his expedition. I remembered all too well how I had squeezed my own people of Aquitaine to finance the Second Crusade, and how my standing had suffered as a result. It was even possible to say that I had never quite recovered my early popularity. I did not wish Richard to suffer a similar fate. Of course, my Crusade, or rather, Louis', had been an utter failure, while Richard's would surely be a total success, but even so . . .

Meanwhile, a week after his brother, John arrived in England, landing at Dover. He came immediately to see me. Marshal had told me of that fatal list. I have written that I did not entirely believe it, but I have also written that it is difficult to be sure of anything where John was, or is, concerned. Now he stood before me, twisting his hands together, and twisting his face, too. "I would have you know that I bitterly regret my father's death," he said. I gazed at him. "Now," he said. "I know not what is to become of me."

"Are you destitute?" I asked.

"What do I have, Mama? Do not speak to me of Ireland. That is nothing more than a vast bog, in every possible sense. For the rest, all has been dreams. I have not even a wife. Gloucester remains a promise, not a possession."

He was sincerely distressed. I took him to my bosom. "I shall speak with the King," I said.

Therefore I must take a good deal of the blame for what happened. But even I was quite surprised by Richard's response. I had appealed merely for some portion to be set aside for John, always the youngest and least provided for of my children – there were even those who openly called him by the nickname I had given him as a babe: Lackland. "That can never be," Richard declared. "He is my sole surviving whole brother. He shall have a portion worthy of his rank."

John had in fact been granted a considerable portion in his father's Will; Richard now gave him six entire counties: Nottinghamshire, Derbyshire, Dorsetshire, Somersetshire, Devonshire and Cornwall. To this huge estate he also added Gloucestershire and South Wales, by completing the marriage of his brother to his cousin Isabel, despite her objections.

All of this vast territory was granted to the royal prince as his alone. He alone was responsible for justice within its borders, nor did he have to account for a penny in tax to the royal exchequer. This at a time when Richard needed all the money he could find anywhere in the kingdom. I am bound to say that I was taken aback by such generosity. "You realise that you have created a kingdom within a kingdom?" I pointed out.

"I have studied this matter, Mother," Richard said. "Was not the principal point at issue between my father and all of his sons the fact that while he gave us all empty titles, he allowed none of us true power and position? My ambition is that there shall never be any point at issue between John and myself. I am King of England. It is fitting that he, my only surviving full brother, should have a portion of my vast lands. And if he is to have them, then he must rule them, absolutely. Answerable only unto me. And, of course, dearest Mother, to you as my vice-regent." A very noble speech, no doubt, expressing noble sentiments. But also, it could be said, a simplistic one. Not for the first time Richard was expressing a total confidence that the status quo would never change. He would marry Alais, and no doubt rapidly beget a son, the moment he returned from the Crusade: there was no question in his mind of his not returning. Equally, John would be content in his vast portion and his beautiful bride, in the certain knowledge that he held such lands in fief of his glorious brother.

But suppose Richard did not come back from Palestine? "Have you spoken with Constance on these matters?" I ventured.

"I have had no communication with Constance save for a brief note of condolence on Father's death."

"Yet is she the mother of the heir to the throne," I reminded him.

"I do not like Constance," Richard said. "I never have. Come to think of it, I never much liked Geoffrey either."

Well, who was I to argue with a point of view which so closely agreed with my own. It was back to my knees to pray that all would be well.

\* \* \*

Richard, however, obviously gave some thought to my reservations, as he privately exacted an oath from John that when he, Richard, departed on the Crusade he, John, would also leave England, and not return until either the King had done so or three years had elapsed, whichever was the sooner. This seemed an eminently satisfactory arrangement, removing all temptation from John to try and enlarge his portion or his power in the King's absence. But at the same time, it largely negated Richard's argument to me that he would eradicate all possibility of a conflict between himself and his brother, for how can you give a man a huge property today and tomorrow tell him that he cannot occupy it for three years, without arousing resentment? Richard of course brushed all argument aside by pointing out that he would be back in a year. Sadly, none of us are able to foresee the twists and turns that the future has in store for us.

I may say here that Richard was equally generous, in his fashion, to his other remaining brother, Ykenai's bastard Geoffrey. Geoffrey had, as I had determined on the occasion of our first meeting, gone into the Church. He had also remained very close to his father, and had indeed been Henry's personal chaplain – one wonders, in view of what I have related about Henry's private life, what this son thought of the confessions made to him by his father? The point is, however, that he was most definitely Henry's man. As had been William Marshal. Now Richard treated his half-brother with an equal amount of generosity, and had him made Archbishop of York.

When I suggested that this also might be going a bit far, he replied. "Above all else, Mother, I admire and wish to encourage loyalty in those who serve." I had to bite my tongue at that. But perhaps he did not reckon that sons served their fathers.

Richard was crowned at Westminster on 3 September, quite the most magnificent business I had ever attended. I organised it without consideration of expense, and it made such hasty affairs as the coronation of Henry and me, or even Louis and me so many years ago, seem mere sideshows. The cost, as I say, was horrendous, and all the while Richard was busily arranging funds for the Crusade. Mere taxes were of course quite insufficient. He had recourse to all the ancient ways of raising money, pledging position and plate. In this regard he was better placed that had been my grandfather, or, indeed, myself: thanks to the prowess of his father he had several very noble, and wealthy, captives to be ransomed. Head of this list was William the Lion of Scotland, who had been held in captivity since 1173, but who was now allowed to buy his freedom, and from all of the ignominious requirements of servitude heaped upon him by Henry, upon payment of ten thousand marks.

I had nothing against this, but it did bother me when learned that Richard was mortgaging everything held in the name of the Crown, from manor-house to castle, to raise the money he sought. It was generally assumed that he was jesting when he announced that he would sell London to the highest bidder, but I have a feeling he was serious. Fortunately, there was no one in the world with quite that much cash available.

Worst of all, however, was what can only be described as a pogrom he launched against the Jews. These people, driven out of their homeland, that same Palestine which was agitating everyone at this moment, some thousand years ago by Titus the Roman Emperor, had become a vast wandering nation, split up into families and family groups, seeking shelter where they could. I have no idea when they first came to England, but as they had never been rejected here, by the end of the twelfth century they formed quite a large community, centred in various cities. Because of their religious beliefs and usages they very wisely kept to themselves, but so far as I am aware they had never attempted to foist those beliefs and usages on the country at large. They were, in fact, the most inoffensive of people, who wished only to be left alone.

Unfortunately, they possessed one characteristic which more than any other set them apart from what might be called normal humanity: an acute business sense. Almost every man or woman I have ever met who aspired to any station has been in debt – but not the Jews. Where your Norman or your Englishman or your Angevin or your Frenchman borrowed lavishly to enhance his outward appearance, the Jews cared little for their physical surroundings while they accumulated. It therefore followed that over any period of time, the wealth of any community gradually found itself in the hands of these people. What is more, the Jews then accumulated more by lending their money back to the still spending Gentiles. This does not make for popularity in the long term – we always dislike those to whom we owe money, especially where the rates of interest are exorbitant.

Richard, or his advisers – I refuse to believe that Richard thought this up in his own essentially gallant mind – therefore conceived the answer to all of his problems. The Jewish community held a large proportion of the available money in England. Of course they paid their taxes like anyone else, but as I have intimated, taxes were not likely to raise the kind of money Richard needed. But the Jewish community was also disliked by nearly everyone, by the upper classes because they all owed money to it, and by the lower classes because of that fear of the unknown which is instinctive in any uneducated mass. It required but a few hired demagogues to tell the mob how the Jews abased the cross and sacrificed babes and generally indulged in every unspeakable practice these people could imagine, to set everyone at their throats.

Naturally the local sheriffs were told to protect the Jews' property, which they did with their soldiers – but the soldiers were under orders to loot the places they protected. While if there was no money forthcoming, the unhappy Jews, and their wives and daughters and sons, were subjected to every imaginable form of physical abuse, a sickening catalogue of rape and torture made the more ghastly by, firstly, the extremely modest attitude of most Jews to their women, and most Jewish women to themselves. For instance, to appear naked before anyone, even a husband, was regarded as being almost on the same level as being raped. And secondly, the peculiar habit of circumcision which appears to leave a Jewish male entirely different to a Gentile. I had of course observed this phenomenon with Saladin – as it is also practised by the Moslems – and found it fascinating. Our "Christian" soldiery found it much more than that!

When I discovered what was going on I protested most strongly to Richard, but he would not be moved. "This is God's work we are about, Mother," he told me. Well, that was a point of view. I could not help but feel that the other gentleman might be rubbing his hands with glee.

However, by whatever methods. Richard raised his

money, and on 13 December he left England for France. Amazingly, he was seen off by huge, cheering and apparently adoring crowds, even if there could have been no one present – except perhaps myself – whose pocket had not been directly affected by his requirements. Such are the qualities of what we are pleased to call greatness. However, I doubt there were any Jews in the multitude.

I joined him the following spring for a formal farewell. But I had not spent an idle winter. It had quickly become obvious to me that my elevation to be chatelaine of England was a purely honorary matter. Richard wished to honour me above all other women, but as he did not regard *any* woman in any flattering light, it simply did not occur to him that any of that sex, even his own tried and true mother, was actually capable of ruling a country. The business was to be done by his two appointed justiciars. This was brought home to me even more by what happened that autumn, when Mandeville died, and Richard immediately appointed in his place, without even consulting me, William Longchamp. Had I been in the mood, I might have regarded this as a slap in the face. Longchamp was already chancellor, and was also Bishop of Ely. He was well known as a hard and ruthless man, who held women in about as much regard as did his master. It was obvious that he was not going to pay much attention to me. As it happened, however, my thoughts were already ranging far afield.

As with so many events in my life, my estrangement from Louis, my flight to the Empress Matilda, my relationship with Rosamund Clifford, to name but three, I find it difficult to trace the exact processes by which they were brought about. I can only say with certainty that where several strands of thought were all inclining in the same direction, it was that direction in which I knew I would eventually go. Ever since Henry had first broached the matter of another Crusade, I had dreamed of a second visit to Palestine. It may be said that in view of my contemptuous strictures on people like Barbarossa returning to the desert at his great age I was being a trifle frivolous here – Barbarossa was a year younger than I. But I was completely fit, and I would not be galloping about clad in full armour! However, Henry had put his foot down on that concept. But he was now dead.

I had decided against broaching the idea with Richard. In the first place I had been overwhelmed at the prospect of being left in charge in England, and in the second I knew that Richard would no more go for the idea than had his father. But if I was not actually going to be left in charge in England . . .

Then I was deeply concerned about the situation regarding the Heir to the Throne. By all the laws of primogeniture, Arthur of Brittany was that heir. But I doubted that he would be acceptable to the lords of England, and even more so if Richard were to be killed or die on the Crusade, when Arthur would still be a minor. There was no one in England going to accept the regency of Constance of Brittany. Least of all would John accept it. Well, if Richard were to die without issue, I would wish John to succeed. But I would far prefer that he didn't have to. As I have suggested more than once in this narrative, much as I loved my youngest son, I did not altogether trust him.

Then there was the business of Geoffrey the Bastard hovering in the wings. How could a priest ever consider becoming King of England? But stranger things have happened, and there could be no doubt that not only had Geoffrey been closer to his father than any of

Henry's other sons – than even me, as a matter of fact – but that he was also immensely popular with the baronage. This thought clearly crossed Richard's mind as well, for before finally leaving for Palestine he exacted an exactly similar oath from Geoffrey as he had from John, that the prospective Archbishop of York would not enter England until the King returned, or until three years had elapsed. Obviously, Geoffrey was no more pleased by this than had been John. Thus it all came down to the one point. For the good of the realm and everyone in it, Richard had to have a son, by a suitably pliant mother, who would be governed by her mother-in-law!

Which brought my thoughts to Alais. I actually liked the girl, but there were so many counts against her one almost needed an abacus to add them up. She had been my step-daughter before she ever got around to being my prospective daughter-in-law. She had been my husband's mistress. Richard actively disliked her, to put it mildly. And she was Philip of France's sister. Just supposing she wound up as Queen Mother of an infant English king, there could be no doubt in which direction she would turn for assistance and advice. Certainly not to me.

But there were two other points of even greater importance. One was that Richard was postponing actually marrying her until he returned from the Crusade. That he had agreed to marry her at all after so many refusals was a concomitant of his necessity to bind Philip Augustus ever closer to him, on such a vast venture. But when he returned from the Crusade, the necessity to marry her at all would no longer obtain, in the short term – something he obviously had much in mind – so the whole sorry charade would commence all over again, with still no acceptable heir in sight. The last point was perhaps more important of all. Alais had been Henry's mistress, on a pretty permanent basis, for something like two years . . . and she had not given birth: as far as I could discover, and I certainly tried, the rumour that she had borne a child for her lover was entirely false – there was no trace of such a babe. Well, Henry had undoubtedly been past his best, and neither Rosamund Clifford nor Lampagie de Porhoet had given birth, so far as I was aware. Still . . .

I was brooding quite deeply on this when I learned of the death of William the Good of Sicily. Instantly all was turmoil in that sunswept isle I remembered so fondly. Joanna had not succeeded in becoming a mother, so the succession was not assured. By rights it belonged to that Constance whom Barbarossa had preferred as a wife for his son to one of my daughters. But she was of course in Germany and the formidable father-in-law who might have been expected to advance her claim was on his way to Palestine. Now it seemed that a bastard grandson of William the Bad, who had undoubtedly inherited all of his grandfather's deplorable habits, had not only seized the throne, but had imprisoned the Queen Dowager. This was quite unacceptable. I might have been imprisoned on two occasions, but both times had been by my current husband, which, sadly, is regarded as fair enough in this uneven world. But I was not having my daughter imprisoned by some lout named Tancred, who would visit upon her heaven knows what indignities.

I complained to Richard, who entirely agreed with me. "I had in any event intended to stop by Sicily on my way to Palestine," he said. "Now I shall simply knock a few heads together." On occasion he could sound just like his father! But while these were certainly the words I wished to hear, I still worried for my baby girl

– as she remained in my heart. Having just lost my eldest daughter by Henry, I was more than normally concerned about my youngest. I wanted to make sure of her health for myself, but she was in Messina and at the time the news arrived I was in Winchester . . .

While all of these thoughts were jostling around my brain, I received a letter from Eleanor. Eleanor was a faithful correspondent, who wrote every Christmas. This time she had more than usual to say. There was the death of Matilda to be mourned. There was Joanna to be considered. There were various domestic matters. And then . . . *'I suppose now that Richard is king, he will simply have to get married,'* she wrote:

*'He really has been very neglectful not to have done this long ago. Of course I entirely understand his feelings about Alais. It is such a pity that he has been encumbered with her for so long. It is more the pity because I have here the girl who would make him a perfect wife. I am speaking of my niece-in-law, Berengaria. She is the daughter of King Sancho of Navarre, and my sister-in-law Blanca, who are great friends of ours. Berengaria has recently been staying with me, and I can tell you that she is not only beautiful, but lively and intelligent. But there it is . . . oh, by the way, she is sixteen years old.'*

When a daughter, who has been a regular correspondent for years and who is therefore entirely *au fait* with all the skeletons in the family closet, writes a letter like that, it makes one think. And coming on top of all my other thoughts it made me realise that it was a time to *do*. Obviously, if my plan was successful, it would mean a quarrel between Richard and Philip. But if the two kings really were lovers, I could think of nothing I would like more than to see them cordially hating each other, as Louis and Henry had hated each other, and

Louis' father and Henry Beauclerk had equally never been friends. Suddenly I was filled with all the energy and passion of my youth.

Of course I had to keep my cards very close to my chest, one might say. It would have negated all my plans had anyone, and most especially either Richard or Philip, gained any idea of what I had in mind. While an even greater complication could arise if Archbishop Baldwin learned of it: Baldwin was intending to accompany Richard to Palestine. I took my instruction from my memory of the Empress. Thus I replied to Eleanor in the most non-committal terms, and as I have said, went myself to France in the spring to be present at the taking of the oath; I dared not move until Richard was actually on his way. Both he and Philip intended to go by sea from the port of Marseilles in the south of France, the science of logistics having advanced a great way in the past fifty years. I wished them well, having no desire myself ever to venture on the briny again, except for very short passages such as Normandy to England. I merely knew that Richard intended to stop at Sicily and sort things out there. I intended to catch him up.

As usual, however, one makes plans and one unmakes them again, through necessity. The Crusade had been meant to start in the spring of 1189. Frederic Barbarossa had indeed set off at that time, commanding an army of thirty thousand men, a formidable force and well led, too, for Frederick had become one of the foremost soldiers of his time, and he remained filled with energy despite being virtually in his dotage; as his second-in-command, like Conrad before him, he took along his son Frederick of Swabia, the rascal who had been intended as a husband for Eleanor, once upon a time. By the time I got to France the Germans had long reached Constantinople, where they wintered. How I envied them. The French and English plans had been thrown into disarray by Henry's death, but yet, as we have seen, Richard and Philip had been determined to leave immediately after Easter, 1190. But now there were the usual delays in getting everything together, and it was past midsummer before they finally set off. This really left me with a lot to do. But the moment I had waved Richard out of sight I was galloping south. I took only a small bodyguard, and of course, Amaria and Blondel. Amaria, poor thing, was now approaching sixty, and found spending all day in the saddle a most wearisome business. But as I was approaching *seventy*, I reckoned that if I could stand it so could she. While Blondel, being not yet twenty-five, was a bundle of energy. And fun.

I sent messengers ahead to warn Pamplona of my coming. I don't know what the reactions of the Navarese court was to the imminent arrival of the Queen Dowager of England, a woman who, if I say so myself, was now famous in both fact and fiction throughout Europe. But they turned out in their thousands to greet me. I had also sent a messenger to Toledo. He had further to travel but then Eleanor, having received my summons, had a smaller distance than I, and in fact we arrived in Pamplona within hours of each other. "Oh, Mama!" she cried. It was some fifteen years since we had seen each other.

"My dearest girl," I said. We hugged each other. Eleanor was now twenty-nine years old, a lovely woman – all my children have been exceedingly handsome, with the possible exception of Geoffrey – who was happily married, and the mother of four delightful children of her own; Henry, who was heir to the throne of Castile, Blanca, Urraca and Berenguela. I say delightful, but this was by hearsay, as they were all still somewhat small and she had not brought them with her, although she had some likenesses to show me.

I could have spent all winter speaking with her, but I was in a great haste. I had not yet told anyone the purpose of my visit, and indeed, I suspect that the good Spaniards had the idea that I was again in flight. Eleanor went so far as to offer me asylum in Castile, where her husband, after inflicting a series of defeats upon the Moors, was supreme. When I told her the real reason for my sudden appearance in her life, her eyes grew round as saucers. "It was you put the idea in my head," I reminded her.

"But can it work, Mama?"

"Well, that depends on the girl, does it not? I should like to meet her."

I met her that very night, at a state banquet given in my honour by Sancho and Blanca. The cream of Navarese society was there, for they were equally flattered at having the Queen of Castile in their midst as the Queen Dowager of England. Berengaria was their only daughter. I found Eleanor's raptures about her beauty a little bit exaggerated; her features were too rounded, and perhaps too soft. But then, this might not be a bad thing. Her complexion was superb, however, and her hair, long and golden, was clearly a throwback to some Visigothic ancestress who had managed to escape the attention of the Moors, unlike mine. As to her figure . . . I had to be sure.

I left the arrangements to Eleanor, of whom her sister-in-law was in great awe. Next morning Eleanor brought Blanca to speak with me privately. "Your Grace does us great honour," the Queen of Navarre began.

"It will be an honour shared," I replied.

"It is our understanding that King Richard is already betrothed," Blanca ventured.

"That is a marriage that can never take place," I assured her, and glanced at Eleanor, to have it immediately confirmed by Blanca's blush that Eleanor had put her in the picture.

"And King Richard looks favourably upon our daughter?" Blanca ventured.

"He looks upon her with my eyes," I pointed out. "As he has never seen her." I am well aware that a recent troubadour has claimed that Richard and Berengaria had indeed actually met, in Poitou, some years earlier, and that Richard had fallen in love with the Spanish princess then. Unfortunately, this is claptrap. Not only had Berengaria never been in Poitou, but Richard had never fallen in love with any woman. Nor was he likely to do so now. However, I still considered it possible to make a woman acceptable to his bed, if allowed the opportunity. "Therefore, as he is content to leave the judgement to me," I went on, "I should like to see the Princess in private."

Blanca looked at Eleanor. "I am sure my mother means with us present, your Grace," Eleanor said.

I had not actually meant that, but I had to accept Eleanor's decision, as without her I could make no plans at all. Thus Berengaria was brought to us, and requested to disrobe by her mother. She was clearly embarrassed at this, but in the presence of three queens could do nothing but obey. We examined her most minutely, physically, and I was delighted. The girl was small-breasted and slender at her thigh, so much so that she almost looked like a boy, but she had the most delightfully shaped backside: both of these were very important considerations where Richard was concerned.

I allowed her to dress again and then questioned her about her education, which was good, her morals, which was superfluous, as she was a Spanish princess and had never moved a step in her life without her duenna at her shoulder, about her ability to compose poetry, which was poor, and about her thoughts regarding my son. "I know nothing of the King, your Grace," she admitted. "Save that he is the greatest knight in the world."

"She will do very well," I told Blanca.

"Think of it, child," her mother said. "You are going to be Queen of England." I thought she might faint.

"I will take the Princess with me when I go," I said. "After we have signed the betrothal treaty, of course." The Queen of Navarre could not object to that established practice. Her husband was delighted, as the marriage contract would naturally include a treaty of alliance with the Angevin Empire, and he was well aware that Aquitaine lay immediately north of his little country, a magnificent friend but a dreadful enemy, were circumstances ever to conspire to bring this about.

This was only one of the aspects of the situation which concerned Eleanor. She came to my bedchamber that night. "Are you really leaving tomorrow, Mama?"

"At the crack of dawn."

"That is such a shame. I would have loved you to come down to Toledo and meet the children. And Alfonso."

"I would love to come, my pet," I said. "But I will have to do so on a later occasion." Not for the first time in my life I was being prescient without knowing it.

"This has been a very rushed business," the dear girl remarked.

"State affairs are always rushed."

"And now you are hurrying off with Berengaria . . . but what *is* the reason for haste? Richard cannot possibly return from his Crusade until next year."

"By then he will be married and a father."

She frowned at me. "You are going on the Crusade yourself? You are taking *Berengaria* on the Crusade?" Clearly she assumed I had lost my senses.

"Well, that will have to be Richard's decision. But I will have them bedded before he sets foot in Palestine."

"But . . ." she was clearly embarrassed. "Has Richard signified that he will accept the girl?"

"No," I said. "I doubt he knows she exists. I would not like this to go any further, you understand."

"But Mama!" She was aghast. "If he rejects her, after you have signed a betrothal treaty, and taken her off . . ."

"There will be the most terrible scandal," I agreed. "And probably war between Navarre and the Angevin Empire. As for the first, one more scandal is really not going to add to my gray hairs. As to the second, it would be a farce."

"Oh, Mama!" She shook her head. "You are as wicked a woman as they say."

"As who say?" I inquired. "As for being wicked, I am a queen, and a mother. I have the welfare of the entire dynasty at stake. Am I to be concerned about morality?"

I could see that she was not happy, but she would not oppose me, and so next morning, cheered by the entire court, Berengaria and I left Navarre. By then I had already made some other arrangements. I summoned Blondel to my bedchamber. Well, he came there often enough, to be sure, but tonight we were to talk business. "You will leave immediately for Sicily," I told him. "I do not care how you go, by horse or by boat, but you must arrive there before the King sails for Palestine."

"I understand, your Grace," he said. "And the message?"

"That he must immediately renounce Alais of France. Tell him that I am coming behind him, with the most vital news, which makes a marriage between him and the Princess quite impossible. Tell him the entire future depends on this."

The poor boy was looking extremely anxious. He knew, of course, my plan, as I had discussed it with him as with Albert and Amaria. "If he rejects the Spaniard, your Grace . . ."

"That is my concern. But he will not reject the Spaniard, I promise you." I gave him a bag of gold and a kiss. "Now, away with you. Haste! Haste!"

He obeyed, and by the time we were ready to leave the next morning, had long gone. We were accompanied through the Pass des Roncesvalles by an escort of Navarese cavalry, but these I dismissed at the border; I had my own escort of Gascons awaiting me there. I also dismissed Berengaria's duennas, much to their annoyance. "We do things differently in England," I told them. Once the Navarese were out of sight, I pointed to the east. "Haste!" I commanded.

Berengaria was concerned, and urged her palfrey alongside mine. "Do we not go to Bordeaux and thence Poitiers?" she asked.

"We go to the King," I told her.

This gave her something to think about, and that night after supper I summoned her to my tent. "Give the Princess a glass of wine," I told Amaria. I had a notion she was going to need it. Berengaria sipped, and sat beside me. "You are going to marry a king," I said. She nodded appreciatively. "And bear him strong sons," I went on.

"If I am blessed, your Grace."

"In your case, blessing is not going to have all that much to do with it. I wish you to listen to me very carefully. What do you know about men?"

She blushed. "Only that they are big and strong and like fighting. And are very hairy," she added.

"And also, I hope, that they are equipped to impregnate women," I suggested.

Her blush deepened. "I have been taught the facts of life, your Grace."

"Good," I said. "However, possibly there are facts of life of which you are unaware, but which are very necessary to understand. Tell me what you know of the sexual act."

For a moment she was speechless. Then she licked her lips. "The man lies on the woman, and . . . makes an entry."

"Go on." She gazed at me in consternation. "I see," I said. "Those are the facts of life, are they? There is a great deal more to it than that, my child, and I may add, fortunately. The man will undoubtedly wish to fondle you. At least," I hastily added, "most men will wish to do this."

"Fondle me, your Grace?"

I demonstrated, and left her more confused than before. But not altogether unhappy. "However," I went on, "there are some men who, in this regard, may well prefer to *be* fondled. My son is such a man." She gazed at me with enormous eyes. "You must do this, boldly," I told her. "When, upon your first night together . . ." I preferred not to dwell on whether or not this would actually be their wedding night, "he comes to you, naked, be bold. Grasp his weapon, not harshly, but tenderly, yet firmly. Stroke it. Indulge it. You will be well rewarded." She gasped. "I am teaching you the way to happiness, my dear girl," I explained. "It follows that if you make my son happy, then you will be happy. And who may know what makes a man happy better than his mother?"

"I understand, your Grace," she said gallantly, although I could tell that she was confused at this addition to her knowledge.

"However," I went on. "There is more that needs to be understood." Berengaria was panting so hard I had Amaria refill her wine goblet. "There are some men," I said, "who are of such sexual capacity that the mere act cannot satisfy them, or make them happy. There are, of course, many ways to make an entry other than the one recommended by the Church. Your husband may well seek some of these. You will accommodate him, if you would make him happy, even if it means going down on your knees."

Her head jerked up and down. "If it will make my husband happy, your Grace. But your Grace . . ." she bit her lip.

"Ask."

"Have you . . .?"

"I have been twice a wife and ten times a mother," I reminded her. "And I have had lovers. In between husbands," I said carefully. Which was all of the answer she seemed to need, as she gazed at me in awe. "However," I went on, taking a glass of wine myself for fortification, "there are also orifices in the female body by which pleasure may be gained with never a risk of pregnancy." Berengaria spilled her wine. "One is the mouth, of course," I said. I could not risk any misunderstanding. "If the King wishes to use this means of gaining pleasure, then you must accommodate him, joyously." Berengaria gulped. "The other . . ."

"Oh, your Grace! Is that not a mortal sin?"

"When one compares what may, or may not, be a mortal sin, Berengaria, with the desires of a man who is King of England, Duke of Normandy, Duke of Aquitaine, Count of Poitou, of Anjou and of Maine, Lord of Ireland and Wales, and who is now on his way to becoming Master of Palestine, it pays one to be pragmatic."

She considered this for several moments, then asked, "If I may be so bold, your Grace, have you . . .?"

"I say what I said before," I told her. "I have been married to two kings and have known other men. Love, in all its aspects, both sacred and profane, has been my joy." Of course I was not going to admit to a girl fifty-two years my junior that I had never been buggered – nor would I have admitted it if I had! "The important thing is," I continued, "that you should in no way be afraid of it, or feel abhorrence for it. What happens between a man and a woman in the privacy of their bedchamber is for them alone to know and understand. Under no circumstances should it ever be confessed. Now, I would recommend that, in your search for happiness, you should make it plain to the King, at the earliest possible opportunity, not only that such an advance on his part would not displease you, but that you would be delighted were he to use you so intimately." Her mouth made a gigantic O. "Now go to bed," I told her. "And dream of Richard." I felt sure I did not need to recommend what parts of Richard she should dream about.

"Your Grace," Amaria said, when we were alone. "You are taking great risks."

"I know it. But this girl is our last hope. She must be to Richard what Richard wants and requires."

"She doesn't have a penis, your Grace."

"One should be enough for two, providing it belongs to the master," I insisted. I could not believe that Richard would ever be anything other than the master, in bed.

The rest of the journey was a vigorous one, for it was now winter, and in places there was snow on the ground; despite this we travelled in great haste, through the lands of the Counts of Maurienne, and thence through the Papal States, past Rome and Naples, to the Straits of Messina. Everywhere I was welcomed as what I now was, the most powerful woman in Europe, and everywhere the lords and bishops, mayors and counts, wished to entertain me. Well, their towns and castles made very useful stopping places, but I never dallied a day, even if I had the utmost confidence in Blondel.

Berengaria and I were now utter intimates. She wished only to talk of love, in all its aspects, and was there ever a happier subject? I naturally continued my theme, and by the time we reached Reggio she clearly did not have a fear in the world of anything sexual that might happen to her. Indeed, by then it had become a business of restraining her until Richard could get his hands on her, judging by the way she looked at the men we encountered or those of our escorts: she seldom seemed interested in anything other than their codpieces.

Sadly, while we were on the road, a great deal was happening elsewhere. We had barely entered Italy when we learned of the catastrophe in Cappadocia: Barbarossa was dead!

My old friend who had become my enemy had

not been killed in battle. Indeed, with his thirty thousand men he had marched on this spring from Constantinople, while Richard and Philip had still not yet left France, having spent the winter quarrelling with the Byzantine Emperor, another Manuel, and had, like his father before him, set out across the highlands of Cappadocia. There was no doubt that he was out to avenge the disaster of 1147 as much as to retake Jerusalem, and indeed, by all accounts, when he had encountered the Seljuks he had put them to flight; he even stormed and took their capital city of Iconium, following which they had made peace, and he had continued his march south without resistance. But then, overcome by the heat, he had one afternoon sought to bathe in the cold waters of a river called the Calycadnus. The result had been a heart attack, and the old man – I use the word in its accepted sense although at sixty-seven he was a year younger than I – had died.

As with Henry, perhaps even more so, my own heart almost stopped beating for a moment when I heard the news. I had, after all, known Barbarossa long before Henry: he was, in fact, my oldest living acquaintance. And I would cheerfully have been his wife. But his death was to prove a disaster in more ways than just personally. As had happened with Conrad's host, the German army had disintegrated following the death of their much-beloved master, and although we learned that Frederick of Swabia had continued his march with the remnants, he could no longer be counted as much value to the Crusade. This would be a blow to Richard, I knew. But equally I knew it was not likely to deter him.

But magnificent old Redbeard, lying dead on the banks of some remote stream in Asia! It made me terribly aware of my own mortality. I was very relieved to reach Messina, and discover that Richard was still there.

Better yet, Philip Augustus was not. He had in fact sailed for Palestine only three days before we arrived.

Richard was waiting for me when I was ferried across the strait. I deemed it best that Berengaria and Amaria travel in a separate galley, until I had discovered the lie of the land. "Mama!" Richard embraced me. "You are the most formidable of women. Why did you not tell me you were coming?"

"I wished to surprise you."

"I am surprised. And delighted. And your gift . . . it is beyond compare."

"My gift?"

"The minstrel. I have never known such pleasure."

"Ah," I said, wondering if I had made a mistake. "He gave you my message?"

"Of course."

"And you did as I asked?"

He grinned. "I am afraid Philip is not in a good mood. He has taken himself off."

"So I have been told. You have definitely renounced Alais?"

"Actually, we haven't discussed Alais."

"Then . . . I do not understand. What has angered him?"

"I would not give Blondel to him."

"Ah," I said again. We discussed the German tragedy as we walked together through cheering crowds to the palazzo he had selected as his own; as I had expected, he found it no more than an irritation. "Tell me of things here?" I asked. "How is Joanna?"

"As well as may be expected."

"You got her out of prison?"

"Oh, indeed. She awaits you."

"And this fellow Tancred?"

"Is up in the hills, uttering threats and making offers in equal numbers. He does not really interest me. I was but awaiting your coming. Now tell me what is this news you have that is so important."

"There is someone I would have you meet," I told him.

As may be supposed, I was fairly nervous. Berengaria and Amaria arrived at the palazzo shortly after us, but were kept waiting while I greeted my baby daughter. She was in surprisingly good health, but was still wearing her widow's weeds, and looked generally in need of cheering up. I hugged her tightly. "Richard says I may go with him to Palestine," she said.

"I think that is ideal," I said. "And now . . ." Berengaria was escorted into the room. "The Princess of Navarre," I announced. Only Richard, Joanna, Amaria, and myself were present. Richard looked at Berengaria, then at me. "I have already signed the marriage contract," I said. He looked at Berengaria again. The poor girl was clearly terrified. "Will you not greet your bride, Richard?" I asked.

He hesitated, then went forward, and took her hand. "You do me great honour, Princess."

Berengaria gave a little curtsey. "As I am honoured, your Grace." She glanced at me, and I gave her a nod. "I would have you know, your Grace," she said, "that it is my sole wish to please you, in every possible way."

Richard came to me in the privacy of the bedchamber he had given me. I waved Amaria away. "Where did you find her, Mama?"

"She was recommended by Eleanor. And when I had seen her, and spoken with her, I knew she was the one for you."

He glanced at me, and having seated himself, now got up again and walked about the room. "You understand that this will mortally offend Philip?"

"I think it is about time you did that." He glanced at me. "You hate Alais, yet you must marry, Richard," I told him. "You must marry, and you must have an heir. But there is no need for it to be a difficult business. I beg you to accept my word that this girl will be like . . ." I drew a deep breath. "She will be as pleasurable to you as Blondel. In every possible way."

Now he turned to face me. "Do you have any understanding of what you speak?"

"I have had that understanding for twenty years, Richard. Do you not think I knew of your relationship with Giles?"

"And you do not condemn me?"

"You are my son. You are the mightiest warrior of the age. And you are King of England. You told me once that you understood your duty. I am asking you to do that duty. Use this girl as it pleases you; she will not object. I give you my word on that. But if you also can impregnate her, then will you truly have done your duty."

He continued to gaze at me for several seconds. Then he said, "I must leave for Palestine immediately. I cannot let Philip get there before me, at least by more than a few days."

"Then you must be married immediately."

"I will take the Princess with me."

"Richard . . ."

"I am taking Joanna as well. She will chaperone the Princess."

"Joanna will oppose you in nothing."

He grinned. "Nor should she."

"Richard, should you take this girl to your bed, and then reject her . . ."

"Nothing will happen at all. We shall simply remain betrothed. But if you are right about her, Mama, I shall marry her."

"Well," I said. "I suppose that is hopeful. When do we leave?"

"Joanna and I, and Berengaria, leave tomorrow, for Palestine. I would like you to leave also, and return to Normandy."

"But . . . I wish to accompany you."

"You cannot. In the first place, dearest Mama, I do not think your health could stand it, at your great age." I snorted. "In the second, I need you at home. I have received word that John is in England."

I raised my eyebrows. "But . . . his oath . . ."

"Exactly."

"Richard," I said uneasily, "do you not suppose it would be best to abandon this Crusade until a more settled time?"

"And become the laughing stock of Europe? Besides, it is what I want to do. What have I to fear with you acting for me?"

Well, that was very flattering, of course, but I remained uneasy.

"It is possible that John intends nothing untoward," he said. "But still, he has broken his oath, and needs to be reminded of this. Now, I do not wish to appear to be over-reacting. I understand that the trouble may have been caused by Longchamp's high-handed behaviour. I have thus already despatched a personal representative, Walter of Coutances, to investigate the situation, and, if necessary, replace Longchamp. I do not wish you involved in this. I wish you to go to Rouen, set up your court there, and keep an eye on things. Only if you are certain that John means mischief must you interfere. But then you must. You are the only person on earth, apart from myself, who can deal with him, Mama. I put this trust in your hands."

What could I say? Not to continue to Palestine was, perhaps, the greatest disappointment of my life. But I have never been one to shirk my duty. "I will take Blondel with me," I said. We gazed at each other. "I wish nothing to come between you and Berengaria," I told him. "I will promise you this: Blondel will be awaiting you, when you return, with your wife . . . and your son."

Richard gave one of his great shouts of laughter. "I will hold you to that, dearest Mama."

Thus I said goodbye to my favourite son and one of my most cherished dreams. But their departure, and mine north, was made the less painful by my awareness that I had a great deal to do. I had a last word with both Berengaria and Joanna, reminding the one of the way to happiness, at least as Richard's wife, and the other that it was her duty to see that the pair were married. Berengaria was of course utterly pliant, Joanna necessarily less so: she was not my daughter for nothing. This was perhaps to turn out unfortunately. But for the time being she understood the seriousness of the situation. Thus off they went, and off I went as well.

Naturally I had even more reason for haste than Richard, but I had the misfortune to arrive in Rome just as the latest Pope, Celestine, was about to be consecrated, and was prevailed upon to attend this most solemn event. This actually served a useful purpose, as I was able to have a chat with this fellow, whose real name was Giacinto Bobo-Orsini, although he now called himself Celestine III. He had been a friend of Becket, but was sensible enough to recognise not only that that was in the past, but that I had already been estranged from Henry when the tragedy had occurred. This we were able to see many things with a common gaze.

However, to my consternation, also in Rome was Henry of Germany, waiting to be crowned Emperor by the new Pope. I could tell at a glance that this Emperor-Elect Henry did not like me. No doubt, like so many built-in enemies, he had been regaled often enough with tales of my misspent life. Well, his dislike I could stand, but I had to presume it would extend to my sons. Not that I could see any way in which the Emperor could trouble Richard: Barbarossa had never been able to trouble my Henry!

Meanwhile I had a great deal to occupy my mind. I duly regained France, late in the year, and preferred to spend Christmas at Bonnevilles-sur-Touques, close to the Channel, a position from which I could receive all the necessary reports as to what was happening in England.

This was not very edifying. All was in turmoil. William Longchamp had naturally taken exception to John's return in defiance of his oath. But how does one expel a prince of the realm, especially when John immediately retired to his six counties, where he was surrounded by his adherents? Longchamp was required to govern southern England in the King's absence, not start a civil war! The situation had been further complicated by the arrival of Walter of Coutances. I did not know this fellow, and had been prepared to accept him at Richard's face value. But now I was told that Walter had sided with John. He apparently hated Longchamp, although it is strange that Richard had not known this. I am more inclined to believe that he was bribed.

Now there arose yet a third complication. Geoffrey the Bastard had decided to follow his half-brother's example, and also ignore the oath he had sworn: he had duly turned up at Dover. There he was seized by Longchamp's sister and cast into a dungeon. This was too much for the people. Geoffrey had always been most popular, he was a churchman, and your mob – usually mainly composed of men – does not like to see one of its own belaboured by a woman. The result was a total upheaval. Longchamp was opposed on all sides, and was forced to surrender his seals as justiciar. These were promptly seized by Walter acting on the authority given him by Richard. The result was that my youngest son, with the support of his older half-brother, was now virtually in supreme control of all England south of the Humber, and there was little prospect of any opposition north of that river, either.

There was as yet not the slightest suggestion that John in any way intended to do Richard any harm, yet he had acted illegally, and I realised that I would have to handle the affair very tactfully. In these circumstances it was reassuring to receive the news that all seemed to be going well with the Crusade. Richard, with his fleet of two hundred ships, had followed Philip across the Mediterranean, but had put in to the large island of Cyprus, where he discovered Guy of Lusignan waiting for him. Guy, of course, whatever his incompetence, or, as far as I was concerned, his villainy, was an important member of any expedition to recover Jerusalem: he was still titular King of the city! Now he and Richard formed an alliance, and Richard proceeded to capture

Cyprus. This was not mere lust for territory, but a sound strategic concept. He conceived that he needed a base secure from Saracen attack, and an island provided this admirably, while Cyprus is no more than a short sail from the Palestinian coast. It was in Cyprus that he married Berengaria, to my great relief. I had the bells rung in Rouen, and awaited eagerly the news of a child.

This was not immediately forthcoming, but everything else was on the up. Proceeding, with his bride and his sister, to the mainland, Richard led the Crusaders in an assault on Acre, and took the city. Following this, and now tacitly at least recognised as the commander of the crusading army, he began the march on Jerusalem. It was at a place called Arsouf that Saladin determined to oppose him. It was a famous battle, and it ended in a complete victory for Richard. I was delighted at this news, which arrived in a letter written from Ascalon, where my son and his bride and sister, with the army, were wintering. *Next spring*, Richard wrote, *we shall be in Jerusalem.* I didn't doubt if for a moment.

Nor was I the least displeased by the news that the quarrel with Philip Augustus had now broken into an open rupture, and Philip had taken himself home. Actually, he may have been impelled in this course by more than the difference with his lover; his wife Isabella had just died. Obviously, to a man like Richard, the death of a wife was of no importance whatsoever when taken in the context of a campaign. Richard indeed seemed to have been quarrelling with all the other commanders, suspecting them, I am sure rightly, of not being as whole-heartedly in the endeavour as himself. He was, of course, his father's son, and while never giving way to such extremes as throwing himself on the floor to eat the rushes, he certainly possessed a temper. It appears that on one occasion he threw down the banner of Leopold of Austria while in a rage. Unfortunately, at this time he lacked all restraint. Neither his wife nor his sister exercised the least influence over his temper, and now I learned that the man who should have kept him in check, Archbishop Baldwin, had died from the heat. I am bound to confess that I found this more of an irritant than a tragedy. Richard nominated one Reginald Fitzjocelyn as his successor, and this seemed a popular choice with the clergy. But Fitzjocelyn died before the end of the year, before he could be consecrated. Then it was decided to leave things in abeyance until the King got home. But I'm afraid these great matters concerned me less than the news that Philip was back in Paris, filled with bile, and eager to cause trouble. I now learned that he had written John inviting him to marry the long-neglected Alais – presumably there would be no difficult in having John's Isabella put aside, in view of their consanguinity – to form an alliance between the pair of them!

This could only be directed against Richard, and I wrote John a strong letter commanding him to do nothing in this direction until the return of his brother, which, if Jerusalem was to fall in the coming spring, could not be long delayed.

It may be imagined that I spent an anxious winter. I was in fact very tempted to disobey Richard and cross the Channel to see for myself what was happening in England, but I decided that a few more months was not going to make too much difference, and I had the assurance of a regular stream of letters from John begging me to believe that he had every intention of awaiting Richard's return before even considering his matrimonial future.

But the spring brought disappointment. Richard duly commenced his advance on the fabled city, but Saladin, if declining again to meet him in a pitched battle, showed great defensive qualities, burning crops and poisoning wells in the Crusaders' path, so that it rapidly became apparent that to continue might entail the destruction of the army. Thus Richard wrote: '*We are back at the coast, and I am afraid that I must accomplish my aim by negotiation. This is a severe blow to me, but on the other hand I have had the great pleasure of a meeting with Saladin and his brother Safadin. Saladin has spoken most kindly of you, and describes you as the most beautiful woman he ever met. I know this will please you.*' Well, my heart was swelling and my eyes were filled with tears.

'*You will be pleased to know,*' Richard continued, '*that Saladin is agreeable to a truce, and indeed we have signed one. It will last for three years, and during it any Christian pilgrims wishing to travel to Jerusalem will be granted safe conducts. I can do no more than this at this time; as for what will happen in three years time, we will have to wait and see. I must tell you that I could have had even more favourable terms had Joanna been agreeable. Saladin's brother, Safadin, a much younger man, was as taken with my baby sister as I suspect Saladin was with you, forty-five years ago. He asked for her hand in marriage.*' Shades of Saladin and myself on the balcony in Antioch! '*I was sure you would not mind,*' Richard wrote. '*Thus I gave my permission, but Joanna absolutely refused to consider the idea of entering a harem. I suppose I could have forced her, but I was reluctant to do that, so . . . I feel the Arab Prince was put out.*

*In any event, dearest Mama, I have finished my work here, at least, as I say, at this time. The fact is that*

*Palestine has been every bit as hot and fever-ridden as you told me it would be, and our affairs are further complicated by the activities of a group of murderous thugs who call themselves Assassins. They have recently done for Conrad of Montferrat. Well, I suppose he is no loss, as he seemed determined to wrest the throne of Jerusalem from Guy – if that empty title has any value now. Thus we are coming home. I have already despatched the Queen and Joanna, as I do not wish them to have to endure another summer here. I myself will follow as soon as I have attended to the requirements of the army. I will write again from Marseilles.'*

I wept for joy.

Richard's letter was written at the end of September, and it seemed reasonable not to expect him until the end of the year. Nevertheless, I prepared a great Christmas feast for his homecoming, and left no one in any doubt that we were going to celebrate a triumph, regardless of his personal disappointment. Berengaria and Joanna arrived home before the festival, both with tremendous stories to tell. I naturally could not wait to get the Queen alone, to ask her about her marriage. "I imagine it is as other marriages, Mother," she said.

I frowned; I did not like the sound of that at all. "Has it been as I prophesied?" I asked.

"Oh, indeed. He uses me in a variety of different ways. When he uses me."

"You mean he neglects you?"

"Well, he is a soldier, conducting a campaign, Mother. He has had very little time for dalliance. Besides . . . he has other interests." She was clearly unhappy. Well, so was I at this unexpected turn of events. Or was it unexpected? "But you knew of this, of course, Mother," the girl went on. "Which is why you prepared me."

"I did what I thought necessary. Tell me this: do you love my son?"

"I could love him, Mother. Did he desire my love?"

"It will be different when he comes home," I assured her. She looked sceptical. "And then you will have many sons," I went on, hopefully. She looked more sceptical yet.

Christmas passed, and I began to worry. I worried even more when men started to turn up in Rouen claiming to have been members of Richard's army. Then Hubert Walter turned up in Rouen. Hubert was a much-respected churchman who had been virtually Archbishop Baldwin's secretary. I had him brought before me. "I seek news of the King," I told him.

"Is he not here, your Grace?"

"Of course he is not here," I snapped. "Did the army not sail together?"

"Yes, it did, your Grace. We embarked together, and the King led us out to sea. But then there came a great storm, and we were scattered."

I remembered such a storm, in the spring of 1149. "Did you not seek the King, afterwards?" I demanded.

"Our orders were to make Marseilles, your Grace."

I dismissed him, and sat there for some time, afraid to think the thoughts that were pressing upon me. "We survived such a storm, your Grace," Amaria ventured. "As did King Louis."

"Yes," I said. "Yes. Richard will have survived."

But where was he?

The answer came a few weeks later, in the form of an

envoy from Philip Augustus. "I bear ill tidings, your Grace," this worthy said.

I kept my face still with an effort. "Speak."

"King Richard's fleet encountered a great storm, your Grace, on its way home from the Holy Land."

"I know that."

"The King was shipwrecked."

My head jerked. "He was drowned?"

"The King made the shore safely, your Grace."

I gave a great sigh of relief. "Then where is he now?"

"The King came ashore on the coast of Dalmatia, your Grace. He had but a few companions, and so determined to make his way across Europe to the safety of his own domains, in disguise. But his identity was discovered, and he was taken before Count Leopold of Austria."

His sworn enemy! But still, Richard was a king. "Then where is the King now?"

"Count Leopold has cast him into a dungeon, your Grace, and says that he will sell the King to the highest bidder."

## Chapter Ten

I am bound to say that my first reaction was one of fury: how may anyone dare to kidnap a king? But fury was very quickly overtaken by apprehension, which soon became fear. There was no prospect of me, or John, or both of us together, wreaking any vengeance upon Austria, separated from it as we were not only by France but the Empire. And talk of selling my son to the highest bidder was not only humiliating but terrifying.

The first thing I needed was information, and I sent off posthaste to Philip to tell me where Richard was being kept. The reply I got from that two-faced wretch was that he could not give me such information as he did not know, but he did know that Richard was being moved from place to place. This was absolutely true. What I did not then know was that this moving about had been recommended to Leopold by Philip, just so I would be unable to locate my son. "I will find him, your Grace," Blondel said.

"How may you do that, you silly boy?"

"I have a plan, your Grace. When the King and I were in Sicily together . . ." he cast me an anxious glance but as my expression did not change he hurried on, "we were wont to compose roundels. Now, one of these was known only to the King and me. If I were to sing it outside of the window of every possible prison in Austria, and someone from inside the prison were to complete the verse, then I would know it was the King."

It sounded a hare-brained scheme to me, and besides . . . "That would take you several years," I told him.

"Does it matter how long it takes, your Grace, so long as we find the King?" He was so fervent I let him go, although I was determined it was not going to be that long before I brought my boy home again.

But of course I had more than one son left, and before Easter John was in Rouen. "I am quite shattered," he said. "How could such a thing happen?"

"The important thing is that it has happened," I told him, "and therefore we must cope with it. Our first business must be to send an embassy to this cur Leopold and discover what he is about."

John stroked his moustache. "He is about villainy, Mama. And I consider our first business must be to put things right here at home."

I frowned at him. "Is there something wrong, here at home?"

"We have no king, Mama."

"Of course we have a king. As soon as we discover what Leopold wants, we will have Richard back."

"Has it not occurred to you, Mama, that Richard may be already dead?"

"Of course he is not dead. We would have heard."

"Would we? Suppose he has died of a fever? Might not Leopold be afraid to release the news?"

I glared at him. "Until we hear differently, the King is alive."

He did some more tugging of his moustache. "While the kingdom drifts, rudderless."

"The kingdom, John, will continue to be ruled by the justiciars, appointed by the King."

"But there is the crux of the matter, Mama. The

kingdom has been ruled by justiciars appointed by the King, and people have been happy to obey them, for that reason. But now they are saying, there is no king. How can we obey men who have been appointed by a king who is no longer our king?"

"That is treason," I pointed out, coldly. "Who has been saying this?"

"People. I can tell you, Mama, there is unrest. And there will be more, unless they have a king to discipline them. Kings need to be seen, and heard, and felt. A king who has disappeared can no longer exert any authority."

"And presumably you see yourself as the king who will be seen and heard and felt."

"Well . . ." he had the grace to flush. "Do you think I *wish* such responsibility? But as I am your son, your only remaining son, Mama, I also understand where my duty lies." He paused, somewhat anxiously, but as I made no reply, hurried on. "I have discussed the matter with Philip, and he is sure that I am right."

"You have done *what*? You have discussed our affairs with that two-faced white-livered rat? When did this meeting take place?"

"We have not yet met, Mama." He was trembling. "We have corresponded. But I am on my way to a meeting with him now."

"Oh, yes? To discuss what?"

"Well . . ." now he was twisting his fingers together. "Philip feels it would be best if I were to do homage for Normandy."

I could not believe my ears. "If *you* were to do homage for Normandy? You are not Duke of Normandy."

"But, you see, Mama, I would be, were anything to have happened to Richard, I would be, wouldn't I? Philip feels it is best that the matter of homage be taken care of now. Did you know that I am to marry Alais?"

I pointed. "You are a treacherous scoundrel, John. God forbid that I should ever have to say that of one of my own children. I will remind you of three things. Firstly, Richard is not dead. Secondly, if he were to be dead, his heir is Arthur of Brittany, not you. And thirdly, in his absence I am regent. He made me so. He asked me only to use my powers if it became necessary. I consider it now necessary. I absolutely forbid you to meet with Philip, or to do homage for any of your brother's lands. As for Alais, I can assure you that *she* knows nothing of this proposed marriage. However, I would dearly like to see her wed, and I will raise no objections to that, as long as proper provision is made for Isabella . . . but there can be no strings attached."

He stamped from the room in a rage.

Obviously finding Richard became more urgent yet, and became more urgent with every day, as I learned that John had disobeyed me and gone to Paris after all. I was still prepared to give him the benefit of the doubt, but when I learned that he had in fact done homage for Normandy, and that, as Duke of Normandy, he was preparing a return to England to take up the reins of government there, backed up by a mercenary army financed by Philip, I realised that once again I had to recapture all the vigour of my youth. It was a sad occasion for me, for while one half of me revelled in the prospect of truly ruling, and in the enormous authority I commanded for the first time in my life, the other half bitterly regretted that I should have to use this authority against my own son.

However, I did not let that put me off my duty. Immediately I received the news from Paris I left Rouen for England. I took with me not only Queen Berengaria and the Princess Joanna, but also the Princess Alais: John was certainly not going to get his hands on her as some part of a deal with Philip. I did not consider I had any need to do anything about poor Isabella of Gloucester, who languished in her own city; she could do nothing more than await events.

I was received with acclamation when I and the princesses landed at Southampton. Everywhere there were cries of loyalty, and I proceeded to London in a triumphal procession. I am sure I cannot be blamed for a brief consideration that if Richard *were* dead, who could possibly be a better or more suitable ruler of the Angevin Empire than myself? How that would make both Henry and Mother-in-law Matilda turn in their graves.

But first, duty. I have related that Walter of Coutances had taken the part of John against Longchamp. But that had been because he had wanted to get rid of Longchamp. He had no intention of surrendering his prerogatives to John, certainly not while the man who had appointed him, Richard, still lived. On the other hand, I doubt he actually intended to surrender them to me, either. He soon learned his mistake, and when I told him what I wanted done he reacted with vigour and efficiency. The realm was mobilised, the coastal areas were garrisoned, and I sent a messenger to John to inform him that if he or any of his mercenaries set foot in England I would have their heads. As to whether I would have gone as far as this where John was concerned I really cannot say. But I certainly meant my threat as far as anyone else was concerned, and his people recognised this and decided against crossing the water.

Meanwhile, I was making progress. I actually received

a letter from Richard himself, in the spring of 1193, informing me that he had been sold to the Emperor. I understood that he could not express his real feelings about all of this, as his mail was certainly being read, but he did convey that Henry was not such a bad fellow after all. Of course I did not believe that, and despatched the loyal Hubert Walter to find out the truth. He had a meeting with the King and reported back that Richard was in good health and spirits, but just how good a fellow the Emperor was I very rapidly discovered when he demanded a ransom of one hundred and fifty throusand marks for the King, failing which, he threatened, he would sell him to Philip, who was quite prepared to raise such a sum.

This was frightening. Quite apart from the thought of Richard being kept forever by Philip as some sort of sexual slave. Philip and John were now rapidly securing as many of our castles in Normandy and the Vexin as they could, and in addition, forming alliances against us; Philip even went so far as to contract a second marriage, with the Princess Ingeborg of Denmark, in order to bring Scandinavia into the conflict. This however turned out to be a disastrous, and scandalous, affair. I have already touched upon Philip's possible relations with his first wife, but she seems to have been a sensible woman, like Berengaria, who realised that to be a queen requires a few sacrifices. Ingeborg was cast in a different mould. She was a Norse maiden who had the strictest ideas on sexual propriety. The result was that after their wedding night she moved out and refused to speak to her husband. Obviously the world was not informed of the truth of the matter, and Philip put it about that she had proved quite unsuitable. Presumably this was perfectly true, as I have no doubt at all that he attempted to sodomise her and that she took offence.

At that time, however, as I had no idea what was going on in Paris except that it seemed the whole world was ranging itself against me, I informed the Emperor that the ransom would be paid, and that June convened a court at St Albans to set about raising the money. To do this it was sadly necessary again to squeeze the populace, who had not fully recovered from being squeezed for the Crusade. But I would accept no negative answers. I applied a scutage of twenty shillings on every knights' fee. Scutage was a tax invented by Henry Beauclerk in his determination to have a permanent standing army, and was a means by which a knight could forego his military service by paying a certain amount of money, which could be used to hire mercenary soldiers, providing there was not a more pressing need elsewhere. I then applied a general tax of a fourth of all revenue and chattels from everyone in the kingdom, including the clergy, which was unique. However, I did grant a concession to the parish priests and allowed them to pay only a tenth. But I took all the plate from all the churches, except where the priests and monks wished to buy them back for cash. I also took the entire wool-crop of the Cistercians and Gilbertines. Naturally I used fines as well, imposing them on all those who had supported John. Amazingly, the good people of England were again disposed to dig deep into their pockets, with only a little grumbling, and in no more than six months I had accumulated the vast sum, which was stored under lock and key in St Paul's Cathedral, to be accounted for by Hubert Walter and Richard Fitz-Neal.

During this time I corresponded regularly with Richard, who continued to be well-treated by Henry and was even allowed to set up his own court, and he wrote to the other members of the family, including a most touching epistle to Marie, who he had always loved more than any other of his sisters. Once again I shed a tear at the hand of fate which had prevented too such tremendous souls from being able to marry. What children they would have had!

At the end of this very busy year, and with the full agreement of Richard, I had the satisfaction of installing Hubert Walter as Archbishop of Canterbury, thus ending the overlong interregnum. Hubert thoroughly deserved the honour, for my house has had no more faithful servant. Indeed, as will be seen, he was perhaps *too* faithful to the name Plantagenet.

I may say that during this trying period I saw little of Berengaria. As she was Queen of England, I had naturally considered it important that she be given her own establishment, and this had been one of my first endeavours. Once I had done that, however, she entirely faded from my society. I know I was very busy, and had little time for domestic matters, yet I gained the impression, mainly through Joanna, that the Queen was not entirely happy, and at least partly blamed me for her misery. Well, I had warned her that marriage to Richard was going to be no bed of roses: it would have been entirely different had she been able to produce an heir. Sadly, I did not know, and neither did Joanna, whether Richard had ever used her properly. At least, she had not done an Ingeborg, for which I suppose we must be thankful.

As I have said, by the end of the year the ransom had been collected, and I set off at once, leaving Hubert Walter and Walter of Coutances in command. We did not make a noise about my departure, and I had every hope of returning with Richard before I had even been missed. This was of course an utterly unreal optimism, and by the time I reached Germany all Europe knew of it; it was now that Philip sent John his famous message, to "beware, for the devil is loosed." I am not sure whether he was referring to Richard or to me! It is generally supposed that he had Richard in mind, but the message was sent *before* Richard's actual release.

To reach Germany, without setting foot in France or French-controlled territory such as Flanders, I had to cross the North Sea. This was the longest voyage I had undertaken since returning from Palestine in 1149, and in January it was no pleasure for a woman of seventy-one. But I celebrated Epiphany in Cologne on 6 January, and on the 16th, the day before the date set for Richard's release, I arrived at Speyer. This was one of the two or three greatest moments of my life. I am not sure what I anticipated: I could not get the image of poor William Marshal, as he had appeared when released by the Lusignans, out of my mind. But as I had nursed him back to the fullest health, I would do the same for Richard, I was determined.

In fact, my fears were groundless. Richard looked as fit and strong and powerful as ever before in his life. We greeted each other tenderly. Obviously we had a great deal to discuss, but before we could get around to it Henry put his oar in. "You understand, your Grace," he said to me, "that there are many who consider I am being ill-advised to loose the Lion Heart again upon the world."

"Oh, yes?" I commented. "You have named a ransom, your majesty, and it has been counted out by your scribes. To renege now would be to reveal yourself as a man of no honour. Hardly a fit son to Barbarossa."

He flushed, but he was a persistent rogue. "I have no intention of reneging, madame. However, as you are a queen and a stateswoman, you must understand that politics is an on-going game. If I release your son, how do I know he will not immediately make common cause with Philip of France against me?"

"I should think the chances of that are as remote as the chances of Guy of Lusignan ever again sitting on the throne of Jerusalem."

"Nevertheless, your Grace, I must have some guarantees."

"Richard will swear an oath never to take up arms against you."

"I am thinking more of his swearing allegiance."

"To you? For what?"

"For his lands, your Grace."

"That is absurd. He has already done homage to Philip."

"Quite. It would be better if he swore allegiance to me."

"Your Majesty, you would be putting us all into the most unsolvable legal muddle. And really, you would have achieved very little."

"Nonetheless. You do realise that I cannot be compelled to let Richard go."

I could have scratched out both of his eyes. But I knew I had to be patient, and diplomatic. "As I have said, I do not see how Richard can possibly swear to be your liege man for our possessions on the continent, having already sworn elsewhere. But I am prepared to have him swear allegiance for England. I assume that will satisfy you?" It did, and a few days later Richard and I were on our way home.

Possessing as we did an Imperial safe-conduct, which not even Philip Augustus would dare defy, we went home by way of Cologne, Louvain, Brussels and

Antwerp, and thence crossed to Sandwich. Our welcome was rapturous; I was both overwhelmed and surprised, as after all, Richard was not really returning from a triumph. But the fact was that John's attempt at a usurpation had put people's backs up. Worse, it had encouraged those barons who supported him to take advantage of the situation, relying on the fact that he would be far too busy trying to maintain his own position to worry about them. Thus there was more than a hint of anarchy in the air, and there were many people who could still remember the tribulations of Stephen's reign, and even more who remembered the comparative tranquillity of Henry Plantagenet's years in power, when inside England at least, a man had needed to fear for neither his life, his property, nor his womenfolk. All dreaded a return to that earlier era, and thus all were prepared to cheer lustily and lend all the support possible, as Richard embarked upon a *chevauchee* throughout the land, demanding the surrender of all the castles held by John's supporters, and generally putting the country to rights. He met with little opposition. John's people were terrified out of their wits. Indeed, the castellan of Mount St Michael off the Cornish coast, just about the most impregnable fortress in England, when he heard that Richard was approaching, dropped dead of a seizure! He also reinstated his old friend Longchamp, almost the moment he landed in England. To avoid any unpleasantness with Walter of Coutances, he sent Walter back to Normandy to act as justiciar there.

I accompanied him on this *chevauchee*. Sad though I was to realise that my attempt to find him an acceptable wife had failed – he did not even trouble to visit Berengaria on his return – I was yet filled with pride to ride at his shoulder and see him recreating the regime of his father. We had the opportunity for several long chats. Obviously I raised the subject of his wife. "You did consummate the marriage?" I asked.

"I did," I waited. He shrugged. "I am sorry, Mother. I am what I am."

"And your heir?"

He grinned. "There's time. When I have settled with Philip."

This was what he wished to do above all, for while he had been in Germany he had learned all about his erstwhile lover's double-dealing. Well, I couldn't criticise his anger. "And John?" I asked.

"Him also," he said. I naturally could not accept that with equanimity; it would have been too pitiful for brother to destroy brother, especially when they were the last two of my sons. However, as with so many of the problems which have lurked round me in my life, it was necessary to act with great caution. So I said no more, but when, after having been crowned for a second time in Winchester on 17 April, a month later Richard sailed for France, I went with him. Richard never returned to England. Oddly, I have not yet done so, either.

In Rouen, to our great pleasure, we found Blondel waiting for us. He looked travel-worn and a trifle haggard, but if his personal mission had been a failure, he was overjoyed to find his lover so well and so restored to power. Richard, who was perhaps more fond of Blondel than of any of the other men in his life, listened to the tale of the minstrel's adventure with great glee, and immediately put it about that Blondel had indeed discovered his prison by singing the roundel beneath the window, and obtaining a response. It is of course a gorgeously romantic tale, and has earned Blondel a modest immortality, however untrue. I did not object to this charade. I just wished the pair of them to be happy.

During this period John was still skulking in French territory, but, knowing John, I also knew that he and Philip would have little in common. I also knew, from my various informants, that Philip was having a lot of private problems, principally on account of Ingeborg. As they had lived apart since their wedding night, he naturally wished to repudiate her. But on what grounds? One would have supposed it was a mere matter of proving that the marriage had not been consummated. But were she to offer evidence in rebuttal, shall we say, it could have been very embarrassing. He was therefore negotiating with the King of Denmark and with the Pope. In these circumstances it is difficult to keep one's mind on the job. I therefore wrote John, and told him this was his last chance to make peace with his brother. And, incidentally, with me!

He came to Rouen almost immediately, threw himself at my feet, and begged my forgiveness. I took him into Richard, and the brothers embraced. Peace was restored, at least within the realm.

I was now seventy-two years old, and beginning to feel that I could take life just a little more easily. Indeed, I decided to retire altogether from affairs of state – as if this is ever possible where there are affairs of state to be attended to. However, I took myself to Fontevrault. There was another reason for this; dear Amaria had died. We had been close companions for so very long, ever since that never-to-be-forgotten night in Antioch when we had been kidnapped by my first husband's minions. Life without her at my side was not the same.

However, even if retired, I had lot on my mind. There were several loose ends lying about which I knew had to be tied up, and it was obvious I was going to have to do the tying. I may say that Richard was now embarked on a wholesale war against Philip, winning battles all over the place, building castles on the model of those he had seen in Palestine, including one rising above the Seine, and called Chateau Gaillard, which was second only to Krak des Chevaliers in strength and magnificence. But he found time to visit me whenever he was in Anjou, and I was able to discuss those matters which were important to me.

First, as a matter of conscience, there was Alais. The poor girl was now in her mid-thirties, her looks were fading, and if she was not still a virgin she certainly did not have a very bright future. I persuaded Richard finally to send her home to her brother, and let him find her a husband amongst his vassals. As we were at war with Philip anyway, his reactions to such an insult did not seem to matter. Less satisfactory was Richard's decision to marry Joanna to Cousin Raymond of Toulouse. I had nothing but contempt for the way this thug's father had behaved at the time of our revolt against Henry, but Richard assured me that the son was anxious to mend his fences with the mainstream of the family, and of course this definitely brought us back into full possession of that long-lost part of my inheritance.

A far more serious problem, as I had always feared might be the case, arose with young Arthur. He had always been much on my mind, but as long as there remained the least prospect of Berengaria producing an heir I had been able to regard him as a threat rather than a danger, and besides, I had been somewhat preoccupied for some time with Richard's problems.

Now that they had all been settled, apart from the obvious fact that his marriage had been a failure, my thoughts returned to the boy. "I think it is absolutely essential," I told Richard, in the spring of 1196, "that we have the upbringing and education of the future King of England. I may say that this is a point of view I shared with your father, but we were distracted into other channels. Now I think that you would be within your rights to claim the boy no matter what Constance may say. After all, the lad is now nine years old. She can no longer claim that he needs to be at his mother's knee."

"You are right, of course," Richard said. "I will attend to it immediately." And this he did. Whereupon we received a most unpleasant shock: young Arthur was no longer in Rennes, but in Paris, whence he had been taken, clandestinely, by his mother. "What's to be done?" Richard demanded. "Philip will never give him back."

And what I had always most feared had come to pass: the next legitimate King of England would be in the pocket of England's most bitter enemy. "There are two things we must do," I said. I knew it would be useless to beg him to have another go at making Berengaria a mother. "We must, firstly, attempt to get Arthur back."

"Not by any concessions," he declared. "I'll owe that rascal Philip nothing."

"That must be your decision. The second thing you must do is make a deposition selecting John as your heir, and give it to me. I will use it only if I have to, obviously. That is, were you to die childless and before we have regained possession of Arthur."

"John," he muttered. "Can that possibly be considered, Mama?"

"John will do as I tell him." I was confident enough of that.

"But will the nation accept him?"

"The nation also will do as I tell them," I asserted. "Besides, they will certainly prefer to have John than Arthur, especially if that means Constance as well."

So it was determined, and I could feel the future was reasonably secure. But that is never certain. Living to a great age has many advantages, and after all, with due respect to the Holy Church, it is always better to be alive than dead. But there are disadvantages too. The principal one, apart from a growing sense of infirmity, even in one such as I who has always been the epitome of health, is that not everyone else is so fortunate. Outliving one's contemporaries is by no means an unsatisfactory process. Some, one regrets bitterly. Uncle Raymond of Antioch was such, and in 1193 Saladin himself died. In many ways they were the two most important men of my life. Others, such as, sadly, my two husbands, I was glad to see the back of. But outliving one's own children is always a matter of great sadness. William had died before I had properly realised he was alive. Hal and Geoffrey had never been close. Matilda's death had been a hard cross to ear. Now I learned of the death of Alix. From a personal point of view, she was the most tragic of my children: I had not laid eyes on her since 1152, when she had been two years old. Then in 1198 Marie followed her sister into the grave. In many ways, once she had got rid of *her* husband, she had been the happiest, most buoyant of my children, as she was the eldest. She was also the nearest to me in looks, and indeed, outlook on life. Her passing left me deeply saddened.

But the crowning tragedy occurred the following

year. That spring I was at Fontevrault, content in that Richard was carrying out some minor campaign down in Poitou, against a recalcitrant baron. This was not even connected with the French wars. Imagine my feelings when I was summoned from my devotions by a messenger from Richard's captain of the guard, Mercadier, to say that I must come at once to Chalus, for the King had been sorely wounded. I may have paused for a moment's reflection that in his hour of need Richard had sent for me, rather than anyone else, including his brother and his wife! I hastened immediately, my mind full of foreboding, but yet recalling my mad dash to Vitry in my youth. But would Richard ever succumb to a mere sickness of the mind?

Alas, not Richard. I knew the truth as soon as I entered the house where he lay, for I had smelt the odious stench of gangrene too often before. I embraced Blondel, ever at his king's side, and then knelt beside my son. "Oh, Richard," I said.

"A chance shot," he said. "Mercadier and I were inspecting the castle, with a view to selecting the best positions for our siege machines, and this fellow loosed a bolt from the top battlement. It could have been the merest chance that I was hit."

"And you did not take it seriously," I said, my mind numb.

"It did not seem so. But now . . ." his hand closed on mine. "You have my Will, Mother. Will you carry out my wishes?"

"They are my wishes as well, Richard," I reminded him.

"Then all will be well. Mother . . . I am sorry about Berengaria."

I let my tears flow freely down my cheeks. "As you

have said, a man must be what he is. You were the greatest warrior of the age, Richard. I believe you would have been the greatest king. Now . . ."

He smiled. "You will have to do what you can with John."

"What I can," I agreed.

"Mother, this fortress must fall. The archer . . . I am sure he did not know what he was about. Forgive him."

I did not reply. There was no man in the world who could possibly not know Richard the Lion Heart, even at a distance. Richard died the next day. I left immediately with the body for Fontevrault, but before I did so, the castle having surrendered, Mercadier dragged the wretched crossbowman before me. "Did you know at whom you were shooting?" I asked.

The man trembled, but was yet defiant. "Him they call the Lion Heart."

"You were not in battle."

"There would be a battle," he answered insolently.

"But you could not wait."

"I wished to see if his heart was in truth greater than that of any man," he declared. "It should have been, seeing that he has lived on others' blood for so long."

I turned to Mercadier. "Do with him as you please," I said.

I later learned that Mercadier had him flayed alive. For this, some have said my conscience should be heavy. As I am both a queen and a mother, it is not.

Richard was buried beside his father and grandmother on Palm Sunday, 1199. By the terms of his Will, his breast had already been opened, and his heart removed, for interment in Rouen. It may well be supposed that I was near to being entirely overcome by grief, but as with so many of the sad events of my life there was simply no time for mourning, and this was in many ways a blessing. Richard and I may have privately determined the succession, but no one else knew of it, and not everyone was going to share our opinion, that was obvious. Indeed William Marshal, who happened to be in Rouen, attended me the moment I arrived, firstly to offer his condolences, secondly to promise me his unswerving allegiance, and thirdly to inform me that he had discussed the situation with Archbishop Hubert Walter, who also happened to be in Rouen at this time, and that the Archbishop had declared unequivocally that the next in line to the throne was Prince Arthur. I could not find it in my heart to criticise dear Hubert, who had always been such a staunch supporter of our house, for wishing to stick exactly to the letter of the law: this had been my own attitude until Philip had got his claws into the Prince. So now I asked William, "And where do you stand in this matter?"

"At your shoulder, your Grace. Your decision is mine." I told him what Richard and I had decided. "At this time, in the midst of a war with France, there can be no other choice but a grown man who is also a doughty warrior," he agreed. "However, your Grace, I must tell you . . . Prince John is at this very moment in Rennes, with Arthur and the Duchess." For Constance had rcently married again, and they were still celebrating.

"Then we must get him here, immediately," I said.

"I will send a messenger. But he must know of the King's death, if he does not already. That means the Duchess of Brittany will also know of it."

"The important thing is to get John out of there," I said. "As long as the Duchess does not know what we are about he should be in no danger."

* * *

John reached me safely, and when I told him that it was my intention he should be the next King of England went down on his knees, buried his head in my lap, and wept. I did not find this very encouraging. Equally was I confounded by the news which reached me from every side, principally the south, where Constance had declared her son King, left Brittany with an army, and marched into Anjou, where they were met by, of all people, Philip, in Le Mans if you please. He had no business being in Angevin territory at all, without invitation. But he claimed he *had* been invited, by *King* Arthur, and in Le Mans he accepted Arthur's homage for Anjou, Maine and Touraine.

I saw Constance's hand in all this, and equally that she was attempting not to arouse my ire by having her son also do homage for Aquitaine, which logically, if he was indeed going to be King of England, he was entitled to do. However, my ire was already aroused. I summoned Mercadier and Richard's army from the south and marched on Angers, myself to the fore wearing a mail surcoat. Shades of my impetuous youth! But I was in my element. John I sent against Le Mans. I intended to seize the whole crew and see what kind of a song they would sing then. Sadly, they got wind of my coming and fled, Philip and Arthur and Constance, for the safety of Paris. They left their army behind, perhaps hoping for a miracle. But I did not deal in miracles, except of my own making. We stormed Angers and took a large number of prisoners. John also had been totally successful. Anjou restored, I sent him immediately to England with Archbishop Walter, and he was crowned at Westminster on 25 May.

I did not accompany him, as there were still pressing matters in hand. I felt it necessary to remind my original subjects that I was still very much alive and kicking, and what is more, more in command of my situation, and of them, than ever before in my life. Thus I performed a *chevauchee* the length and breadth of Aquitaine, the terrifying Mercadier and his soldiers always at my side, and was greeted with acclamation by my people. How many of them, I wondered, were old enough to remember the fifteen-year-old girl who had fled them in such haste in 1137, or could reconcile such a memory with this seventy-seven-year-old warrior queen who now called for their obedience?

Of course, we live in an absurd world. Philip and I were at war, certainly physically if not by any declaration. Had I caught him in Angers I would have dealt harshly with him. But, as Duchess of Aquitaine, he remained my liege lord. He now summoned me to his court at Tours to do homage for my lands. He was entirely entitled to do this, and if I did not obey him, he would be entitled to declare me deposed and encourage any number of adventurers to chance their arms against me. I may say that William, Blondel and Mercadier took the point of view that as the King of France was undoubtedly going to do this anyway, we should ignore him. I thought otherwise. Not only did I wish to be seen by the world to be doing everything by the book – if, once I had sworn allegiance, he *then* sent people against me, *he* would be in the wrong – but I also wished to come face to face with this cur for the first time.

So to Tours I went. I took with me a great mesnie, and my arms and banners spread across the countryside. The people gawped. And Philip was most courteous, himself raising me from my kneeling position before him, kissing me upon each cheek, and addressing me as "dear Mother." I actually was, of course, his stepmother.

He was indeed a comely youth, and I even detected in him certain elements which might, in time, grow to greatness. This did not mean I in any way forgave him for his crimes, the more so as Constance of Brittany and her misbegotten son were in the throng behind the King. However, the deed was done, and I returned to Rouen, where I formally invested John with the Duchy of Aquitaine, before again retiring to Fontevrault. For the second time I conceived that I had done all that was needed to set the kingdom to rights. And for the second time I was mistaken.

But first, another domestic tragedy. Joanna appeared at Fontevrault, heavily pregnant, and also desperately ill. She had fled her husband, who had turned out – as I had always feared – to be a true son of his detestable father. Her tale of his mistreatment of her made me very angry, especially when they were added to the stories of his double-dealing, as while appearing to be in our camp he had always secretly been Philip's man. My relief that my baby daughter should have escaped him, however, was tempered by the understanding that she was unlikely to survive. Nor did she. She died in childbirth, and the babe, a boy, followed his mother a few hours later. Oh, if only she could have made the decision to go into Safadin's harem! Quite apart from the effect it might have had on history, how happy she would have been.

So, as the new century dawned, not without the usual prognostications of doom and disaster, out of all my ten children I was down to two. However, at least they appeared settled and healthy. And with the coming of a new age, as everyone confidently predicted, even Philip seemed anxious to call a halt to wars and rivalries. Thus early in the year he and John had a meeting at which all of their differences appeared to have been resolved.

Philip accepted the fait accompli of John's accession as King of England, John then did homage for his Continental lands, and Arthur, as Duke of Brittany, nothing more, was forced to do homage to John. I was not present at this occasion – I was still mourning Joanna – but I can imagine that Constance must have been fit to spit.

However, I was almost immediately embroiled in the consequences of this peace-making. For it was determined to link the two royal houses, the Capets and the Plantagenets, by marriage. Philip's son by Elizabeth of Hainault, Louis, was now twelve years old, and was giving every indication of being a youth of martial tastes, quite unlike his father and grandfather. Indeed there were those who already called him the Lion Heart, no doubt hoping that he would take after my Richard. It was determined that he should be married to a princess of my house, and there was only one available – Blanche of Castile. But initial feelers put out by both John and Philip south of the Pyrenees had not immediately been greeted with shrieks of joy, and so the two rascals, my son and my stepson, now invited me to do what I had done with the Queen Dowager, Berengaria, rush to the south, and return with the prospective bride.

I should say that as I was now approaching seventy-eight, I gave something of a gulp at this request. However, I have never been one to shirk either a duty or an adventure, even if I may be forgiven for supposing this had to be the very last adventure of my life. It very nearly was. I set off in all haste, wishing to be across the Pyrenees before winter closed the passes. I was accompanied by only a small mesnie; Mercadier and a body of troops were to meet me on my return with the Princess, when I imagined I would be in more need of protection. I could not imagine, in the present state of affairs, anyone attempting to waylay the senior Queen Dowager of England!

But I had reckoned without those mad people, the Lusignans. Guy of course had never returned from the Holy Land, or rather, Cyprus, which was as near as he could now get to his erstwhile "Kingdom". The Gascon Lusignans were now headed by a fellow called Geoffrey, who had a younger brother named Hugh, known as Le Brun. Whether he actually had Moorish blood I would not like to say, but he was certainly swarthy and ill-favoured. I disliked him on sight, but this may have been because when we met I was suddenly surrounded by his people and my progress brought to a halt. Blondel, ever at my side, promptly reached for his sword, but I could see that we were outnumbered, and shook my head. Instead of fighting I addressed myself to this brown lout. "What mean you, sir, so to waylay the Duchess of Aquitaine?" I demanded.

"Why, your Grace," the scoundrel said, "I would invite you to my castle for a season."

"I am in great haste, sir," I said.

"Yet must I insist, your Grace."

There was nothing for it. I saw no point in issuing threats. These are seldom of much value. It is far better to accept the circumstances, bearing in mind always the intention of avenging oneself the moment the opportunity arose. Naturally I considered the several possible reasons for such an abduction, but was forced to reflect that, even more than thirty-odd years earlier, it was hardly likely he sought me for his bed; I might have been the most famous lover in history, but I was old enough to be his grandmother!

In fact, all Hugh de Lusignan wanted was a formal

recognition from me that their county of Le Marche was not a part of Aquitaine, something his forebears had strenuously tried to maintain over the past hundred years, but which my forebears, and indeed, myself, had staunchly refused to concede. No doubt to his surprise, I readily made the concession on this occasion, and was thus on my way again very shortly. "How can you permit such a thing," Blondel grumbled.

I smiled. "I have permitted nothing. He has regained title to his property. But he is a Lusignan, and will soon commit some crime or other. At which time I will regain Le Marche by force of arms, and settle with that wretch at the same time, too."

"Has anyone ever told you that you are quite the most remarkable woman who ever lived, your Grace?"

I kissed him. "Why, many men. Including yourself, my dear boy."

We crossed the Pyrenees, and were welcomed somewhat anxiously in Navarre. This was not because Berengaria had ever unburdened herself of her marital problems to her mother – or if she had, Blanca had clearly reflected that to wind up as Queen Dowager of England, with all the wealth and respect that went with such a title, had to be worth a bit of sodomy. In any event, the Court of Navarre clearly attached no blame to me. Their concern was that since the last time I had been in Pamplona, Sancho had fallen out with his brother-in-law Alfonso, and indeed the pair had been at war.

As far as I understood it, the provocation was entirely Sancho's, but I did not consider it my part to interfere in what was virtually a domestic squabble, as long as Eleanor was not affected by it. I was still in a hurry, and so continued to sunny Toledo, a splendid city nestling in the arms of the River Tagus, and a place of great historical interest, as it had been the capital of the Visigothic kings of Spain before the Moorish conquest. Here I was made welcome by Eleanor. Her husband was away campaigning, at which indeed he spent much of his time. For Castile had been going through a difficult period. I have related how my son-in-law, upon attaining his majority, had promptly undertaken a series of successful campaigns against the Moors. Possibly rendered over-confident by these triumphs, he had got himself into a scrape at a place called Alarcos, in 1195, and been roundly beaten. Castile had seemed on the point of collapse, and as I have indicated, the neighbouring Christian states of Leon and Navarre had sought to take advantage of this. But Alfonso had rallied his people, defeated his treacherous brother-in-law, and re-established his authority. However, the situation remained fluid, as I had observed in Navarre, and Eleanor, while willing to be persuaded into the match, was anxious about my return journey, which necessitated traversing Navarese territory with a Castilian princess. "Nonsense," I assured her. "No one is going to interfere with me. Besides, by now, Mercadier is waiting at the pass with his people."

It was now for the first, and sadly, up till now, the last time, I had the great pleasure of meeting Eleanor's children. They were a delightful lot, full of spirit and confidence. I felt the future of Castile was in safe hands. Blanche herself – I would not call her by the Spanish Blanca – was just coming up to thirteen; she was thus approximately the same age as her future husband. She was a lovely girl, and had been properly educated by her mother, which is to say that she had no fears of her approaching fate as Queen of France. How my memory drifted back to when I had been informed that was to be my portion. I had been no older, and I had had no mother to guide and advise me. But Blanche had everything going for her. Where I had been pitchforked into being a queen before I was truly ready for it, there was no sign of Philip Augustus dying in the near future – worse luck – and therefore she would be able to serve a long apprenticeship. And where I had had the misfortune to be married to a would-be monk, Blanche was going to the bed of a would-be soldier. I felt I could have every confidence in her future, as well.

Sadly, I was not able to deliver her personally to Paris. Having spent several months with Eleanor, and at last being able to meet Alfonso, when he returned home in the New Year, it was early spring before we set off, and I determined to pause in Bordeaux – when one attains the age of seventy-nine one is always conscious that each glimpse of a treasured memory may be one's last – to celebrate Easter. This turned out to be a mistake. We had now been joined by Mercadier and his people. This grim soldier had become one of my very favourite people, absolutely loyal to the memory of Richard, and thus absolutely loyal to me. Now, while we celebrated the most holy of festivals, he was struck down by the hand of an assassin. His men were so angry it was with difficulty I dissuaded them from pulling down the city. Indeed, I felt like doing this myself. But I was perhaps more tired than I had realised by my exertions over the past six months. Now I wanted only to turn my back on the world. I handed Blanche into the care of the Archbishop of Bordeaux, bade her a tearful farewell, and retired to Fontevrault.

In fact, I very rapidly regained my spirits, and this was just as well, because I was almost immediately faced with a fresh set of problems. It may be recalled that

Henry, in one of his ranting fits, had once declared that John was the only true Plantagenet amongst his sons, by which he meant that John was the only one who unmistakeably took after his father. I had never denied this, and being the optimist I am, had been prepared to hope that John would, in the course of time, reveal all of his father's great talents, and not too many of his equally great vices. Well, I am bound to say that in this first year of his reign my last remaining son had revealed very little talent – it was I who had secured his throne for him by driving his enemies from the field. Now I returned to discover that he had certainly revealed his inheritance of his father's outstanding vice.

It appears that in my absence he had made a *chevauchee* through Aquitaine, in the course of which he had stopped at the castle of Angouleme, where Count Aymer held sway. The King was of course lavishly entertained, and made the acquaintance of Count Aymer's beautiful daughters, and they were, in fact, very good-looking girls. One of them certainly roused the cockles of John's heart, to put it as delicately as I may. Before anyone could say snap, John had departed Angouleme, with the young lady in his baggage, and on regaining England, had her crowned queen by an obedient Hubert Walter!

This was quite the most outrageous act anyone had ever heard of, and made Henry's seduction of Lampagie de Porhoet appear like a page of old-fashioned chivalry taken straight from the pages of Tristan and Isolde. Let us consider what my headstrong – although the strength obviously stemmed from the other end of his body – son had done. And undone.

In the first place, he was still officially married to Isabella of Gloucester, even if they had not co-habited for years, and if, in view of their consanguinity, it would have been a simple matter to have the marriage annulled. But he had not wasted the time to do that. Thus he had at the least committed bigamy. In the second place, this girl – her name was also Isabel – was only twelve years old! In the third place, she was betrothed to be married. But, looked at from my point of view, this was the only saving grace about the whole thing, for she was betrothed to none other than Hugh le Brun of Lusignan, a man with whom I was determined to get even. But John was not acting as my agent here; he did not yet know of my meeting with Hugh. And in the fourth place, of course, one did not snatch a child virtually off the streets – there was no trace of royal blood in the Angoulemes – bed her, and have her crowned queen of the greatest kingdom in Europe, all in passing, as it were.

I could be under no misapprehension that this business was going to cause a lot of trouble. And it did. Aymer wished to complain and so did Hugh Le Brun. I wrote urgent letters to John begging him to come to France to sort the business out, but he ignored me. No doubt he was entirely wrapped up – presumably literally – in his twelve-year-old, bigamal-bride. Meanwhile, I wrote letters in every direction, attempting to ascertain how many of our vassals were going to stand by us in the clash that was obviously coming. This clash was somewhat delayed, for Philip was now deeply involved with the Papacy over his own matrimonial problems – getting rid of Ingeborg so that he could marry his latest lady-love Agnes of Meran. He was becoming quite an heterosexual in his middle-age, but it will be seen that, unlike John, he was prepared to do everything legally.

His bed sorted out, he took action in the spring of

1202. John had by now returned to France, and he and I had had a brief and stormy meeting. "Do not speak to me of duty, Mama," he shouted angrily. "All my life I have been required to do my duty. Now I am King."

"By the Grace of God," I reminded him. I should have added, and your mother!

"Will you arrange for my marriage to Isabel to be terminated?" he demanded.

"Which Isabel?" I inquired, coldly. He stormed off in a huff.

Of course I intended to sort things out for him, as I did not doubt I could. But Philip got in first, by summoning his liege man, John, to a judicial court. When John, who had taken himself off to Rouen, refused to attend, Philip acted with a determination which surprised everyone. He had of course anticipated some such position arising, and had his plans all laid. John's lands of Aquitaine, Poitou and Anjou were declared forfeit; the French King immediately accepted the homage of Arthur of Brittany for these lands; he knighted Arthur himself and declared him the legitimate King of England; and he launched his army in an invasion of Normandy. This was an even greater crisis tham I had anticipated. It was obvious that although my eightieth birthday approached, I had to take the field or watch everything I had spent a lifetime creating crumble into the dust. I reflected only briefly, and I am sure I cannot be blamed for the decision I made. Normandy was John's, and he must fight for it. I sent him a message to do just that and leave the rest to me. Anjou was also his, rather than mine. But Anjou would fall to whoever won the war anyway. My true interest was in Poitou and Aquitaine, my ancestral lands. And if I held Poitiers against all comers, then Philip's plans would come to naught. It should be understood that I had no fear of encountering Philip Augustus in battle. I knew this over-ambitious lout too well, and I knew he had no stomach for a real fight.

Thus with a small escort I left Fontevrault to ride for Poitiers. We travelled fast, and in a single day were at the town of Mirebeau, with Poitiers no more than a march ahead of us. We had ridden hard, and at eighty-one is not quite as resilient as when, shall I say, one is sixty. I therefore chose to rest here for a day before continuing, being under the misapprehension that my movements were unknown to anyone. Besides, Mirebeau Castle was one of my favourites, and was in the care of none other than Hubert de Rais, the son of my old companion in arms, Flaubert – sadly, not by Isabeau of Poitiers. But clearly I was being watched, and equally clearly there were traitors within Mirebeau itself, who had summoned my enemies upon learning of my arrival. Thus I was called from my bed in the small hours by Blondel, who was looking quite shaken. "Your Grace," he said urgently. "The town is taken."

I was dressed in a few seconds, and hurrying to the battlements. Everywhere in the streets beneath me there were banners and armed men, and a goodly number of these were actually clustered just beyond the drawbridge. Two of the banners I recognised immediately: one belonged to the Lusignans, and the other to Arthur Duke of Brittany: my principal enemies had come together to corner me.

Now Hubert came hurrying up. "Your Grace," he gasped, "they are demanding entry."

"How many do they muster?"

"Several thousand men, your Grace. And we have but three hundred."

"We have stone walls and arrows and swords, Hubert," I told him. "Refuse them."

He went off, and I made a quick circuit of the walls, to discover what I wanted. Like so many castles, Mirebeau was situated on the edge of the town, and on its outer side overlooked green fields. And so confident of their success had been Arthur and Geoffrey, that they had taken all their people into the town itself, to assault the main gate of the citadel: even Theobald of Blois had known better than to do that when he had moved against me in Angers, fifty years before. Thus beneath me was a postern, with no one in sight. I held Blondel's arm. "Do you walk a horse through that gate, Blondel, and ride like the wind for John."

"And leave you here, your Grace? I shall never desert you."

"I am sending you, Blondel, because it is upon you more than any other man that I rely. Besides, John will know that it is urgent, if you are my messenger. Find my son, and bid him march to my aid with all his strength. Do not fail me, Blondel."

"But . . . why do you not come with me?"

"At my age? I would be nothing more than a hindrance. They would follow and catch us in hours. But as long as I am here, they will be here, seeking my capture."

"But your Grace, if the castle were to fall . . ."

"Do you suppose I am afraid of rape?" I demanded. "But it will not fall, as long as I live and breathe."

He argued no further, but left immediately, while I returned to stand above the gate. They recognised me quickly enough. "Good Grandmother," Arthur called. "Why do you mistrust me? I but seek your safety and honour. Open these gates and come out, that I may kneel at your feet."

"And then?" I inquired.

"Then? Why, good your Grace, I offer you safe conduct to wherever you wish to go."

"So long as it is somewhere of your choosing," I suggested.

This discomfited him, as he could not immediately think of a reply, and by this time the Lusignans were growing impatient. "You had best come out of there, you old hag," shouted Hugh's brother Geoffrey. "Before we come in and get you, when it will go hard with you, I promise you."

"I have seen better men than you crumbled into dust at my feet," I told him. "Get you gone, before I come out and get *you*." After that exchange there could of course be no agreement between us, not that I would ever have allowed one in any event. They immediately began to arrange their forces for the attack, and now at last entirely encircled the castle; it did not seem to occur to them that they were too late.

Hubert remained concerned. "If the King is in Normandy," he said, "we are speaking of several days before we can be succoured. And if he has returned to England . . ."

I knew that what he was really considering was our situation should John not bother to come to our aid. This would not have been altogether out of character, and the possibility was of some concern to me as well. But I was not about to let anyone know that. "The King will be here," I said.

In fact he was there, far sooner than anyone had expected. The Lusignans and Arthur did some desultory shooting of arrows, which effected nothing, and then retired for the night. The next day was the same, and it became obvious that, taken by surprise by the refusal of an eighty-year-old beldam to surrender to their superior force, they had sent off for the siege machines they had neglected to bring with them. Naturally, they anticipated no danger, as when last heard of John had been in Rouen, a matter of two hundred miles north of Mirebeau, nor was it supposed he would readily leave his Norman capital with Philip Augustus masking it with a French army.

But John at last revealed that he had in him at least some of the energy of his father and the military genius of his brother. He had determined immediately what was the focal point of this war: it was possession of Arthur. That possessing Arthur and rescuing his mother happened to fall into the same category, as it were, merely simplified things. Thus Blondel, galloping north and wearing out a succession of horses to do so, reached Le Mans, eighty miles north of Mirebeau, within twenty-four hours of leaving my side – and there found John and all his array, already marching south at full speed. Continuing apace, my rescuers were in Mirebeau at dawn two days later, entirely surprising the besiegers, who were actually at their breakfasts. The ensuing battle was very brief, and the next man to summon my gates to open was the King of England. "Oh, John," I said. "Oh, my dearest, darling boy."

We embraced. "Did you suppose I would leave you in the lurch, dearest Mama?" he asked. "I have someone I would have you meet."

The child Isabel was with him! She really was a delight, and although clearly terrified at the thought of meeting me, was undoubtedly a girl of both spirit and good sense. "My lady, your Grace," she said, when we had embraced. "I desire only to make your son happy." This from a twelve-year-old girl! I'm afraid I fell in love with her as quickly as John must have done, and forthwith endowed her with the cities of

Saintes and Niort, as she had received no dowry from her own people.

There remained our enemies. The Lusignans, as I have related, were actually at their breakfasts when attacked. Now the brothers and Arthur were dragged before us. This was the first time I had ever actually met Arthur, as opposed to shouting at him from the top of a battlement. He had grown into quite an attractive youth, but had too much of his mother in him.

"Well, wretched boy," I said. "What have you to say for yourself? How do you excuse drawing your sword against your lawful King? Not to mention your grandmother."

"I have no lawful king, Grandmama," he said. "I am lawful King of England. As for you, I intended you no harm."

I could have slapped his face, but restrained myself. But it is difficult to know what to do with someone so recalcitrant. "Take him away," I said.

"And these?" John indicated the Lusignans.

"Ah, yes," I said. "Well, my brown friend, when last we met you insisted that I be your guest for a season. You are now my guest, and I make the same demand of you. But your season will be for the rest of your natural days."

Hugh was too terrifed to speak. But his brother was made of sterner stuff. "You have no right," he protested.

"I have every right," I told him. "I have the right of your liege lady over her vassals. I have the right of a Queen against whom you have rebelled. And I have the right of a lady whom you chose to insult. Be thankful I leave you your heads."

"I will deal with them," John said, when the prisoners had been removed.

"I would not have Arthur harmed," I said. "He is our flesh and blood."

"I shall not touch a hair on his head," John promised. "But you will agree that he must be kept securely."

I sighed. "I know that must be so. But treat him as gently as you may." As we were alone, I could permit myself a smile. "He is right, you know, about being the lawful king."

Dare I say I consider my story told? I am back in Fontevrault, and I am content. True, Philip Augustus still rages and puts armies in the field, but now he can estimate John at his true worth, a master of the art of war, and he can I think be dismissed from our minds.

I have sorted out the business of John and the two Isabels, and he is now happily married. It is a treat to see them so.

Eleanor also seems content enough. I hope John and Isabel have as large a family.

Blanche is proving a success in Paris.

I am sorry that Arthur has to be kept in prison, but hopefully in the course of time it will be possible to release him.

And I? I have my memories. What memories! I defy any other woman to claim she has lived as full of life as I. Is it over? I doubt it. Not so long as I have Blondel to sing songs to me and remind me that I am probably the most successful woman who ever lived!

# Epilogue

Eleanor of Aquitaine never did return to England, or see her grandchildren again. She died 1 April 1204, just short of her eighty-second birthday. She was buried in Fontevrault Abbey, beside her husband, her mother-in-law, and her favourite son.

When she died, her dream was already falling apart. But it is probable she was not aware of this. She did know, for it happened a month before her death, that with John away in England Philip Augustus managed to capture Richard's "impregnable" stronghold of Chateau Gaillard – some historians consider this may have hastened her death.

It is unlikely she knew that Arthur was already dead. While few people doubt that the young prince was murdered, no one is quite sure how and when; the most likely date is 3 April 1203, when John, always his father's son, fell into a drunken and ungovernable rage, probably murdered the boy with his own hands, and threw the body into the Seine. Certain it is that Arthur was never seen again after that date. His sister Eleanor was confined for the rest of her life, as were the Lusignans.

With the restraining hand of his mother withdrawn, John embarked upon that strange career of mingled energy and lethargy, glimpses of genius and relapses into savagery, which punctuated the next dozen years.

He was indeed a reincarnation of Henry II, but one turned inside out. His reign was a disaster, and his early death unregretted.

In complete contrast, his sister Eleanor prospered throughout the rest of her life. Having restored his kingdom, Alfonso VIII resumed his campaigns against the Moors, and at Las Navas de Tolosa in 1212 gained the greatest victory of the entire reconquista; the Moors never recovered. Their daughter, Blanche of Castile, became one of the famous queens of history. Her husband led the opposition to John and actually invaded England to enforce a papal interdiction. He became King of France as Louis VIII following the death of Philip Augustus in 1223. When he died three years later, Blanche acted as regent for her infant son. This son, Louis IX, was the first French monarch to be canonised. Widely recognised as the most chivalrous man of his time, he became the arbiter of Europe, and his reign is considered the golden age of medieval France.

Eleanor would have been proud of her great-grandson, but equally would she have been proud of her great-grandson of England, Edward I, the "English Justinian", the grandson of John and Isabel of Angouleme. In these two men were to be found all that had been great and noble in her own character. She had no reason for regrets, for she had lived and fought, and ruled, and above all, she had *loved* on a scale equalled by no other woman, of any time.